THE CONDUCTOR

BOOK 1 OF RIAN KRIEGER'S JOURNEY

ROGER A. SMITH

MILFORD HOUSE
an imprint of Sunbury Press, Inc.
Mechanicsburg, PA USA

MILFORD HOUSE

an imprint of Sunbury Press, Inc.
Mechanicsburg, PA USA

For information about special discounts for bulk purchases, please contact Sunbury Press Orders Dept. at (855) 338-8359 or orders@sunburypress.com.

To request one of our authors for speaking engagements or book signings, please contact Sunbury Press Publicity Dept. at publicity@sunburypress.com.

FIRST MILFORD HOUSE PRESS EDITION: JUNE 2022

Set in Adobe Garamond Pro | Interior design by Crystal Devine | Cover by Ashley Nichole Walkowiak | Edited by Abigail Henson.

Publisher's Cataloging-in-Publication Data
Names: Smith, Roger A., author.
Title: The conductor: book 1 of Rian Krieger's Journey / Roger A. Smith.
Description: First trade paperback edition. | Mechanicsburg, PA : Milford House Press, 2022.
Summary: Philadelphia, 1835. 11-year-old tomboy Rian Krieger is getting an education in her father's factories. She is swept into the city's racial and economic turmoil when mentors introduce her to the Underground Railroad, the seamy world of fire brigades, and the abolition movement. Then Rian and a new friend plot to help a house slave escape to freedom.
Identifiers: ISBN : 978-1-62006-581-5 (softcover).
Subjects: FICTION / Historical / General | FICTION / Historical / Civil War Era | FICTION / African American & Black / Historical.

Product of the United States of America
0 1 1 2 3 5 8 13 21 34 55

Continue the Enlightenment!

For Linda and Gloria

The kind of real-life heroes we need today

"Bird's Eye View of Philadelphia" drawn from nature and on stone by John Bachmann. (Courtesy of the Free Library of Philadelphia, Rare Book Department.)

1835

MONDAY, JUNE 22

· RIAN ·

"So, what was the real reason you beat up Billy Schiffler?" Uncle Adrian asked the question as if he were asking, *"What do you think Andy Jackson ate for breakfast?"*

Nuts, eleven-year-old Rian Krieger said to herself. *How did he know?*

Rian tracked the ferry's wake as the Falcon powered across the Delaware River. The pilothouse blocked the rhythmic *choosh! choosh! choosh!* of the *Falcon*'s steam engine, making it possible to talk if they wanted. Rian had no interest in a chat. Instead, she watched Philadelphia's waterfront slowly recede. Her uncle leaned against the pilothouse wall, puffing on his pipe as if he had all the time in the world.

Rian peeked around the corner and considered escaping to safety next to Jules, who stood facing Camden near the bow. A headwind blasted her with an earsplitting *choosh! choosh!* and the musty smell of draft horses and oxen. She turned back. "I thought you wanted to look at the steam engine."

"Plenty of time for that. Let's talk first."

Rian folded her arms in front of her. She wished her uncle would just leave her alone. She tried to concentrate on the calming sound of water splashing off the side paddlewheel a few feet to her left. "I told you. Billy called me Barn Door because of the space between my front teeth."

"He's called you that since you were eight. It was my job to take care of you for three days, and on day three, you managed to get yourself kicked out of school. This isn't going to go well when we tell your father. So, I ask again, why'd you punch Billy in the nose?"

Rian watched a seagull float effortlessly overhead, wishing she could fly with him rather than be in this conversation. She took a deep sigh. "You can't tell *Vater*."

Adrian held his hand over his heart. "If that's what it takes, I swear to God and hope to die; I won't tell my brother."

Rian hesitated one last time before taking the plunge. "He called me a dirty mick girl."

Adrian Krieger snorted. "Really? That's it? What part did you object to?"

Despite her desire to remain angry, Rian smiled for the first time that morning. "Probably not the dirty part. I'm always dirty." Indeed, her pants and shirt, clean when she put them on this morning, were dirt-stained from her scuffle with Billy. *And a little bit of his blood*, she noted with pride.

"So, the mick girl part?"

Rian nodded. "I'm only half Irish. I beat him fair and square in a race to the flagpole and back, so he called me names. That's when I hit him. It was an insult."

"Of course, it was an insult, but so what? There's an insult for everyone in this city."

"Then why didn't he call me a krautbreath?"

"So that's what passes as an insult when you're eleven, huh?"

"You know what I mean. Why didn't he insult my German half?"

"I don't know. What do you think?"

Rian gave a tentative kick to a mooring line coiled next to a cleat. "Because the Irish are the bottom of the barrel. They don't know how to read. They get all the worst jobs in the city."

"Your mother wasn't that way."

"If that's true, how come we don't see any of my Gallagher relatives any-more? It's because *Vater* doesn't like the Irish."

"I don't think that's true, Rian."

"He's never hired an Irishman in the shop."

"That's because Irish and Germans don't get along."

"Blacks and Germans don't get along either, but Jules is *Vater's* foreman. What's the difference?"

"Jules saved Otto's life when we first got to America. They've been friends ever since. And believe me, Jules has his hands plenty full keeping the men in line."

"But he does it. That proves that you can put two groups together and make it work, but *Vater* doesn't do it with the Irish. He doesn't do it because he doesn't like them."

"Sounds to me like you don't like them. Are you ashamed of being half Irish?"

"I don't know. Maybe. I don't know the Irish very well."

"Your best friend is Conor McGuire. He's Irish."

"Conor's different. His parents both died in '32. In the epidemic, same as Mother. He spends all his time at our house or at the shop. I never go to his place."

"And why is that?"

"Because his brothers hate me."

"And why is that?"

"Because my last name is Krieger, not McGuire or Murphy or Donovan."

"Hmm, seems like this conversation's circled around to where it started. What about the girl part? Was that an insult too?"

"Kind of."

"Why kind of?"

"I'm better than Billy at everything. I'm smarter than he is. Faster. He doesn't even know how to ride a horse. So, he calls me Barn Door and teases me because I like to wear boys' clothes. It's about the only thing he's got. And the mick part."

"So was the girl part an insult or not?"

Rian shrugged. "I'll fine as long as I can still beat him up."

"That probably isn't a very good long-term plan. Sooner or later, he's going to get bigger than you."

"But I'll still be smarter."

"Yes, you will."

"What's *Vater* going to do with me since I won't be allowed back in school?"

"Beats me. He's intent on you getting a good education. He wants you to marry someone from the crowd he's been having lunches with recently at the United States Hotel."

"Ugh," said Rian. "That's stupid. What are you going to tell him? About this conversation?"

"Hmm, I think your question should be, 'what are we going to tell him?' That's why I dragged you along to meet him in Camden. It will give us all time to talk before we get back to Philadelphia. I don't think he's going to be pleased. But just so you know, I'm glad you popped Billy. You probably should have done it a long time ago. C'mon, let's have a look at that steam engine."

•   •   •   •   •   •   •   •   •   •   •   •   •   •   •   •   •   •

· SEAMUS ·

Seamus Gallagher stood in the same ditch on Mulberry Street that he and five other men had been digging for the past nine days and was now thirty-six inches deep and eighteen blocks long. He placed one foot in front of the other and swung his pickaxe, which kicked up a large chunk of dirt and rock. He moved slightly forward and repeated the motion. His friend Dylan followed with a shovel, lifting out the dirt and rocks Seamus had loosened.

When completed, the ditch would stretch two miles, from the Schuylkill to the Delaware. Then a crew of skilled pipefitters would lay gas pipes and make sure there were no leaks. Only then would Seamus, Dylan, and whoever else got picked that day return to fill in the ditch. Until that time, Mulberry Street would be a wreck.

While construction continued, horses and carriages were supposed to travel only from east to west. However, with no constables to enforce the restriction, many members of the impatient class acted as if the rule didn't apply to them.

By next year, coal gas manufactured in a plant next to the Schuylkill River and piped underground through trenches like this would light the major streets of Philadelphia, but coal gas wasn't on Seamus's mind at the moment.

It was 11:00 in the morning. The heat of the day was upon them, and Seamus had taken off his shirt. At 19, he had a mature physique to match his good looks.

Dylan leaned on his shovel, taking one of his frequent breaks. "You're awful quiet today, Boyo."

"Shut up, Dylan. I'm thinking."

"Another one of your get-rich schemes?"

Seamus swung his pick extra hard to go after a particularly pesky rock. "Not at the moment. More like a not-be-poor scheme. Gotta figure out how to pay me rent."

Before Dylan interrupted his thoughts, Seamus had been mulling over a conversation with his mother before daybreak this morning. He sat on her bed, stroking her hair as she lay in a ball under two threadbare blankets. The family had long since stopped heating the apartment, and even this late in June, it was still bone-chilling in the morning.

"Ma, I told you. Don't worry. It's going to be all right."

"Don't try to fool a storyteller, Seamus. We're two months behind on rent. Landlord's given us until Friday to pay up. Where are we going to get that kind of money?"

"I'll think of something. Maybe I can shake something loose on the docks tonight."

"I should go back to the factory."

"Ma, they fired you when you got sick. At least you're not coughing as much as you were. Hell, breathing in all that dust made you sick in the first place."

"Not much choice. Gotta pay the rent somehow."

"No way you're going back, even if they'd have you. We'll figure this out. Maybe we can bring somebody else in to help pay the rent."

"You're dreaming."

Seamus acknowledged that this particular idea might not have been his best. He and his mum already shared their apartment with his three sisters and two brothers.

Their apartment was two rooms in a mansion that used to be owned by a wealthy Philadelphia merchant. Like many members of the upper crust, as commerce and crime from the wharves on the Delaware River encroached on the neighborhood, he sold the house and moved to a more fashionable area west of Seventh Street. The new owner broke the house up into eight apartments. Most of their fellow tenants were just like them: poor, uneducated Irish precariously clinging to the bottom rung of Philadelphia's economic ladder.

"Ma, I gotta go. If I don't get there by sunup, they'll pick somebody else. Nora's not working today. She can take care of you. And don't even think of going back to the mill. I'll figure something out."

Dylan again brought Seamus out of his thoughts. "There's that fancy-pants house down near Washington Square we've been scoping out. Maybe it's time to do a little burgling."

"They've got a pretty big dog. She's a bit of a deterrent. I'm thinking we see what we can swipe on the docks."

"Big risk, big reward. Ain't that what you always say?"

"At this point, I'm just looking for enough to get even with me landlord."

"Jaysus, Seamus. Weren't you almost tossed out last winter?"

"I just wish it weren't so hard for us Irish to get a respectable job. Is that too much to ask?"

"Don't know what good that would do you. Whataya want to be? A baker? A carpenter? A bricklayer? They don't seem very happy at the moment. They're all on strike today if you haven't noticed."

"Well, yeah. But at least they've got a glimmer of something better. Maybe a ten-hour day if they're lucky. You and me? Every morning we don't know if the straw boss is going to pick us. Then, if he does choose us, we get to dig this ditch from sunup to candlelight."

"So, what's your alternative?"

"I don't have one yet. Wish you'd shut up. I can't figure anything out with you yammering at me."

· ·

· OTTO ·

"Board!" the brakeman yelled from atop the train's third and last passenger coach.

Otto Krieger walked past the first two passenger cars. Both relatively new, they had filled quickly. The last coach was beaten up and shabby. The rear-facing bench seat in the middle compartment was unoccupied. He tossed his satchel up to the brakeman, who lashed it to the roof with the other baggage.

Otto stepped back a few paces to look at the car with a critical eye. It couldn't be more than three years old because the *Camden & Amboy Railroad* had been operating only since 1832, but the paint, once a bright red and turquoise, was now dull and peeling. *I can design a better carriage than this, and my craftsmen are much more skilled than whoever slapped this piece of junk together.*

Otto poked at a board on the side of the coach with his lumber estimating stick. The board had warped so badly that it was pulling away from the side of the car. *This wood was never properly dried. Never properly painted.* On a hunch, he walked toward the front of the car and spotted a bracket that used to connect to a wagon tongue. *It is no longer used, but they never bothered to remove it. They have been running this car since the C&A was nothing but horse-drawn carriages. Come on, Stevens, it is time to update your rolling stock.*

"Hey, mister, you getting on or not?" the brakeman yelled down to him.

Otto gave him a perfunctory wave and stepped up into the coach's middle compartment. *Perfect. Far enough away from the locomotive to catch up on some sleep.*

A man, a woman, and a young girl about Otto's daughter's age occupied the forward-facing bench. Otto sat opposite the three, mildly disappointed to be traveling with his back to the locomotive. The train started with a jerk, momentarily yanking back the heads of the three people opposite him.

Otto was about to shut his eyes when the man said, "Excuse me, aren't you Otto Krieger?"

"*Ya.* Yes, I am," Otto replied. He extended his hand to the gentleman. "I am sorry, your face is familiar, but I do not remember from where." As he did every time he engaged in conversation with a new acquaintance, he stuffed down a bit of chagrin, as his English was heavily laden with the inflections of his native Wurttemberg.

"I am Randolph Tucker of Charleston. We met at your factory a couple of months ago when I ordered a new carriage."

Otto's ear was not particularly attuned to accents, but he could hear the slow, relaxed manner of the South in Tucker's speech. "Of course, the landau. You are George Shippen's brother-in-law. Yes, we finished your carriage two weeks ago. I think you will be very pleased with it. If I remember correctly, you had just purchased a house on Spruce Street."

Tucker nodded. "I hope the workers have finished the repairs. It needed some work."

"And now you will be with us for the summer?"

"Yes, we come up for the social season every year. Excuse me; I neglect my duties. This is my wife, Penelope, and my daughter Olivia."

"Delighted to meet you," Otto said to Mrs. Tucker, tipping the brim of his top hat. "I hope you will enjoy your time in Philadelphia."

"Oh, I grew up here, Mr. Krieger. We have summered in Philadelphia since Olivia was one, so that's ten years now. Randolph finally decided it was time to buy a house rather than rent."

Otto shifted his attention to Olivia and gave her a twinkly smile. "I have a daughter just your age. Today is her last day of school. Perhaps you two will be able to spend time together during your vacation. Did you sail from Charleston to New York City?"

"Yes, usually we sail directly to Philadelphia on the *Carolina Princess*, but it was in drydock for repairs, so we sailed to New York on the *Morning Star* instead."

"And will your parents allow you to attend any of the balls during the summer season?"

Olivia blushed and looked at her knees. "No, I'm not old enough yet, but I'm looking forward to it someday. Does your daughter get to go?"

An image of Rian wearing a dress flashed in front of Otto. He loved those occasions, but he could not separate them from the perpetual scowl Rian displayed when doing so. "Rian has not yet expressed interest in such things. Perhaps you can nudge her in that direction."

"I would be delighted," Olivia responded. She pointed to Otto's stick. "Is that a cane?"

"No. It is called a lumber estimating rule. When I sailed to America from Wurttemberg, the only thing I brought was a bag of tools. This lumber rule is the first tool I made in my new country. See these notches? If I hold this stick at arm's length and look at a standing tree, I can estimate the amount of lumber that can be milled out of the tree. It is one of my prized possessions, but I just use it as a walking stick these days."

"It's kind of chunky for a walking stick."

Otto chuckled. "Indeed, it is. It is made of hickory, the same as our president." Otto handed the lumber rule to Olivia. "Here, feel the heft of it. No one bothers a gentleman when he carries a cane such as this."

"Have you ever had to use it to fight off bad guys?"

Otto took back possession of the stick and sat back in his seat. "Not in a very long time."

Randolph Tucker put his hand on his daughter's knee to tell her she was occupying too much of Otto's attention. "You just got on the train in Bordentown, Mr. Krieger. Did you have business there?"

"Well, actually, I have been away from Philadelphia for three days. I had an appointment with the Camden & Amboy Railroad president in Hoboken on Saturday. I spent the night in New York, then yesterday I took the ferry to Amboy and caught a train to Bordentown for an appointment here first thing this morning."

"And what was your appointment this morning?"

Otto stuffed down a shard of annoyance. *I have lived in America for fifteen years, and I still am amazed at how Americans believe they can ask even the most personal questions.* "I visited a manufactury that builds railroad cars."

"And why was that?"

Otto considered dodging the answer but decided to plunge ahead. *The word will get out soon enough anyway.* "I am thinking of getting into the same business. It seems the future of railroads is bright. Making passenger cars would be a bit of a leap for Krieger Coach, but well within my shop's capabilities."

"The shop owner, he let you into his place of business?"

"More than that. He gave me a grand tour. He wants to sell me his operation, but I told him I was not interested."

"And why was that?"

"His shop is more antiquated than mine. He has not invested in capital goods in twenty years. His tools and machinery were fit for a factory in the 1700s, but not our modern age."

Tucker nodded, tacitly agreeing with Otto. "So, you intend to build railroad cars. Will you still make horse-drawn carriages?"

"Oh yes, for the time being."

A glowing cinder blew in the window and landed on Penelope's cape. She brushed it off with a grunt. "If you start making new train cars, Mr. Krieger, please figure out how to keep the burning coals out of the passenger compartments."

Otto again touched the brim of his hat. "Duly noted, Mrs. Tucker."

"I assume you know my brother George is involved with the new railroad that will run from Philadelphia to Baltimore."

Tucker took his wife's hand, a signal for her not to intrude in the men's conversation. "Yes, perhaps George Shippen can help you out. You will probably need capital to finance your expansion. I'm sure his bank will be receptive."

Instead of letting Tucker steal the conversation, Otto responded directly to Mrs. Tucker. "Your brother has been encouraging me to invest in his railroad for months. I am inclined to do it. With the addition of the Baltimore railroad, Philadelphia will have railroads extending to the north, west, and south."

"Mother, perhaps Mr. Krieger and his wife can come to the ball at our house."

Her daughter's impetuous comment caught Penelope off guard. "I am sure that Mr. Krieger has better things to do than come to one of our parties."

"I thank you for your thoughtfulness, Olivia. Sadly, my dear wife died in the cholera epidemic three years ago. I have not attended parties for a long while."

Olivia hung her head. "I'm sorry. I didn't know."

"Of course, you did not know. I am used to my situation now, and I spend time with my daughter. We play violin together most every evening."

A wave of melancholy washed over Otto. The conversation with the Tuckers had reached a natural conclusion. He closed his eyes and retreated into himself. As he had done since Deirdre died, he spoke to her before he drifted off to sleep. *This isn't going well, Beloved. Our daughter is fiery and willful. I made a mistake: I allowed her to wear boy clothes in the shop because she got her dresses so dirty. Now she wants to wear her shop clothes all the time. The other day, a customer mistook her for a boy. Thankfully, that won't work for very much longer.*

Wenn sie nur ein Junge wäre [If only she were a boy]. The carriage maker knew he would never share that thought with anyone, not even Deirdre. *But you would have known what to do, my love.*

Otto heard the brakeman's footsteps overhead. Then the train started a descent down a slight grade. The passenger car swayed, allowing the sun to warm his hands occasionally. The notes struck by wheels on rails rose as their car passed over a wooden bridge. Otto lapsed into a dreamless sleep.

· ·

· JULES ·

Jules Freeman watched Adrian and Rian as they inspected the *Falcon*'s noisy steam engine, thirty feet aft. Rian affectionately leaned on her uncle's shoulder while they chatted with the ferry's mechanic at his post behind the railing that separated the engine from the ferry's deck. All three raised their voices above the *choosh! choosh!* of the steam engine, but the headwind carried their words aft, and Jules could not hear their conversation.

Although the warmth of this first day of summer was gratifying, his mind was back at the shop. *I should never have left the men. It's hard enough for a Black man to keep a bunch of krautbreath in line on a normal day, but they were an especially sullen bunch this morning.*

He rarely left the factory during business hours, but Otto had been insistent when he left: *Meet me at the train station in Camden at 12:30 on Monday.*

Adrian sauntered to Jules's side and turned to watch Rian as she continued yelling back and forth with the mechanic.

Jules casually pointed toward Rian. "Did you find out what was going on?"

"No surprise. Billy Schiffler called her a dirty mick girl, so she popped him one."

"Good for her. Otto's not going to be pleased, though."

Adrian shook his head. "No, he's not. And I certainly didn't need this distraction today of all days. Are you still sorry we're taking this little excursion?"

Jules nodded. "With strikes cropping up all over the city? I think this is the worst time to be away from the shop. But I'm just the foreman. You two are the owners. You should be the ones who are worried."

"First, we'll hear how Otto made out with his appointments. Then we'll tell him about Rian. Then we'll figure out how to avoid a strike at Krieger Coach and Krieger Forge. What's there to be worried about?"

Rian finally tore herself away from the ferry's mechanic and ran up to join them at the boat's bow. "Hi, Jules. Did Uncle Adrian tell you he's going to build a steam engine?"

Adrian looked at his niece in mock exasperation. "Rian! Well, I said I could build one. I don't think it would be that difficult."

Jules stared at Adrian. "Are you serious?"

Adrian shrugged his shoulders and smiled, revealing nothing.

The Falcon's whistle sounded, prompting Jules to turn, face into the wind, and watch the river-town outline of Camden grow. As the ferry approached

Cooper Point, a much smaller version of the wharves they had left in Philadelphia a short time ago loomed directly ahead.

Jules braced himself for the collision as the ferry approached the landing, but it pulled in smoothly and gently nudged the dock. *Well done, Captain,* he thought to himself.

Two deckhands stepped from the boat to the dock and secured the bow and stern. Then they winched heavy planks from the deck to the wharf so passengers and cargo could disembark. The mechanic continued tending the steam engine, which gave up its energy to the blue sky with a lengthy whoosh.

The passengers, horses and drays, oxen and carts, and workers with wheelbarrows left the boat, moving on to the next legs of their journeys. The band of three hung back and then sauntered off the boat in no particular hurry. The last passenger off the boat, Jules stepped onto New Jersey soil, the first time he had left the relative safety of Philadelphia in months.

As Adrian, Jules, and Rian worked their way up the gravel slope from the wharf, the smell of cooking meat wafted down the embankment. Jules led the band up away from the river to a rotund man with a grease-stained apron. He was tending a large cast-iron frying pan set directly on coals surrounded by a ring of stones. Jules leaned into the smell of the cooking meat and smiled. *"Schnitzel?"*

"Ja," responded the cook. Although Jules had asked the question, the cook ignored him and addressed Adrian in German. "I bought this pork from the butcher this morning. This boat was hungry. They almost cleaned me out. If you take all that's left, I'll throw in this loaf of bread."

Unwilling to be excluded, Jules said in German, "If we *don't* buy you out, you'll have to wait for the next ferry, and that's more than an hour."

The vendor again ignored Jules and returned his attention to Adrian. "The *John Bull* should arrive soon carrying twenty passengers or more. Those folks will buy the rest, and I can sell this loaf rather than give it to you, fine gentlemen." As he made eye contact with Adrian and even fleetingly with Rian, the exclusion of Jules, the Black man, was obvious.

Adrian ignored the slight and nodded, agreeing to the deal. "When is the *John Bull* due?"

The schnitzel man tugged a penny paper out from under a stone, placed the small loaf of bread on it, and pried it open with his fingers. "Soon. If it doesn't break down or run off the tracks, it can make the trip from Amboy in five hours. Not bad when a stagecoach takes fifteen."

"Does it break down often?"

The schnitzel man shrugged. "It derailed two years ago, and two people were killed. So, a lot of people still take stagecoaches even though they are slower. Stick around. The locomotive is noisier than the boat you just crossed the Delaware on." He spooned the last of the schnitzel and its gravy onto the bread.

Adrian paid the man and put his money clip back in his pocket. "Thanks for lunch."

"Thanks for cleaning me out. Now, I'll go home early and see my missus. Show her my sausage." He laughed at his own joke as he handed Adrian the bread- and schnitzel-laden newspaper.

In a silent rebuke to the man's insults, Adrian held out the newspaper first to Jules, then to Rian, for them to take first bites, then turned away and muttered, "I imagine this guy's sausage isn't any bigger than his schnitzel." Jules and Adrian shared a laugh as they started walking up the hill.

The trio finger-ate the bread and schnitzel as they walked in lockstep up the gravel slope.

Jules looked ahead. A beefy, barrel-chested man stood at the top of the hill; a pistol tucked in his waistband. He wore a shabby coat and vest, and draped over his shoulder was a set of iron shackles. Hand on the butt of his pistol, he stared hard at Jules, causing him to fall out of step with his companions momentarily. Jules quickly corrected to return to their pace.

Adrian noticed Jules's stutter-step and followed his gaze up the hill. "Who is that gump?"

"That gump is Austin T. Slatter. He's no one to fool with."

"What's he to you?"

"He's a slave catcher."

Adrian slowed his pace. "Do you want to turn around?"

"Nope, that's what he wants me to do. Just act like everything's okay. And if he drops my emancipation papers on the ground, don't stoop down to pick them up."

Rian detected the urgency in their exchange. "What's wrong?"

"Hush, Niece," said Adrian. "Later."

The slave catcher put up his hand to signal them to stop. He addressed Adrian. "This your African?"

"No, he's a free Negro. The foreman at my brother's factory."

The man stared at Jules. "I'm looking for a buck that fits his description. You got papers, boy?"

"Yes, I do," said Jules as he reached toward his breast pocket.

"Hold on a minute, Jules," said Adrian, as he turned his attention to Jules's antagonist. "Who are you, and what right do you have to stop a free man going about his business?"

"My name is Austin T. Slatter, and I have been hired by numerous people in Maryland and Virginia to recover their property. I'm looking for a runaway that fits this African's description."

"Let me see your documentation."

Slatter stared back at Adrian for three seconds, spit a stream of tobacco juice that landed between Adrian and Jules, and reached into a pocket inside his jacket. He handed a folded sheet of paper to Adrian. "Third one down," he said without looking at the sheet.

Adrian perused the paper and handed it to Jules. "This says the man you are looking for a dark-skinned Negro who is 5'10". My friend is taller than I am, which would make him at least 6'2". And I wouldn't call him dark-skinned."

"Owners of escaped slaves are describing their property from memory. Sometimes warrants have their details wrong, but the warrant legally entitles me to demand this African's papers."

Jules reached into his breast pocket, pulled out a yellowed piece of paper, unfolded it, and presented it to the man. "It's okay, Adrian. We'll be here all day until I do this."

Slatter perused the paper. "What's your name, boy?"

"It tells you right there on the paper."

Slatter's eyes bored into Jules. "I know what the paper says. I want to see if you know. These papers could be forged. Tell me your name."

Jules sighed. He had been through this routine a hundred times before. "My name is Jules Freeman. That paper says my name is Jules Howland."

"Why the difference?

"I changed my name fifteen years ago."

"How come?"

"I guess I didn't like my slave name."

Slatter glared at Jules, seemingly a hairbreadth away from striking him. "Where were you born?"

"Greene County, Virginia."

"How old are you?"

"Don't know for sure. That document says I was born in 1798."

"How come you're not a slave anymore?"

"I bought my emancipation."

"Emancipation, huh? That's a pretty fancy word, boy. You like putting on airs, don't you?"

"Are we done here?" interjected Adrian.

"We're done when I say we're done." He returned his attention to Jules. "Your owner. What was her name?"

"His name."

"Don't be smart with me, boy. What was his name?"

"My enslaver's name was Marion Pruett."

"What are you doing in New Jersey?"

"I don't think that's any of your business."

Slatter put his hand on his pistol. Before he could do anything else, Adrian grabbed the man's wrist. "You pick a fight with Jules; you pick a fight with me. I think you would regret it."

In answer, Slatter let the paper fall out of his hand. It floated down to their feet. "Well, I guess we are done here. For the moment."

With the standoff seemingly resolved, Adrian released the man's wrist.

Unwilling to stoop to pick up the emancipation paper, Jules stood his ground and stared back at the slave catcher. Adrian adhered to Jules' caution and remained on guard. Rian solved the dilemma by bending down to retrieve the paper.

The slave catcher grunted. "Well, Mr. Putting-On-Airs, I spend a lot of time in Philadelphia. I'm sure I'll be running into you again. Next time, maybe you won't have your white friend to protect you."

"I look forward to it," said Jules.

Adrian tugged on Jules's arm. "Come on. I can hear the train."

As they walked toward the tracks, Jules realized that Adrian still held the newspaper containing the remnants of the schnitzel and bread. "You had one hand on Slatter's wrist and the other hand filled with schnitzels. What were you going to do if he tried to pull his gun?"

"I hadn't quite figured that out yet, but it would have been a waste if I had to smash good food in his face."

Jules laughed, partly at the thought of Slatter with a face full of schnitzel, but more to burn off the stink of the encounter.

· ·

· RIAN ·

Rian read Jules's emancipation paper as they continued toward the railroad tracks. Although entirely handwritten, it looked like an official document to her unpracticed eyes. At the very bottom, it was signed by

Cyrus R. Talbot
Prothonotary
Greene County, Virginia

Rian rubbed her finger over the outline of an American eagle and a circle of tiny stars embossed over Cyrus Talbot's name.

"Jules, I thought you were born in Calvert County, in Maryland."

"I was."

"But this paper says Greene County, Virginia."

"I know. It's forged."

"The whole thing is made up? Is anything on this paper true?"

"My age is a best guess. Everything else is fake." Jules made a half-hearted attempt to tug the paper out of Rian's hands.

Rian turned her body away from him and continued reading. "Why'd you make it up?"

Adrian put his hand on Rian's shoulder. "Niece, quit asking questions that are none of your business."

"No," said Jules. "It's time she learned these things. Rian, I ran away from my enslaver fifteen years ago, before you were born. Your father and your Uncle Adrian know. So does Aaron Bassinger, but no one else at the shop knows. Even though it's been fifteen years since I was a slave, if I were found out, I could be taken back to Maryland and forced back into slavery."

In response, Rian borrowed one of her friend Conor's favorite words. "Jaysus. And that gump could have just arrested you right on the spot and taken you back to Maryland?"

"If he knew who my enslaver was. He would have to take me to a magistrate first and prove that I was a runaway. I keep this paper on me all the time. I have to be careful everywhere I go, especially when I leave Philadelphia."

"So, this signature, Cyrus R. Talbot; that isn't real?"

"No, it isn't."

"Who signed it?"

"Maddie."

"Maddie, your wife?"

"Yes, Maddie, my wife."

Rian again ran her fingers over the embossed stars. "How did she make these?"

"Maybe I'll show you sometime." Jules plucked the paper from Rian's hand, folded it, and tucked it into his breast pocket. "Thanks, by the way, for picking this up."

Rian put her hand in Jules's big, welcoming mitt. "Austin T. Slatter would have bashed you on the head if you'd bent down to pick up the paper, wouldn't he."

"How'd you figure that out?"

"That's what I would have done if it had been Billy Schiffler and one of his idiot friends. You always lose when it's two against one, so you've got to take one of them out early."

Jules and Adrian stopped in their tracks. Adrian turned to her. "How many fistfights have you been in, Niece?"

Rian looked up, momentarily calculating. "I don't know. Seven. Uh, eight if you count the one Conor and I were in together. Mostly they've been draws. Billy's was my first win."

"How many of them did you start?"

"It depends on how you look at it."

"What do you mean?"

"Big kids pick on the little kids. The boys pick on girls. Some boys pick on Tom Mott because he's a Quaker, and they know he won't fight back. I always tell them to stop being a bully. If they don't, then I start swinging."

"So, by your reckoning, the bullies start the fight when . . ."

"When they don't stop being a bully."

"How many of these fights does your father know about?"

"One, but that was a couple of years ago."

Adrian started walking again, prompting Jules and Rian to do the same. "Well, Niece, I know your father will be disappointed, but I think your grandfather would have been pleased."

"Really? Why?"

"Do you know what *krieger* means in German?"

"Of course. It means *warrior*."

"Well, your grandfather Heinrich Krieger—Otto and Kurt's and my father—was a cavalry officer during the Napoleonic Wars. He never backed down from a fight. I bet a hundred times I heard him say, 'I'm a Warrior by name and a warrior by nature.' He would have heard your tale and said 'Bravo.'"

"I don't think *Vater* is going to say that."

Adrian pulled Rian toward him in an avuncular fashion and put his arm around her as they walked. "No, definitely not."

"So, Jules," said Rian, "how did you know that Austin T. Slatter would drop your paper?"

"Two years ago, I saw Slatter sitting in a rocking chair on the porch of a boarding house on Cedar Street in Philadelphia. Two men I knew, but not very well, walked by the rooming house—black men, just like me. Just walking. Slatter left the porch and demanded to see their emancipation papers. They showed them to him. Didn't cause a fuss. Rather than hand them back, Slatter dropped the papers in the gutter. When one of them stooped to pick them up, Slatter cracked him on the head with the butt of his pistol, then challenged his friend to continue the fight. Of course, he declined. Slatter just laughed, turned his back on the men, and returned to the porch."

"That is one nasty son-of-a-bitch.," Adrian commented as they continued up the hill.

At the top of the hill, the trio arrived at the train station, which was a wooden platform about one hundred feet long. Fifty feet away stood a small building with a sign above the door that said "Tickets Merchandise Victuals." The *choosh . . . choosh . . . choosh* of the *John Bull* grew louder and drew their attention down the railroad tracks. Rian could see a plume of smoke moving toward them above the trees but not yet the train.

Adrian followed Rian's gaze up the tracks and took out his pocket watch. "Well, despite the delays for schnitzel and the slave catcher, our timing is perfect. So, tell me again why Otto asked us to meet him here?"

Jules pointed toward the approaching plume. "He wants us to see as many train cars as possible before he starts designing new ones. All the *Camden & Amboy* cars were made in New Jersey. Maybe we'll see something we haven't seen on the *Philadelphia & Columbia*."

"So, as the owner of Krieger Forge, I guess I'm looking at wheels and the undercarriage."

"What can I do?" asked Rian.

"You, dear Niece, can tell your father that you got kicked out of school this morning and that I didn't feel like leaving you alone in the factory because the workers are feeling a bit surly today."

• • • • • • • • • • • • • • • • • •

The *choosh . . . choosh . . . choosh* grew louder, drawing Rian's attention to the noisy machine clanking toward them. She had not yet ridden on a train, but they weren't unfamiliar to her. The *Philadelphia & Columbia's* eastern terminus was only an eight-block walk from her house, and she and her father had lately taken more than a few after-dinner strolls to the station on Vine Street. When the last train of the evening entered Philadelphia, Otto would comment on the various railroad cars, which ones were well built, and what flaws he spotted in their design.

Rian absorbed her father's lessons but was equally intrigued by the loco-motives. They struck her as an ungainly melding of a cart and furnace. They belched soot and ash. They clanked and screeched. But they also had an allure. They were good at what they were designed to do.

The locomotive *chooshed* to a halt at the platform. Like the *Philadelphia & Columbia's* engines, the *John Bull* was a mechanical marvel and a workhorse; fourteen feet long, with a smokestack that rose almost that high. The engine driver stood in the open air directly behind the boiler. The locomotive pulled a tender with two barrels set on end and almost empty of firewood. The tender, in turn, pulled a flatbed car filled with wooden boxes, mail sacks, and luggage, followed by three carriages, each holding eighteen people or so. Last came an open gondola car occupied by two white horses. As the train slowed, six men and women stood up, brushing straw off their shoulders.

Jules, standing next to Rian, studied the train as well. He muttered "Shit" when he saw the people with the horses.

Rian followed his gaze. "What?"

"Just a little tough seeing my people riding with the animals. Suppose I should expect it."

"Those Negroes? Why don't they ride in the passenger cars?"

"Because they aren't allowed."

A well-dressed boy about Rian's age leaped over the side of the gondola while the train was still moving. He sprinted to catch up to the last passenger car and opened the door for its occupants when the train halted. A man in his mid-thirties descended from the coach without acknowledging the boy. The man brushed cinders off the shoulder of his frock coat, briefly surveyed his surroundings, turned, and offered his hand to an attractive woman descending from the coach.

The woman addressed the boy. "Topper, where is Matilde? She should be here attending to me. I'm covered with cinders."

"Sorry, Missus. One of the horses stepped on her ankle when we pulled into the station. She's walking it off, but she'll be here directly."

"Topper," said the man. "Go tell Matilde to hurry up. Then attend to the horses. Make sure you do your job."

"Shit," Jules said again in a low voice.

"What this time?"

"I can tell from that man's accent. He's from the South. Deeper South than where I grew up. All the people in that open car back there are not free Blacks. They're slaves."

"How can they be slaves? Isn't New Jersey a free state the same as Pennsylvania?"

"Nope, it's not. New Jersey went for gradual emancipation thirty years ago. If you were born after February 15, 1804, you had to be freed on your twenty-first birthday. So, if you were unlucky enough to be born a day earlier, you'll be a slave for life."

"Unless you run away."

Jules looked around to see if anyone was listening. "Keep your voice down, Child." He cocked his head toward the last car of the train. "Those folks with the horses, they're not New Jersey slaves. They're from the South. I'm betting South Carolina."

"What are they doing up here?"

"I dunno. Maybe we'll find out."

A young girl hopped from the carriage. Rian didn't have any friends who were girls, but this one struck her as being quite pretty, with auburn hair and blue eyes. Both her coat and dress came down to just below her knees, befitting a young woman about her age. Rian paid very little attention to fashion, but she acknowledged the girl was quite fetching.

People disembarked from the compartments of all three coaches. The brakeman lowered peoples' bags to a station attendant. Railroad workers and two men from the gondola transferred the wooden boxes from the flatbed car to a wagon. The engine driver jerked the spout from the water tank over the tender and started adding water into the barrels. Another station attendant threw billets of firewood up to the fireman, who threw them into the tender. Topper and another man led the two white horses toward the river.

Rian looked for her father. He finally emerged from the same compartment as the pretty girl.

· · · · · · · · · · · · · · · · · · ·

· OTTO ·

Otto caught sight of Rian with his brother and Jules as he descended from the coach. He strode directly to them, already with a head of steam. "*Rian, was machst du hier* [Rian, what are you doing here]? You are supposed to be in school. And why are you not wearing a dress?"

Adrian took a step toward his brother. "Uh, that was my decision, Otto. Rian had to leave school today, and I didn't want to leave her roaming the shop."

"And why did she have to leave school early?"

Adrian looked at Rian, but she was looking at her shoes. "She popped Billy Schiffler in the nose for calling her Barn Door. That started a bit of a scuffle, which she won, by the way."

"Billy Schiffler, the son of the bank president?"

Adrian pulled Rian protectively toward him. "Yes, Otto, the man you often eat lunch with at the hotel."

"This happened at school?"

"Yes."

"Is that Billy's blood on your shirt?"

Adrian continued to answer for Rian. "Yes, I imagine it is."

"So, you were not wearing a dress at school?"

"Uh, Otto, that may have been my fault. Rian told me that since it was the last day of school, they would be playing games all day, so it was okay if she wore her shop clothes."

"Rian, were any of the other girls wearing pants?"

"No," his daughter responded.

"Adrian, if she was kicked out of school, why did you not just leave her with Aaron at the shop? She spends half her time there anyway."

"Things at the shop are a little tense at the moment, Otto. The whole city's in an uproar, and I thought it would be better to keep her with us."

"So, the strikes have spread?"

Adrian nodded. "But our men were working away when we left. We might be okay."

"Then we should get back. Skip looking at these cars. The one I rode in is junk anyway."

Jules looked back down the hill toward the river. "There's no rush at the moment, Otto. The ferry's not back yet, so we'd just be waiting down at the landing for another fifteen minutes or so."

"Then let us get to it. Rian, you and I will discuss your actions later."

As they turned to walk toward the train, Randolph Tucker approached the group. "Herr Krieger, I seem to have lost track of Olivia. You didn't see where she wandered off to, did you?"

"I'm sorry, Mr. Tucker, but I have not."

"Hmm, she's probably back with my Africans."

"Excuse me?"

"My slaves. They were on our train, back with the horses. Household staff, my groom, plus some others to continue repairs to the house."

"Mr. Tucker, you know slavery is illegal in Pennsylvania."

"Oh yes, well aware. But that's only a problem if they remain in the state for more than six months. We'll be long gone before that time. Excuse me, I have to find out what has become of Olivia."

Tucker left before Otto had a chance to introduce his greeting party. *But my daughter looks like a street urchin, and Tucker probably would not be interested in Jules.*

"*Hör mal zu* [Listen]," Otto said to his greeting party, "I am interested in overall impressions of all the railroad cars. What appears to be well designed and well-constructed? What would we do differently with our cars? Rian will stay with me, and we will look at the passenger cars."

Adrian pointed to the underside of the flatbed. "I'll look at anything that involves iron and steel. That means I'll need to get under the cars. I suggest that Jules join me and learn how the cars are built from the wheels up."

"That is a good plan. Thank you for coming, by the way."

"Otto, one thing."

"*Was ist das* [What is that]?"

"What we're doing is going to look a bit suspicious."

"Yes, I am afraid we will have to be a little cagey. I have a plan. If anyone confronts you, tell them I lost a handkerchief on the train, and we are looking for it."

"That's a pretty flimsy plan, Otto."

"It is the best I could come up with. Rian, you will stick with me."

• •

Otto made measurements with his lumber rule. "Sixty inches wide, Rian." or "Eighteen inches between seats, Rian." His daughter entered the figures onto a sheet of paper. *My daughter was kicked out of school for fighting today. My daughter wears boys' clothing. My daughter tucks her hair up into her cap and is mistaken for a boy more often than not.*

"What are you going to do with all these figures, *Vater*?"

"Adrian and I are working on a proposal to a railway company to build carriages for them. We think we can offer a better carriage at a lower price than the ones that are currently in service." *Although she's unladylike, combative, and defiant, my daughter has the Krieger brains. She asks me these questions to keep me from asking about the fight. Well, we will get to that.*

"So why are we stealing other people's ideas?"

"We are not. This is more like learning from their mistakes. My designs are going to look nothing like these cars. Here, sit on this bench. Tell me what you think."

"I'm smaller than you, but there's not much legroom even for me."

"Why do you think that is?"

"Maybe they had to make this coach small to cut down on weight."

"Good guess," Otto replied. "Here is what I think. The men who designed this passenger car had previously designed only stagecoaches. They just slapped a different set of wheels on it and called it a day."

"But you've only designed carriages. What's the difference?"

Otto appreciated his daughter's engagement and already felt his ire at Rian's fisticuffs dissipating. He would deal with the events of Rian's morning later. "The difference, *Liebling*, is that I know I must design a totally different beast. Stagecoaches are pulled by horses. They are driven over rocky roads. Weight on the new coaches will still be an important consideration, but not the most important. My cars will be more spacious and designed to roll along steel rails. Okay, we are done here. We should get out before the conductor asks us what we are doing."

By the time they descended from the car, Adrian and Jules had worked their way to the front of the train. At first, kneeling near the wheels of the flatbed car, Jules found something interesting and shifted his position to lie on his back to look up toward the car's underside. Adrian examined the John Bull. Otto and Rian joined Adrian.

"The *John Bull's* a lot different from the ferry's steam engine," Rian said.

"Yeah, a bit," responded Adrian. "This is a fine machine, but it's five years old. There have been a lot of improvements since then."

Rian looked down at the rails. "How come this track is different?"

Adrian looked down, then returned his gaze to the locomotive. "Different than what?"

A blast from the *Falcon's* whistle announced its arrival back on the New Jersey side of the Delaware. Otto craned his neck down the slope. *We still have fifteen minutes yet.*

"You know," Rian responded to Adrian. "The *Philadelphia & Columbia's* track. At the depot."

"In Philadelphia?" Adrian looked at the track more critically. "You're right. It is different. That's a good question, Rian. Otto, take a look at these rails. I bet they can carry a heavier load than the ones in Pennsylvania."

Otto glanced at the rail. The tracks in Philadelphia were thick strap-iron standing on edge and nailed to stout boards, not nearly as beefy as this all-iron stock. These rails were thick and forged in the form of an upside-down T.

"Hey!" The *John Bull's* engine driver strode aggressively toward Jules, who was lying on his back, head resting on the rail and staring up at the underside of a carriage. "What are you doing under there, boy?"

Jules got up slowly and faced the engine driver. He said nothing.

The engine driver pushed Jules in the chest with both hands. "I said, what were you doing there?" Jules was forced back a step but made no effort to defend himself.

Otto strode from the *John Bull*, using his estimating rule like a cane. "Excuse me! Is there a problem?" He shifted his grip on the stout stick so that the heavy end rested on his shoulder. Rian followed behind him.

"This African was fooling with the train. We've had problems, and now I know why."

"I'm sorry, sir, but that is not so. I arrived on this train fifteen minutes ago and seemed to have misplaced my handkerchief. My friend was just helping me look for it."

The conductor didn't believe Otto's story. He balled both his fists, seemingly preparing to strike at Jules. "The African is your friend, huh. Well, I want you and your African friend away from my train."

Otto's voice was calm, but he tightened his grip on his lumber rule. "Take it easy, sir. We have done no harm to your train."

The engine driver had been willing to assail Jules when Jules was alone but was reluctant to take on two, especially when one of them carried a stout stick. He hesitated. Then the standoff became volatile again as the train's fireman, attracted by the ruckus, strode to his co-worker's side.

"What've we got here, Ned?"

"I caught this krautbreath and his African messin' with the car."

The fireman chose to focus on Jules. "What were you doing with the car, boy?"

"Watch out!" yelled Rian, a split second before the fireman took a swing at Jules. The engine driver charged at Otto. Jules parried the fireman's blow, and it had no effect. Otto swung down hard with his lumber rule, clubbing the engine driver on his shoulder hard enough to drop him to one knee. Otto returned to Jules's side, crouched slightly, and prepared for a second assault by either trainman. They still looked ready to fight, but their first attempt didn't breed confidence. Jules stood his ground, not breathing hard. Otto crouched, prepared for combat but not particularly threatening.

A crowd gathered. Some people looked unfriendly, some merely curious. Otto noticed Randolph Tucker's daughter was among them. A man whose plaid pants and bright green vest identified him as an Irishman joined the two trainmen. Then a fourth man—big, beefy, dressed in a shabby suit and with a set of iron manacles draped over his shoulder—elbowed his way through the gawkers and joined the railroaders.

Otto sensed that with the addition of the two and a few of the onlookers egging them on, the trainmen might try something again. *This is not good.*

Adrian casually walked to Jules's side and stared at the four antagonists. *Three against four.* Rian, weighing all of seventy pounds, sidled up beside her uncle, father, and Jules.

"Well, well, well," said the beefy man as he leered at Jules. "If it ain't Mr. Putting-On-Airs. Didn't think opportunity was going to knock on my door quite so quickly." He pulled the manacles off his shoulder and dangled them menacingly at his side.

"Excuse me," said Olivia Tucker

"I think we can take these fellas," said the Irishman.

The engine driver crouched, girding himself to re-engage. "I think you're right. On the count of three. One . . ."

"Excuse me," Olivia repeated.

"Two . . ."

"Excuse me, Mr. Krieger," Olivia said a third time as she strode between the fireman and the Irishman, waving an embroidered handkerchief high in the air. "I think I found your handkerchief."

The mood momentarily broken, the trainmen, the Irishman, and the man with the manacles straightened and stepped back.

Without breaking his gaze from the trainmen, Otto held out his hand for the handkerchief. "Why, thank you, Miss Tucker. I have been looking all over for this."

The engine driver, rubbing his shoulder, didn't seem to have much stomach for a fight. "I don't believe your story about a handkerchief one bit. Just keep your African friend away from the train. We've had trouble."

With a fight now unlikely, the crowd began to disperse, although the trainmen backed off only a few feet.

"Lucky a second time, boy," said the man with the manacles. "This will make our next meeting even sweeter."

"Sorry for the misunderstanding, sir," Otto said to the trainmen. He shifted his attention to his allies. "I have to go get my satchel. Come on, all. Let us stick together." As the group returned to the platform, he said, "Rian, Adrian, Jules, I would like you to meet Miss Olivia Tucker. I want to thank you, Olivia, for helping to get us out of a nasty jam. Here is your handkerchief back, my dear."

The group arrived at Otto's satchel, sitting by itself on the now deserted platform.

Randolph Tucker leaped up the platform steps. "Olivia! Where have you been? I've been looking for you for fifteen minutes."

"I am sorry," said Otto before Olivia could respond. "I lost my handkerchief on the train and was looking for it. Olivia found it and just returned it to me."

Tucker grabbed his daughter by the wrist. "Someone said there were fisticuffs a few moments ago."

"Just a misunderstanding, apparently," said Otto.

Tucker jerked Olivia toward the river. "Come along. We're going to miss the ferry."

Otto, Rian, Adrian, and Jules followed Tucker and his daughter at a distance. They passed their recent antagonists, who were still telling their side of the story to the few crowd members who remained to listen.

Adrian impulsively stopped and addressed both the trainmen. "Uh, one thing. I noticed that your rails are different than our rails in Philadelphia. Where were they made?"

Otto briefly feared the confrontation would start all over again. However, after a short pause, the engine driver said. "England. You can't get anything like these rails in America." The engine driver turned away from Adrian, shaking his head.

Otto kept walking, a relieved smile on his face. Finally, he said, "I wish Kurt had come along with us. We could have used him." Kurt was the largest of the three Krieger brothers. Although a reluctant brawler, his size alone would have intimidated the trainmen.

Adrian pulled Rian toward him and threw her into a playful headlock. "Who needs Kurt when we've got Rian. Thanks for your help, girl. I don't think they would have backed down if you hadn't joined us. Otto, you've got a warrior on your hands."

Despite his recent irritation with his daughter, Otto had to admit that she was definitely a Krieger. "*Ein Krieger mit Namen und ein Krieger von Natur aus* [A Warrior by name and a warrior by nature]," he said just loud enough for his group to hear. *Wenn sie nur ein Junge wäre* [If only she were a boy], he thought to himself for the second time that morning.

Another blast of the ferry whistle announced its impending departure, and stragglers started moving down to the dock.

Otto paid for the group's passage. They formed the tail end of the procession to the ferry. Rather than move past knots of people who had witnessed the altercation and were eying his group with varying degrees of hostility, he opted to keep them at the rear of the ferry. He picked up the conversation, happy to continue speaking in his native German. "I am sorry this happened. The fact is the railmen have had problems. They are in bitter competition with a stagecoach line and a canal. The railway is winning, but there are suspicions that thugs are being sent to meddle with the cars and rails."

Adrian watched the deckhands untie the mooring lines from the dock. "We weren't doing anything wrong."

"We were not damaging the railway cars, but we were not looking for my handkerchief either," replied Otto. "The trainmen knew that and would have been happy to give Jules a good thrashing just because he's Black. I apologize, Jules, for getting you into that."

Jules shrugged. "Just another day for me, Otto."

With a final blast of its whistle and a surge of power, the ferry left the dock. What had been its stern was now its bow.

Rian tugged on her father's sleeve. "*Vater*, may I go up to the bow and talk to that Olivia girl?"

Otto was a bit surprised at his daughter's request. *She rarely chooses to spend time with girls her own age.* He looked toward the bow of the boat and spied Olivia and Topper, the slave boy who had opened the coach door for Randolph Tucker. They were looking back at his group, and Topper was pointing at Rian. "Of course, *Liebling*, but come back here before the ferry docks so we can all leave the ferry together."

Jules continued the conversation after Rian's interruption. "So, who's the man you were riding in the coach with? Olivia's father."

"His name is Randolph Tucker. The landau we finished a few days ago? That is his. He is going to pick it up sometime this week."

Jules sighed as he looked back at the receding docks of Camden.

Otto sensed Jules' annoyance. "*Was die Sache* [What's the matter?]"

"Isn't it obvious? I wish you didn't sell your carriages to slave owners."

"Well, I did not know he was a slave owner when he ordered it. Second, if I chose not to do business with everyone who was pro-slavery in Philadelphia, I would not have any customers. A little disturbing that Tucker can bring his slaves up with him for an extended stay, though."

"You think every Negro walking around Philadelphia is free?"

"Not every one of them, but I assumed if they were slaves, they were just passing through with their masters."

"They can stay here for six months. Been that way forever."

Otto chose to change the subject. "Who was the guy with the manacles?"

"His name is Austin T. Slatter. He's a slave catcher. He stopped me when we got off the ferry. He was just looking for trouble."

"Your papers did the trick?"

"Yeah, but then Adrian and I told Rian the truth about them."

"Do you think that was wise?"

Jules watched Rian as she made her way forward toward the bow. "Who lined up with us when it was four against three?"

"My daughter. And then that little Olivia Tucker diffused the whole thing. I do not think I thanked her enough."

Adrian turned his gaze away from the receding Camden. "Tell us about your trip."

"I met with Robert Stevens at his office in Hoboken. He was receptive to us building coaches for the *Camden & Amboy*, but only if we can sell them at a lower price than others are offering."

"What about quality? That's what you were hoping for. Was that a factor?"

Otto flicked a piece of pigeon shit off the handrail and into the water. Confident that he would now not soil his frock coat, he turned and leaned against the rail. "Durability, yes. Comfort, not as much. He has a monopoly in New Jersey. No other railroads can be built to compete with him. He knows the *Camden & Amboy* offers the fastest travel time between New York and Philadelphia. The stagecoach cannot come close. Canal boats are much more spacious but are even slower yet. So, he has little incentive to make passengers more comfortable. He is only interested in price. Craftsmanship has always been our selling point for the carriages we build. I don't know how we can translate that to railroad cars if all Stevens is worried about is price."

"How about the factory owner in Bordentown? Are you going to buy his machinery?"

"Pff. On the one hand, it was a waste of time. On the other, if that's who we are competing with, I think we might be able to make it in the railroad world."

· ·

· RIAN ·

Rian weaved her way toward the bow, past horses and drays, half a dozen wheelbarrows, and a team of oxen harnessed to a wagon. At about midships, she nodded to Mr. and Mrs. Tucker standing next to a wagon filled with boxes from the train. A man whom Jules had identified as a slave held the reins of the two white horses that had been in the rear car of the train. She dodged around more animals and people, past the noisy steam engine and the pilothouse, and approached Olivia and her companion.

Rian shyly clasped her hands behind her back. "Hi, I'm Rian."

"I'm Olivia."

"Thank you for helping us out earlier. How did you know about the handkerchief?"

Olivia shrugged. "I heard your father tell the engine driver that he lost one. Even I knew it wasn't true, and I'm only eleven."

Olivia's accent entranced Rian. It was slow, lazy, melodic. "How come you helped us out?"

"I figured the fight was really about your father's Black friend. Negroes are always getting ganged up on at home. It's shameful. I try to stop it when I can." Olivia's companion nudged her. "Oh, this is Topper. He's got a lot of questions."

Rian turned to Topper. He smiled at her shyly. "Are you a boy or a girl?"

The question didn't seem like a challenge to Rian, just an expression of curiosity. "My name is Rian. It's Irish. I'm lucky because Rian can be either a boy's or a girl's name. A lot of people think I'm a boy when they first meet me because of my clothes. I tuck my hair up into my cap, and they can't tell."

"If you're a girl, how come you don't wear dresses?"

Because I hate them, I can't do things I want to when I'm wearing them. People treat me differently. I don't like the way they feel on my skin or even the sound they make. "When I'm in my father's shop, dresses get dirty. It's easier to wear boy's clothes. My uncles call me a tomboy."

Topper pointed at the red stains on her shirt. "Is that blood?"

"Yeah, a boy at school called me names, and I punched him."

Topper's eyes widened as if he could never imagine punching a white boy for calling him names. "Does your family get into fights a lot?"

"Mostly me. But sometimes because of Jules because he's Black."

"Jules. That's the big man you got on the ferry with?"

Rian nodded.

"Is he a slave or free?"

"He's been free for about fifteen years. I've known him all my life."

"How did he get free?"

Rian had just learned the lie, but none of its details, so she made them up on the fly. "He bought his freedom. His master let him work as a carpenter during the evenings, and he saved the money."

"Do you wish you were a boy?"

"Sometimes." Rian was tired of having the focus on her. "Are you a slave?"

"Yes."

"How come all the slaves in the last train car didn't just jump out? You could have been free."

"We talked about it, but no one wanted to do it."

"Why not?"

Before Topper could answer, Olivia's father appeared out of nowhere, grabbed him by the arm, and said, "Topper, I told you before to do your job. Get back to the horses."

"That's my fault, Papa," Olivia interjected. "Topper's never been to Philadelphia before, and I wanted him to see the city from the water because it's so beautiful."

"Topper isn't here to admire the view; he's here to take care of the horses. Olivia, you should know better." Tucker gave Topper a shove and followed him back toward the horses.

"I'm sorry, Papa," Olivia said to her father's back. She stomped her foot in frustration, crossed her arms, and looked at Rian. "Topper didn't get a chance to say it right. I imagine our slaves all wanted to escape. My mammy—she's the one who really raised me, not my mother—her real name is Rose—she says that my father brings only one member of a slave family when we come to Philadelphia. That way, if one of them escapes, he can punish their loved ones who were left behind. No one tries to escape."

Olivia's explanation seemed rather far-fetched to Rian. "Has he done that before? Punished the family?"

"Once that I know of. I was too little to understand. A field hand was sent to help load a shipment of our rice onto a ship. He tried to stow away, but he got caught. Papa's overseer whipped him good, then he tied his woman to a post and whipped her almost as much. Gave his little boy some licks too."

Olivia's story made Rian queasy. She chose to change the subject. "Seems like you try to stick up for Topper when he gets in trouble."

Olivia nodded. "I have to. He's my brother."

Rian felt Olivia's statement wash over her. She couldn't make sense of it. "I thought Topper's a slave."

"He is. He's really my half-brother. Mammy says my father had his way with her daughter when Mama was pregnant with me. Topper and I have grown up together."

"Does your mother know this?"

Olivia nodded. "Of course, everyone knows. They just don't talk about it. Sometimes, I hear Mama and my father arguing at night, though. He promises to stop, but he never does. I hate him."

Rian couldn't imagine hating her own father. Olivia was telling her things that Rian wouldn't have shared with anyone. She didn't know what to say. Instead, she watched a crewman work his way down the Falcon's deck, scooping manure up with a shovel and tossing it overboard into the Delaware River.

"That Irishman would have liked to join the fight against your family," Olivia commented.

Olivia's statement jerked Rian back to their conversation, which had taken a new turn. "Jules says that most whites won't give the Irish the time of day, but when they both can gang up on a Negro, they're happy as cutlets to get together."

"My father doesn't care for the Irish much, but he hires them to do black powder work on the farm. That way, if someone gets blown up, it doesn't come out of Papa's pocket." Olivia turned and looked to the west. "We always sail up the Delaware into Philadelphia. This is the first time we sailed to New York first. I've never been on this ferry."

"So, you've been to Philadelphia before?"

"We live outside of Charleston. In South Carolina. But we summer here every year. It's too hot in Charleston. So many people get sick there during the summer that my parents bought a house on Spruce Street so we can get away from it."[1]

The ferry was about to reach the northern tip of Windmill Island. In a few minutes, the expanse of Philadelphia's waterfront would be visible.

Uncle Adrian sidled up to the two of them. "Mind if I join you? The view from the bow is the best."

---

1. So many Charlestonians had purchased houses on Spruce Street between Ninth and Tenth Streets that it was called Carolina Row by locals and summer residents alike.

"Olivia, this is my Uncle Adrian."

Olivia smiled shyly, then turned her gaze to follow Adrian's as they rounded Windmill Island. She gasped as she saw the ships and docks on the opposite shore.

"Oh, it's beautiful."

Hundreds of sailing vessels crammed the waterfront, their masts so abundant that the docks might as well have been a forest. Single masted sloops. Two-masted brigs and schooners. Cranes to haul cargo on and off. Rian spied workers, still tiny to the eye, idling on the docks, which was unusual. Typically, they would be bustling about like ants at this time of day. Far to the south, just more than a mile, stood the colossal ship houses of the Philadelphia Navy Yard.

Half a dozen steam ferries, some larger than theirs, crossed every which way on the Delaware. Rian could see their decks laden with coaches, wagons, horses, livestock, wheelbarrows, and people. The ferries moved with the relative speed of insects in contrast to the majestic progress of two larger ships-of-sail. Huge, stately creatures, the ocean-going vessels ignored the insects as they embarked on their months-long journeys.

Adrian put his hands on the railing. "This is one of my favorite views in the world. The river was iced over for two months until late March, and no shipping could get in or out. That ship right there . . . the one being towed away from its berth, that's the *Vestal*, my brother Kurt's ship. He arrived two days ago with rice and cotton from Savannah."

"Uncle Kurt stays with *Vater* and me when he's in port," Rian interjected.

"There's the *Alice May* from New Bedford. She arrived yesterday with a load of whale oil. That's the Caledonia, just in from China. She's got a little bit of everything: silks, spices, porcelain, tea, kites, fireworks. There are ships here with goods from all over the world: wine from France and Spain, tobacco and cotton from the South, indigo from Bengal, rum from St. Croix, toys from Bavaria, hides from Uruguay, mahogany from Central America."

Olivia shifted her attention to another ship that a tug with ten oarsmen had towed to the middle of the river. Its crew was unfurling its sails to start its journey down the Delaware River. "What do they carry out?"

"Mostly manufactured goods made here—steam engines, textiles, carpets, flour, glass, steel. Even Otto, Rian's father, is involved. When he went back to Wurttemberg to see our two half-sisters after their mother died, he made some contacts in Hamburg. That led to orders for four landaus, some of the most luxurious carriages he's ever built. They're finished except for installing the hardware from my shop, and they'll go onto that ship over there, the *Elizabeth*, before she sails tomorrow."

"It's all so beautiful from here."

"Indeed, from this vantage point, it's hard to believe there's so much turmoil in the city. Hang on, Miss Tucker. You arrived in Philadelphia at a very interesting time. Rian, it's time for us to return to your father at the back of the ferry."

. . . .

· OTTO ·

Otto watched Rian and Adrian talking with Randolph Tucker's daughter at the bow. The contrast between the two girls could not have been starker. Rian looked like a street urchin, a boy urchin to boot. Olivia struck him as at ease with who she was.

When Rian was born, Otto had been a bit disappointed when Dierdre gave birth to a girl. On top of that, since the Lord had chosen to give them a girl, Otto wished that she looked more like Deirdre's Gallaghers than the Krieger side of the family, for his wife and her sisters were raving beauties. But that was not his daughter's lot.

Rian's green eyes, high cheekbones, and light brown hair that turned blond in summer were all enviable features. But as she grew older, traits that had helped to make generations of Krieger men handsome were not working well for Rian. Her face was square, not rounded. She had slightly olive skin, hardly desirable when women tried to keep themselves as pale as possible. Most notably, just like himself, her uncles, and her grandfather, Rian sported a gap between her two front teeth.

Rian's abhorrence for dresses drove Otto into fits of distraction. *Another battle I lose all too often. I better get rich making railroad cars because riches may be the only way for Rian to marry into a good family. Time to stow these worries for the moment, Otto. You have more pressing things to worry over.*

Besides Rian's education and the economic turmoil in Philadelphia, Krieger Coach was on thin financial ice. The Hamburg landaus were key to getting him onto a solid footing. He wouldn't breathe easy until the carriages were safe aboard the *Elizabeth*.

Jules leaned against the railing and followed Otto's gaze toward Rian. "So, what are you going to do with her?"

"I have no idea. Keep her close for the moment. One of my problems is that she is so willful; even when she defies me, she makes no effort to hide it. I suppose I should meet with the headmaster. Perhaps I can talk him out of expelling her."

"I have some thoughts if you don't jump down my throat."

"Jules, I am desperate. I will consider anything. I want her to be educated. How else will she be able to marry into a proper family?"

"I don't know about the husband part. But I think she can get a pretty good education right in the shop."

"And be influenced by the men on the shop floor? I do not think that is a good idea."

Jules looked skyward as if asking the good Lord for patience. "Not them. Us. Look, she already has arithmetic skills. Aaron can teach her bookkeeping. Adrian started teaching her how to make molds and cast brass over in his shop. There's got to be chemistry involved there someplace."

Otto put up his hands defensively. "There is no need for a young woman to need chemistry."

Jules plowed on, undeterred by Otto's interruption. "I'll take time with her on the carriage shop floor. She'll get algebra and geometry through the woodworking we do every day."

"What you describe does not sound like a rounded education to me."

"Let me finish. We can quiz her on current events that she reads from the penny papers. You can make sure she reads both English and German pennies. She'll get geography every time we ship a carriage to a new part of the world. She sees Professor LaForce three times a week for French, Latin, and Greek lessons. You're teaching her how to play the violin. Every time you take her out on an excursion like this, it's an opportunity to learn something."

Most nights, after Otto returned from the shop, the two of them played duets borrowed from the works of Bach, Beethoven, and Mozart. "We do enjoy our evenings of practice together."

"So, how much more does she need to learn?"

"I do not know. Manners? Needlepoint? I just do not know what a little girl is supposed to learn. Maybe I should just pay her Aunt Colleen to raise her."

"That's a terrible idea, Boss. We both know that your sister-in-law doesn't have the polish to groom Rian for the drawing rooms of Philadelphia society. Besides, it would break Rian's heart. She wants to be with you. She needs to be with you."

"But look at her. How does she learn to become a young woman?"

"Boss, you've got a lot on your plate right now. You don't have to solve all of this by dinner time."

"*Ach, mist* [Oh, Crap]!"

"What?"

"Dinner. You just reminded me. My next-door neighbor is hosting a newspaper publisher from Boston for dinner tonight. Her husband scheduled a business trip down South, so she asked me to join them so there would be no sense of impropriety. Now, with Rian's problems, I'm not sure I want to leave her at home tonight. I think I should just write a note and bow out. She has an adult daughter who can chaperone."

"Which next-door neighbor? Lucretia Mott?"

"Yes."

"Who's the man she's hosting?"

"I don't know. Someone named Garrison. I was not paying much attention."

"William Lloyd Garrison? He's the most influential abolitionist in the country. He's the publisher of *The Liberator*. You can't bow out of that dinner! They'll probably recruit you into the cause!"

"Jules, I know abolition is dear to your heart, but I am busy running a business, and we are about to get bigger. I think I have made a clear statement about how Blacks and whites should live and work together in this country. You have been Krieger Coach's foreman since we hired our first worker. You are a great foreman. But I do not have time to engage in anti-slavery activities any more than you do."

Jules stared at Otto with a stony expression. Otto felt an invisible wall arise between them. *This happens all too often. I say something the wrong way, and his mood changes. I misstep somehow, and I don't know how to change things back.*

During a lengthy silence, Otto watched Adrian and Rian walk toward them.

Finally, Jules lowered the wall. "How well do you know Mrs. Mott?"

"We often eat dinner with her family, both at her house and ours. She is a handful. A Quaker. Outspoken. Hates slavery, same as you. She's lately been traveling around the state speaking against it, even to promiscuous audiences.[2] She has six children, so things are a little more hectic at her house than ours."

"Don't cancel out. Write a note asking her if Rian could join you. She won't mind having one more mouth to feed. Mr. Garrison is speaking at Bethel

---

2. A promiscuous audience was a mixed gathering of men and women. Most Americans in this era considered it unseemly for a woman to address both men and women at a public event.

African Methodist Episcopal Church tomorrow night. Maddie and I were planning on going."

Otto considered Jules' advice, then stooped to fish a sheet of paper and pencil out of his satchel. "All right. You have convinced me."

As the *Falcon* approached the Walnut Street wharf, Otto expected to hear the sounds of the city above the *choosh, choosh, choosh* of the ferry's steam engine. Sensing that Rian was of a similar mind, he put his arm around her so they could wordlessly share the moment. But no bells rang. No horses neighed. No wheels clattered. No cranes creaked. No whistles blew. No workers yelled. The sounds of the city were music to him, just like the violin concertos of Beethoven and Mozart, but there was no music playing at the moment. Something was wrong.

As the ferry kissed the dock, Otto noticed Rian's best friend Conor McGuire on the wharf. Conor had emigrated from Ireland with his family eight years ago. Both his parents died in 1832. His three older brothers were raising him, but they were doing their best just to survive. Conor's care was not their top priority. He slept at the Krieger house as often as in his brothers' crowded apartment. Before charity school let out for the summer, Conor would often come to the carriage shop in the afternoon and spend hours there. Conor and Rian swept up or sharpened tools that Otto's workers would leave for them. Otto suspected that now that school was out of session, Rian and Conor would be inseparable.

Otto's group was the last to descend the gangplank when the ferry docked. Conor was dressed much like Rian and could pass as a homeless waif. As usual, his auburn hair was uncombed and punctuated by an unruly cowlick. He shifted his weight uneasily from one leg to the other, a sign that he was the bearer of news, and by the look of it, it wasn't good. "Afternoon, Mr. Krieger. The strike has spread, sir. The dockworkers are out. Your workers walked right after lunchtime." Conor shifted his attention to Adrian. "Yours too, sir."

Otto absorbed the news of his striking workers, not showing any signs of worry to the others. "Hmm, unfortunate." He pointed the group away from the water with his lumber estimating rule. They walked off the wharf, past warehouses that should have been bustling with activity, and stopped at Water Street.

Otto put his satchel down. "We will separate here. Adrian, Jules, and I must head to the shops and deal with the workers. Rian, I would like you and Conor to deliver this note to Mrs. Mott. While you are at it, take my satchel back to the house. Stick together. You can catch an omnibus on High Street to Ninth. Here's enough money to get both of you on the omnibus. Do not tarry. Rian, I want to speak to you about your problems at school today. Conor, I want you to take personal responsibility for getting my daughter back to Krieger Coach as soon as possible."

• •

· SEAMUS ·

"Wish I knew which prayer did it," Seamus said to Dylan. He took another swing with his pickaxe.

"Whataya mean?"

"This morning, I didn't know how I was going to pay me rent. I said a prayer to the Virgin. Then I appealed to God directly. Then I prayed to St. Jude. He's the patron saint of lost causes."

"Well, you got that right. You're a lost cause for sure."

"No, you idiot. Paying me rent was the lost cause. Now I've got three quarter dollars in me pocket, enough to hold the landlord off for a few days. That gives me time to figure out me next gambit."

"So, you think the Lord cares about you enough to drop a rock in the middle of the street?"

Seamus set down his pick and reflexively looked for the straw boss but couldn't find him. *Of course. He isn't here.* "It's a lot more than a rock. Think about it. I say me prayers. Then Mr. Richie-rich, with his fancy-pants store on High Street, decides after all this time that he's changed his mind and wants gas lighting, and he needs a side-ditch dug to his place before the pipe fitters get there."

"Which apparently is tomorrow."

Seamus nodded, grateful that Dylan was keeping up with his train of thought. "Then Richie-rich comes by and bribes O'Shea to take the rest of the crew down to High Street."

"Which you wished included you because of all the pretty girls that do their shopping on High Street."

Seamus, warming to his subject, refused to allow Dylan to throw him off his narrative. "But no, O'Shea tells us we've got to get the ditch as far as Third Street, then we can leave, even if it's before candlelight."

"Which you decided was a good deal because that would give you time to case out the docks before dark."

"But then that wagon drops this huge rock in the street, a little too close to the ditch for an eastbound carriage to squeeze by. The wagon driver keeps going, oblivious to the mayhem the rock is about to cause. There shouldn't be any eastbound carriages because of the mess we're making. But certain members of the impatient class don't think the signs apply to them, and they just drive right down the street like they own it."

Shortly after the boulder dropped onto the street, two carriages passed the spot simultaneously. Neither driver wanted to give way to the other, thus prompting the eastbound carriage, which wasn't supposed to be driving down the street, to veer dangerously close to the ditch. Too close, as it turned out. Both right wheels dropped into the ditch to their axles and threw the carriage driver onto the ground. Fifty feet away, Seamus and Dylan jumped out of the ditch and ran to offer their services. Ten minutes later, Seamus and Dylan had levered the carriage out of the ditch, and each had a quarter dollar piece in their pocket.

"Seamus, we should move that rock," Dylan said as they walked back to their tools.

"Let's leave it, Boyo. You never know; we might get lucky again."

They got lucky twice more. The second time Seamus, still shirtless, helped a comely young woman out of a precariously teetering landau with its top down. Dylan, a step slower than Seamus, offered assistance to her father.

After muscling the carriage out of the ditch, Seamus appraised the damage. "Your rear wheel looks to be a little whopperjawed, sir. Me uncle owns a carriage shop on the corner of Walnut and Twelfth—Krieger Coach. You might want to pay him a visit and see what he can do to fix this."

The man thanked Seamus and pressed a quarter dollar into his palm. The lass rewarded Seamus with a backward look as the carriage departed.

Seamus smiled at the young woman and gave her a wave. "Come on, Dylan, let's take a water break."

They walked to the corner of Mulberry and Third Street, where Seamus pumped a bucket full of water, took a tin cup off a hook, and dipped it into the bucket. He sat on a bench so he could keep his eyes on their tools.

A parade of workers noisily crossed Mulberry Street, heading south on Third. "What's the sign say?" asked Dylan.

Seamus stared long and hard at the sign. "It says 'painters union on strike.' You need to learn to read, Boyo."

"Why should I when I've got you?"

"Because, you idiot, me own education is a bit limited. I won't always be around to do your reading for you."

"Where do you think they're heading off to?"

"Dunno. Probably to hook up with some other unions. Seems like every union in the city is looking for higher pay and shorter hours. They don't know how good they've got it."

"We should do that."

"What?"

"Go on strike. We need to get paid more. Then you'd be able to pay your rent."

"Dylan, I like the way you're thinking, but ditch diggers aren't like the coal haulers over on the Schuylkill. They've blocked off the docks and threatened anyone who crosses the line to take their jobs. We can't do that."

"Why not?"

"How many men were here before sunrise, hoping the straw boss would pick them?"

"I don't know, twenty?"

"And how many did O'Shea pick?"

Dylan looked heavenward, trying to recollect. "Seven, including you and me."

"So, if all seven of us went on strike, we just don't show up in the morning. Then what would happen?"

"I guess O'Shea would pick seven other guys. But what if all of us Irish banded together and went on strike. Then what would happen?"

"That's the problem. If we ever tried that, they'd start hiring Africans, and the coloreds would work for even less than we will. We can't win in the day-work game, Dylan. We've got to think of something else. C'mon, Boyo, let's get back to work. The ditch isn't going to get to Third Street by itself."

• •

· RIAN ·

Rian and Conor walked north on Water Street. Rian carried her father's satchel for half a block, then handed it off to Conor. "Here, you take it for a while."

"Your da didn't seem very upset by the strike, but he's sure pissed at you for something. What did he mean when he said *your problems at school*?"

"I punched Billy Schiffler in the nose. Then we got into a scuffle."

"Who won?"

"I was winning, but teacher pulled me off him. Then I got taken to the headmaster's office. He sent someone to get Uncle Adrian because *Vater* was on his business trip. He told Uncle Adrian he was kicking me out."

"Rian, that's three schools you've been kicked out of. First German school, then Catholic school. Now it looks like you'll be going to charity school with me."

"Maybe I'll just wear what I'm wearing now and run away to sea. People would think I'm a boy. I could become a ship's carpenter like Uncle Kurt."

"Even I know that's a stupid idea. Hey, are you even listening to me?"

A hundred steps after Rian off-loaded the satchel to Conor, she noticed how much the atmosphere on Water Street had changed in the three hours since she was here last. When she, Adrian, and Jules had walked to catch the ferry to New Jersey, she had to weave around freight wagons drawn by teams of six horses, huge barrels on dollies, carts filled with bags of grain, and even a young sow led on a leather leash. Now the street was relatively quiet. "Holy mackerel. The street is really different with the dockworkers out on strike."

"That's what I was telling your da, idiot. The stevedores followed the coal haulers' lead. They went on strike a couple of hours ago. No one's loading or unloading ships all along the wharf."

Looking to their right, Rian noted that the doors to all the warehouses were closed and padlocked. Usually, they gaped open at this time of day, revealing bales of cotton or cowhides, barrels of who-knows-what, and machinery of various descriptions awaiting their ships.

When they crossed Chestnut, a makeshift barrier of barrels and a wagon drawn crosswise blocked the street to the pier. A group of workers stood guard, some smoking cigarettes or pipes, some brandishing tools that could easily be used as weapons, all looking sullen. One man spit tobacco in the path of a well-dressed gentleman who happened to be walking by. Rian caught a glimpse of ships' masts with furled sails. Cranes, which normally at this time of day would have been laden with goods, sat idle.

To Rian's left, the atmosphere was quite different. Shops that catered to mariners were still busy; apothecaries, taverns, dentists, and a temperance house next to a hotel with women hanging out the windows. The aromas of cooking food with a myriad of unfamiliar spices assaulted her. Two Chinese sailors, their hair in a single braid, bartered with a merchant using wild gestures. Other sailors in exotic garb spoke languages that she couldn't identify. Some walked purposefully; others idled with prostitutes.

Conor looked to the right, toward the docks. "Me brother Mikey's probably in there somewhere. When he got up this morning, he wasn't sure anything would happen. He was itching to strike, but he had to keep his yap shut because the straw bosses don't pick the hotheads. Now look."

Rian didn't know what to think. On the one hand, the workers deserved more pay or shorter hours. On the other hand, the Krieger Coach and Krieger Forge workers were striking over the same issues, which would be a hardship for her father. "What about Redmond?"

"He's with the coal workers. I haven't seen him since they went on strike two weeks ago."

Rian halted at the corner of Water and High Streets. "This is where Kurt's ship was docked this morning. I guess he was lucky he got out when he did."

"When is he due back?"

"Not sure. Maybe two or three weeks. Usually, his boat sails to Charleston. But sometimes it keeps on going to Savannah." Rian looked down High Street and spotted a gaily painted horse-drawn carriage that could carry a dozen people inside. A steep, curved staircase at the rear invited the adventurous to climb to its top deck, which had room for perhaps ten more. "There's our omnibus."

"This is going to be a first. I've never ridden on an omnibus before. Let's ride on the upper deck."

The two walked a short block to Front Street. As they were about to board the omnibus's rear platform, a voice from behind them said, "Why hello, Rian. Where's your father?"

Rian turned around to see Harold Foote, a newspaper reporter for the *Philadelphia Independent*. He was thirty years old or so. His frock coat was stained and well worn. He wore shoes that had been patched numerous times and not by anyone with great skill. "Hi, Mr. Foote. He had to go to his shop. His workers went on strike."

"Hmm, as have many others. So, what are you doing?"

"I'm taking my father's bag back to our house. He was on a business trip to New York."

Rian paid the conductor for Conor and herself with the coins her father had given her, and they climbed the curved staircase to the upper deck. As they walked down the aisle to a bench seat, Rian murmured to Conor, "Get ready for a history lesson." Conor suppressed a giggle.

Harold followed them to their seats and picked up the conversation. "What was your father doing in New York?"

Rian liked Mr. Foote but had a sense that she should keep her father's business within the family. "I don't know. He had some meetings. He had to go directly to the shop to deal with the workers."

"The strike has put many people on edge. I just heard that the city workers have joined the others. I figure that means about 20,000 workers on strike. I can't imagine that it can go on like this for much longer."

"But not the omnibus drivers, I guess."

"No, the omnibuses are wildcats. They're independent operators. Take our driver, for instance. He owns this rig. He starts when he wants, and he knocks off for the night when he wants. There would not be any advantage for him to strike. They're really just getting started."

"Getting started?"

"How old are you, Rian?"

"Eleven." Rian nudged Conor subtly, eliciting a smile from Conor but no other reaction.

"Then, to you, it probably seems like omnibuses have always been in Philadelphia. In fact, it's only been a couple of years. I first saw them in Paris in 1830. The idea spread to London, then New York, and just lately here. Now every major street in the city has at least one omnibus, and some like High Street have three or four."

By this time, the compartment below had filled, and the omnibus was on its way. Only Rian, Conor, and Harold Foote occupied the top deck. Their vantage point afforded a perfect view. At 100 feet wide, High Street was one of the broadest streets in Philadelphia. Scores of semi-permanently constructed market stalls occupied the middle of the thoroughfare between Front and Eighth Streets. Today, despite the general strike, the stalls throbbed with activity, both shoppers and vendors.

Rian caught fleeting glimpses of various goods in the stalls; farm produce, pots, pans, dishes, fabrics, knives, toys, crates, tools, and candles. Genteel shoppers with colorful clothing and parasols created a kaleidoscope of colors. Rian saw silks and satins, ribbons and tassels, and rich cloaks, even on such a warm day. She spotted Olivia Tucker and two other women at one of the stalls that sold fresh produce.

"I saw that girl get off the *Falcon* ahead of you guys," commented Conor.

Rian stood and turned to watch Olivia until the omnibus had traveled so far away that she was lost in the crowd of shoppers. "She's nice. Her name is Olivia Tucker."

"I've never heard you call a girl nice before. You usually don't like them."

"I don't know; she's different. She's plucky."

"Plucky. Like you."

A parade of workers heading south on Fifth Street stopped to let the omnibus pass. A sign said, "No More Sun to Sun."

"I don't get it," commented Rian. "Everyone works sun to sun in the city. Workers are paid by the day, not the hour. If it's light, you work. Sure, the hours are long during the summertime, but you get it back in the winter when the days are so much shorter."

Harold Foote leaned over the back of their bench. "Well, if that's how it really played out, you'd be right. But the problem is that both the rivers freeze up during the winter. No ships on the Delaware and no coal boats on the Schuylkill go in or out, so the bosses just lay the workers off. So, the workers can work fifteen hours a day during the summer, but not at all during the winter. The bosses win every time. Maybe the strike will even things out a little bit."

The omnibus approached the corner of Seventh and High Streets. Foote continued, "I think TJ would approve."

"TJ?"

"Thomas Jefferson." Foote pointed to a brick building on the corner. "That's the Graff House. Jefferson wrote the Declaration of Independence there in 1776. We wanted freedom from tyranny. Here we are, sixty years later, and tyranny is still alive and well."

"Well, thanks for the history lesson," interrupted Rian. "This is Ninth Street, where we get off."

"Of course. Rian, please give your father my warmest regards."

With that, Rian and Conor descended the stairs to the rear platform and jumped to the street just in time to bump into Conor's seventeen-year-old brother Redmond.

"Conor, this is perfect. I need you. You can help us out."

"Redmond, what are you doing here? I thought you were on strike with the coal workers."

Redmond waved a fistful of paper bills. "Getting provisions at the markets. The boys are hungry. We're keeping the scabs away from the docks on the Schuylkill, but the bigwigs aren't letting us out either. Me and Declan McGinty tried to sneak out to get us some food. Some of their pugs caught Declan and were wailing the tar out of him until our boys rescued him. Now that you're here, you can take Declan's place. I'll be able to bring more food back." Then Redmond noticed Rian. "What are you doing with her?"

"Helping her take her father's satchel back to their house. Then going back to the factory to help out."

"Conor, you shouldn't be helping the Kriegers. You shouldn't pal around with her like you're all buddy-buddy. Stick with your own kind."

"I'm half Irish," Rian blurted out.

"Yeah, well, your last name's Krieger. How much Gaeilge[3] do you speak?"

Rian hung her head. "Not much. My mother died when I was eight. She used to sing Gaelic songs to me."

---

3. Irish Gaelic.

"Conor, how much Gaeilge do you speak?"

"*Go leor le fáil* [Enough to get by]."

"And how old were you when both our ma and da died?"

"Eight."

"So, there you have it, Rian. You're nothing but a high and mighty, filthy little *ispini*,[4] and your kind's about to get knocked down a peg."

Rian saw red. She dropped her father's satchel and took a swing at Redmond.

· ·

· OTTO ·

Otto watched briefly as Rian and Conor worked their way north on Water Street. Then he, Adrian, and Jules turned and headed west on Walnut, each lost in their thoughts.

Adrian broke the silence. "Otto, your carriages are supposed to be loaded onto the ship tomorrow morning. All the hardware from my shop is ready but needs to be installed. If your workers have joined the strike, there's no way that we can get the carriages to the *Elizabeth* before she sails. And that assumes the stevedores will even load them. If we don't deliver, we can't tap the letter of credit. If we don't get paid soon, you're going to miss your payment to the bank. They're not going to be happy if you default again."

"One step at a time, Adrian. If the stevedores aren't working, the *Elizabeth* won't sail. Let us see what is going on at the shops."

Before Otto, Adrian, and Jules could cross Front Street, a highly polished landau pulled by a matched team of black horses and driven by a coachman in full livery stopped next to the trio. With its top down, it was easy to identify its only occupant: George Shippen, Chairman of the Board of the Bank of Industry. Shippen leaned out. "Krieger, I assume you've heard the news."

Otto had mixed feelings about Shippen. Two years ago, he had entered Otto's shop without an appointment and ordered a phaeton without dickering about the price. He was the first person of "society" who had taken an interest in him. Shippen seemed oblivious to Otto's heavily accented English. He had since recommended Krieger Coach to numerous friends. Late last year, he ordered this landau from Otto, which Krieger Coach delivered two months ago. On the negative side, Shippen always seemed to be involved in a risky investment scheme that he wanted Otto to join. In addition, Shippen frequently voiced opinions and prejudices that Otto didn't agree with and often found offensive.

---

4. Irish for sausage.

"George. Hello. Yes, we were just heading to the factory."

Shippen shrugged, the only indication that he had heard Otto. "I'm heading right by your shop. Please jump in. It will give the two of us the opportunity to talk."

As the landau was a four-seater, Shippen could have offered a ride to Jules and Adrian, but by saying "the two of us," Otto knew that his invitation did not include Adrian and especially not his Black foreman.

"We can hoof it from here, Otto," said Adrian, his inflection indicating he would rather walk with Jules than ride with Shippen. "We'll see you in a few minutes."

Shippen ignored Adrian.

Otto hauled himself up into the landau. Shippen signaled the driver to start by slapping his hand on the side of the carriage. Before Otto's rear hit the seat, they were underway.

"Krieger, this news is very distressing."

"That my men have joined the strike?"

"The anarchists are taking over. I said two weeks ago that we should have crushed the coal workers or there would be problems."

"They do have some legitimate grievances, George."

"Nonsense." Shippen rapped his walking cane on the floor of the carriage for emphasis. "They would only use the time to get drunk earlier. The working classes have no aspirations. Booze and breeding more of their kind; that's all they are interested in."

Otto chose not to take the bait. "What other unions have joined the coal workers?"

Shippen refused to get derailed from his rant. "That's when we should have taken action. The Protestant Irish and the Catholic Irish hate each other just as much as the rest of us hate them. We could have used that to break the strike at the wharves on the Schuylkill before it spread. *Divide ut regnes*, Krieger, divide and rule."

"Sorry you feel that way, George. I remind you, my wife was an Irish Catholic."

"Oh, Krieger, don't get caught up in semantics. I don't hate them as individuals. Just as a class. You know as well as I do—there are two types of Irish, deserving poor and vicious poor. There's a world of difference. I don't hate our house staff. They're all Irish. The deserving poor might get a helping hand when they need it, but they need to get a job in short order. It's the vicious poor I'm talking about. They don't show up for work when they don't feel like it. They drink away their wages rather than feed their families. They deserve nothing from me save a kick in the ass. Let them die in the gutter, for all I care."

Otto tried a second time to change the subject. "Who walked out today?"

The carriage passed a law office, its wooden trim scraped of old paint but no new coats yet applied, and no tools, tarps, or ladders visible. Shippen gave the scene a glance and a disapproving *tsk*. "You know about the house painters, of course. Then the plasterers, bricklayers, masons, hod carriers, carpenters, blacksmiths, plumbers, and leather curriers. All workers paid by the day. The printers this morning, which meant the strike had spread to the pieceworkers. Other pieceworkers have since joined them. Auger makers. Saddlers. The cordwainers were already on strike for higher piece rates. The stevedores smelled the dock owners' fear. They threw in with the rest. Then the workers started walking out of smaller shops like yours. I can't tell you how fast this is growing. It's out of control."

Emphasizing Shippen's point, their carriage halted abruptly, forced to stop by a parade of striking workers that left Washington Square and turned ahead of them onto Walnut Street. Led by a fife and drum corps, each group carried a flag or a banner identifying its union or profession. Workers remained dressed in their distinctive garb and carried the tools of their trade. Bakers in white. Carpenters with their saws. Painters with paint-stained clothing and brushes. One banner stated, "From 6 to 6, ten hours work and two hours for meals."

Otto pointed to the banner. "Honestly, George, that does not seem too much to ask."

Shippen was visibly irritated by the delay. "Nonsense. Look at them. I'm telling you, you must not give in. Your workers have walked. So, you lock your doors. Don't let them come back in until they're starving."

"I am not going to do that, George. Plus, I have my own finances to worry about."

"Schiffler tells me you have a payment due on Wednesday. I hope the strike doesn't affect that. We've already restructured your loan once."

"I have four landaus at the shop right now. As soon as I load them on the *Elizabeth*, I can tap half the letter of credit sitting in Schiffler's office. The bank will be able to release the funds, I will immediately pay the bank, and I will have a little extra."

"So, you're just going to concede a ten-hour day? Give all your hard-won profits to these slackers?"

"They are not slackers. They work hard in my shop. If I pay them the same amount for a ten-hour day as I currently pay for sun to sun, I will certainly have to tighten my belt, but we will survive."

"You make a good living because you are smart and willing to take risks. I heard that you are going into the railway carriage business."

Otto tried not to show his surprise. "I guess you have already seen your sister."

Shippen nodded. "I just drove by to welcome them back to town. Imagine my surprise when my sister knew more than I did about one of my most important clients. So, are you going to make the leap or not?"

Otto was flattered by Shippen's statement but not sure Shippen was sincere. "I haven't decided yet."

"I think you would be smart to do it. You know I appreciate the craftsmanship that went into this carriage, but the future is in railroads. Krieger Coach can supply railroads all over the world. And if you want to make some real money, you should buy stock in the *Philadelphia & Delaware County Rail-Road Company*. Or, if you want to venture just a little further away from home, try the *Wilmington and Susquehanna Rail Road Company*.[5] There's some real caché there because we've hired William Strickland to survey between Wilmington and Baltimore. His men should start their work next month. I've been telling you for years that the early investors will be the ones who make the big money, so you've already missed that boat."

"I may join you after the dust settles, George. But first things first: get the landaus on the *Elizabeth* and deal with my workers."

"Fair enough." Then, as he was prone to do, Shippen changed the subject. "My son says that your daughter is going to barely finish the school year. She keeps cutting school."

Forced to return to an unpleasant subject, Otto briefly shut his eyes. "I think it is worse than that. She was kicked out today. She punched Billy Schiffler in the nose."

"Whoa-ho, I imagine Edward Schiffler's going to have something to say about that. Honestly, Krieger, you need to rein her in soon. She already looks like an orphan half the days. She needs a good education. She'll never grow up into an eligible young lady unless she learns some manners and starts to play the part."

"I still have some options."

"Don't forget about Frau Gilbert's School in Switzerland. My Prudence was like your daughter. Willful. Defiant. I sent her off to Lucerne. They broke her in two years."

---

5. In the early days of railroads, corporations did not agree on the proper spelling for railroad. In the next few pages, you will see Rail-Road, Rail Road, Railroad, and Railway, all of which reflect how the entities were named in their incorporation papers.

"I do not believe Rian needs to be broken."

"Now you're getting wrapped up in semantics again, Krieger. I mean, broke her like a spirited filly. That's what men want: a woman who is compliant. Intelligent but trustworthy. Now Prudence is married to a Prussian count. That's what you want for Rian, isn't it? The fairytale?"

Otto was unwilling to make any concessions about his daughter's upbringing. "Well, here we are. Thanks for the lift." Otto descended from the landau.

"Think about what I said, Krieger. The first ones in will make the real money."

"Thank you for the opportunity, George. I am thinking about it."

"And don't give your workers a thing." With that, Shippen again smacked his palm on the side of the carriage, signaling the coachman to proceed. They were off.

Otto watched as the landau pulled away. He and Shippen inhabited two different worlds, yet Shippen was dangling access to his world out to Otto for reasons that Otto didn't quite understand. Otto came to America with only a bag of tools and the clothes on his back. Although he had done well in the past fifteen years, he was still an outsider looking in on upper-class life. Shippen, of British stock, was born to wealth and circulated comfortably among the wealthy. Part of Otto wanted that life for himself and Rian. He was flattered by Shippen's attention and knew that further interactions would lead to more commissions from Shippen's peers.

Just as Otto finished his thoughts, Adrian and Jules joined him and watched the landau turn right on Tenth Street.

"How's Shippen like the landau?" asked Jules in German.

"Well enough, I guess. He complimented me just before he tried to get me to buy stock again."

Adrian shook his head. "What's it called this time?"

That made Otto smile. "I do not remember. I cannot keep them straight anyway. Sometimes it is the *Wilmington & Susquehanna Rail Road Company.* Last month it was the *Baltimore & Port Deposit Rail Road.* Then it was the *Delaware & Maryland Rail Road Company.* I do not know if it is the same rail line or a new one or if they have combined.

Adrian elbowed his brother slightly. "The parade held you up. We were never far behind you. You should have walked with us."

"Shippen wanted to talk."

"Brother, what are you doing with him? That man is no good."

"I'm not sure. I do not agree with some of his opinions, but he knows how to make money."

"Or get his hands on your money. Be careful, Brother."

"His venture is intriguing. This could be the way we get rich."

"Jules and I were just talking about that. We might have some ideas."

Otto became tired of the discussion. "There will be plenty of time to talk about this. We need to hear what the workers have to say."

· ·

· LUCRETIA ·

Forty-two-year-old Lucretia Mott contemplated problems both big and small as she swept the brick walk from her house to the street. The five children still at home needed tending, as children do. She had been asked to speak at meetings of numerous anti-slavery organizations in Pennsylvania and New York and had to decide if and when that was possible.

Of immediate concern, her house was a wreck because a crew of plasterers had joined the strike and walked off the job late last week, leaving her household in uncharacteristic disarray. As a testament to her character, she sided with the workers despite the mayhem.

Not quite five feet tall, she wore a full-length dress that would have been considered stylish had it been any color but "Quaker grey." She wore a white bonnet that completely covered her head and provided a bit of shade for her face.

Rather than attack the mess inside, she chose to sweep the walk. *At least I'll be able to tell the difference when I'm finished*, she consoled herself.

As Lucretia worked her way to the end of the walkway, she spotted Rian Krieger lugging a heavy satchel northward on Ninth Street. Lucretia called to her son, "Thomas! Rian is here with a heavy bag. Come with me to help her out!"

They met Rian halfway down the block. "Hello, Rian, I assume that is thy father's satchel. My dear, when is thee going to start dressing like a young woman instead of a ragamuffin? And how did thee get that bruise on thy cheek?"

Rian put down the satchel. "Conor's brother called me a filthy ispini. I took a swing at him. He blocked it and punched me back. It wasn't much of a punch. He could have hit me a lot harder. But I think I made my point."

"Rian, I don't know what to do with thee. Violence is never the answer to these situations."

Rian held out a folded piece of paper. "My father asked me to give this to you."

Lucretia unfolded the paper and read Otto's penciled query. "Is thee going back to the shop, Dear?"

"Yes."

"Thy father has asked if thee could attend dinner tonight. Apparently, this isn't the first bout of fisticuffs that thee has gotten into today. Please tell thy father that my house is in an uproar because the plasterers walked off the job, and I cannot entertain Mr. Garrison in my home. Ask him if it would be all right if we move the dinner to thy house. I will bring everything over. All he has to do is show up. I will keep it simple. I'll bring only Tom with me so thee will have someone to talk to as well."

"Who will take care of the rest of the kids while you're with us?"

"Maria is seventeen. She is quite capable of running the house while I am next door."

"I'm sure your plan will be fine, Lucretia."

Lucretia noted that Rian had finally called her by her first name. Quakers did not adhere to the same formalities that most people in Philadelphia did.[6]

"Tom will help thee get thy father's bag upstairs. Then come next door. I will give thee some ice to put on thy cheek."

· · · · · · · · · · · · · · · · · ·

· RIAN ·

Rian muscled half the satchel's weight upstairs while Tom Mott assisted from below. "Thee has to stop hitting people, Rian."

"You didn't mind it when those boys were ganging up on you last fall."

"I would have been all right. Now they tease me worse. They say that I let a girl do my fighting for me."

"What do you say to that?"

"I don't say anything. I just keep walking. It's only teasing. We will all grow older. The teasing will stop someday."

Rian got to the top of the stairs and backed toward her father's bedroom. "That's not how I look at it. I think the teasing stops when I shove it back down their throats. That makes them think twice when they want to tease me the next time. Besides, the teasing doesn't stop. It gets meaner."

"What does thee mean?"

"Billy called me a dirty mick girl. I got kicked out of school for fighting because I'm a girl. Boys fight all the time, and they never get punished. This morning Jules got ignored, then almost got beat up because he's Black. The

---

6. Quakers did not use titles like Mr., Mrs., or Miss.

workers hate the owners. The Germans hate the Irish. The Irish hate the Blacks. And fifteen minutes ago, Redmond McGuire called me a dirty ispini. I'm sick of it."

Tom took control of the bag and placed it on a bench at the foot of Otto's bed. "What happened to Conor, anyway?"

"His brother Redmond said he had to decide: which is he? Irish or a friend of the rich? That meant me and *Vater*. Redmond said he couldn't be both."

"And Conor chose his brother."

"Well, he left with Redmond to get more food for the coal haulers, so I guess he's more Irish than a friend."

"I don't know, Rian. He spends more time at thy house than at his home. Thy father feeds him. He sleeps at your place half the time. He goes to thy father's factory when he's not in school. Maybe he just thought his brother needed him more at the moment."

"But my father told him he had to make sure I got back to the factory right away."

"Is that something thee is not able to do by thyself?"

"No."

"Then maybe, if thee is truly Conor's friend, thy job is to do that. And don't get into trouble on the way. That shouldn't be a problem even for thee. It is just over a mile."

· · · · · · · · · · · · · · · · · · · ·

· OTTO ·

Otto, Jules, and Adrian entered Krieger Coach from Walnut Street. Ten paces in, they found sixteen workers from both shops, all idle, some sullen.

Otto addressed the men. "You did not join the parade." He hoped his words would start a conversation, not a confrontation.

At the sound of Otto's voice, Aaron Bassinger, bookkeeper for both shops, stepped out of the office. He called no attention to himself.

Ernst Winther, one of the older workers, stepped forward. "There will be more parades before this is over. We knew you'd be here as soon as you got back from New York. We want to talk."

"We are willing to talk. Thanks for sticking around. How about if you elect two representatives from each shop to meet with us in my office right away?"

"No," came an immediate reply from Hans Schmidt, one of Otto's younger employees and a bit of a hothead. "No, you speak to all of us."

"If that is what you want, we can do it that way. Tell us what you want."

"Right now, we work sun to sun," said Ernst. "You give us an hour to go home for breakfast and supper. This time of year, if we get eight hours of sleep, which we don't, that gives us no time at all to spend with our families and educate ourselves. How are we supposed to get ahead if we're not even home in the daylight hours?"

Otto crossed his arms. "A banner in the parade said they wanted ten hours of work, plus an hour for breakfast and an hour for supper at noon. That would give you plenty of time to walk home, eat your meals, and get back here ready to work. Your workday would be 6:00 to 6:00, Monday through Saturday. Is that what you are asking for as well?"

"Yes, that's it . . ."

"There are other things," Hans spit out before Ernst had finished. He pointed to Jules. "We don't want to take orders from a Schwarz." Then Hans pointed to Aaron. "We don't want to deal with that Jew over there. And no bogtrotters."

Otto stiffened and hesitated. "Give us a minute." He turned to his brother, and they walked away from the workers toward one of the almost completed landaus. Jules joined Aaron at the door to the office, both with arms folded in front of them.

Otto leaned his back into one of the carriage wheels. "Did you read those projections that Aaron prepared? The ones that factored in a ten-hour day?"

"Of course. It's going to hurt in the short term. Less profit at first, but I can raise my prices a bit. Krieger Forge'll get by. How about you?"

"Not quite the same. I cannot raise my prices too much because there are too many one-man shops in the city. They just pay themselves, so they do not care what the strikers ask for. I think my only hope is to get bigger."

"And make railroad cars?"

"Railroad cars, carriages, it does not make a difference. I need to invest in more machinery. Make these men more efficient."

"That's money you don't have."

"I have some, but not enough. I can talk to Edward Schiffler at the bank about another loan."

"Schiffler. Whose son Rian just punched in the nose."

"I doubt that he will let a schoolyard brawl get in the way of business. If he objects, George Shippen will set him straight."

"Shippen. The bank board's president. A man I don't trust."

"Then I guess it is a good thing you do not have to take out a loan."

"What about the other thing?"

"What? Jules and Aaron and the Irish?"

Adrian nodded.

"*Über meinen toten körper* [Over my dead corpse]."

Adrian smiled in agreement.

Otto and Adrian approached the workers. "Adrian and I have conferred," Otto announced. "If you are willing to get back to work right away, we can accept a ten-hour day plus two hours for meals, six days a week, starting immediately."

"What about the other demands?" said Hans. "Kick the African and the Jew out, and you will never have any trouble in this shop."

"We can make sure you never have to take orders from a Black man again. Any of my people who are unwilling to work with Jules are fired as of right now. Aaron stays. As far as the Irish go, I have never hired any Irish, so I do not know what you are worried about. But for the record, I am willing to hire any man who shows up every day, stays sober on the job, and works as hard as you all do."

"Otto and I are in agreement," added Adrian. "So, gentlemen, the decision is yours. If you choose to leave, take the tools you came with. Never come back. Five minutes."

The workers looked stunned.

"Are you kidding me?" bellowed Hans. "Four coaches are sitting on the floor that have to be shipped by tomorrow. If we don't work, they don't get completed. We can get everything we want if we just hang together. They have to give in."

Otto rested the heavy end of his lumber estimating rule on his shoulder, an indication that he had no intention to give further ground. "It might take all night, but we can finish those carriages by ourselves if need be."

Fifteen workers responded to Hans by looking at the floor, and Otto knew that the strike was over. Now it was just a matter of how many would leave. Hans angrily tossed a wagon wheel spoke across the factory, but it harmlessly hit the wall.

Three minutes later, Ernst Winther walked over and shook Otto's hand. "Thank you for listening to us, sir. We'll be happy to stay, except for Hans. I believe he's burned his bridges."

Otto looked Ernst directly in the eye. "I am happy that it has worked out this way. Thank you for sticking with us. How would you feel about working directly with Jules? I will be out of the office more often, and we need some age and wisdom to keep some of the younger men in line. I will pay you a dollar more a day."

Otto could see the mixed emotions on Ernst's face. A dollar more a day was a lot of money, especially when the workday was two hours shorter.

Ernst squared his shoulders. "Well, I guess the world is changing. Not crazy about working with him, but I'm okay to give it a try."

"I think any man willing to put in a solid day of work is worthy of respect, no matter the color of his skin."

"Don't know how some of the others will take to me working with him."

"Well, you already know what my response to that is. You can feel free to show them the door."

"I'm not going to fire my own kind, sir. It's not in my nature."

"I appreciate your honesty, Ernst. I will take care of the firing if it comes to that. It is time to get back to work."

Otto walked over to Hans, who was still seething. "Never come back, Hans."

"Fuck you!" was Hans's only reply. As he stormed out the door, he swept his hand across a workbench, upending a box of wood chisels. The box crashed onto the concrete floor, causing the chisels to clatter and scatter.

Otto stooped to pick up the chisels, noting that some had sustained nicks in the fall. *That man has no respect.*

Adrian wrapped up his own conversation with his men, and they returned to Krieger Forge next door. He watched with a frown as Hans made his exit, then walked over to Otto and silently handed him a small oval brass plate.

Krieger Coach
Philadelphia U. S. A.

Otto smiled. "Did you make this?"

"Of course. Figured if we're going to keep selling coaches overseas, we might as well have our name on them."

"How many did you make?"

Adrian pointed to a stack of three other plates on a workbench. "Four. For the landaus that are going out tomorrow."

"I like this. We should put them on all our coaches from now on."

"I was hoping you would say that."

Otto turned to search for a hand drill and screwdriver. "I think we should start right now."

It took half an hour, but afterward, the two brothers were able to stand back and admire their handiwork just as Rian walked into the factory.

"Beautiful plaques," Rian said. "They should go on all Krieger Coaches."

"We were just talking about that. Take a look, *Liebling*. We fled from Wurt-temberg fifteen years ago without a penny in our pockets. Now we are shipping the finest carriages built in Philadelphia back there with our name on them." Otto grabbed a rag from a nearby bench and gave one of the plaques a final swipe. "Come join us in the office."

· ·

· LUCRETIA ·

Lucretia was preparing dinner for the evening when she heard a knock on the door. A minute later, Tom ushered William Lloyd Garrison into the kitchen.

"William, how good to see thee again. Thee is early."

Garrison noted the disarray caused by the striking plasterers but chose to ignore it. "Yes, I know we will be dining with some people who may not share the depth of your convictions, and I wanted to approach you about a matter of some delicacy."

"I thank thee for thy discretion, but I believe Otto Krieger is prone to favor our cause. Tell me what is on thy mind."

"Yesterday, I attended a meeting of the American Anti-Slavery Society in New York. Lewis Tappan unveiled a plan to saturate the country with abolition-ist pamphlets. He is talking about fifty thousand copies a week."

That number astounded Lucretia, prompting her to sit at her kitchen table. "That sounds impossible. How many presses does he have at his disposal?"

"That's the thing. It all has to do with a fortuitous confluence of innova-tions. Just months ago, printers could print a mere two hundred sheets an hour on hand presses. Now, some of the New York dailies have installed steam-pow-ered printing presses. They can produce a thousand copies an hour. And that wouldn't be possible if rag paper—most of it made here in Philadelphia, mind you—hadn't improved in quality and uniform thickness in the past few years. Lucretia, we are planning a revolution, and our revolution wouldn't be possible without these innovations. We will be able to print twice as many pamphlets for half the cost as in years past."

"This is very interesting, William, but why must thee tell me this in private?"

"The American Anti-Slavery Society's intention is to start by blanketing the North with pamphlets. After that, we will do the same to the South. Philadel-phia will be among the last to receive the pamphlets."

"That sounds like a perfectly reasonable strategy."

"And we would like to send thousands of these pamphlets directly to you and have you and your fellow members of the Philadelphia Female Anti-Slavery Society figure out how to distribute them throughout the city."

· · · · · · · · · · · · · · · · · · · ·

· OTTO ·

Otto, Rian, and Adrian joined Jules and Aaron in the office, a cramped room off the production floor with two desks, a drafting table, and a few chairs.

"An eventful day, gentlemen, but a good day," said Otto.

"Were you tempted to throw us out?" asked Jules.

Otto smiled. "Not in the least. Adrian and I would rather go back on the floor than give in to those demands. Asking for shorter hours is one thing. Telling me who I can employ is another. I do not think most of them thought that one was going to go over."

Jules looked a little worried. "I'm not sorry to see Hans's backside. He's been a thorn in my side since you hired him."

Otto leafed through the mail that had arrived while he was gone. "Then it is good he is gone."

"Doubt we've heard the last of him, though. He's got a mean streak."

Adrian changed the subject. "Brother, Jules and I were talking while you were riding over here with Shippen. Rian pointed out that the rails on the *Camden & Amboy* are stouter than the rails to Columbia."

There were a couple of interesting pieces of mail but nothing that demanded Otto's immediate attention. "What about them?"

Adrian continued. "There's no doubt that the strap-iron and wood rails on the *Philadelphia & Columbia Railway* aren't nearly as good as the ones we saw today. Stouter rails like those in New Jersey—shaped like an upside-down T—can carry more weight, and they're certainly more durable."

"I agree. So?"

"If you can carry more weight, you can build a heavier engine."

"A heavier engine means more power," added Jules.

Adrian nodded. "And more power means we can pull a heavier load."

Otto crossed his arms and leaned back on his desk. "So, where are you going with this?"

Adrian looked at Jules, got a nod, and plowed ahead. "We think Krieger Coach should build enclosed coaches, not open like everything made today.

That way, passengers won't get covered with dirt and cinders, and they won't freeze during the wintertime."

"We already talked about this," said Otto. "Enclosing the carriages will add too much weight. No steam engine will be able to pull them."

"No steam engine that has been invented yet. Why build a carriage that half the buggy makers in Philadelphia can make? We should be planning a year, two years in advance."

"Why build carriages to be pulled by a locomotive that has not been invented yet?"

"Because someone will build that locomotive within the next two years. Probably within months. Look at how much more powerful stationary steam engines are now than just a couple of years ago."

"So, we just assume that steam engines will become more and more powerful?"

"Yes."

"How are you so sure?" Otto noted a twinkle in his younger brother's eye.

"Because I'm going to do it."

Otto walked around the desk and sat down heavily in his chair. "You have never even made a stationary steam engine, much less a locomotive. What makes you think you can build a locomotive that is worth a shit?"

Adrian was undeterred. "Half of the hardware we turn out in the machine shop already matches the tolerances in the parts we saw on the *John Bull* today. Making the parts is not the problem. We need an engineer who can design the thing. I had a beer with Heinrich Aldrich the other day. He makes steam engines for Baldwin. He doesn't like working there. I think I can get him to come and work for us."

Otto shook his head. "I am going to have to keep you and Jules apart. You are dangerous when you get together. You want to build enclosed cars, so you need more power. To get more power, you need heavier engines. To carry heavier engines, you need stouter rails. It does not work if you cannot forge stouter rails."

Adrian and Jules looked at each other. "Yeah, we haven't figured that one out yet. Railroads will have to buy them in England, the same as they did for the *Camden & Amboy*, but it would be great to make them right here. It would take a lot of capital."

Silence.

Aaron Bassinger, the bookkeeper who had been only listening to the conversation up to this point, spoke up. "I have a thought. My cousin arrived last month from Westphalia. They aren't terribly kind to us Jews over there these days. He is a metallurgist. He worked for a steel manufacturer named Krupp. He might be part of your solution."

"Westphalia. So, now you want us to hire a northerner?" said Adrian facetiously.

"So, a Jew is okay, but a northerner maybe not?" Aaron retorted sarcastically. "But, no, I wasn't thinking about 'hire.' I was thinking about a partnership. Jacob has some money. And the Jewish community in Philadelphia is pretty close-knit. We may be able to scrape together enough to get us started."

Otto noticed Adrian and Jules hesitate. He had not yet indicated what he thought about the idea of moving into the locomotive and rail manufacturing business. His enthusiastic participation would be pivotal. If he didn't endorse it, it was not going to work.

There was a long silence as Otto pondered this new future.

Finally, Otto said, "We will need a bigger shop."

· ·

· LUCRETIA ·

Lucretia, her son Tom, and William Lloyd Garrison walked all the dinner courses to Otto's kitchen, and the meal was hot and ready to serve when Otto and Rian arrived. After introductions, the group dug into a hearty beef barley soup, roast beef, bread, mashed potatoes, and spinach. Lucretia had forgotten how much Mr. Garrison craved being the center of attention. He had been telling a story without interruption for five minutes.

"So, I speak for over an hour, using notes I had agonized over for days. People started leaving after fifteen minutes. I had no idea what was going wrong because everyone there had come to hear my views on abolition. It was a disaster. By the time I finished, I bet there weren't twenty people left. Fortunately for me, and I dare say for the anti-slavery movement, Lucretia and James cornered me right after my speech. Now bear in mind, I barely knew these people. They counseled me to throw away my notes and speak from my heart. Two evenings later, I did exactly that and received thunderous applause at the end. Any accolades I have received as a speaker since are all because of this dear lady."

Otto wiped his mouth with his napkin. "I understand that you will be speaking at the Bethel African Methodist Episcopal Church tomorrow evening, Mr. Garrison."

"Yes, we hope for a sizable crowd. Will you attend?"

"I have many work obligations. I do not think I will have the time. My shop foreman intends to, however."

"That is a good sign. We honestly don't get many members of the working class at these lectures."

"Jules—the shop foreman—is Black. I doubt that others from my shop will attend. I suspect they do not share his sympathies."

"Hmm, a Black man in charge of whites. James Forten, one of *The Liberator's* major supporters, is well known for running a mixed shop over on the waterfront. But he is a Black man, and he would be expected to hire members of his race. Is it common in Philadelphia for a Black man to be in charge of whites in a white-owned business?"

"I do not know of any other instances. It is a source of friction. Just today, I fired a man who refused to take orders from Jules, even though we had just conceded a ten-hour day. He stormed out of the shop, burning his bridges on the way out. I will never take him back."

"*Vater*, what does 'burn his bridges' mean?" asked Rian.

Lucretia had to marvel at how poised Rian was at the dinner table. Though the etiquette of the day dictated that children remain silent at the dinner table, that was not how she ran her household and, clearly, not how Otto ran his. She was pleased that Rian had changed out of her "ragamuffin clothes" and into a dress but had to admit the bruise on her cheek belied any pretense of femininity.

"Burn your bridges. It harkens back to the time of Julius Caesar. He burned his bridges behind him to ensure his legions were with him one hundred percent. It means that there is no retreat, no going back."

"So, you won't hire Hans back?" Rian asked.

"No, definitely not. That was an easy decision. He was a grouser and a bit of a troublemaker. He was far from my best worker. Things will run more smoothly with him gone."

Garrison belatedly dug into his meal. "And where do your sympathies lie regarding emancipation, Mr. Krieger?"

Otto placed his fork on his plate and leaned forward. "I favor immediate emancipation, not gradual emancipation. I do not think slaveholders should be compensated for their slaves the way Great Britain did two years ago. I do not think free Blacks should be recolonized back to Africa."

"Hear, hear, Mr. Krieger. I don't think there is a sliver of daylight between your beliefs and mine. Once all these things are accomplished, we can establish schools and help educate these poor brutes so they can take their rightful place in society."

"I disagree with you on that point. Perhaps there is daylight between us."

"What would you do when millions of slaves are suddenly freed?"

"Why, I would get out of their way."

"You would expect them to educate themselves?"

"I believe I would. Jules Freeman was educated by his own kind. He speaks English better than I do."

"So, the white man just leaves the Black man to his own devices?"

"Well, no, when I said, 'get out of their way,' I meant stop throwing impediments into their path. Open up the trade unions. Stop forcing them to live only in certain districts. Educate their children in the same schools. Loan them money at the same rate as an equally competent white man."

"Well, I find no need to split hairs with you, Krieger. My goodness, Lucretia, you said you thought Mr. Krieger favored our cause. I believe he should become an agent and start spreading the gospel."

"Thank you for the compliment, Mr. Garrison, but I am a little busy with other projects. I also find that large groups of people have difficulty understanding me through my thick accent. I will leave the proselytizing to you and Lucretia. Besides, I have no illusions. Changing what is in the hearts of so many of us is a Herculean task. It will not be over in our lifetime."

Lucretia passed the mashed potatoes to Otto. "I hope the strike ends soon. My house is a wreck."

Otto helped himself and passed the bowl to Tom. "I ran into Harold Foote on the way home. He said he rode with Rian and Conor on the omnibus. Harold told me the general strike is over. It was the public workers walking out that guaranteed the workers would win the day. The Common Council caved in. The ten-hour day will be the new norm in the city. So hopefully, you will get your house back soon, Lucretia."

"Well, that would be a relief. Perhaps the plasterers will show up tomorrow. If I'm lucky, they'll be finished, and the house painters will be in and out before James returns. I'll be grateful to have some order. It's been in shambles for weeks."

"I am a bit mystified, really," said Garrison. "A few weeks ago, there was a similar strike in Boston, but it never took hold beyond the carpenters and one or two other unions."

Otto spread a generous slather of butter on his bread. "Well, here the strikes spread like wildfire from the coal docks on the Schuylkill to many other trades. It became a real force. I bet word of this is going to travel to other cities. We will see more such strikes before it's all played out."

Lucretia put down her fork. "I find the attitude of many people to be quite patronizing, And the penny papers aren't helping. I read in one paper today that a sixty-hour week would be harmful to the workers. They would use all their extra time for useless and unworthy purposes. That means drinking alcohol, of course. Instead, I believe they will use the time to educate themselves better, learn a skill, and be with their families."

"I think the world is changing before their eyes," said Otto. "And not always for the better. Twenty years ago, a cordwainer was a skilled craftsman who made shoes in his own shop. He set his own hours and his own prices. He had significant standing in the community. Status. Respect. Now, almost all shoes are made in factories. The independent cordwainer—the guildsman—has been put out of business. Now cordwainers are employees who labor in factories. They work long hours for not nearly as much pay. They cannot set their own schedules. They do not have the status in our community that they used to."

"But we, the customers who buy the shoes, help that happen because factory-made shoes are cheaper," interjected Lucretia.

"So, which would you rather have? More prosperous independent guildsmen or cheaper goods?" asked Garrison.

Lucretia placed her knife and fork on her plate and crossed her arms. "I, for one, favor the workers. But I have no idea how to stop this trend."

"Well, the workers won this round," said Otto. "But I fear that their struggles will continue. The employers are in their own competition to create cheaper goods. The easiest way to do that is to cut wages. One group that is feeling its oats right now is the Irish. It was the Irish day workers at the coal docks who started this. Not only did they strike, but they threatened anyone who wanted to take their place. I do not believe a coal boat on the Schuylkill has been unloaded in three weeks. That means 75 vessels tied up at docks and not moving. Almost nothing has left the Schuylkill for almost a month."

"Are any of Deirdre's relatives with the coal workers?" asked Lucretia.

Otto shrugged. "I am not sure. She had five brothers and four sisters. So, I bump into them and my nieces and nephews occasionally. I am sorry to admit this, but we are not very comfortable with one another. Deirdre and I had been married ten years when she died, so I got to know them pretty well. But without her, we do not make much effort to see one another."

"Why not?"

"Good question. Many reasons. Deirdre and I fell in love and were able to bridge the gap between Irish and German. Even though I do not attend church very often these days, I was baptized as a Catholic, so our religion was not a factor. But I do not think the Gallaghers like me very much. As difficult as our lives were in Wurttemberg, I was taught to read and write. I was expected to learn a skill. I do not think a lot of Irish immigrants are that lucky. They come to America with no skills. They do not read. Many do not care to learn. So, they compete with the Blacks for the lowest paying jobs in the city. They work in factories. They dig ditches. Heck, if it were not for the Irish, we would not have half the canals in the country now. But it is dangerous, backbreaking work. It is honest labor, but I do not envy them."

Lucretia passed the empty meat plate back to Otto. "Hard work and the animosity from the nativists who don't like those of the Roman Catholic faith make for a difficult life. Yet thee must have endured similar slights."

"If I were a church-going Catholic, I would likely be ostracized, just like the Irish. Catholics are outnumbered by Protestants in Philadelphia. We are Papists, so our religion sets us apart. We are accused of taking orders from the Pope and having greater allegiance to the Church than America. Many people do not trust us for that alone. It can be difficult."

"As a Quaker, I have some affinity for thy feelings. We often find ourselves assaulted for our beliefs. Ironic, since Pennsylvania's founder was a Quaker."

Otto cut more roast beef for the table. "Even when there is a common religion, there is still a chasm of distrust between Irish and Germans. Because I knew them through Deirdre, I feel connected to her family, but I admit they are a different breed. I worry that because they cannot get good jobs, they descend into professions that worsen things. They have formed tight-knit gangs involved in burglary, extortion, and violence."

Otto seemingly realized he had taken the conversation to a dark place and changed the subject. "Where did you say James was off to, Lucretia?"

"He sailed on the *Waterloo* to Charleston early last week. Savannah next. Home hopefully next week."

"Business, I assume?"

"Yes, he is visiting cotton brokers and other merchants in both states. Honestly, since he's been gone, I've had some misgivings."

Otto finished the second cutting of roast beef and passed the plate. "How so?"

"Cotton is a crop produced by slave labor. By buying cotton, we are helping to support that evil institution. I'm not sure I want to be a part of it anymore."

"Are you saying buying cotton in James's wholesale trade, or all goods made of cotton?"

"Well, this is a brand-new idea to me. But I think I mean all cotton."

"That would be difficult. So much of our clothing is made of cotton. What would you do?

"I'm not sure. I'm still working it out in my mind."

"And so much of James's business is based on cotton. That could cripple his company."

"In my mind, the immorality of slavery is more important than our family's comfort. But, as I said, I haven't worked all this out in my mind yet, and I daresay James will be shocked when he comes home to hear this."

Rian rooched in her chair. "*Vater*, I have a question. Today Uncle Adrian said something about hiring someone from the northern part of the German Confederation. It sounded like he didn't like them."

Lucretia was at a loss. The conversation had taken a turn that she didn't understand. "What is thee talking about?"

Otto set down his fork and put his elbows on the table. "When a person like you, Lucretia, asks one of us, 'Where are you from?' we say 'Germany.' You don't know the difference between northern Germany and southern Germany. But if another German asks me the same question, the answer would be a lot different. The German Confederation is made up of about forty states, some with millions of people, some no bigger than cities. So, I would tell a fellow German that I am from Wurttemberg. Our bookkeeper's cousin would say he is from Westphalia. The problem is that northern Germans and southern Germans do not necessarily like each other."

"My goodness," said Lucretia. "Does everyone need someone to look down upon?"

"That has certainly been my experience. Folks from the south of Germany think Northerners are cold. They eat a lot of fish. Their landscape is flat and dreary. Their beer tastes different. They are boring snobs. The Northerners say we Southerners are stupid and unsophisticated. We have strange accents. We are lazy, uneducated, more conservative. They say we think with our hearts and not with our brains. I say we are hot-blooded. And then there is the religion issue: Northerners are mostly Protestant; most Southerners are Catholics."

Shortly thereafter, the dinner broke up.

As Lucretia made her leave, she asked Otto, "How is Jules these days?"

"He is well. My most trusted employee. He thinks like an owner. I wish I had more like him. How do you know Jules?"

"His wife Maddie and I worked together to found the Philadelphia Female Anti-Slavery Society a couple of years ago. I've had meetings with her regularly ever since."

"He has never mentioned that to me."

"I guess that shouldn't be a surprise. I would describe him as supportive but wary."

"What do you mean?"

"The Black community in Philadelphia is getting stronger, growing in numbers, and building a significant middle class. As far as Jules is concerned, they would be much better off being invisible. I think he's afraid that if the Black community starts calling attention to itself and the great evil of slavery, that will cause problems."

"He may be right, Lucretia. I see it every day at the shop. As much as I love the man, mixing Black and white has caused many problems. Hans—the man I fired today—all that was really over his unwillingness to work for a Black man. If Jules were not Jules, I would have fired him long ago."

"Otto Krieger, thee talks like such a hard-hearted businessman, but I don't believe thee. Thee is very loyal to those who are loyal to thee. Thee has lived in America for fifteen years, but thy southern German shines through. Thee makes thy decisions with thy heart."

"I accept the compliment, Lucretia. Thank you for preparing the meal for Mr. Garrison and us. You are a wonderful neighbor and a good friend."

"I have one other parting thought: how does thee know how many other Jules Freemans are out there who are just as capable when given a chance? Or Irish, for that matter? Everyone, regardless of their religion or skin color, should have the opportunity to support their families and prosper in this country."

"Your lips to God's ears, Lucretia. Your lips to God's ears."

· ·

· JULES ·

Jules was in a pensive mood when he left the shop. He had stayed at Krieger Coach until the men had mounted all the hardware on the carriages, and they were ready to wheel out of the shop first thing the next day. He admired the brass plates that stated: "Krieger Coach, Philadelphia U.S.A." on each landau. *Nice touch*, he said to himself. *Wonder if I'll ever put my name on anything this fine.* He and bookkeeper Aaron Bassinger were the last two to leave.

Yes, as Otto said, on balance, it had been a good day. But not without its bumps. People had called him every disparaging name for "Negro" he had ever heard and some new to him. The man selling schnitzels slighted him. The altercation with Slatter threatened his freedom. He had been lucky to avoid a fight with the trainmen. He had shrugged off the hostile stares of people on the ferry. Shippen didn't acknowledge his presence and certainly would not have given him a ride in his carriage. Hans wasn't willing to take orders from him because he was Black. This was the life of a Black man in Philadelphia in 1835. If Jules had chosen to fuel his life with resentment, these events would have given him plenty of kindling.

His mother's words rang in his head. He could barely remember her voice these days, but her many Ashanti proverbs remained with him. *There is no medicine to cure hatred.* That was his mother's legacy to him, the wisdom of a centuries-old empire distilled down to a few proverbs. His mother was captured and sold into slavery when she was twenty. He was born in Maryland and sold away from her when he was twelve. *A wise man who knows proverbs reconciles difficulties.*

So, Jules chose to concentrate on the good things. He had a loving wife and six beautiful children. He was good at his job and well paid for his efforts. His position as foreman was a source of status in the Black community. The Krieger brothers respected his opinions about matters in their shops and gave him all the responsibilities that one would expect of a trusted foreman. As much as a white man can have the same standards for white and Black, that is what they did. Although he didn't work for Adrian, Otto's brother was frequently in the carriage shop, and he and Jules often collaborated.

Otto and Adrian had lined up shoulder-to-shoulder with him when the trainmen confronted him. Heck, even Rian joined them. Otto had not blinked when Hans said he wouldn't work for a Black man. Firing Hans was what he hoped Otto would do, but Hans had fired himself by walking out the door.

One less nasty krautbreath I have to worry about. Jules could name only a handful of Black men who had authority over a white man in the city. He had found that things ran more smoothly when his orders came across like a suggestion. Most of the workers at Krieger Coach worked with him with no outward signs of resentment. Only twice had he been forced to solve a problem on the shop floor with his fists, but he would be willing to do that again if necessary.

Jules's second master had trained him as a carpenter and hired him out to neighbors. In April 1820, his master, a man who had treated him about as well as masters treated slaves, died of pneumonia. Jules became the possession of the man's sister, who told him she would soon sell him. A few days later, without a plan or much knowledge of geography beyond Calvert County, he started walking north instead of walking to his job. Traveling by night, he carried a sack of clothing in one hand and a toolbox in the other. He arrived in Philadelphia seven days later with only a glimmer of what it meant to be a free man. 'Philadelphia' was almost a dream to him, a place that he'd heard of where slaves were no longer slaves.

"A carpenter, are ye?" These were the first words spoken to him by a white man when he arrived in Philadelphia. *"Suspect you'll be needing a job."*

"I guess I do. You know of anything?"

"A job and a place to live to boot. Follow me."

Naively, Jules followed the man down a warren of alleys that became so narrow that daylight was almost shut out. Without warning, he was set upon by two men who pummeled him from behind. To defend himself, he dropped his sack and his toolbox. Before he knew it, his guide had grabbed his toolbox and run away farther down the alley. Their part of the heist complete, his two assailants also faded away.

In the next few weeks, Jules survived, but he learned that trust had to come slowly. He encountered individuals of both colors who were willing to help him. These people asked for nothing in return. He learned—gradually—that they were not a danger to him.

Because he had a skill, he did get a job within a few weeks. With his modest earnings, he bought a few second-hand tools and fabricated some others. He even bought back his old draw knife, which he found at the stall of used goods on High Street. Rather than make a fuss, he dickered with the man until he got a fair price and was thankful to have his 'old friend' back.

Three months after his arrival, Jules had steady employment, a place to live, and a girlfriend. He was sitting on a brick wall, taking a break from fixing a door for a customer and reflecting more on his good fortune than the many bad things that had happened to him. His lunch of bread and cheese lay beside him on the wall.

"A woodworker, are ye? Suspect you'll be needing a job." The familiar voice was not directed at Jules. Instead, the man addressed a tall, blonde-haired galoot of about twenty carrying a toolbox.

"Ja," said the man. *"Can you help me?"* His English was so bad that Jules could barely understand him.

"Aye, a job and a place to stay."

"I have two brothers and a sister."

"Let's take care of you first, Darlin'. We'll take care of your kin later. Follow me."

With a wave of his arm, the man signaled blondie to follow him down an alley. Jules sat for a moment, but knowing what was about to happen, he picked up his carpenter's mallet and followed them at a distance down the alley.

Different alley, same routine, Jules thought to himself as he walked as purposefully and quietly as he could. A few moments later, he heard the sounds of a scuffle and started running, screaming all the way. In seconds he came upon two men who had already turned to face him. However, the sight of the large Black man wildly wielding a hefty mallet was all they needed to see before they turned and rushed past blondie and out of sight. Blondie was in a tug of war with the guide, each with a firm grip on the toolbox. Jules advanced and took a mighty swing at the guide's shoulder. Contact. The guide yelped, released his grip on the toolbox, turned, and ran away.

Thus began the friendship between Jules Freeman and Otto Krieger.

When he returned to his worksite, Jules's tools and bread and cheese were gone.

So, for better or worse, this was what Jules Freeman had come to expect in his life. Keep your dukes up. Count your blessings. Acknowledge kindnesses. Give kindness when you can. Tamp down your dreams. And, as Otto frequently said, never let the bastards see you bleed.

Today was a perfect example. Otto Krieger trusted him and respected his council. However, in the discussion about the future of Krieger Coach, there was never any mention of Jules being anything but an employee. Jules knew many Black businessmen, but with only one exception—the sailmaker James Forten—their operations were small. They were barbers, tavern owners, landlords, caterers, and shopkeepers. He sensed that as long as they didn't get too big, too prominent, he and they would all be okay. But as soon as members of the Black community started attracting attention to themselves, somehow, they were always cut down to size.

Just don't get too big for your britches, Jules. Yet even as he said that he knew that perhaps he was already too big for his britches. Even his modest successes were enough to make him a target. The Irish especially seemed to resent him. Mostly he ignored their taunts and disrespect. He kept his head down. He fought back only when he felt threatened. Instead, he chose to resist in another, more secretive way that stemmed back to his history.

$\cdot$ $\cdot$ $\cdot$ $\cdot$ $\cdot$ $\cdot$ $\cdot$ $\cdot$ $\cdot$ $\cdot$ $\cdot$ $\cdot$ $\cdot$ $\cdot$ $\cdot$ $\cdot$ $\cdot$ $\cdot$

Dinner with Maddie and the kids was always a rollicking affair. As a former slave ripped away from his mother at age 12, Jules took his parenting cues from his beautiful wife. Maddie was a third-generation free Black whose grandparents had become emancipated during the American Revolution.

Maddie sighed in exasperation at her children's antics at the table. "All right, my mighties, you are obviously in no mood to sit at this table any longer. Go outside and play. I don't want to see any of you until candlelight. Now go." Without further prompting, the children grabbed their plates, placed them in the washtub, and rollicked out of the house.

Jules wistfully watched them leave. "It still makes me uncomfortable for them to be out of sight for hours at a time."

"They'll be fine."

"I just worry, that's all. Slave catchers are all over this city. I ran into one of them today."

"No one's going to snatch them."

"It happens. They grab the kids, and before they know it, they're picking cotton in Charleston."

Maddie sighed. "It doesn't happen in Moyamensing. None of our neighbors would allow white men to take a screaming kid out of the neighborhood. Moyamensing is about as safe a place for our kids to grow up as there can be."

"Safe unless there's a scrap over a fricking merry-go-round. You know that it was just dumb luck that none of our family was harmed during the riots."[7]

As a result of the Flying Horse riots, scores of Jules and Maddie's neighbors left Philadelphia, but the Freemans remained resolute. The riots reinforced Jules's belief that they were safer if they didn't stick out too much. Maddie, who had never known slavery, came to another conclusion. She believed that the only way to end such heinous acts of violence was through activism. The two did agree on their hatred of slavery and their moral obligation to end it.

---

7. The Flying Horse riots occurred in August 1834. An enterprising character had built a carousel, called the *Flying Horses*, that was housed in a large building at Seventh and Cedar Streets, on the northern edge of Moyamensing. The *Flying Horses* became a popular neighborhood attraction, used by both Blacks and whites. The two races had coexisted peaceably at the carousel for months.

But during a heat wave in August, an Irish family and a Black family had a dispute over place in line. Words led to a fist fight, which quickly became a melee between Black and white. All the next day, rumors flew around both the Irish and Black neighborhoods. That evening, hot heads congregated at the Flying Horses. More fights broke out. The building and merry-go-round were destroyed.

Blacks retreated to their neighborhoods in Moyamensing. Whites, mostly Irish, gathered just outside the Black areas. Fueled by drink and hatred, they destroyed the house of a prominent Black family and broke windows along many side streets. One local constable comprised the entire police force for the area, and he was not inclined to stick his neck out to protect a bunch of 'coloreds' in the face of a raging mob.

The mob returned the following evening. Rioters tore down a Black church and destroyed a grog shop and lodging house that served both Blacks and whites. Unsatiated by this destruction and armed with clubs and paving stones, they flowed through the streets of Moyamensing. They forced their way into the houses of scores of Black families, skipping their white neighbors. They threw furniture and occupants alike into the street. The furniture was busted up or stolen. The occupants—men, women, and children—were beaten. The rioting continued for a third evening, but by this time the mayor of Philadelphia had sworn in a posse of three hundred special constables to make a show of force in the community.

With the children gone, the house became blessedly quiet, quiet enough that Jules noticed faint footsteps coming from upstairs. "Houseguests?"

Maddie nodded. "They arrived around noon."

"That's the third this month. How many?"

"Three. A man, a woman, and a young boy. I assume their son, but I'm not sure."

"Where are they from?"

"Calvert County. Same as you. The Quaker delivered them. He got them from the waterman."

"Did you ask them?"

"No. I figured you would want to do it."

"How are they?"

"Jumpy. Hungry. Scared. No need for a doctor that I can see."

"How come now?"

This was a question Maddie and Jules always asked the fugitive slaves who came through their doors. They had heard everything in the book. A beating. A threat of a beating. A flogging. An amputated hand. A family member about to be sold off. The threat of being sold south. Repeated rape by a master or a master's son or an overseer. Poor food. No food. Miserable living conditions. Cold. Ongoing humiliations, both large and small. Or just the unwillingness to be a slave. Sometimes this was the visitor's first success after repeated attempts at gaining freedom. Maddie and Jules's home had been a haven for fugitive slaves for more than a decade. After the first year, Maddie started keeping a diary of her interviews with each runaway who came through the door. It was now over one hundred pages long.

"Master was going to break up the family. The man—Barnaby—was going to be sold south."

"How long do you expect to have them here?"

"A day or so. I've got to make sure there's a place for them in Reading. I sent word a few hours ago."

"Do the children know?"

"Martha, Grace, and Rufus do. Jeremiah, Missy, and Gladys are too young to understand it. They'll get it soon enough. They all know to keep their mouths shut."

"I suppose I should go up and meet them." With that, Jules climbed the stairs, knocked, and opened a bedroom door. He saw two adults, both of whom seemed to be in their mid-twenties, and a child of four or five.

"Good evening. My name is Jules. Welcome to my home."

"Thank you, sir. How long do you think we'll be here?"

"At least a day. Then we'll keep you heading north. But from now on, you'll be safe. No one can touch you here. I understand your master was going to sell you south."

"Yes, sir. I wasn't well-behaved enough." *Well-behaved,* Jules knew, was code for a slave who didn't act like a slave.

"Well, you're a free man now. You'll never have to go south. Soon enough, you'll never have to worry about that again."

"Thank you, sir."

"I have a question for you. Did you ever hear of a slave owner named Michael Taney?"

"No, sir. Where did he live?"

"He had an estate in Calvert County. How about a slave woman by the name of Hattie? Probably had the same last name: Taney."

"No, sir. Who's Hattie Taney?"

"She's my mother." Every time a "houseguest" passed through Jules and Maddie's home in the past ten years, whether they were from Calvert County, Maryland, or not, Jules asked them the same question. "Have you ever heard of Hattie Taney?" Every time, he received the same answer. "No."

• •

· SEAMUS ·

Seamus had never seen so many patrons at Clancy's Saloon before. The throng was jubilant. The strikers had won. The ten-hour day was the new standard for workers—even many day workers—in Philadelphia. Whiskey and beer flowed and sloshed. A pair of fiddlers played near the door, but he could barely hear them over the din.

Seamus stood at the bar, feeling quite mixed about the day. He had paid his landlord three quarter dollars and bought himself a week's grace. But the ten-hour day was not in his future. *Ditch diggers don't have that kind of leverage.*

Hugh Callaghan, president of the Moyamensing Hose Company, sidled up to Seamus. Moyamensing, which its residents called Moya, was one of the poorest districts in Philadelphia. Free blacks and Irish lived cheek by jowl in Moya in a hodgepodge of animosity and distrust.

Hugh signaled Clancy to freshen Seamus's glass. "Looks to me like you need some cheering up, Kid. Come talk to me in the back room. We can have a little private conversation."

Hugh had never invited Seamus into his office, and Seamus had no idea what to expect as he followed him through the saloon and into the back room. There were two other men there. One was counting money and making entries in a ledger. The other—big, beefy, with a pistol and brass knuckles arrayed on a table before him—sat idly near the back door, reading a penny paper.

Hugh sat down at a round table in the center of the room and signaled Seamus to sit opposite him. "So, the vote on new members is coming up in August. You going to cast your lot with us, Kid?"

"I'd like to. Gotta worry about me ma and me brothers and sisters, though, and we're pretty tight to the line."

"Seamus, I've had me eye on you ever since your da died. Join the hose company, and you'll never have to worry about paying the rent again. We take care of our own."

Seamus took a sip of his whiskey. "How's that work?"

"It's not just the fire business, although that's our most lucrative endeavor. As long as we're the first fire brigade to train our hoses on a fire, we get paid a commission by the insurance companies for saving the building. And since Moya is our territory, we're generally the first ones on the scene. Course, if it's an African house, we don't bother putting out the fire. We just train the hoses on the houses next door."

"How come you don't put out the fires at the Black houses?"

"I guess you'd have to say it's a matter of policy. We don't like them, don't like living next to them, and don't want to give them any reason to want to live next to us. If business is slow, sometimes we'll even set a fire in one of their houses just to give the boys some practice." Hugh chuckled. "Then they're all too happy to see us come running."

"What if another fire company comes to put out the fire at the Africans' house?"

"Ah, they might get a bit of resistance from the boys."

"Doesn't sound very fair."

"I don't think the world worries about fair, Kid—the world worries about power. Right now, the only power us Irish have is to stick together. If that means kicking the Africans when they're down, so be it. But fighting fires is just one slice of the pie we've got our fingers in."

"What else?"

"I heard you're doing a little pilfering on the docks lately. Better watch that. Our territory goes up as far as Walnut Street. Start lifting anything south of there, and me boys aren't going to be happy."

"What if I join up?"

"Ah, now that's a different story altogether. A couple thousand years ago, a wise man said, 'when you conquer territory, divide the profits.' We still follow that philosophy. The higher up in the organization you are, the larger percentage you get from our activities. Course, you'd start at the bottom, just like everybody, but from the moment you join us, you'll be earning more than you are now with your current evening activities. Like I said, I've had me eye on you. You're a bright lad, Kid. You aren't afraid of a fight. I suspect in a few years you'll be me right-hand man."

"That's very flattering, Hugh. I think Dylan and I both want to join."

Hugh set his empty glass down on the table with a clatter, indicating the interview was coming to a close. "Now Dylan, he's another story. He's not the sharpest knife in the drawer."

Tuesday, June 23

· JULES ·

It was 5:30 in the morning, the day after the strike ended. Jules, Otto, and Rian had beat the rest of the workers to the factory by half an hour. They stood in the middle of the shop, taking in the beauty of the four shiny landaus. Otto appreciatively ran his hand along the curved surface. "Rian, I think they are ready. Time to go to the stable and get the horses. We need eight, so it will take you a few trips." Rian dashed out.

Otto opened and closed the door of one of the carriages a few times, testing the precision of the fit. "They look good, Jules. You have done a great job on them. And on time, no less."

"I was worried. The varnish is barely dry."

Reflexively, Otto touched the rear quarter panel. Sure enough, the wood was smooth and not at all tacky. "The strike did not help."

"A few of us had to work late last night. I think the men wanted them to look good. After all, they're being shipped to Hamburg. I'm the only one in the shop who wasn't born in one of the principalities." *That's why I had to learn to speak German. There was too much being said that I didn't understand.* "Most of the workers came here without a penny in their pocket. Now they're sending something they're proud of back home. Gives them some bragging rights. Otto, I know we're pressed for time, but I want to take each landau for a spin around the block before we deliver them to the docks."

"Afraid you missed something?"

"We just installed the hardware yesterday. The carriages have never been out of the shop. Never been pulled by a team. There's always something."

"Okay, but they need to be on the docks by noon. Captain Ellsworth told me he is sailing out with the evening tide, and he needs to load the landaus before the last of the cargo."

"That's plenty of time. As soon as I test one, Rian can take it to the docks."

"No. I want to take them all together. I told the stable I needed eight horses for the morning. I want everyone to see a procession of four coaches heading right down High Street on their way to the docks. That is the best advertising

Krieger Coach can have. This afternoon all of Philadelphia will know that we have four rigs on that ship."

Rian arrived, leading two horses, and helped Jules and her father hitch them to the rig. "*Vater*, I thought you fired Hans yesterday."

"I did. He burned his bridges, remember?"

"Well, he's standing out on the corner across the street."

"He is probably hoping I will hire him back. Hold off on getting the next horses, Rian. Jules wants to take each of the carriages around the block before delivering them to the *Elizabeth*. We can use this team until then. Want to drive the first one?"

Rian answered by immediately climbing up into the seat at the front of the carriage.

Jules walked beside the landau as Rian drove from her perch high in front. He was proud of this commission. Although it wasn't the first order Krieger Coach had sent to another country, it was the largest, and no expense was spared. He knew that Otto had gone out on a limb with this one.

Rian and Jules exited the shop through the big sliding door and turned left on Walnut. After a short distance, they turned left on Twelfth. Walking at a rapid pace beside the landau, Jules observed how the wheels rotated without a trace of wobble. He was pleased with what he saw.

From the left-hand side, Jules checked the hardware attached to the elliptic spring. All was well. He admired the landau's graceful curves, the deep rich browns of the wood, and the black of the metal springs and hardware.

They turned left onto Locust. Jules ran ahead of the team and walked backward, taking in the whole scene from the front. The leather of the harness and traces shone. Even the horses seemed to understand the importance of the occasion. They pranced.

They turned left again onto Eleventh. Jules shifted to the right side, working his way back, looking at how the spring absorbed the shock of the cobblestones. Just as they reached the corner of Eleventh and Walnut, Jules noticed Hans Schmidt leaning against a lamp post. They had almost circumnavigated the block and were within two hundred feet of the shop when Ernst Winther sprinted out the shop door and ran in their direction.

"Jules, something's wrong," Rian called from the driver's seat while pulling back on the reins.

Rian had brought the landau almost to a complete stop when the right rear corner of the carriage sagged abruptly. Jules cringed at the sound of metal scraping against wood.

Ernst reached them moments later. "Jules, Hans messed with the rigs last night."

"All of them?"

"All the ones that are supposed to be on the ship this morning."

. . . .

Half an hour later, Jules approached the standing desk outside the office with pencil and paper in hand. Aaron Bassinger was muttering something to Otto, shaking his head as he pored over the company ledger. Otto watched the workers as they scrutinized each of the four carriages. Even Rian and Conor McGuire were crawling under one rig, looking for damage.

"What happens if we don't get them on the *Elizabeth* this morning, Aaron?" asked Jules.

Aaron removed his bifocals. "It'll be bad. This was a big order for us. The problem is the way the contract reads."

"That is my fault," said Otto. "The only way I could close the Hamburg deal was if they did not pay any money upfront. So, we have a lot of resources tied up in those four carriages, and we have not received a penny yet."

Aaron again perused his ledger as if there might be some detail he had missed. "Well, I talked to Schiffler the other day. It's all sitting in the bank, waiting for us to deliver them to the ship. If we don't deliver today, we don't get paid the first half. Who knows when the next ship leaves Philadelphia for Hamburg? If we can't tap that letter of credit this week, we can't make our payments to the bank. Or payroll, for that matter. Not sure that would go over very well with the men. So, we're already on thin ice. And we don't see the other half until Ellsworth returns with a letter certifying the delivery. That's two months from now if we're lucky."

Otto eyed Randolph Tucker's carriage, parked in the corner and covered by a tarpaulin. "What about that?"

"Let's see." Aaron flipped back a few pages and ran his index finger down the ledger. "November 20th. Tucker paid us one-half upfront. We'll get the second half of that as soon as he takes possession. Maybe you could contact him and get him over here today."

"But that will not solve all our problems."

Aaron closed the ledger, a signal that he had mined all the information he could get out of it. "Nope, but it'll give us some breathing room. It would be better if we got those carriages on the ship today. If we get half the letter of credit this week, we've got the wind at our backs. It would be the first time since I've been here that I can see clear sailing. We've got orders for nine more carriages. Some are already half built."

"Can we hurry those along?"

Jules saw this as a good time to jump in. "We could if you didn't make outrageous offers to your customers. Gold plated hinges? Ivory inlay? We could have had those carriages out the door weeks ago, but there's no ivory to be found in the city. No one in America does gold plating, so we had to send Adrian's hinges off to England. You've got to check with us before making these commitments."

"I do not remember you complaining when I came in with the contract."

"Admittedly, it seems like every time you go out for lunch with Shippen or Biddle or Strickland, you come back with another order from someone, but honestly, Boss, try to make it a little easier on the production side of your business in the future."

Otto pointed to the paper in Jules's hand. "What did you find out?"

Jules consulted his notes. "Here's what we've found so far. Hans messed with each of the carriages. Each one is something different. Let's see. On the first one—the one Rian was driving—all the bolts connecting the three-quarter elliptic spring to the spring iron were removed. That's on the right rear. It would've been worse if Rian hadn't stopped when she did. But there's damage. The rear quarter panel has a pretty good scar on it where the wheel scraped up against it. Ernst already has someone sanding it out. It won't take half an hour.

"He ran a knife through the canopy of the second one. We wouldn't have found that until we popped it up on the docks. He cut some leather straps on carriage number three. Sawed almost completely through the center shaft on number four. If that had broken while the horses were hooked up to it, I'm afraid it would have been messy. Gotta admit he was creative."

"Any ideas?"

"Some. Your brother has two workers making new nuts and bolts in his shop. We need four of each. The bastard either took them or hid them. If we're lucky, the new ones'll be done in an hour.

"We have another landau in the queue for delivery in three weeks or so—same dimensions. The canopy's already here but not installed. We can steal that and put it on number two.

"We have a few yards of leather straps in the shop. We just need to cut new traces to length, and we'll be fine. That takes care of number three.

"When our guys were making the center-shafts, I had them make five so that you could pick the four you liked the best. I know you wanted these four coaches to be perfect. We've still got the one you liked least. The guys are looking for it now. That'll be our first compromise."

Otto gazed at the activity on the shop floor. "Okay, that is the good news. I already can see the bad news."

"Yeah. I'm pretty sure we can get them all to the ship on time, but they won't be finished. The bolts on number one won't be painted. The quarter panel and the center shaft won't be varnished. Are you willing to compromise on this delivery? Give them a few tasks for their local guys to complete in Hamburg?"

"No. Our name is on those plates. 'Krieger Coach.' I am not sending them out unless they are perfect. We cannot even put the first coat on anything because the dust on the street will ruin it."

"I knew you were going to say that. So, here's another idea. But you're not going to like it. We send a worker on the ship to apply all three coats. Set them up with a little black paint for the bolts and a bucket of varnish for the center shaft and the quarter panel. Three to four weeks to cross. Each coat gets days to dry in between. Even when you consider how damp it will be in the hold, there's plenty of time for three coats."

"Are you kidding?"

"Hell, no, I'm not kidding. I'd go myself, except Maddie would kill me."

Aaron looked back at his ledger. "Jules has got something there. Compared to what we're going to make on these coaches, the cost of sending a worker over and back to Hamburg is minuscule."

"Well, not you, Jules," said Otto. "The shop runs because of you. I would do it, but I have too many meetings coming up. One of the workers?"

"Trouble is we're already down one man, and now we've started running ten-hour days. It means some of our orders will be late."

"Anyone else?"

"I can go," said Rian. Up until this time, Jules had barely noticed her at his side. *Typical. She parks herself nearby, soaking in everything the adults have to say, learning, always learning.*

Otto whooped. "I am sorry, *Liebling*, I am not sending you on the high seas for eight weeks."

Jules laughed and pulled Rian close to him. "We almost had it. She has the skills. Rian and Conor did some of the finishing on these coaches."

"No. That is final. An eleven-year-old girl on a ship by herself. I will not consider it."

"Then how about Conor?" said Jules. "Same skills."

Otto pondered for a long moment. "Conor, did some of this work?"

"Yes. Sanding and finishing. I checked his work and never had to correct him. He even knows a little German. He'll be able to get by while he's in Hamburg."

Otto hesitated, then yelled, "Conor, come on over here and talk to us!"

· ·

· RIAN ·

Rian walked out of the factory with Conor. "Excited?"

Conor nodded. "This'll show me brothers. Your da is paying me a lot more money than they earned when they were eleven. I'll be out of their hair for two months. I'll get to visit Hamburg. I can't wait."

"I'm really jealous. I should be going with you. Listen, about yesterday. . . ."

Conor waved her off. "I felt like I was between a rock and a hard place. I figured Redmond needed me more than you did. But Rian, he shouldn'ta said those words."

"And I shouldn't have hit your brother."

"And he shouldn'ta hit you back. How's it feel?"

Rian touched her swollen cheek. "It was just the back of his hand."

Conor hugged Rian and started jogging south on Twelfth Street.

Rian watched Conor until he was two blocks away. When she turned to re-enter the shop, she noticed Topper holding the reins of the two white horses that were on the train yesterday. Rather than return immediately to the factory, she walked across the street.

"Hi Topper, what are you doing?"

"Master's going to pick up a buggy. Olivia told me your daddy owns this place."

"Yup. How's the Tuckers' place on Spruce Street?"

"For me, it's better than down home. I'm in the basement with the other servants. It's cooler down there at night than upstairs, so I like it better. I don't think the Tuckers know what they're missing. I miss Mammy. She's my gramma. It looks like you got in another fight."

"It didn't last long. It was more a discussion that got out of hand."

"Glad I don't get into your kind of discussions. I don't like getting cuffed around."

"Do you get cuffed around a lot?"

"Master gives me the back of his hand every once in a while."

· ·

· OTTO ·

Otto retreated to the office to write a note to Randolph Tucker, asking him to take possession of his landau at his earliest possible convenience. As if in answer to his prayers, Tucker entered the office with a polite knock. "Mr. Krieger. Good. Your boy told me you were here."

Otto rose from his desk and shook Tucker's hand. "Ah, that boy is actually my daughter Rian. She often dresses in boy's clothing because it is so dirty in the shop."

"No, I mean the big African at the desk. He was a bit abrupt with me. I think you should tell him in no uncertain terms it was no way to treat his betters."

"That man is Jules Freeman, my shop foreman." Otto was used to slights and insults flung at Jules in his presence. Sometimes it bothered him, sometimes not. This time it raised the hackles on the back of his neck. "I would also call him my good friend. I am sorry you felt slighted."

Tucker crossed his arms. "Your foreman. An African in charge of whites. Do you think that is wise?"

"It has worked well for fifteen years. He is excellent at what he does." *Time to change the conversation, Otto.* "Are you here to pick up the landau?"

Tucker dodged the question. "It looks like you have had some problems this morning."

"Nothing we cannot handle."

"Well, here's the thing. It occurs to me that you may have some cash flow problems due to the incident. I would be happy to pick up the landau today and pay cash for a reduced price."

"How much of a reduction were you thinking of?"

"Twenty-five percent."

Otto felt his blood start to boil. "I do not think that will be necessary. When can I expect you to pick up the carriage?"

"Later on this week. When I get around to it."

"Then good day to you, sir. If you will excuse me, I have duties to attend to. Please feel free to let yourself out."

· ·

· RIAN ·

Rian followed Aaron Bassinger into the office. Her father was sitting at his desk, running his hands through his hair in frustration.

"Who was your visitor?" Aaron asked.

"Randolph Tucker. He stopped by to tell me he would pick up the landau and pay cash right away for a reduced price. I told him no."

When Rian was in the office, she usually holed up in a corner and listened to the adults' conversation. She found she learned a lot that way. But this time, she had valuable information. "I just spoke to his groom out in front. He was with the two white horses they brought from South Carolina. Topper said they were picking up the carriage today."

Otto thumped his fist lightly on his desk. "So, he could have been a good man and helped me out of a tight situation. Instead, he tried to squeeze me when he thought I had no alternatives. *Dieser bastard* [That bastard]!"

Aaron went to his desk and sat down. "I think you are the victim of your own success."

"How so?"

"You have cultivated clients who have more money than they know what to do with. They buy your most expensive carriages, but they also think they are entitled to do whatever they want, to whomever they want, with no consequences. You're swimming with sharks."

"I can handle the sharks."

"Just make sure you don't become one of them."

Rian's father didn't like the direction the conversation was going. "Aaron, someone must go talk to Captain Ellsworth to make sure he has room for Conor. I want to stay here and make sure we get back on track. You okay to go?"

"Happy to. A couple of things, though. We've got to figure out how much we'll pay Conor for this. We threw out a number, but he was so excited about his adventure that he never nailed it down."

Otto chuckled. "I do not think now is a time for me to become a shark, but if all our negotiations were with eleven-year-olds, we would be rich by now. Now that you mention it, though, I guess we should start paying Conor when he is working here. I thought he was just sweeping up and sharpening tools."

"We already do pay him. For a couple of months now. Jules made the suggestion. We pay Rian, too."

Otto turned to Rian, a quizzical look on his face. Rian shrugged her shoulders and smiled.

"We didn't want to bother you with details," added Aaron. "And something else comes to mind. Conor will have a ton of time on his hands when he's on the ship. Putting a coat of varnish on every three days won't take him long. I'm a little worried about that. He tends to get into mischief if you leave him untended for a long while."

"Ellsworth is a good man. He has a cabin boy. When I crossed with him last year, the cabin boy had chores, but Ellsworth also spent quite a bit of time tutoring him. Everything. Navigation. Mathematics. History. How about if we ask him to treat Conor like a cabin boy? He is a good lad. This will be a good experience for him. It cannot hurt to ask. I bet the captain will be happy to do it."

Aaron started walking toward the door. "Okay, the sooner I go see Ellsworth, the sooner we know if this harebrained scheme will work."

"Close the door on the way out, please." Rian's father turned his attention to her. "*Liebling*, it has been very busy since you met me at the train yesterday. It is time for us to talk."

Rian cringed inwardly. *What's he going to yell at me first about? Hitting Billy? Getting kicked out of school? The cuff on the cheek that I got from Redmond?*

"This afternoon, you and I will go to your school and talk to the headmaster. I will ask him to reconsider his decision to kick you out of school."

"I understand, but he was pretty mad yesterday."

"Maybe he has had time to cool off."

"Well, there is something else you don't know yet. This isn't the first time I've gotten into a fight at school." *And that doesn't count the ones I've had out of school.*

Her father sat back and crossed his arms. "How many other fights have there been?"

"Three."

"Refresh my memory. Why did you get kicked out of German school?"

"Because our teacher spoke Low German. He didn't like it when I spoke back in High German."

"And why did you get kicked out of Catholic school?"

"Because the nuns were unfair. They had different rules for the boys and the girls."

"You got into a fight."

"That was one of the different rules. No boys ever get kicked out for fighting."

"Jules thinks that I should not bother meeting with the headmaster. He thinks you should come to work with me every day. He says you can get a good education right here in the shop."

"*Vater*, I would love that. I would do anything you want. Or Jules, or Uncle Adrian. I'll sweep floors. I'll sharpen tools." *And I'll never have to wear a dress again.*

"No matter what, you will be sweeping floors all summer long, plus additional tasks that we cook up. But come September, you will be back in school."

"What if the headmaster doesn't let me back in?"

"There is a finishing school in Switzerland. I may have to send you there."

Rian's mood went from elation to new depths in a heartbeat. "That would be terrible."

"Then first, we try to get you back in school. Then you have to get through a summer without hitting anyone."

"What if someone is being ganged up on? Like yesterday with Jules, and you, and Uncle Adrian?"

"No fights. Period."

Jules entered the office and shut the door behind him. "Everyone has a task. I think we are going to make it." He noticed Rian. "Ah, have you had a chance to ask Rian yet?"

"Not about what you want to know, but now is a good time." Otto leaned forward and put his elbows on his desk. "*Liebling*, there should have been more damage to the rig you were driving this morning. How did you stop the landau so quickly? Jules said you pulled the reins and the brake even before the carriage fell apart."

Rian exhaled, grateful that the subject had changed. "Sometimes, I sense that something is going to go wrong just before it does. I don't know how I know. I just know. Yesterday, I knew the trainman would throw a punch at Jules before he started."

Her father nodded at the recollection. "Yes, I remember. What about today?"

"I saw Hans on the street corner. He shouldn't have been there. Ernst came running out of the shop. That's all I know. Conor calls it my 'danger sense.'"

"Well, your 'danger sense' saved us a lot of heartache this morning." Otto turned to Jules. "Why did Ernst come running out of the shop?"

"Hans told him and a bunch of the guys that he snuck in last night and messed with the landaus. Ernst came into the shop right away, looking for you and me. He couldn't find either of us but found Aaron. Aaron told him Rian and I were already taking a spin around the block with the first rig."

"Hans told Ernst and other men he did this?"

"So Ernst says."

"But only Ernst bothered to tell us?"

Jules sat down in a chair next to Rian. "Yup. I don't think we can let this one pass."

Otto ran his hand through his hair. "No, not at all."

"Go to the alderman? We should be demanding justice."

"We could do that, but I have another idea. Jules, I want you to let the rest of the workers know that if Hans's plan had worked, we would not have been able to make payroll this week. We likely would have gone out of business."

"From what I heard Aaron say, that could be true."

"Maybe. But I want them to believe it. I want them to understand that Hans's actions could have cost them their jobs. They need to decide whose side they are on."

"That it?"

"No. Not at all. Rian, what is Seamus Gallagher doing these days?"

"Cousin Seamus? Digging ditches for the gas lines, I think. I saw him over on Mulberry Street a couple of days ago."

Jules shook his head ruefully, knowing what was about to come. "What are you thinking, Otto?"

"I think it is time we hired an Irishman."

. . . .

· SEAMUS ·

Seamus Gallagher was back in the same ditch as yesterday, taking swing after swing with his pickaxe. They would be finished with Mulberry Street in two more days, and the pipe layers would come over to do their work. Then Seamus and six other men would return and fill in the ditch.

Seamus continued to put his back into each swing of the pick, but he was barely breathing hard. "This time next year, a lot of the streets'll be lit by gas. Just like Paris. Some of the shops, too."

Dylan was at his usual position behind Seamus, shoveling the dirt that Seamus had already broken up and not working nearly as hard. "How would you know? You've never been to Paris."

"Yeah, but I've heard the stories. It's beautiful. And the girls there just love young Irish lads like us."

"You're full of crap, Seamus. Slow down. This street ain't gonna last forever. We've only got two blocks to go. Besides, you're making the rest of us look bad."

"This work ain't so hard. It's not like we're going to run out of streets. Besides, the only way I know I'm going to get picked every morning is to work harder than you."

A presence appeared above Seamus and cast a shadow across him. "Good afternoon, Seamus."

Seamus looked up, dropped his pickaxe, and climbed out of the ditch. "Well, Uncle Otto, I was just thinking about you. I bet our ditch here is good for your business. Saw three rigs get busted up just yesterday."

Otto smiled. "We will fix them if we made them. These days we are more interested in building new. How is your mum?"

"She's okay, I guess. Got fired from the mill, which I think was a good thing. Course, we need the money, but she's not coughing nearly so much. The cotton. It just gets in your lungs. I don't know how the girls stand it. I'd rather be digging ditches in this beautiful sunshine."

"What time do you get off, Seamus?"

"Not 'til candlelight. No ten-hour days for a ditch digger." *No bargaining power for us boys with no skills*, he thought to himself.

"I want to buy you a beer."

O'Shea yelled from halfway down the block. "Hey, Gallagher. No jawing with the swells! Get back to work!"

Seamus ignored the straw boss. "Irish drink whiskey, not that swill you call beer."

"I am okay to sip some whiskey if your lads will serve me."

"I think your money will be good at Clancy's."

Otto responded with a quizzical look.

It's on Plum Street, just off Pasture."

"I have not been that far south in a while. Name a time."

"Give me time to take me tools home. Wash meself up a bit. See you at 8:30. Don't worry about Clancy. He won't bite you. But you might want to dress down a bit."

. . . .

· OTTO ·

"I'm sorry it came to this, Herr Krieger, but I had no other choice."

Otto Krieger and Rian sat in the office of Hyram Chadwick, Headmaster of the Eighth Street Common School. "No other choice?" Otto retorted. "Of course, you had another choice. You did not have to expel my daughter."

"Well, technically, I did not expel her. She punched the Schiffler boy on the last day of the school year. I dismissed her for the day but made it very clear to your brother that she would not be readmitted in the fall."

"And you will not reconsider your decision?"

Chadwick put on his glasses and picked a sheet of paper off his desk. "Herr Krieger, let me quote from a report from Rian's teacher. 'Rian was, at best, a mixed blessing in the classroom this year. She is as smart as a whip. She has to read something only once to remember it. Arithmetic seems to come naturally to her. Yet repetitive drills bore her to the point of rebellion. She has no patience for students who don't grasp new things as quickly as she does. She is obstinate. At one point, I asked her to help teach some of the slower students, but she refused. Worst of all, during recess, she prefers roughhousing with the boys to staying inside with the girls. Those interactions have led to three brawls, after each of which she has refused to apologize.'"

"I just learned about these fights."

The headmaster took off his glasses. "I assure you, there were witnesses to each. They were brawls. Rian started all of them. And that gets us to the straw that broke the camel's back. On Monday, after many warnings, she engaged in another fight, this one with fists flying, with Billy Schiffler, son of the board of education's president."

"I talked to Mr. Schiffler. He says this fight was just kids being kids. He does not want this incident to affect Rian's future."

The headmaster had obviously prepared for this meeting. He picked another piece of paper off his desk. "And then there is her attendance sheet: your daughter attended only half the school days this year. Going back to last year, I see a similar pattern." Chadwick shifted his focus on Rian. "And where do you go when you decide to miss a school day, Rian?"

"I go to my father's shop, Krieger Coach. I help the workers. Sharpen their tools. Clean up. I learn things."

Chadwick raised his hands in a hallelujah gesture. "And there is the confirmation, Mr. Krieger. Despite her obvious intelligence, your daughter clearly gravitates to the trades. I suggest that you embrace this rather than fight it."

"No, that is not the future that I want for my daughter. I want her to get a good education so that she will be accepted into Philadelphia society."

Chadwick stared back at Otto with an expression that Otto could not interpret.

"I wish you could forgive her a bit. Her mother died when she was eight. I do not know how to raise a little girl."

"It's not as though you don't have other options, Herr Krieger. You are a Catholic. Your church runs a school three blocks from here. Or think about a German school. Many German-speaking families in Philadelphia send their children to private schools where they can be schooled in their native tongue. Clearly, these should not be unpalatable options."

They would be acceptable options, yet Rian has already been expelled from both. "No, I will not send her to either of those schools."

Chadwick toyed with his glasses on his desk. "Since last year, a charity school down in Moyamensing has opened up. She could go there if you sign a paper declaring yourself to be a pauper. No one will check up on the deception."

"No, I will not do that. My business is not yet prosperous, but I am far from being a pauper. Let me ask you a question: when boys engage in fights, do they get thrown out of school?"

"They are frequently dismissed for the remainder of the day. It provides time for them to cool off."

"But are they expelled from an entire school year?"

"Our standards for girls are different from those for boys. Boys are, by nature, more aggressive. We try to channel their aggression through sports and physical activities. What is considered a laudable trait in boys is unsuitable in girls. And let me be clear; Rian was not expelled from school. She was dismissed for the remainder of the day yesterday. She was told she would not be asked to return in September. We do not want an expulsion to go on her record."

"Could you please give her one more chance? Edward Schiffler told me to tell you that he would favor that decision." Otto handed Chadwick a folded sheet of paper. "I have a letter to that effect from him."

Chadwick read the letter. He shut his eyes, pinched the bridge of his nose, and then looked at Rian. "Rian, against my better judgment, I will allow you to return to school in the fall. But, and this is a big but, you must keep your nose clean all summer. If I hear of one fight that you engage in, no matter where it is, I will revoke your reinstatement. Do you understand?"

"Yes, sir."

"Do you doubt my sincerity?"

"No, sir."

"Then I must get on with the rest of my day's responsibilities. Good day to you both."

• • • • • • • • • • • • • • • • • • • •

· OTTO ·

Adrian ducked his head into the office. "Has Aaron run the new numbers yet?"

Otto sifted through a stack of papers on his desk and found the sheet Aaron had left when he and Rian met with the headmaster. "Yes, he says the new payroll for the year will knock us back a bit. I have no choice but to go to the bank for an additional loan."

"Well, if Krieger Coach goes into the railroad business, you will have to do that anyway."

"True enough, but with these new wage rates, I believe the only way I am going to be able to make a profit is if I invest in more machinery. The men will have to become more productive."

"How is machinery going to make them more productive?"

"A steam-driven shop, just like the mills that drive a score of machines that weave cotton. But our shop will drive drill presses, saws, and planers."

"Otto, you are crazy. You've spent fifteen years building a workforce of craftsmen. They do their drilling and sawing and planing by hand. You design beautiful carriages, and they build them by hand. The finest carriages in Philadelphia, probably all of America."

"Well, I do not know about that."

"The men will not put down their hand planes to run a rough-cut board through a machine. This whole lot you just won over with a ten-hour day will quit on you and find work with someone who values the traditional ways of doing things."

"I disagree. Look around. Philadelphia is changing before our eyes. When the four of us got off the boat fifteen years ago, there weren't half the factories that there are now. I bet even a quarter. And almost all of those were driven by water along the Schuylkill. The steam engine has changed everything. Now you can put a factory in any place you want and drive it with steam. We need to learn new ways of doing things, and so do our men."

"You said yesterday that we were going to need a bigger shop. Now you're saying a bigger shop and a huge investment in machinery."

"Actually, three bigger shops. For railroad cars, locomotives, and track. And each of us will have debt up to our eyeballs for the first few years."

"Jesus, Mary, and Joseph. I'm not sure I signed on for all that." Adrian flopped into a chair.

"Think about it. Get back to me. Aaron is already talking to his people. His cousin is on board. A few of his people have expressed interest in investing in the rail business."

"How did you make out with the headmaster?"

"Okay, for the moment. Rian will be allowed back in school in the fall if she avoids all altercations this summer. Trouble is, she got into two fights just yesterday. I will have to keep her close all summer long so she does not screw things up."

"What are you going to do?"

"Bring her here with me every day. Jules thinks she could get a good education in the shops. Learn bookkeeping from Aaron. Practical things from him, you, and me."

"Doesn't sound like a bad idea to me. Her curiosity alone is going to make sure she becomes educated. She was fascinated by the steam engine on the Falcon. Wanted to take it apart. Hell, she could name most of the parts already. Kept asking the mechanic what he was doing."

The thought of spending more time with his daughter did have its appeal. "I will speak to Aaron about the bookkeeping when he gets back. But she interacts with senior staff only; me, Jules, Aaron, and you in the metal shop, Adrian. I do not want her fraternizing with the men on the floor."

"I think that's wise."

. . . .

· RIAN ·

"Uncle Adrian, did you lie to me?

Adrian watched two workers who were about to pour molten iron from a casting ladle into a mold for a bar that they would eventually mill into bolts. He turned to find his niece with her hands on her hips. "In what respect?

"Did you tell *Vater* about our conversation on the ferry?"

"Absolutely not. Why would you think so?"

"Because the next day after I tell you I think *Vater* doesn't like the Irish, he says he's going to offer my cousin Seamus a job."

"Sorry to disappoint you, Niece, but your father did that all on his own."

Rian kicked at a stout block of wood that held the largest anvil in the forge. "What?"

"Why'd it have to be Seamus?"

"What's the problem with Seamus?"

Rian crossed her arms. "One day three weeks ago, I didn't go to school. I went to the shop instead."

"Probably more than one day. You barely went to school all spring."

Rian was undeterred by her uncle's distraction. "Jules read in the harbor list in the *Independent* that the *Hannibal* had arrived from Rio de Janeiro and docked at the Flintham Pier. He told me to go to the pier, talk to the *Hannibal's* quartermaster, see if they had the load of mahogany that they were supposed to have, and ask when it would be unloaded."

"You've run that sort of errand a lot. So what?"

"So, I'd just crossed Dock Street on Walnut. It was crowded. All sorts of men. Businessmen, workers, delivery guys. All of a sudden, Cousin Seamus comes hell-bent for leather around the corner from Second and runs right toward me. He sees it's me, stops, takes off his jacket and hat, balls them up, and shoves them in my stomach. 'Just keep walking,' he says. Then he puts his hands in his pocket and starts strolling in the direction he was going."

"Why'd he do that?"

"Not two seconds later, two gumps come flying around the corner. They were looking for a guy in a hat and coat. They'd been chasing him. They lost him."

"How do you know?"

"He found me at the shop that afternoon and asked for his hat and jacket. He fished in his jacket pocket and took out a money clip. There was a lot of money in it. He offered me a whole dollar just for carting his stuff around for an hour."

"Did you take it?"

"Yes, but I gave it to Conor. He and his brothers didn't have any food."

"So, let's get back to your problem. You wish Otto hadn't hired Seamus because . . ."

"Because he's the kind of Irish *Vater* told Mrs. Mott and Mr. Garrison about at dinner last night. He leads a life of crime."

"Admittedly, I don't know Seamus very well, but I think he's a smart young man who needs a break. Now your father has given him one. Let's see what he does with it. I think you should trust your father's judgment. Give your cousin a chance."

· · · · · · · · · · · · · · · · · · · ·

· SEAMUS ·

That evening, as Seamus entered the dark saloon, he gave a quick nod to Clancy. The saloon keeper reached for a bottle of whiskey and poured a glass. Seamus noted that Otto was already seated at a table in the back. He stepped to the bar. "Quiet night."

"I think the boys did their celebrating last night after the city council caved in. Didn't expect much tonight, but it's early yet. Gent over there's looking for you. German accent."

"That's me Uncle Otto."

"Deirdre's husband?"

"That's the one."

Clancy poured a bit more of the dark liquid into Seamus's glass. "If you're having a meeting with your uncle, you'd best have some more fortitude. How long's it been since Deirdre passed?"

"August of '32. Same as me da."

"Those were bad days. Lord took a lot of good people that year."

Seamus threw a coin on the bar. "Not sure it was the Lord that took them all."

Clancy slid the whiskey over to Seamus, who used the glass to give a slight salute to the saloon keeper and headed to the back of the room. His uncle was sitting at a table with two benches with high backs, ideal for a private conversation.

"Evening, Uncle Otto. See you found yourself a beverage."

"Good evening, Seamus. Thanks for meeting me. Nice place. Clancy was friendly until I asked for you."

"He watches out for us. But no current entanglements for me. I like this pub because it's a short walk home."

With a wave of his hand, Otto asked Seamus to sit on the bench opposite him. "You cleaned up pretty good. Good thing the city council didn't pass that resolution."[8]

"Aye. It only lost by two votes. I think it was stupid. Even I know a bath is a good thing. But today, it was just a slosh around me armpits. I'll have to get over to the river sometime soon and take a proper dip."

"Where are you living these days?"

"Me mum and brothers and sisters have a place just north of here."

"Nice area."

"Used to be. The previous owner was pretty rich, but he built a new place somewhere west of Seventh. More toward your neighborhood. That's the trend now. The richies are moving out. Building new away from the riff-raff."

"How is it?"

"It's what we're used to—lot of our own kind about. You learn who you can rely on and who to avoid. We share the house with seven other families. The owners pack us in pretty good. Lot of those old houses are now rentals. Irish get some. Africans in others."

"When did you move? I had no idea."

"January. Me old landlord found he could squeeze more Africans into the same space. We got the heave-ho."

---

8. In 1835, the Philadelphia City Council considered, but failed to pass, a measure to ban bathing, which was considered by many citizens to be unhealthy.

"I wish I had known. I could have helped you move."

Seamus shrugged and leaned back on his bench. "It wasn't a hard move. We don't own that much stuff."

"I'm afraid that since Dierdre died, I haven't kept in touch with the Gallaghers the way I should. Deirdre and your dad were so close. He's the one I knew the best. The cholera hurt a lot of families that year."

"Not sure it was cholera. I guess you haven't heard the rumors."

"What rumors?"

"Duffy's Cut. Where me da was working. Fall of '32. They were digging the cut and laying track for the *Philadelphia & Columbia Railway*. All Irish. Sixty of 'em. Most of them had just got off the boat from Ulster a couple of months previous. Cholera swept through the camp and killed most of them in a couple of days."

"That is what I thought."

"Not all of them, though."

Otto said nothing, but he raised his eyebrows.

"Turns out that when so many of them got sick and died, neighbors came in and killed the rest, sick or not. They were afraid the cholera was going to spread. Wanted to make sure it didn't. After all, it was only Irish."

"Do you believe it?"

"Dunno. Irish are expendable. No one cares about us. How'd you make out in the strike?"

"We agreed to a ten-hour day yesterday, same as everyone else. I am pretty sure we can get by with it. Think we beat the town council's decision by a couple of hours."

"Heard you had some problems this morning."

"That news traveled fast. We took care of it, but that is really the reason I wanted to talk to you."

That got Seamus's attention. "I haven't roughed anyone up in a while. A little pugilism might be fun. How many of me boys do you need?"

"Just you and me ought to be enough. I just want you to make sure no one else interferes in my . . . discussion."

"Count me in. When do you want to have this discussion?"

"Soon, but that is not really why I wanted to talk to you tonight. Do you know how to read?"

"Passably. Me learning came mostly from me da. When he died, that was about it. Unlike Deirdre, Mum never learned to read or write."

Otto contemplated this as he took a sip of whiskey. "That never stopped her from telling a good story, though. How are you with arithmetic?"

"Same. I can get by."

"I wonder if you would be interested in working for me at Krieger Coach?"

"Hmm. The strike's over, and you're hiring. Didn't see that coming. Interesting. Why me? Why now?"

"As of yesterday, I am down a man."

"There's plenty of good Germans who'd like to build carriages. Probably even come with skills."

"True, but this morning I learned that my own kind was not watching out for me. Actually, they were not even looking out for themselves. So, why not hire an Irishman? That is where you come in. I have neglected Deirdre's family long enough."

"That all?"

"No, that is not all. Lately, we have been thinking Krieger Coach is going to get a lot bigger. I need people I can trust. You are family."

"Uncle Otto, I'm a ditch digger. I wake up every morning, and I don't even know if I'm going to get picked to be on a crew. What do you want me for?"

"You underestimate yourself. I was watching you when you were digging that ditch. You work harder than anyone else. You motivate them. You are a natural leader. I can teach you the skills. I can even teach you how to read and write better. I cannot teach you how to lead."

"Why do I feel like you're still not telling me something?"

Otto took another sip of his whiskey. "You are sharp for a nineteen-year-old. Yes, there is one other thing. If Krieger Coach is going to grow, we will be at this for a long time. The Irish proved with the strike that they are a force now. You—the Irish—are only going to get more powerful. I need to know that in the future, I can work with you. Neither of us—Germans or Irish—are going away."

"What would I be doing?"

"Starting with the basics on the shop floor. More responsibility when you demonstrate you are ready for it. When we start to expand, I expect you will be a person I can rely on when we hire. Especially amongst the Hibernians." There was no pejorative connotation to the word *Hibernian*. It harkened back to Roman times when the Latin name for Ireland was Hibernia.

"Ispini and bogtrotters under the same roof. What makes you think the two can get along? Most of your lads are Protestants. We all take orders from the Pope, you know."

"I have already bridged that gap. My men know I am Catholic, and they don't seem to care. I guess it helps that I do not go to church that often. Sure, there will be some problems. It will be your job to keep your boys in line. My guy Ernst Winther can take care of our Germans."

"This sounds like an offer I would be foolish to turn down."

"That is what I was hoping you would say. One thing, though."

"What's that?"

"You would have to take orders from a Black man."

"Jules Freeman? Of all the Negroes in Philadelphia, he may be the only one I'd be willing to take orders from."

"You know him?"

"From years ago. A bunch of colored kids were wailing the tar out of me. Nothing, really, but I thought they were going to kill me at the time. Jules came upon us and threw the kids off me. Sent them running."

"Did he know you were my nephew?"

"Doubt it. He may not even remember it. That sort of stuff happens all the time around Moya, especially with kids."

Otto took another sip of his whiskey. "When we start to hire more Irish, think working for a Black man will be a problem for them?"

"Sounds like we're a ways away from that, Uncle. Let's take it a step at a time. Hey, one thing, though. I'm spending a lot of time with the Moyamensing Hose Company. Expect I'll get voted in this summer sometime. I won't be cutting my ties with them."

"That's a pretty rough crowd."

"We watch out for each other."

Otto leaned forward and looked Seamus right in the eye. "I need to know that none of their shenanigans will creep into the shop."

"I'm pretty confident that wouldn't happen."

"Then, as far as I am concerned, you can start work as soon as you want to quit digging ditches."

"You don't quit a job as a ditch digger. You just don't show up when they pick crews in the morning. There's always more workers than they need. How about tomorrow?"

"Six o'clock."

"Yeah, I saw the banners. Six to six with time off for two meals. Six days a week. Beats digging ditches from sun to sun. Hey, if you're hiring more of us in the future, keep your eye on Rian's friend Conor. He'll be the kind of worker you're looking for in a couple of years."

"Actually, he is already on the payroll. Right now, he is sailing to Hamburg with the four landaus that we delivered to the *Elizabeth* this morning."

"What'd Rian say about that? A whole summer without her best friend isn't going to be to her liking."

"She was a little down this evening. When I told her I was meeting you here after dinner, she said she was going to go to bed early."

· · · · · · · · · · · · · · · · · · · ·

· JULES ·

Jules and Maddie approached Bethel African Methodist Episcopal Church on Lombard Street in a sedate stream of mostly Black Philadelphians. Robert and Harriet Purvis stood on the front steps, greeting attendees as they entered.[9]

Jules had to marvel at the couple. Purvis was so light-skinned that he could pass for white. There was no doubt that the lovely Harriet was Black. That contrast alone made them stick out when they traveled together in the white sections of town. Harriet was the daughter of James Forten, whose flourishing sail-making business made him one of the wealthiest Black men in North America. That, combined with Robert's fortune, put the couple at the peak of Philadelphia's Black elite.

Jules sidled up to Robert, turned, and faced the incoming stream of lecture-goers. "How was dinner?"

"Too bad you weren't able to join us. I'm sure you and Garrison would have hit it off."

Jules scanned the crowd to assure himself that no one was listening. "Sorry about canceling at the last minute. Our conductor didn't show up on time."

Purvis cocked his head just enough to acknowledge Jules's involvement with the Underground Railroad but made no more mention of it. "Harriet's parents filled in for you. It went fine. Garrison entertained us."

"Is he inside already?"

"Yes, he wanted to get here earlier than the bully boys. It's just two blocks from our house, so we all accompanied him."

---

9. Just 24 years old, Robert Purvis was already one of the leaders of Philadelphia's Black community. He was born in Charleston, South Carolina, the son of William Purvis, a wealthy English cotton merchant and Harriet Judah, a woman whose ancestors were Jewish and Moorish. In South Carolina, one drop of Black blood meant you were legally Black. As mixed-race marriages were illegal in the state, the couple was forced to move with their three sons to Philadelphia.

Robert's father died when he was sixteen. Robert's mother made sure that her sons continued their education and immersed themselves in Philadelphia's free Black community. Robert, whose light skin allowed him to pass easily across color lines, took great pride in his African heritage and involved himself in America's abolitionist movement. Reflecting his wealth, his home on the corner of Ninth and Lombard was opulent.

"Is he expecting trouble?"

"I think he always expects trouble. We scanned the pennies that usually would be stirring up the locals. There wasn't anything, but he's cautious wherever he goes. Did you know he has a price on his head?"

"How much?"

"Five thousand dollars."

Jules whistled a long, slow note of amazement.

"Four years ago, the Georgia state legislature cited him for mailing copies of The Liberator down South. They blamed the paper for inciting Nat Turner's rebellion.[10] The Georgia state legislature put a bounty on his head for anyone who could kidnap him and bring him to Atlanta."

"Poor guy should have eyes in the back of his head."

"Yeah, he might as well be Black."

Jules chuckled at Robert's joke as he scanned the crowd. He caught a fleeting glimpse of someone who could have been Rian Krieger in the crowd but then lost track of the person. He and Maddie entered the church, and he forgot the incident.

10. In August 1831, the enslaved Nat Turner killed his master Joseph Travis and his family in their sleep. His intent was to spark a slave rebellion in Southampton County, Virginia, where Blacks outnumbered whites. Seventy-five enslaved and free Blacks joined the rebellion, which resulted in the death of 50 or so whites and some Blacks. It was put down after four days, but Turner evaded capture for seven weeks. Upon capture, he was tried and hung. Four years later, Nat Turner's rebellion still reverberated throughout the nation, belying the Southern myth that slaves were happy, and stoking fears that similar bloody rebellions could occur again. Thus, Garrison and his newspaper were vilified throughout the South.

Wednesday, June 24

· RIAN ·

The next morning at 5:30, Rian and Otto started their new daily routine by walking to the factory together. Her father began talking before they reached the end of the block. "Rian, I hired Seamus Gallagher last night."

"What's he going to do?"

"Start the same way we start anyone who has never worked in the trade: sharpening tools."

"Does he know how to sharpen a chisel?"

"I do not know. Probably not."

"Who's going to teach him?"

"You."

"Why me?"

"Because you have been sharpening the men's tools since you were seven years old. You are very good at it. You like to do it. You have taught two other men how to do it."

"Three."

Otto didn't break his stride. "I stand corrected. My point is that you are the logical person to do it. Plus, it would be good for you and your cousin to get to know one another better. Is that enough reasons?"

"I'm not sure we're going to get along."

"Why do you say that?"

"He doesn't know how to read. He doesn't think the way we do. He doesn't like Black people."

"He does know how to read, just not very well. Aaron is going to work with him on both reading and arithmetic. You do not know how he thinks. You will have to gauge that for yourself. And he knows he is going to be taking orders from Jules, and he says he is fine with it. I want you to give him a chance."

"I'll do my best, *Vater*." *I told Uncle Adrian on the ferry that I didn't know any Irish people. I guess now's my chance.*

"Good, that is settled. Now, about your time in the shop. Do not think your education is going to stop because it is summertime. You and I will walk to the shop together every morning in time to get there at 5:45. That will give you time to read the morning pennies. Jules says he will bring in Mr. Garrison's *Liberator* as well. Sometime during the day, Jules, Aaron, or I will quiz you on what you have read. If any of us are not satisfied with your answers, you will be sent to the library for further study."

"I can do that."

"I expect you can. The balance of every morning, Aaron has agreed to teach you bookkeeping. In the afternoon, Jules will teach you woodworking and pat-ternmaking. Adrian will take you over to the forge and start you making screws or angle brackets or casts of who-knows-what. In the evening, you and I will re-turn home around 6:30, and after dinner, we will practice our violins together. You will continue your Latin, Greek, and French lessons with Professor LaForce three times a week."

"That sounds good."

"You agree to it? Wholeheartedly?"

"Of course." Rian was elated. *Conor's going to be gone all summer. I have no other friends. And not one single mention of a dress.*

. . . .

"Have you ever sharpened a chisel before?" Rian asked Seamus.

"I've never even held a chisel before."

"Okay, this is a flat bench chisel. I just sharpened it yesterday. Look at the blade; tell me what you see."

"It's about an inch wide. The blade tapers down to an angle."

Rian noted that Seamus used the word *taper* correctly. "That's called a bevel. For this chisel, we want the bevel to be about 25 degrees."

Seamus looked lost already.

"Don't worry about it. You'll figure it out soon enough. What else do you see?"

"The edge is true as a die. The angle at the very bottom of the bevel gets a little steeper."

"Good. That's called a microbevel. That's the part that does all the work. The microbevel must be as sharp as possible." Rian picked up another chisel. "Now, this is one of the chisels that Hans knocked off a workbench as he was leaving yesterday. Tell me what you see."

"It's got a little nick in it."

"Good. Today, we're going to repair the nick."

"But it's just a little nick."

"But that little nick means that every stroke one of the men takes will encounter resistance. Every surface will be flawed. They would have to be sanded out. That can take hours."

"Makes sense. Let's get started."

Two hours later, Seamus was putting the finishing touches on the fifth chisel that Hans had damaged during his angry exit. Rian had to show Seamus something only once, and he got it. *Oh sure, he had to practice a bit. Okay, he had to practice a lot, but he did it, did it, did it until he got it right.*

Seamus took five more strokes on the whetstone. "Take a look at me microbevel. How'd I do?"

"Cousin Seamus, it looks perfect to me. We've been working half the morning; it's time to try one out." Rian locked a walnut board from the scrap pile into a vice. She pushed the chisel forward on the edge of the board, generating a dark, thin ribbon of wood. She handed Seamus the chisel. "Here, you try."

Seamus mimicked Rian's motions, creating a similar ribbon. "Well, this is satisfying."

"Satisfying when it's good and sharp. You've done a fine job on these."

"Seems to me that a good chisel's like a fellow Irishman."

"What do you mean?"

"It's obvious, isn't it? You take care of your chisel, and it'll take care of you."

Rian thought about Seamus's statement. "Is that how the Irish think?"

"We stick together. We've had to. Been under the boot of the English so long it's the only way we've been able to survive."

"But you live in America now."

"Aye, but as soon as me family stepped on these beautiful shores, there was always someone else happy to take the place of the English. Someone with their foot just itching to bear down on the backs of our necks."

"If that's what it's like, I don't think I'll ever know what it's like to be Irish."

"I've got some thoughts about that, Cousin. First, count your blessings. But second, you don't need three hundred years of misery at the hands of the English to be Irish. It seems to me you express your Irish half pretty well already."

"What do you mean?"

"Why it's obvious, isn't it? From what I hear, you dole out punches at the drop of a hat."

"Uncle Adrian says that's from my German side."

"Hmm, then maybe you got it from both sides. Your ma was a scrappy one. She came to me ma's defense more than once when they were kids."

"That's good to hear."

"Another thing; you're pretty thick with Conor McGuire. He's as sharp a chisel as you could ever have in your drawer."

The thought of Conor, at the very beginning of a months-long voyage to Hamburg and back, saddened her. "I miss him already."

"Well, stick with your cousin Seamus. This summer is likely to fly by. Together we'll make sure you learn to appreciate your Irish half."

"Did Uncle Adrian tell you to say that?"

Seamus slid the chisel one more time down the edge of the board, peeling up a thin walnut ribbon. "I don't know what you're talking about."

SATURDAY, JUNE 27

· RIAN ·

Rian sat at her table and steamed. "This is stupid," she muttered.

It had been three days since her first official morning at the shop. Her father had purchased a small table at a used furniture shop on Locust Street and placed it next to Aaron Bassinger's bookkeeper's desk in the Krieger Coach office. Rian liked her new old table but not Aaron's teaching methods.

"It isn't stupid. It's practice," Aaron replied, not looking up from his ledger.

"It's a column of figures. Adding dollars and cents is the same as adding any other two-decimal numbers. I can do this with my eyes closed."

"I doubt that."

"Try me."

Aaron looked sideways at Rian, tipped his head in an "I'll show you" gesture, and turned a page of his ledger. "I've got five figures here. You say you can add them up in your head without looking at them?"

"Try me."

"$25.50, $28.95, $30.00, $17.17, $1.05."

"$102.67," Rian said without hesitation.

Aaron's mouth turned into an upside-down U. "Impressive."

"I could have done more. But you know what? Just plain numbers don't mean anything."

"What do you mean?"

"The numbers don't mean anything because they aren't related to anything. They're just numbers. Let me do some addition that helps you out."

"Three days ago, on Seamus' first day of work. What did you do?"

"I taught him how to sharpen chisels."

"Was he good at it right away?"

"No, he had to practice."

"So, that's what I'm having you do now. Practice. It's the same process I do in my ledger."

"But at the end of the morning, Seamus had six sharp chisels to show for his practice. All I've got is a bunch of wasted paper."

Aaron consulted his ledger again. "The five numbers that I read to you. They are the cost of the major component for a shaft and harnesses for two horses for a phaeton that your father designed. You're telling me that if your numbers were real, not just made up, you wouldn't spend the morning muttering?"

"No, I wouldn't mutter a bit."

"I'll make you a deal, Missy. I'm going to give you a problem. Solve the problem, and I'll let you make entries into the company's ledger. Don't solve it, and you have to go at the pace that I set for you. Deal?"

"Deal."

· ·

· OTTO ·

Otto and Seamus waited in the darkness of an alley across the street from the Sansom Street Brauhaus. Ernst Winther had told Otto that Hans Schmidt drank there almost every evening, often with a few of the workers from Krieger Coach. It had been four days since Hans had damaged the carriages the night before they were shipped to Hamburg. It was time to rebalance the books.

Otto was dressed in his everyday suit, the same clothes he wore both in the shop and at lunch in the United States Hotel. He carried his stout lumber estimating rule that he used as a walking stick but occasionally needed for other purposes.

Seamus broke the silence. "Just to be clear, you're not going to kill him, right?"

"No, no one is going to die tonight. I just want to make sure that he and his remaining friends at the shop learn that there are consequences for what he did this week. I could have gone to the alderman to get justice, but I find this to be more . . . personal."

"When's the last time you got into a fracas?"

"I had a bit of a dustup last week at the Camden train station. Before that? Years, I suppose."

"Good to see you're not afraid to mix it up a bit when the occasion is called for, Uncle."

"Not my preference, really. Back when it was just Jules and me building wheelbarrows, things were different. It felt like I had a brawl every other week. I slept in my shop more than once to keep the thieves out. Back then, I was always scrambling. I had to fight for everything I got. I cut corners. I was always one step ahead of the bill collector. This seems like a step back to those days.

"You sure you want to do this?"

"Just because things look rosy at the moment does not mean I forget where I came from. I remember the first time I priced out a carriage. I did not know how to do half the things I told the customer I could do. I flat out lied. If it had not been for Jules's knowledge and skills, we could have gone under any number of times. He would get so angry with me. I would come to the shop and tell him that we were going to make a carriage for someone and have it ready in six weeks. He would fuss and fume, but we always figured out how to do it. The more we did it, the better we got."

"So, you weren't a carriage maker back in Wurttemberg?"

"No, I was a lumber estimator—great skill to have. With this stick here, I can tell you how many board-feet are in a standing tree. Jules is the one who talked me into the carriage business. Actually, it was originally wheelbarrows, wagons, and sleighs, but we always had our eyes on the expensive rigs. That is where the money is."

"And now you want to leave all that behind and go into the railroad business."

"I think we will be able to do both for a while. Then we will see."

Seamus's attention switched to the door of the saloon. "Somebody's coming out of the Brauhaus."

"I think that is our man."

"There's two others. Looks like Gunther and Niels."

"Good, I do not mind a few witnesses. They will make sure an accurate story gets back to the shop. You do not have to do anything, Seamus. Just make sure they do not jump me from behind."

Hans Schmidt careened his way across Sansom Street as Otto walked out of the shadows. "*Hallo, Hans. Es ist Zeit für Rückzahlungen* [Hello, Hans. It is time for paybacks]."

Hans made the mistake of taking the first swing.

Good. If the alderman gets involved, I can just plead self-defense.

Wednesday, July 8

Philadelphia Mourns Loss
Of Chief Justice John Marshall
Exclusive to the Philadelphia Independent by Harold Foote

The citizens of Philadelphia were saddened to learn of the death of John Marshall, Chief Justice of the Supreme Court, who died locally on July 6. Mr. Marshall had traveled to Philadelphia from his home in Virginia to receive unspecified medical treatment.

Mr. Marshall's tenure started in controversy and sparked additional contention through landmark decisions under his guidance as Chief Justice of the Supreme Court. He was initially appointed to the position by President John Adams on Adams's final day in office after he and the Federalist Party had been defeated in the election of 1800. Marshall surmounted his rocky start as one of Adams's "Midnight Judges" and built the Supreme Court into a co-equal third branch of the government, a counterbalance to Congress and the presidency.

Critical decisions during Marshall's tenure include *Marbury v. Madison*, which established the Supreme Court's authority of judicial review—the ability to declare acts of Congress to be unconstitutional. *Fletcher v. Peck* was the first case where the Supreme Court declared a state law unconstitutional. *McCulloch v. Maryland* cited the "necessary and proper" clause of the Constitution to justify the expansion of federal powers beyond those explicitly identified in our Founding Document.

These decisions and many of Marshall's other written opinions were groundbreaking and deemed highly controversial by many citizens. What is undeniable is that Marshall, our fifth and longest-serving Supreme Court Chief Justice, was a revolutionary thinker who deftly enhanced the status of the Supreme Court over 34 years.

A cortege in honor of Mr. Marshall will occur in Philadelphia today at 3:00 pm and will be marked by the ringing of the State House Bell. All citizens are encouraged to line the streets along the route on Chestnut Street.

•   •   •   •   •   •   •   •   •   •   •   •   •   •   •   •   •   •   •   •

· LUCRETIA ·

Choosh! Choosh! Choosh! The sound of ferries crossing the Delaware competed with the daytime cacophony of the docks.

Lucretia Mott waited on the Spruce Street wharf with some apprehension when the *Waterloo* tied up at its berth. She feared that James might not respond favorably to her thinking about slave-free produce. James was on deck, holding his carpetbag and looking pleasantly surprised to see his wife on the wharf.

Upon descending the gangplank, James dropped his carpetbag and embraced his wife. "My dear, this is very modern of thee, coming to the docks unescorted."

"It's perfectly safe here. I wanted to be the first person to greet thee upon thy return."

"I'm so pleased. It makes me feel important. How long has thee been waiting?" The couple started walking west on Spruce Street, away from the docks.

"I just arrived. The semaphore towers[11] sent word as soon as the *Waterloo* entered the bay yesterday, so I knew thee was arriving today; I just didn't know when. I sent Rian Krieger and Thomas to the Navy Yard to monitor incoming ships. The *Waterloo* was one of the first ships to arrive this morning.

"Rian, huh. She's a firecracker. I daresay she's the one who took the lead on that assignment. What was she today, a boy or a girl?"

"Oh, she wore her ragamuffin clothes, of course. Honestly, sometimes I don't understand why Otto allows it. It's so unladylike. But today, it came in handy for us. I was pleased to have them go together and to be frank, despite how she dresses, I think Rian has a lot more street smarts than Thomas."

"Indeed. Where are they now?"

"Thomas is playing with his sisters. They are anxiously awaiting thy return. They've missed thee so. I imagine Rian just headed off to her father's shop. So, how was thy trip? Thy letter said thee had some misgivings."

"More than misgivings, I'm afraid. Charleston was bad, and Savannah was worse. I met with Johnson, of course, about our contract to buy his cotton. The price is reasonable, and there's no economic reason not to buy it. It's a good deal for both of us. I'm just sick about this."

Lucretia hooked her arm into his. "Sick about what?"

"I made it a priority to visit some places I'd managed to avoid in previous trips. Pointedly avoided, I'm ashamed to say."

---

11. Since 1809, a series of towers constructed from Cape May to Philadelphia had given merchants notice of arriving ships a day in advance. Mechanical arms in different configurations could spell the letters of the alphabet. The optical telegraph communicated tower-to-tower, and a message from Cape May could travel the hundred miles to Philadelphia in less than an hour.

"Thomas, where did thee go?"

"A public slave auction in Charleston. I visited two plantations outside of Savannah."

"How bad was it?"

"Lucretia, they were worse than I'd even imagined."

"I'm not sure I want to hear this."

"The conclusion I have come to is that slavery is as destructive of the slaveholders as it is of the slaves. The slave owners just don't know it. At the slave auction, most of the crowd was there just for the spectacle. They had no intention of buying. A young male slave, perhaps 20, was at the auction block. His back was horribly shredded from lashings; some healed and scarred, some raw. The gawkers assumed the lashes meant the man had been defiant, and he was therefore worth less. His master inflicting unbelievable cruelty upon him was not even a consideration. I saw a mother sold to one owner and her daughter sold to another. The poor woman was heartbroken. She pleaded not to be separated from her daughter. That amused the crowd. They yelled to her that her daughter would be used by the new owner for his carnal desires and then discarded like a broken-down horse."

"Oh, James. I'm so distraught."

"It gets worse. On the plantations in Georgia, the slaves were barely clothed. Food was a gruel of grain and not much else. I found a particular distaste for one of the plantation overseers, but I have the impression that his actions weren't unusual. If a slave tried to escape, he punished not only him but his family. Horrible whippings. Then he would rub pickle juice in the wounds. I heard of another slaveholder who was notorious even among his neighbors. When the slave was recaptured, he would tie the poor wretch down on an anthill where he was horribly bitten thousands of times. He left one young man who wanted only to be free, tied to a post until he died, pecked to death by birds. He wanted to send a message to any other slave who even thought about escaping."

"What are we going to do?"

"My time on the *Waterloo* has given me much time to think and pray on this subject. I can no longer justify making a living from a product produced by slaves. I'm not going to renew my contracts this year."

"I agree."

"You do?"

"Yes, of course. Thee has been pondering the morality of this from a business side. Thee is no longer willing to build a livelihood from a corrupt, soulless institution. I've been thinking and praying about this same subject, but from the domestic side. What moral justification can there be for supporting the institution of slavery by buying its products? My answer is that when I buy a bolt of cotton cloth, I am as corrupt as the slave driver who applies the lash."

James drew her closer to him. "We should spend a month apart more often."

"Pardon me?"

"The two of us have taken this time apart to come to momentous conclusions. The implications are almost too big to contemplate."

"Thy business will become difficult."

"I can find other things to import from other parts of the country. Or the world, really. If thee doesn't buy cotton, what will we wear?"

"Wool in the winter. Linen in the summer, I suppose. Thee has all those ties to cotton brokers in Georgia and the Carolinas. What will thee do?"

"Write to them. Tell them why I am no longer willing to do business with them."

"That will end the friendships, of course."

"Yes, but think about it. There is a larger goal than no longer profiting from the fruits of slavery. Our goal is to end slavery altogether. This will only be possible when people like us declare ourselves to the world. We will no longer support the institution of slavery, even many steps removed."

"So, we tell our friends as well. Set an example. Be public about it. Bring our sentiments to the anti-slavery societies."

"Without a doubt. No purchasing or wearing cotton."

"Then no more sugar either."

"Ow. That one's going to hurt. Yes, no more sugar. Well, let us not dwell on business so soon after my homecoming. A momentous day, nonetheless. Shall we table the discussion until later?"

Lucretia nodded, amused that James spoke as if he were chairing an Anti-Slavery Society meeting.

"Tell me, what other news have I missed? How has the construction on the house gone? How are the children?"

"Thee has been at sea. Has thee heard about John Marshall?

"The Chief Justice?"

"Yes. He died two days ago, here in Philadelphia. A cortege will escort his casket out of town this afternoon. I guess then his body goes back to Virginia."

"Sad news. A great man."

"A great man, assuredly. But also a slave owner."

"Isn't it interesting? So many people we consider to be great men—the generation of Washington, Jefferson, Madison—were also slaveholders. It is such a pity that they couldn't have been so great that they could see slavery for its corruption. What else? What of the house?"

"Construction is complete. The house was a wreck for a few weeks, but the plasterers finished up once the strike ended. The plaster dried. The painters came and went. We moved out for a few days while all that was going on. Maria and Thomas stayed next door with the Kriegers. Thomas loved that because he was able to carouse with Rian a bit. Otto runs a looser ship than we do, but I approve of how he is raising Rian, except for how she dresses, of course. Elizabeth, Martha, Little Anna, and I did fine with Big Anna. Little Anna put up with the mayhem better than I expected. I think she has come to terms with the loss of my dear sister and is now settled into our family. Now the furniture is back in place, so thee is returning to a home of domestic tranquility."

"It must have been difficult."

"Yes, but I had other things to worry about that took my mind off the mayhem. I chaired a few meetings of the Female Anti-Slavery Society and cooked a meal for William Lloyd Garrison, though we switched it to Otto's house because of the plasterers. I've also received requests to speak at various Quaker meetings in Pennsylvania and New York. We should talk about that soon as well."

"My beloved wife. Thou art a force."

· ·

· OTTO ·

Otto and Adrian Krieger; Aaron Bassinger, the bookkeeper and hopeful steel railman; and Aaron's cousin Jacob rode to the vacant lot in Spring Garden in a landau and a landaulet, both built by Krieger Coach. The mile trip from the current shops to the new site took less than five minutes. One of Philadelphia's preeminent architects, William Strickland, was waiting for them when they arrived.

At forty-seven years old, Strickland stood tall and thin. Thick mutton chop whiskers bracketed his narrow face and long, aquiline nose. Although he might not be considered a handsome man, the effect worked in his favor. More importantly, he struck the confident pose of a man who was unintimidated by a grandiose challenge. His professional resume included some of the era's preeminent construction projects, including large public buildings, canals, railroads, and dams.

"Okay, I've done my best to change your minds, but I'll say this one last time. There is no logical reason why Krieger Coach, Krieger Locomotive, and

Krieger Rail all have to be housed on the same plot of land. The three entities should be established in separate locations that give the greatest access to incoming raw materials and labor, and then ease of shipment of completed products. Two out of three would be acceptable. All three would be preferable.

"Krieger Rail will use huge amounts of iron and coal as the primary raw materials for its rails, not to mention the fuel to fire the furnaces. The most advantageous site would be somewhere on the Schuylkill River. Krieger Coach won't use nearly that volume of resources, but you'll want to be near skilled workers. You should be south of here. There are plenty of viable locations not far from where Krieger Coach is now. Krieger Locomotive will want access to both workers and resources. You should be somewhere over by the wharves on the Delaware so you can ship your finished locomotives to Buenos Aires or Dublin or wherever you dream of selling. Here, you're in the middle of nowhere, halfway between the Delaware and the Schuylkill, with none of the advantages."

Strickland looked expectantly at his audience and saw four smiling faces.

Otto spoke for the group. "I am sorry, William. We have spent hours talking about this these past two weeks. Aaron, Adrian, and I have worked together for the past ten years. Adrian's shop is a separate business, but we are essentially under the same roof. We are used to wandering in and out of each other's space all day long. You have to admit, we are talking about allied manufacturies. We believe that what we lose in access to shipping or workers, we will make up in our ability to collaborate and innovate together. Our decision is made."

Strickland responded to Otto with silence. He scanned the big empty block as if envisioning it with factories in place.

Otto continued. "First of all, we are only one block from the railway. I am told we will likely be able to build a spur that will supply us with all the iron and coal that we need. Finished goods can go west to the Schuylkill or east to the Delaware. It is only a mile either way. You have done your due diligence, William. Let us proceed."

"Okay, let's see what you're thinking. I see you've brought some plans."

Otto unrolled a large sheet of vellum and laid it out on the boot of the landaulet. "These are just for placement only." The group crowded around the drawing. "We envision Krieger Rail as the longest of the buildings, extending the entire length of the block. Raw materials in this end, finished rails sixteen feet in length out this end. That is approximately one-half of the block. One quarter, here in the north, will be Krieger Coach. The other quarter, where we are standing now, will be Krieger Locomotive. Alleys here and here separate the three buildings. Wide enough to accommodate importation of machinery, but close enough that we can easily move between buildings for consultations."

"Hmm. This is a good start. I can work with this. I'm not a lawyer, but I have a firm recommendation. Since you insist on occupying the same parcel of property, I would suggest various layers of corporate entities. One corporation, with you all as the primary stockholders, owns this parcel in its entirety, along with whatever structures we build on the property. Then each of you creates your own corporation. Well, actually, Krieger Coach already exists. Krieger Forge becomes Krieger Locomotive. And the four of you are all stockholders in the newly created Krieger Rail, along with many lesser stockholders. That way, if one corporation goes out of business, or if one of you wants to sell, it doesn't jeopardize the whole."

"So, you are willing to work with us?"

"I would be flattered to work with you. I've always wanted to design a factory. I've done banks, canals, an asylum, railroad beds, the Delaware Break-water, but never a factory. You may not know this, but in 1825 the Internal Improvements Society sent me to Europe to learn whatever I could about European canals before we started the Pennsylvania Canal. I came home convinced instead that the future lay in railroads, not in canals. Judge Kane and some of his cohorts didn't like my conclusion and modified my report's recommendations. However, I am convinced that you gentlemen are on the right track, if you'll pardon my pun. But I do have a question."

"Go ahead."

"How big do you intend to get?"

"How big?" Otto looked around at his fellow entrepreneurs. They nodded. "We intend to be in the vanguard of innovation in this industry—in rails and locomotives, and even rolling stock. We think we are going to get very big."

"I'm inclined to agree with you. And if that is so, you might consider an option to buy that parcel of property across the street. I think in a few years, you're going to need it."

· ·

· RIAN ·

Rian was sitting at her desk when Aaron Bassinger returned to Krieger Coach after the meeting with William Strickland. She was dressed in her shop clothes, although her long brown hair flowed down her back.

"Hi, Aaron."

Bassinger shed his coat and hung it on a hook. "I thought you and Thomas Mott were standing look-out at the Navy Yard today."

"We did. Mr. Mott's schooner was the first ship up the river this morning. We ran to Thomas's house and told his mom. She dropped everything and headed to the wharf. She was pretty excited."

"Not surprised. He's been gone for a long time. So, you didn't take time off to play with your friends. I figured my assignment might keep you away from the office for a while."

"Summertime's not much fun without Conor. I wish *Vater* had let me sail to Hamburg with him."

"So, since you're here, I assume you're working on my request. I believe I asked you to cost out a bid for that cabriolet for Mr. Demerit."

Rian was certain that Aaron had assigned her that task assuming that she would never take on such a complex job. She started it a week ago just to prove him wrong. "That's what I'm doing. I'm almost finished." After another minute, she handed him her draft.

Aaron took the paper, an incredulous look on his face. "You've got different prices for oak, mahogany, and hickory. How did you come up with those prices?"

"We get our mahogany from Honduras, so I looked at the last bill we paid for wood right off the boat. I added one percent just because. We generally buy small quantities of oak and hickory from Dierdorff Lumber, so I walked over there and asked Mr. Dierdorff what his current prices were."

"What about the hardware?"

"Uncle Adrian's shop makes all our hinges and springs and so on. A cabriolet is lighter and smaller than a landau, so I just took the figure Uncle Adrian charged for the landaus we shipped to Hamburg and cut it by a third. It was the best I could do since Uncle Adrian was with you this morning."

"What's this figure here? 'Additional expenses'?"

"I just made that up. I figured that there are certain expenses that we should charge that don't have anything to do with making the cabriolet."

"Like what?"

"A percentage of everything that it takes to run the shop. Coal for heat, new tools, candles, insurance, taxes. That kind of stuff."

"How did you get that figure?"

"One of the first things you had me do when I started helping you two weeks ago was filing paid bills. I thought it was pretty interesting. Yesterday, I went through every bill we've paid over the past year and added them all up.

Then I divided by the number of carriages we made over the same amount of time. Well, actually, every carriage, slay, wheelbarrow, and cart."

"Where did you get that number?"

"Jules keeps a running list of the things we've built out in the shop. He showed it to me a long time ago. I figured all the additional expenses should be built into every bid. I found a couple of bills that were misfiled, by the way. I put them on your desk."

Aaron took off his glasses and cleaned them with a handkerchief. He took two minutes to study Rian's work. "Well, Rian, if this bid had been submitted just as you've written it, I think Krieger Coach would have lost about $300."

"What do you mean?" said Rian, crestfallen.

"You didn't factor in any cost for labor. If you had submitted this as a final bid, you would have cost Krieger Coach a bundle of money."

Rian assumed her plans to do real bookkeeping died with her failure to create a good bid. She hung her head. "I'm sorry. I didn't even think about that."

"Understandable. I keep payroll files in a separate box on that shelf over there. Rian, don't be sorry. I'm proud of you. There's not a man in this shop except your father or Jules who could have gotten this far on this project. You understand the mechanics for determining how much a carriage as complex as a cabriolet will cost. You figured out on your own that the cost of building a carriage is much more than wood and springs. You are eleven years old. This bid is an impressive accomplishment. Despite your monumental error, I believe you are ready to make entries directly into the company ledger. Congratulations."

Rian jumped up from her chair so quickly that it tipped over backward.

Aaron put a damper on her enthusiasm. "Did you read the penny paper this morning?"

Rian's father, Jules, or Aaron had been asking her this question every workday for three weeks now. She enjoyed the challenge. "Two of them. One in German, one in English."

"Give me the two top stories from each."

Rian sighed as if Aaron's request was a burden.

Aaron was undeterred. "Let's hear it."

"Hmm, for English . . . Chief Justice John Marshall died two days ago. He came to Philadelphia for some medical treatment. He was staying at Mrs. Crimm's boarding house on Walnut Street. Mr. Foote wrote that article."

"What does the Chief Justice do?"

"I'm not sure. I know he's important."

"Yes, he is. And Mr. Marshall is the greatest of the five Chief Justices the United States has had so far. By tomorrow I want you to be able to tell me both sides of the discussion, 'Why John Marshall was a great Chief Justice.'"

"Oh, Aaron, come on!"

"Rian, even though school's out for the summer, it doesn't mean your education goes on hold. That's a year-round thing. Okay, what else?"

"The sickly season has started down South, so folks from Charleston, South Carolina, and a bunch of places in Virginia have already started to arrive for the summer. I remember some of the names of the Southerners. Now that the Tuckers have arrived, it kicks off something called the social season, whatever that is. I think that's the same Tuckers that bought the landau."

Aaron grunted, implying a lack of interest in that topic. "The German papers?"

"Workers are striking in other cities. Just like the ones here three weeks ago."

"Where are they?"

"I can't remember them all. New Brunswick, New Jersey. Seneca Falls, New York. Hartford, Connecticut. Someplace in Massachusetts."

Aaron settled into his chair, indicating that he had no intention of making this a perfunctory conversation. "What are they striking about?"

"Same as here. The ten-hour day."

"Have any of the strikes been resolved?"

Rian shrugged. "I don't think so. Are you going to ask me to point them out on a map?"

"No, we'll save geography for another day. You still owe me another article from a German paper."

"They talked about the general strike."

"Old news. Give me something else."

"Halley's Comet?"

"What's that?"

"A comet that's supposed to show up sometime later this year."

"Really. How do they know?"

Rian brightened because she had read this article in detail. "Because of Edmond Halley. He was an English astronomer in the early 1700s. He did some research and found records of comets that appeared about every 76 years going back for centuries. He believed that it was really the same comet. And if that was so, then it would come back in 1758. Then he died."

"So, he never saw his own comet?"

"Nope."

"Did the comet come back in 1758?"

"Yup, in 1758 going toward the sun, and then again in 1759 on its way back out again. It goes all the way past Jupiter before it turns around again. And guess what? It's supposed to show up this year sometime."

"This is all very interesting. Why is it important?"

"Some people think it means bad things are going to happen."

"What do you think?"

Rian shook her head. "I think it's just a comet. But I think it's a fun thing to know about."

"I agree. Okay, it's time for you to get out of here. I've still got to check your math from the bid. Did you leave tracks?"

"Yes, Aaron. I made a worksheet."

"Go, bother Jules. I'm sure he can use some help on the floor."

· ·

· SEAMUS ·

Seamus sat on the shop floor, surrounded by the parts of a disassembled foot-powered lathe. He tested the fit of a new bearing for the crankshaft—*God bless Adrian's shop. They made exactly what I asked for*—which was in turn connected to an eighty-pound flywheel.

"What are you doing, bogtrotter?" Seamus recognized the voice coming from directly behind and above him. It was Jürgen, one of the ispini who had been particularly vocal in his dislike of the Irish.

Seamus ignored the insult. He had been called a lot worse in the two weeks since he started working at Krieger Coach. "The bearings for the crankshaft were failing. It wasn't an easy fix, so I had to take the whole machine apart. Then Krieger Forge made two new bearings right on the spot."

"Did Ernst tell you to do that?"

"Nay, but if someone didn't fix it, it would have broken soon enough for sure."

Seamus reached for the second bearing, but Jürgen toed it away from his grasp. "Kind of uppity of you, doing something like taking a machine apart without being told. You should have a better idea of what your place is here."

Seamus decided he would be better off talking to Jürgen eye-to-eye. He stood up slowly, on the ready if Jürgen took a swing at him, then pointed toward two Germans working at lathes, each with a foot on a pedal that kept a flywheel spinning rapidly. "Look over there. What do you see?"

Jürgen looked briefly. "I see two good German men doing their job. A job no mick should ever be allowed to do."

"You know what I see? I see two machines that are sure to break if someone doesn't work on them soon. Look at the flywheels. They're both wobbling. The bearings are a weak point. If the crankshaft comes out of them or breaks, one of your isipinis will get hurt."

Jürgen looked again at the machines and returned his attention to Seamus. "Those flywheels have been wobbly ever since I started work here. You should stick to sweeping floors."

"So, you've got a problem with what I'm doing?"

"I've got a problem with you, Mick. Your kind is nothing but a bunch of Africans turned inside out."

Seamus shook his head. He knew the Irish were on the same rung as the Africans. He'd heard the "inside out" insult before. And the abuse went both ways. Want to insult an African? Call him *smoked Irish*.

Seamus stepped away from the strewn machine parts to give himself room to maneuver. "So maybe we should take care of your problem right here right now."

"I was hoping you would say that." Jürgen whistled, attracting the attention of a handful of other ispinis who left their machines and surrounded Seamus.

Seamus was confident that one-on-one, he could beat Jürgen in a fistfight. Five against one would be a bit of a stretch, but he was willing to take the licking if it proved he belonged on the shop floor.

Both the lathe operators left their machines and joined the group. *Great, seven against one.*

The flywheels of the two lathes continued to spin, their foot pedals rhythmically pumping up and down without the operators.

Jürgen took a fighting stance. The other six closed in on Seamus.

Saint Francis, I could use you about now. If ever there was a lost cause, I think this is it.

As if Saint Francis had heard Seamus's plea, the crankshaft of one of the still rapidly spinning flywheels disengaged from its left bearing. The flywheel tore away the leather belt that connected it to the lathe, dropped and dug into the shop floor, tearing the right leg off the lathe. The lathe collapsed. The flywheel, crankshaft, and right leg spun wildly toward the workers, knocking one man off his feet before it finally came to rest between Seamus and Jürgen.

Seamus walked over to the man who had been knocked on his ass. He held out his hand to help him up. "Are you okay?"

The man nodded and gratefully took Seamus's hand.

Seamus turned to the group. "Does anyone besides Jürgan have any problem with me looking after these machines?"

Six men who had moments ago surrounded Seamus intending to thrash him turned to go back to their work. One clapped him on his back on his way by.

· ·

· OTTO ·

An hour after his meeting with Strickland, Otto sat with George Shippen and Edward Schiffler in the restaurant at the United States Hotel.

"I hope you don't mind, Krieger," said Shippen, "but I took the liberty of inviting Schiffler. As the Bank of Industry's president, he knows more about the day-to-day workings than I do. If there are questions that I can't answer, Schiffler certainly will be able to."

Shippen's remarks were interrupted by the waiter, who delivered a mutton pie to each of the diners. He surveyed his meal and returned his attention to Otto. "How did you make out the day your men went on strike?"

"Knuckled under to the ten-hour day. Aaron ran new numbers. Things will be tight for a while. I think many people were more negatively affected than Krieger Coach. No coal left the Schuylkill for two weeks, which idled many factories. The home of my neighbor Lucretia Mott was in an uproar for days because the plasterers walked off their job."

"Ah, yes. Our local rabble-rouser. How is she doing?"

"She seems well. Happy to have her house back now that the strike is over. I think that when James returns, they will leave shortly for a tour of upstate New York. She has a series of speaking engagements."

"Only to other women, I hope."

"I don't believe so. Apparently, the Quaker tradition encourages women to speak their minds within their congregations."

"Good Lord, I'm not sure I approve of that. Strikes me as very unseemly." As he often did when he dined with Otto, Shippen gazed about the room to see who else was conducting business nearby. "I see we're dining in the presence of the great Nicholas Biddle."[12]

Shippen raised his glass in mock salute to the President of the Second Bank of the United States. "Poor bastard. Here he is, a beaten man, still trying to drum up support for his dying bank." Forty-nine-year-old Nicholas Biddle, seated across the room with a gentleman whom Otto didn't recognize, returned the gesture.

Otto also raised his glass and smiled warmly at Biddle. "You do not buy his argument; that without his bank, there will be too much money in the system?"

"So, you've been talking to Nicholas the Great? I think that is a pile of hogwash. Banks like my Bank of Industry can act very responsibly without oversight from Second National. He overplayed his hand. He should never have involved himself in the presidential race in '32. Once Jackson was re-elected, the handwriting was on the wall. Second Bank is dead. Biddle just doesn't know it yet."

"You do not see another recession in the future?"

"My God, Biddle manufactured the last recession to scare us away from a second term with Andy Jackson. No, I see nothing but economic expansion for years to come, which probably should lead us to talk about your own proposed expansion."

"Yes, as you know, we see the three entities—Krieger Coach, Krieger Locomotive, and Krieger Rail—working closely together. Neither my brother nor I have nearly enough savings to finance the entire expansion, so we are coming to you for assistance."

"I'm sure the bank board will be happy to help two of the up-and-coming members of our German community."

Schiffler leaned back into his chair, tipping it back on its two rear legs. "However, I do not approve of putting Africans in charge of operations.

---

12. Nicholas Biddle was one of the most brilliant men in America and a financial genius. President Monroe appointed him to run the Second Bank of the United States in 1822 when he was 38. He imposed modern banking systems on an institution that had previously been ineptly run. With his steady leadership, the American money supply stabilized, and the economy grew.

However, though Biddle demonstrated vast financial acumen, he was politically ham-handed. In recent years he had suffered at the hands of President Andrew Jackson. Jackson hated the Second National Bank, which he blamed for precipitating a recession fifteen years previously that had financially ruined him and many of his neighbors.

The fact that Biddle was not running the bank during that time didn't matter to Jackson. Even though Biddle's discipline had helped the American economy avoid a recession that was plaguing Europe, Jackson was adamant. He wanted the Second National Bank to die. Against the counsel of many of his advisors, he had recently crippled the bank by withdrawing federal funds and distributing them instead to various "Pet Banks" around the country.

Sweeping floors is one thing. Giving orders to whites is another. I just don't think that makes sound business sense. I'm sure I could get you a lower interest rate if you cleaned up your payroll a bit."

Otto turned cold. "You are kidding, I hope." True to his warrior name, he instantly girded himself for battle.

"No, I'm deadly serious," responded Schiffler.

"Two weeks ago, I fired a man who made the same demand." Otto shifted his focus to the Bank of Industry's board chairman. "George, you should know me better than this."

Undeterred, Schiffler persisted. "And we understand that there are Jewish investors in the rail venture. Honestly, couldn't you have picked a better group of associates? Who will want to do business with you when they find out that Krieger Rail is a bunch of Jews?"

"We are not hiding who we are. My name will be on the building because we intend to become a dominant force in all phases of the railroad industry. People will do business with us when we offer a better product at a fair price. Besides, the loan Krieger Rail is asking for is minuscule. The Jewish community in Philadelphia has raised most of the capital already."

Schiffler pressed. "Krieger, you are making a huge mistake. If word gets out that we denied your loan application, no other bank in Philadelphia will touch you."

Otto took his napkin off his lap and placed it on the table. "Perhaps I will have to find that out for myself. I will be happy to walk over and talk to Biddle right now."

"Now, now," interjected Shippen. "Let's not get ahead of ourselves. Edward, I don't think the people Otto chooses to associate with should get in the way of the bank's endorsement of a very promising enterprise. Krieger is demonstrating loyalty to those who work for him. That is a trait that I admire. We can overlook this for the time being."

Otto brought his temper back from a boil. "I feel very strongly about this. If you cannot accept it, I will go talk to Biddle."

Shippen continued. "The Board will express concern, but with assurances from me, I think they'll be amenable."

Otto's guard was now up. "And, since you are the one who brought up interest rates, I assume you will offer me the same low rate you would offer any of your best clients?"

Shippen waved the back of his hand as if the interest rate was of little consequence. "Krieger, if you want to become a dominant player in the railroad industry, I suggest you make the leap into railroad ownership. I still have stock available."

"Much of my savings is going to go into the new venture. But I promised you that once the strike was resolved I would make a decision. I think a modest investment will be possible."

"That's good. Between the new Krieger enterprises and my railroad, we will make a rich man out of you."

Thus, the meeting, which had become momentarily frosty, ended on a positive note and with a handshake. The two bankers excused themselves and departed. As Otto's next meeting was also at the United States Hotel, he remained behind.

Shortly thereafter, Nicholas Biddle approached the table. "Good afternoon, Otto."

Otto stood and shook the hand of the man whom he admired but didn't know particularly well. "Mr. Biddle, how good to see you. Did you have the special?"

"The mutton was a bit tough, but it tasted fine. I always look forward to the cooler months when the hotel serves oysters. That's my weakness. I would like to introduce you to my lunch companion, Henry Inman, the portrait painter."

"Why, Mr. Inman. It is a pleasure to meet you. I was under the impression that you had moved back to New York City."

"I have. I am just back cleaning up some loose ends. Biddle and I were catching up before I return to New York tomorrow."

"I heard that you had recently painted a portrait of Mr. Biddle. I have not seen it yet."

"Oh, that portrait," interjected Biddle. "He added about twenty pounds to my frame."

Inman chuckled. "Well, my goal was to make you look prosperous."

Otto smiled at Inman's joke. "I have seen an engraving of a portrait you painted of John Marshall. I am sure you are mourning the death of our great Chief Justice."

"We were just talking about that. He was a great subject. Very handsome."

"And we will miss him," added Biddle. "McCulloch v. Maryland changed the nature of our republic. The debate over strict interpretation versus loose interpretation of the Constitution will rage for a hundred years. However, his dominant intellect assured there would be any debate at all. If it weren't for Marshall, I wouldn't have a job because the Second Bank wouldn't exist."

"Well, sir, may you and the Bank have better days."

"Thank you, Otto . . . You were conducting business with our friend Shippen?"

"Yes, my brother and I are hoping to expand our shops. George and I have been doing business for a few years now."

"Be careful. You know I don't like his bank. I've looked into the railroad he's trying to put together. I think there is a future for a railway between Philadelphia and Baltimore; I just don't think Shippen's the man to do it. Beware of his chicanery."

"Thanks for the warning, Mr. Biddle." *But your caution comes just a few minutes too late.*

. . . .

· RIAN ·

Jules stood at a workbench, examining fourteen wagon wheel spokes lined up side by side.

"Rian, did you sharpen those spokeshaves like I asked you to yesterday?"

"Uh-huh. One of them took a long time. It had a pretty good chip in it. I think I got it, though."

"That explains it. Take a look at these spokes. What do you see?"

Rian took a few seconds to examine the array of spokes. "Hmm, they're not all the same color. I think these three are red oak. The rest are hickory. These two are a little fatter in the middle. This one has a pretty good gouge in it."

"If you were the boss, what would you do?"

"What do you mean?"

"What would you do if you were me?"

Rian fingered the pieces of wood. "I'd pick the twelve spokes I like the best. That's what you usually do, right? Have the men make more than you need so that you can use the best ones?"

"Go ahead. Pick."

Jules patiently waited while Rian deliberated for more than a minute. "I can't pick."

"Why not?"

"Because there aren't enough good ones. I wouldn't mix the oak and the hickory. I would throw this one away because of the gouge. You could shave these two down a bit. Then they'd be okay."

Jules smiled like a teacher whose student had correctly answered a trick question. "Good eye. You're still the foreman. Now, what would you do?"

Rian hesitated again. Finally, she said, "Jules, I don't want to get anyone in trouble."

"No one's going to get into trouble. What would you do?"

"I'd show them to the guy who made them. Tell him they're not good enough. Teach him why they're not good enough. When you taught me how to shave a spoke, you started me out measuring with calipers. I doubt that this guy used them."

"Okay, good answer. Thank you. I've got to keep this order on schedule. Want to help?"

"Sure, but I can't stay too long. I've got to get to the library."

Jules straddled one of two shaving horses that sat next to one another and locked the first spoke into place with his feet. "What's Aaron got you doing now?"

"I've got to be able to know both sides of the argument if John Marshall was a good Supreme Court Justice."

"Ouch. Good luck with that. I wasn't crazy about the man."

Rian sat down next to Jules and locked her spoke into place. "Why not?"

"Because he enslaved my fellow Negroes."

"Oh, sure. That."

Jules pulled on his spokeshave and shaved a ribbon of wood off the spoke. "All these men who signed the Declaration of Independence and wrote the Constitution are American heroes. Well, some of them are not heroes to me."

"Even George Washington?"

"Even George Washington. He was an enslaver, just like the rest of them. You know that if a slave remains in Pennsylvania for more than six months, then that slave becomes free?"

Rian took her own satisfying stroke on her spoke, peeling a ribbon of oak away from it. "Yeah, I think I learned that the day we met *Vater* in Camden. Mr. Tucker said something about it."

"Well, when Philadelphia was the US capital city and Washington was the President, he used to swap his slaves back to his place in Virginia every few months so that he didn't have to free them."

"I guess I need to think about this."

"The problem is that when this country created its heroes, no one asked any Black people what they thought."

"So, then who are your heroes?"

Jules hesitated for a few seconds. "No one's ever asked me that question before. The first thing I thought of—right as soon as you asked it—was Maddie's two grandfathers."

"Tell me about them."

"Both her grandfathers won freedom for themselves and their families by fighting in the Revolutionary War. Something we keep under wraps and talk about only amongst the family is that one fought for the British, the other for the Patriots."

"Did they know each other?"

"Only after Maddie's parents fell in love."

"Did they get along? I mean, they were enemies and all."

"I never met either of them, but I doubt they considered each other enemies. The real enemies were their enslavers."

"How did they become free?"

"Well, Lemrich, the one who fought for the British, joined Lord Dunmore's Ethiopian Regiment. Dunmore had promised freedom for the escaped slaves of the revolutionaries. He served bravely in the Ethiopian Regiment starting in 1775. Later on, in the Loyalist Queen's Rangers, he helped to defend British-held New York City."

"Did he ever fight against Maddie's other grandfather?"

Jules shook his head. "When the British army evacuated from New York, they encouraged Tories and freed slaves alike to leave with them. Lemrich and his family sailed to Nova Scotia in one of the last British ships and lived there for fifteen years. Things got a little difficult there, and they returned to the United States in 1798. They bumped around for a while before ending up in Philadelphia, but they talked about his time with the British only at family gatherings."

"What about her other grandfather?"

"His name was Scipio. He gained his freedom when the Rhode Island legislature voted to pay slave owners to voluntarily give up their slaves to fight for the patriotic cause. The 1st Rhode Island Regiment was an integrated outfit that saw only a little action. Story goes, though, that Scipio liked military life, and he stayed in the army after the Revolution drew to a close."

"How long was he in the army?"

"That all came to an end in 1792, when our beloved United States Congress passed a law that excluded Negroes from serving in the military. He mustered out and moved his family to Philadelphia."

"Do you have any other heroes?"

"Sure, lots of them."

"Who?"

"How about if we save this discussion for another day." Jules released his spoke and eyed its new dimensions. "Okay, I've got to re-teach one of the men how to make spokes. You should get over to the library before I think up something else for you to do."

. . . .

· LUCRETIA ·

Lucretia Mott knocked on the door of the Freemans' house, a two-story structure on the corner of Twelfth and Fitzwater Streets in Moyamensing. Maddie Freeman opened the door wide for her to enter. "Mrs. Mott, thank you for coming all this way."

"It's my pleasure, Maddie Freeman. Thank thee for having me. But two things. First of all, it was my turn to come to thy neighborhood. When we started these meetings, we agreed that it would be every other one—my house, then thy house." She took a moment to determine that the downstairs of Maddie's house had four rooms. "Which is lovely, by the way."

"We were finally able to buy it just last year. We are very happy here."

"I haven't been to Moyamensing since before the Flying Horse riots. It seems that Black and white are coexisting peacefully at the moment."

"Oh, I guess you could call it an uneasy truce. The Irish are arriving in increasing numbers and settling in Moyamensing. Many native-born Americans don't like them any more than the free Blacks. You would think there would be a natural alliance between the Irish and Negro, but whenever the Irish have the opportunity to kick us, they seem to do so."

"A pity. What is it about human nature that demands to have someone else to look down upon?"

Maddie shook her head. "You said there were two things you wanted to talk about before we got down to business. What was the second thing?"

"Doesn't thee think we can now start calling one another by our first names? Dear me, we are engaged in this lofty conspiracy together. We've already established so much trust between us. I would like to be considered among thy circle of friends; close enough to call thee by thy given name."

Maddie extended her hand to Lucretia. "Nice to meet you. I'm Maddie."

"And I am Lucretia. Good! We've gotten that out of the way. One of the great benefits that I have derived from walking alone in this city of contradictions is the time to think. I resolved to raise this issue with thee as I was walking here. I've already accomplished that. Let's get on with our business."

"Yes, the pamphlets."

Lucretia handed a small booklet of eight pages to Maddie. "Mr. Garrison has sent a sample of what the American Anti-Slavery Society is printing. They're going to mail thousands of them. He says directly to individuals all over the country. In a few weeks, he'll send more to us for distribution here in Philadelphia."

Maddie eyed the pamphlet, which contained engravings of Negroes being abused by white enslavers. "Oh dear. This is going to raise some eyebrows."

"I sincerely hope so. Some of the references are pretty graphic. Mutilations. Slave owners having their way with slave women. A slave mother killing her children rather than allowing them to be sold away from her. Is thee going to be able to stand behind this?"

Maddie crossed her arms. "There's nothing here that's untrue. Jules will have some misgivings."

"How so?"

"He thinks the Black community in Philadelphia is doing all right by keeping our heads down and not calling attention to ourselves. More of our men seem to have decent jobs. Some are even business owners. It's only when we start reaching beyond our grasp that bad things happen. Like last year with the Flying Horses riots. I think Jules would rather attack the problem one escaped slave at a time, where nobody can see."

"Have you had many travelers this month?"

Maddie smiled. "We call them house guests. Yes, lots. And another is supposed to arrive this evening. We just put them up for a night or so and keep them moving north. Very few choose to stay in Philadelphia the way Jules did. Too close to Maryland. Too easy to get snatched and taken back."

"So, will Jules let thee speak if we start passing out pamphlets at public meetings?"

"I'm not sure if *let* is a good word to use. Our marriage is more like a negotiation. We try to find common ground that we are both comfortable with. Or maybe *equally uncomfortable* is a better description. I think he is proud that you and I and the others formed the Female Anti-Slavery Society. Having Black women and white women sitting down together to attack the abomination of slavery is progress. Public speaking? If it were just women, he would probably be okay with it. A meeting that brings together men and women? That may be a bit of a stretch. I'm sure he would be afraid for my safety. Yet you speak to groups of both men and women."

"I benefit from a long Quaker tradition of encouraging all members to speak their minds. Lately I've gained a reputation for speaking against slavery, so I have received invitations from other meeting houses in New York and Pennsylvania. I'm planning another tour for next month."

"And Mr. Mott supports you?"

"Definitely. He encourages me. But it isn't without controversy. There's a division, even among Quakers."

"I had no idea."

"A few years back, James and I followed Elias Hicks and broke away from the Orthodox Friends. We believe that the Inner Light should guide us, not the teachings of another individual. We are referred to as Hicksites, but in general, thee can assume we put what is right ahead of what would make us prosperous. Which is why James is planning to get out of the cotton business."

Maddie placed the pamphlet on the kitchen table. "A bold move. A laudatory move. Will it affect your circumstances?"

"Oh, I expect there will be considerable belt-tightening. I have to admit, that makes me a little apprehensive, but I am convinced we are on a proper course."

· · · · · · · · · · · · · · · · · ·

· RIAN ·

Rian had completed her research on John Marshall. She was walking out of the Philadelphia Library on Fifth Street, directly across the street from the State House. Just as she reached the bottom step, five kids about her age ran by, obviously excited about something.

Trey Shippen was the biggest and most athletic boy in her class at school. He was the son of the chairman of the board of the Bank of Industry, who had bought two carriages from Krieger Coach. His name was actually George Shippen III.

Billy Schiffler was a bully and a weasel. It was because of him that she got kicked out of school.

Rian didn't know Emmanuel Rauch very well but thought he was a good guy. Tom Mott was her next-door neighbor. And the girl—Olivia Tucker—sped by close on the boys' heels.

"Where are you going?" Rian called after them.

"Funeral for some dead guy. We're going to see if we can ring the bell." Trey yelled back over his shoulder but never broke stride.

"What bell?" Rian asked.

"In the State House. C'mon!"

Rian ran after the group, crossing Sixth Street, and entered the grounds of the State House. She caught up to the gaggle as they entered the vast building. "Trey, are we allowed in here?"

"Who cares? Emmanuel knows Major Jack. He said it was okay."

"Who's Major Jack?"

"The steeple keeper. He told Emmanuel he could ring the bell when the funeral goes by the State House. That's just about right now."

Rian followed the raucous group farther into the building and then stopped abruptly. "Isn't this where the Declaration was signed?"

Trey hesitated only briefly. "What declaration?"

Rian peered reverently into a room that contained twenty or so desks and chairs and a low platform that held a table and more chairs. She was surprised at how shabby it looked. "The Declaration of Independence, Stupid."

Trey noticed a narrow staircase and hit it at a run, skipping the first two steps. "I don't know. C'mon, it's going to start without us."

Tom, Billy, and Emmanuel followed him at the same clip. Olivia, wearing a pinafore and blouse appropriate for the sweltering day, hung back. "Do you remember me? We met on the ferry. I'm Olivia Tucker. I'm Trey's cousin," she said in her syrupy accent.

Rian nodded, acknowledging that she remembered Olivia. "Your father finally picked up his new landau last week. Have you ridden in it yet?"

"Just once. It's wonderful." Olivia joined Rian as they peered into the room where the Declaration of Independence was signed, and the US Constitutional Convention was held. "My father had to go back to Charleston. Our overseer died in an accident. Mother and I walked over to Shippen House to visit Aunt Ida and Trey this morning, but Trey wanted to play with his friends, and Mother let me go with him."

"What about Topper?"

"He's at Spruce Street. He has to take care of the horses."

Rian liked Olivia. She was more interesting than any of the girls at school, but Rian's real interest at the moment was the State House and its history. Rather than race after the boys, she walked up the stairs, trying to imagine the great minds all gathered in one place to create the Declaration of Independence and then again to draft the Constitution of the United States. *And yet, Jules says some of them were slaveholders.*

When the bell started ringing, she hurried her pace a bit. Olivia stayed on her heels. The girls followed the sound of the tolling bell. They worked their way up a series of increasingly narrow staircases and finally entered a small room with a thick rope hanging in the middle.

Peering up another twenty feet or so, Rian could see the bottom of a bell that looked to be about four feet across. Big sonorous *dongs* enveloped the room. Given her recent research at the library, Rian believed they were an appropriate salute to the late Chief Justice, whether he was a great man or not.

A skinny old man with a long grey beard leaned against a wall. He looked bored and barely paid attention to the kids. Rian assumed he was Major Jack, the steeple keeper.

Billy was pulling the rope and showed no sign of giving it up. Trey, who was much larger than Billy, muscled him aside, saying, "My turn." After six or seven pulls, he turned the rope over to Emmanuel Rauch. Emmanuel discovered that if you hung on to the rope, the movement of the bell could lift him a few inches off the floor.

Major Jack continued to lean against the wall, his eyes closed.

Dong!

Emmanuel handed the rope to Rian despite Billy's protestations.

Dong!

After five pulls, Rian handed the rope to Olivia, who got one pull before Billy Schiffler grabbed the rope and shoved her aside with his shoulder. "No! Girls don't get to do this."

Major Jack ignored these goings-on.

Dong!

Since Rian had already rung the bell, she didn't stop to think that Billy's "no girls" decree hadn't included her. Nevertheless, his statement incensed her. She thought only fleetingly about her father's threat to send her to Switzerland if she got in another fight; so briefly, it was almost no thought at all. Without giving Billy any warning, she punched him in the nose and grabbed the rope. Stunned, Billy fell backward onto his rear.

Rian handed the rope back to Olivia. Olivia, somewhat stunned, pulled on the rope five or six times and then looked around to see who wanted the rope next. For lack of takers, she handed the rope back to Rian.

Looking Billy right in the eye, Rian hung on to the rope as it pulled her off the floor. Her defiant stare dared him to try to take the rope away from her.

Dong!

Billy held his hands to his nose. Blood poured from between his fingers. "You gave me a bloody nose, Barn Door! I'm going to tell my father! You're never gonna come back to school!"

Clong! The State House bell suddenly sounded very different.

Major Jack opened his eyes and jumped from his place at the wall, a look of panic on his face.

"What have you done?"

Clong!

"Nothing," said Trey. "We were just pulling the cord like you said to!"

"You kids need to go! Now!"

The six youngsters scrambled down the narrow staircases and dashed out of the State House. Rian was not sure what, if anything, she had done wrong, as far as the bell was concerned, but knew for sure she was going to pay the price for hitting Billy.

"You're in real trouble now, Barn Door. I'm going to tell my father you hit me without any warning. He's the president of the school board. He told me what the headmaster told you. I guess you're not going to be allowed to come back to school after all."

It's worse than that, thought Rian. As a result of her punch, the prospect of being sent away to school in Switzerland now loomed, but Billy didn't know that. Rian was not about to give Billy any satisfaction if he tattled. "Good. I'm having more fun in my father's factory anyway."

Taking Rian's retort at face value, Billy changed tactics. "Barn Door broke the bell! Barn Door broke the bell!"

"It wasn't my fault. I was just pulling on the rope."

Looking across the State House green toward Walnut Street, the group could see the end of the funeral procession for John Marshall as it continued west. "Who died, anyway?" asked Billy, whose bloody nose seemed to be drying up.

Rian, fresh off her library research, knew the answer. "John Marshall. He was the Chief Justice of the Supreme Court."

Billy was unimpressed. "Whatever that is. You're just a stupid girl, Barn Door. Why don't you get out of here? We don't want you."

"Leave her alone, Billy," said Trey. "Jesus, don't you ever learn? She's beaten you up twice in two weeks."

"She didn't beat me up. Why are you sticking up for a stupid ugly mick girl, Trey? You must be in love with her."

"Shut up, Billy, or I'll punch you too."

"Trey loves Barn Door! Trey loves Barn Door!"

"I do not!" Trey made an aggressive lunge toward Billy. Billy stepped back defensively, but he tripped and fell to the ground.

Trey laughed but held his hand out to Billy and helped him up. "C'mon, let's go over to the square."[13]

The group ambled across the green, cutting between four untethered Milking Devon cows that were more intent on munching the green's lush grass than wandering around Philadelphia. As the kids turned right on Walnut, a junk wagon dropped a tin can onto the street. Trey scooped up the errant discard. "C'mon! We can play kick the can!"

Trey, Billy, Tom, and Emmanuel ran across Walnut Street, but Rian noticed Olivia lagged behind them. Uncharacteristically, Rian peeled away from the boys to keep Olivia company.

"Thanks for walking with me," said Olivia. "My father doesn't like your father."

"My father doesn't like your father."

"My father thinks your father shouldn't allow a Negro to give orders to white people."

"My father thinks no one should own slaves. He thinks all Negroes should be free."

Olivia didn't respond for about thirty seconds. "So do I."

"You do?"

Olivia nodded.

"Does your father know?"

"I would never dare tell him that. My mammy tells me it's just a secret between us."

"Your mother?"

"No, my mammy, she's a slave. She's really the one who has raised me. Not Mama."

"Is that why you think slavery's bad? Because of your mammy?"

Olivia shook her head. "Not really. I confessed to her a couple of months ago that I thought slavery was cruel. We've talked a lot about it since. Are you really going to get kicked out of school?"

"Probably. I don't care. I don't like it very much anyway. My father has me working in his factory this summer. It's supposed to be kind of a punishment for fighting, but that's what I'd like to do instead of going to school. The

---

13. Originally laid out by William Penn's surveyor in the 1600s, the field at Sixth and Walnut had been used to graze cattle and as a burial ground for Blacks. In 1825, reflecting increasing prosperity in the neighborhood, walking paths and gardens were installed and it was renamed Washington Square in honor of the first president.

problem is, *Vater* says if I get in trouble again, he's going to send me to finishing school in Switzerland."

"What's a finishing school?"

"I dunno. I think it prepares girls to become good wives. I would have to wear a dress all the time."

"I guess you wouldn't like that very much."

"Not at all. I'm going to have to figure out how to get out of it."

As they entered Washington Square, Rian thought the trees and shrubbery would provide perfect hiding places for kick the can, even in the daylight.

Billy Schiffler didn't feel the same way. "We don't have enough kids to play kick the can."

Trey, the leader, was undeterred. "We can find some other kids. C'mon."

However, as the band meandered through the garden paths, they could find no other kids their age to play a game. That is until they came upon a group of four Black kids, all their age or younger.

Billy put his hands on his hips. "What are you Africans doing here?"

The tallest of the Black kids protectively stepped in front of the others. "We're allowed. You don't own this park."

Trey muscled ahead of Billy. "Cut it out, Billy. Do you guys want to play kick the can?"

Before they could answer, Billy turned on his heels and started to walk away. "I don't want to play with Africans. If they're going to play, I'm leaving."

"Oh, come on, Billy. It'll be all right. It's just kick the can."

"I think this is stupid. I'm not playing with any coloreds."

Trey seemed unphased by Billy's threats. "Okay, we'll play without you."

Billy immediately caved. "Well, maybe I'll play for a little while, but I've got to get home for dinner soon."

Trey turned to the Black kids. "So, do you guys want to play?"

The oldest of the kids stood his ground. "Maybe."

"C'mon. It'll be fun. We have to know everybody's names. I'm Trey. This is Billy, Olivia, Emmanuel, Tom, and that's Rian."

"I'm Rufus. That's my brother Jeremiah and my sisters Missy and Gladys."

All those names sounded familiar to Rian. "Is your last name Freeman?"

Rufus continued to speak for his siblings. "Yes. How did you know?"

"Your father works for my father."

"You're Rian Krieger? Father says he taught you how to make wagon wheels."

"He's taught me a lot of stuff. He talks about you all the time."

Billy, who had conceded to play kick the can with a bunch of Black kids, wasn't interested in the getting-to-know-you nonsense. "Okay, come on. If we're going to play, let's play."

So, as had been the case since tin cans came to America in the 1820s, the kids had to agree on the rules for kick the can: boundaries, where home is, where the jail is, how high the 'it' person has to count while the others hide.

The first two rounds proceeded without incident. Rian was 'it' the first game. When she spied someone hiding, she called their name and raced to beat them home so that they had to go to jail. With five kids in jail, Rian had to roam a little farther from home to find other hiders. She strayed too far, and Trey sprinted home, kicked the can, and the jailbirds flew the coop. Rian started all over again and finally got everyone in jail.

Trey became 'it.' He got everyone into jail the first time. Then Billy was 'it.'

Things still went smoothly until Billy spied Rufus, and the two of them sprinted for home. Rufus kicked the can just before Billy got home. "Free!" he yelled. The jailbirds flew.

"No fair. I beat you home. Everyone has to go back to jail."

Rufus turned back toward Billy. "No way. I kicked the can. They're free. Start counting."

"I beat you."

"Did not."

Trey declared a time-out. Rian walked back to the jail. "Billy, he beat you by a mile."

"Shut up, Barn Door. He did not!"

Trey joined the argument. "Billy, I saw it too. He beat you fair and square."

"You're going to side with an African?"

"That's got nothing to do with it. He beat you."

Rufus gathered his siblings, turned, and started to walk away. "Jeremiah, Missy, Gladys. Let's go home. It's time for dinner."

"No! I beat you! Admit it! You have to go back to jail!" With that, Billy picked up a rock and threw it at Rufus's head. The rock hit Rufus so hard that he fell face first onto the pathway.

· ·

· OTTO ·

Otto returned to the office after his meetings at the United States Hotel.

Aaron Bassinger was working at his ledger. He took off his glasses and placed them on the large book. "How did your meetings go?"

Otto chose not to divulge Schiffler's antipathy toward Negroes and Jews with Aaron. "Good, I think. The Bank of Industry wants to work with us. Interest is yet to be determined, but they will have to be competitive because I said I would otherwise talk to Nicholas Biddle. I also took two new orders, a buggy and a sleigh. Not a bad lunch."

"Otto, you should just set up an office at the hotel. That's where you make all your deals anyway."

Otto smiled at Aaron's dry humor. "Oh, no. Things are far too interesting around here. And with the new factories, they will get even more exciting. What did you think of our meeting with Strickland?"

Aaron started shifting papers on his desk, obviously looking for something. "I don't think the meeting could have gone any better. Lining up Philadelphia's most sought-after architect was a real coup. I guess it's time to start looking for contractors to build the factories."

Otto nodded. "Yes, right away. Even before we have plans from Strickland. The strike caused a bit of a backup, and there is a skilled labor shortage in Philadelphia anyway."

Aaron finally found the sheet of paper he was looking for. "I want you to look at this." He handed the sheet to Otto. "It's a draft of a quote for the cabriolet that Mr. Demerit is interested in."

Otto scanned the paper. "You forgot labor costs."

"I didn't do the work on this, but I thought you should see it."

"Seamus said his math is only passable. He has come a long way in two weeks."

Aaron shook his head. "It wasn't Seamus. Look at the handwriting."

"Rian?"

Aaron nodded. "She's eleven years old, and she constructed a quote for a carriage that I have double-checked and I would be willing to stand behind. Plus the labor, of course. Otto, she had no help on this. She did it to prove she could do it. Your daughter is a stubborn, gifted child."

Otto sat on a chair in front of Aaron's desk. He didn't look at Aaron. In a subdued voice, he said, "I do not want you to teach her bookkeeping to train a new employee. I want you to help sharpen her mind. To keep her stimulated. To shape her into a young woman who will attract a man. This is too much."

"Otto, I've been a bookkeeper for two decades. I've trained a dozen clerks. I've never had a student as sharp as your daughter. She has been with me for two weeks. I see no limits to what she will be able to do."

"No."

"No, what?"

"No, that is not what I want for her."

"But what does she want?"

"She is eleven years old. She is too young to determine what she wants."

Aaron leaned back in his chair. "Then I need some guidance on how to proceed. I gave her this problem because she rebelled at my practice sessions. The deal was that if she couldn't complete it, she would have to proceed at my pace. I never dreamed she would be successful. With your permission, I would like to treat her as I would any other accounting trainee. I will give her tasks as she demonstrates competence. I will always be looking over her shoulder."

Otto shook his head. "Aaron, I am so sorry. I know how difficult my daughter can be. I myself have made so many concessions."

"Otto, I am not looking for an apology. There are university professors who teach a lifetime and never have the experience of teaching a student of her caliber. This is a privilege for me."

"But she is a girl. This is contrary to everything a woman should be doing."

Aaron leaned forward, placing his elbows on his desk. "I'm not sure your next-door neighbor would agree."

"Lucretia Mott? She is formidable, to be sure. And all evidence is that James gives her his full support."

Aaron merely responded by arching his left eyebrow. *And therefore . . . ?*

Otto smiled. "Maybe she just needs the right man."

Aaron shrugged and smiled.

"Where is my daughter, by the way?"

"I was quizzing her about her reading in the pennies this morning. She didn't know what the Chief Justice of the Supreme Court did, so I sent her to the City Library to do some research."

Otto brightened. "Now, that is the sort of thing I hoped would happen when Jules proposed this whole scheme to me. How much trouble could she get into doing research at the City Library?"

. . . .

· RIAN ·

Looking horrified by what he had done, Billy turned and ran away. Emmanuel Rauch also left.

Rian ran to Rufus, who hadn't moved, but blood was gushing from a wound on the back of his head.

Trey grabbed Olivia by the arm. "C'mon, we should go."

Olivia didn't take her eyes off Rufus and the kneeling Rian. "No. I'm going to stay here. You can go."

"I told Mother we would stick together. You don't know the city."

Rian lost patience with Trey. "Go if you want to. I'll make sure Olivia gets home."

Jeremiah shook Rufus's shoulder, saying, "Rufus, wake up. Rufus, wake up." Gladys was crying. "Is he dead?" asked Missy.

Trey backed away from the scene, then turned and ran away. Tom Mott remained but seemed unable to do anything.

Disappointed by Trey's departure, Rian returned her attention to Rufus. "He's breathing. We need to get him home."

"Unh," moaned Rufus.

Olivia looked up from the semi-conscious figure. "How far's your house from here, Jeremiah?"

"I dunno. Nine or ten blocks."

Rian said, "No way we're going to be able to carry him that far. We need help. Tom, see if you can find someone to help us."

Tom Mott approached a man carrying a walking stick. "Excuse me. Could you help us, please? Our friend got hurt." The man kept on walking without responding.

Another man kept walking.

And another.

And a man and a woman walking together.

Tom ranged farther away to find an adult who could help them. Finally, he came running back to the group with Seamus Gallagher walking behind him.

"Rian, what's going on?" asked Seamus.

Rian looked up to see her cousin. "Seamus, we need help. Rufus is hurt bad. Billy Schiffler hit him in the back of the head with a rock."

"Didn't know you hung out with coloreds, Rian."

"We were just playing kick the can. Can you help us?"

Seamus looked over his shoulder as if he was concerned about who might be observing this interaction. "Coloreds and Irish don't exactly get along, Rian."

"Seamus, this is Rufus Freeman, Jules's son."

"Oh, Jaysus. This just got complicated. All right, where do you kids live?"

"In Moyamensing. Fitzwater and Twelfth," said Jeremiah.

"Okay, that's down near me own neighborhood. Rufus, if I load you on me back, can you hold on?"

"Unh," said Rufus.

"Okay, here we go. Kids, I need your help. When I crouch down, load him on me back. Then keep walking behind me, because if he lets go, you'll have to catch him."

"Rian, what should I do?" called out Tom Mott.

Seamus turned and looked at Tom. "I think this army's big enough, lad. You run along home." Tom hesitantly turned and headed north.

The motley group set off on the ten-block trek to the Freeman house. Almost forgotten by Rian, Olivia held Gladys's hand as they walked. The farther south the group walked on Seventh, the less familiar and more forbidding the streetscape seemed to Rian. Most of the buildings were three stories tall, and none were well-maintained. Looking sideways between major streets, she saw narrow alleyways filled with garbage. Adults and kids shared the alleyways with chickens and pigs. One alley would be populated primarily by whites—Irish by the sounds of them—and the next by Negroes.

When they crossed Tenth Street, the buildings became a bit less congested. There were even some vacant lots. Rufus started to come around. "Lemme down."

"I think it's best that I carry you the rest of the way, lad."

With a block to go, Missy and Gladys sprinted ahead to get their parents. Moments later, Jules and Maddie came flying out the door.

Jules reached for his son. "What happened?"

Rian assumed the role of reporter. "Billy Schiffler hit him in the head with a rock. I don't think he meant to hurt him. We were playing kick the can in Washington Square."

Maddie, ever gracious, looked at the three visitors. "That's a long walk. Please come in."

The group entered Jules and Maddie's house, and Maddie led them into the kitchen. "Put him down here. How long was he out?"

All eyes were on Rufus. Rian continued her report. "I don't know. Maybe five minutes. But he started talking only about a block ago." Suddenly, Rian caught a movement out of the corner of her eye. She looked across the kitchen to see a Black man, barely clothed in tattered rags. His back was against the wall, and he was holding a knife.

"Father . . . ," said Missy.

"Not now, Missy."

"Father, look."

With that, everyone turned. With the room's attention directed at him, the man in tatters held his knife higher as if to tell everyone to stay away from him.

Maddie was the first to react. "Why, Cousin Elmo. You're early. We weren't expecting you until this evening." She walked calmly toward him, put her hand atop his knife hand, and gently pushed it lower. "You must be so tired from your trip. Let me show you to your room." She escorted the man upstairs.

Jules returned his attention to Rufus. "Missy, please wet a rag and bring it here. Seamus, how did you get involved in this?"

"Made the mistake of taking a shortcut through the square on me way home. Rian convinced me. Not sure I would have helped until she told me he's yours."

"I'm in your debt."

Seamus sat on a kitchen chair. "You don't remember, do you?"

"Remember what?"

"You pulled a bunch of colored kids off me when I was about this age. Sent them running."

Jules looked up from his injured son. "That was you?"

"Aye. I was scared shitless. Thought I was going to die. I never thanked you. Just ran away. I guess this evens things out a bit."

"Thank you, Seamus. Yes, this evens things out a lot."

"Please don't be spreading this around the neighborhood," Seamus said with a twinkle in his eye. "Me boys wouldn't take well to me helping out a colored kid. They'd think I was going a little daft."

"Afraid your secret's already out. I bet a hundred people saw you walk down here, both Black and white."

"Hope it doesn't hurt me reputation."

Jules looked Seamus right in the eye. "Just makes your reputation bigger, that's all."

Jules turned his attention to Olivia. "And who are you? I noticed you were holding Gladys's hand when you arrived. I want to thank you for your thoughtfulness."

"I'm Olivia Tucker. We've met before, at the railroad station in Camden."

Jules straightened up, but Rian couldn't tell what his thoughts were. "She was the one with the handkerchief," she said.

"You are Randolph Tucker's daughter."

Olivia nodded but didn't say anything more.

Seamus made his way toward the hallway. "Rufus looks like he's coming around. Don't think he should do much tomorrow. Rian, you and your little friend here, we should be taking our leave."

In three blocks, Seamus said, "Okay, this is where you turn to head north to your own neighborhoods. You kids know the way?"

Rian looked straight north up Ninth Street. "Yup, we can get there. Seamus, thank you."

Seamus gave a perfunctory wave and started to walk away. Then he stopped and turned. "I don't think anyone needs to know about Cousin Elmo. That's nobody's business but Jules and his wife."

As Rian and Olivia walked north, Olivia said, "I don't think Cousin Elmo's a cousin."

Still walking, Rian turned to her. "What do you mean?"

"I think he's a slave."

Rian didn't understand. "Do Black people have slaves?"

"No, I mean an escaped slave. I think Rufus's parents are helping slaves escape."

Rian kicked at a stone and sent it flying ahead of them on the brick sidewalk. "Are you going to tell?"

"Tell who?"

"I don't know. Your father?"

Olivia kicked the same stone. It clattered ahead of them on the bricks. "I don't think so. I'm sure my father wouldn't approve of someone helping a slave escape. How about you?"

Rian was perplexed. "Is Jules doing a bad thing? My father and Jules are pretty good friends. I don't think I'm going to tell. How come you stuck with us?"

Olivia kicked at the stone again. "What do you mean?"

"How come you didn't leave like Emmanuel and Trey did when Billy knocked out Rufus?"

"I guess I was worried. I didn't want to leave you alone. If it had been Topper, I wouldn't have left him if he got hurt."

The stone-kicking game went on for another three blocks. Rian decided Olivia was pretty good at it. She walked Olivia to the Tucker mansion.

· ·

· JULES ·

Jules and Maddie watched Seamus, Rian, and Olivia walk west on Fitzwater from their front door. Jules folded his arms. "Do you think she knows anything?"

"Olivia? How old is she? Eleven? Kids at that age are pretty oblivious. Look at our children. They don't know we have house guests half the time."

"But when they do, they know enough not to talk about it. That little girl's father is a slave owner. If she talks, we could be in real trouble. I could poke at Rian. Try to figure out what she thinks Olivia knows."

"I'd let that sleeping dog lie. The two of them may have accepted the whole incident at face value, that the poor man with the knife was our cousin Elmo. Let's just leave it at that."

Friday, July 10

· OTTO ·

As had become their habit, Rian and Otto walked home together at the end of the workday. It had been two days since Rian cracked the State House bell.

"Rian, it is time for us to talk.

Rian noted that he didn't refer to her as *Liebling*. "Okay."

"I received a note from the headmaster today. He tells me you got into another fight the other day."

"It wasn't much of a fight, *Vater*."

"Did you punch Billy Schiffler in the nose again?"

"Yes, but he deserved it. He wouldn't let Olivia Tucker . . ." Then she thought better about continuing because she was afraid that the discussion would lead to her breaking the bell. "He wouldn't let Olivia play with us because she's a girl."

"I suspect there were other courses of action that you could have taken than hitting Billy. I have written a letter to Mrs. Gilbert's Finishing School for Young Women in Lucerne, Switzerland. I told them I would like to enroll you in the school in September."

"*Vater*, please . . ."

"No, it is too late for 'Vater, please.' You knew what the consequences would be if you continued to get into fights. Come September, you will be on a ship to Europe. That is the only way that I can see for you to become a proper young lady."

FRIDAY, JULY 17

· RIAN ·

A week later, as Rian and her Uncle Kurt walked east on Locust Street, she spotted Olivia and Topper walking in the same direction across the street. "Olivia! Uncle Kurt, that's my friend Olivia. Let's go talk to her. Maybe they'll want to come with us."

Uncle Kurt was the tallest and beefiest of the three Krieger brothers, sunburned and muscled from long hours working as a ship's carpenter aboard the schooner *Vestal*.

Olivia and Topper stopped and waited for Rian and her uncle to join them.

"Uncle Kurt, this is Olivia, and this is her half-brother Topper. They are the two I was telling you about. The ones I met on the ferry. Olivia, Topper, this is my uncle Kurt. His ship just got in yesterday. He's got a day off today, and I talked him into going to see Joice Heth. Do you want to join us?"

"Who is Joice Heth?" asked Olivia.

Rian pulled a penny paper out of her pocket. "There's an article about her in today's *Pennsylvania Inquirer*." She started reading.

"The citizens of Philadelphia and its vicinity have an opportunity of witnessing at the Masonic Hall, one of the greatest natural curiosities ever witnessed, viz: Joice Heth, a negress, aged 161 years, who formerly belonged to the father of General Washington. She was born near the old Potomac River in Virginia and has lived in Paris, Kentucky, with the Bowling family for ninety or one hundred years. She has been a member of the Baptist Church for one hundred and sixteen years and can rehearse many hymns and sing them according to former custom.

All who have seen this extraordinary woman are satisfied with the truth of her age's account. The evidence of the Bowling family, which is respectable, is strong. However, the original bill of sale of Augustine Washington, in his own handwriting, and other evidences which the proprietor has in his possession, will satisfy even the most incredulous.

A lady will attend at the hall during the afternoon and evening for the accommodation of those ladies who may call."

Olivia looked at Topper, who nodded in agreement. She turned to Rian and Kurt. "Mother is visiting my aunt. My father returned from Charleston yesterday, but he went back over to the docks to make sure a shipment of our rice gets unloaded properly. He took his horse, not our new carriage, so he didn't need Topper. We're playing hooky together. Topper isn't supposed to leave, but I talked him into going out with me. We think going with you would be perfect." The group started walking toward Broad Street. "Where did you sail to this time, Mr. Krieger?"

"Call me Kurt. We went north this time. Unusual for us. New York, New London, Boston, then Yarmouth, Nova Scotia, and back."

"What did the ship take from Philadelphia?"

"A little bit of everything. Mostly things manufactured here in Philadelphia. Carpets, bolts of cloth, lanterns, plus about fifty bales of cowhides."

"What did you bring back?"

"Hides, butter, and cheese back to Boston from Yarmouth. Shoes and textiles out of Boston. On and on."

Olivia hooked her arm into Rian's. "I haven't seen you since the day of Mr. Marshall's funeral."

Rian was grateful Olivia didn't mention either the broken bell or the incident with Rufus.

Olivia continued. "Did you get in trouble for hitting Billy?"

Uncle Kurt couldn't resist butting in. "Oh, yes, she did. My brother still hasn't cooled down."

"He's going to send me to Switzerland."

"Even I think that is a bad idea," said Kurt, "but Otto seems determined."

The group arrived at the Masonic Hall on Broad Street. Rian's eyes took a bit of time to adjust to the half-light of the hall's lobby. A man sat at a desk with a sign that said "TICKETS 25¢. Children half price."

"Sorry folks, the African has to stay outside," the man said.

Kurt adjusted his shoulders and leaned over the man. "Oh, come on. We walked all the way here to see Joice Heth."

"Sorry, rules is rules."

Olivia had a better handle on what arguments worked best in Philadelphia. "He's actually a slave. He belongs to me. I would like to take him in."

The man's demeanor changed. "Well, in that case, there's no rule against a person bringing her personal property in with her. You'll still have to pay for him, though."

Kurt fished coins out of his pocket and paid the man 62½¢. "Is this going to be worth it?"

"Judge for yourself. She looks pretty goddamn old to me."

The four curiosity seekers walked through a double door and entered a dimly lit lecture room. Someone was singing a song, but Rian, surveying the room, did not immediately detect who.

> When I survey the wondrous cross
> On which the Prince of glory died
> My richest gain I count but loss
> And pour contempt on all my pride.

To the left, permanent risers hosted three rows of perhaps twenty chairs. Only three chairs were occupied; one by a woman reading a book by candlelight, the other two by a couple who were talking and chuckling with each other. To the right, wooden stanchions connected by a hemp rope separated two male spectators from Joice Heth. It was then that Rian realized it was the main attraction who was singing:

> A mighty fortress is our God,
> A bulwark never failing:
> Our helper He, amid the flood
> Of mortal ills prevailing.

Rian walked to the rope to take a closer look at the 161-year-old woman. She sat in an armchair, wearing a dress that was tattered and dingy. Her feet were bare, with toenails thick and yellowed. Her voice was clear, perhaps her only aspect that didn't come across as ancient.

As the woman sang, Rian could detect no teeth. Her left arm was draped across her chest, seemingly useless. Her withered hand was closed tight, with four-inch fingernails that extended back above her wrist. Her right arm hung at her side, not having enough strength to raise it to lie on the arm of the chair. A bonnet did a poor job of trying to cover a bushy head of grey hair. Her sunken eye sockets implied that her eyes were closed or no longer present.

When Joice stopped singing, one of the men, who seemed to know her, said, "Joice, tell us a story about George Washington."

"Ah, little Georgie," Joice immediately responded. "His daddy sold me to Mrs. Atwood before Georgie was born. I saw him when he was a baby a coupla times, though. He was a good boy."

"So, what do you think?" the first man said to the other.

"She certainly looks old enough. I have to say, Lindsay, there's not much of a crowd here. And the fact that Washington's father once owned her isn't a very big draw. She says she met him only a couple of times. How can you expect me to pay $3000 for something that brings in"—the man looked around the lecture hall—"six paying customers; two of whom are canoodling in the back, three of whom are children, and one of those is a Negro?"

"And that is why I want to sell. I have very little talent for this business. But I assure you, she is the genuine article and can make the right showman a significant amount of money."

The potential buyer turned to Kurt. "Let me ask you, sir, what brought you here today?"

"My ship is in port for the day, and I volunteered to accompany my niece to whatever she wanted to do today. She read an article in the *Inquirer* about your attraction here. She talked her father into letting her out of the shop today."

"Do you have any doubts that she is 161 years old?"

Kurt assessed Joice Heth. "Let's just say that she could be by the looks of her. It would be nice to have some proof, though."

"Actually," the man named Lindsay said to Kurt, "I have a bill of sale right here." He produced a yellowed piece of paper that Kurt read, then passed over to the girls.

> *"February 5, 1727*
> *Sold to Elizabeth Atwood, my half-sister and neighbor,*
> *One negro woman, named Joice Heth, aged fifty-four years,*
> *For and in consideration of the sum of thirty-three pounds lawful money*
>   *of Virginia.*
> *Augustine Washington, County of Westmoreland, Virginia."*

"The document looks genuine," commented Kurt, who turned his attention to the potential buyer. "So, are you going to purchase her?"

"If Mr. Lindsay reduces his asking price significantly, say to $1000, I believe I can raise the funds. I'll have to sell my interest in my grocery store in Connecticut and perhaps borrow some additional funds. You wouldn't be interested in becoming an investor, would you?"

"Perhaps. I have some money stashed away. My expenses are minimal. What makes you think you can make a go of it when Mr. Lindsay here seems to be struggling so?"

"Let me tell you a story. My grocery store. In Bethel, Connecticut. The sign in my window says my goods are 25% cheaper than any of my competitors. Is it true? Usually not, but customers flock to my store."

"I don't see how that lesson applies to this woman."

The man dismissed Kurt's riposte with a wave of his hand. "I'll need to change her story a bit." He gestured theatrically at Joice Heth. "This ancient was not merely once the chattel of Augustine Washington. Oh, no. She is the former nursemaid of the *Father of Our Country*. She was the first person to swaddle him in a blanket upon his birth."

"Is that true?"

"It will be by the time Joice and I create some stories together. She watched Little Georgie take his first steps. She was there when he cut down the cherry tree as a six-year-old. She was there on the tragic day his father died. The people will love it."

"How will the people find out about it?"

"The same way you did; from the newspaper."

"But those stories. They aren't true."

"But they will be believed once they appear often enough in the pennies. Might you be interested in loaning me the funds? You would save me a trip back to Connecticut, and I would offer highly favorable interest."

"I may. Let me think about it, Mr. . . . ."

The man offered his hand. "Barnum. Phineas T. Barnum. I'm spending the night at the United States Hotel. Reach me there by late tomorrow morning if you are interested."

Rian had been listening to the conversation between her Uncle Kurt and Mr. Barnum, somewhat horrified by the man's lack of commitment to the truth. "Let's get out of here," she said to Olivia.

Olivia and Topper readily agreed.

"We're heading outside," Rian said to Kurt as she handed the bill of sale back to Mr. Lindsay. The three walked through the double doors and into the lobby just in time to bump into Randolph Tucker and a young woman Rian didn't recognize.

"Papa?"

"Olivia? Topper, what are you doing here? I told you to tend the horses."

"That's my fault, Papa. I talked Topper into coming with me. He didn't want to come, but I twisted his arm."

"Topper, you are going to get a whipping when I get home."

All of eleven years old, Olivia straightened to her full 54 inches and said, "I don't think so."

"What?!"

"I don't think you'll whip him. Do whatever you want to me, but if you do anything at all to Topper, I'll tell Mama that you didn't go to the docks to check on your rice today like you said. Instead, you headed straight for a whorehouse and found this . . . this prostitute."

"Olivia, we will talk about this later."

"You promised Mama you wouldn't do this anymore."

"Olivia, I . . ."

"I overheard you arguing. She said she was sick of you galivanting around town with whores. You promised you would stop."

"Olivia, it is time for you to go home."

Olivia turned on her heel. "I'm going. C'mon Topper."

"And who is your friend?"

Rian stopped in mid-stride and turned toward Randolph Tucker. "I am Rian Krieger. I'm the one who suggested that we come here."

"I suppose that is something I will have to talk to your father about."

Olivia resumed her attack. "If you want to face Mama's wrath when I tell her, go ahead."

"Leave, Olivia. Take Topper and your little friend with you."

· · · · · · · · · · · · · · · · · ·

Five minutes later, Kurt met Rian, Olivia, and Topper across the street from the Masonic Hall. "You all left too early. A man and a woman had a big row right in front of us. Boy, she had him back on his heels. That alone was worth the price of admission." Then Kurt noticed Olivia was crying. "What's the matter?"

"That man who was arguing with that woman is my father. She's a prostitute."

Kurt looked from Olivia to Rian.

Rian shrugged. "Don't look at me. I'd never known anyone who visited a prostitute until five minutes ago. I thought it was only sailors down by the docks."

"Hmm," said Kurt. "Come on, kids, we should leave before Mr. Tucker comes out. I got the impression they won't be in there long."

As the group walked back along Locust Street, Olivia told Kurt what had happened. Kurt protectively put his arm around Olivia's shoulders. "There, there, Little Tiger. You stuck up for Topper and your friend. And your mother, for that matter. I believe your daddy's got his hands full. It sounds like you acquitted yourself admirably. Wish I'd been there to see it."

"I hate him. He may not do anything to Topper this time, but he holds grudges. He's mean. He always finds a way to get even."

"Well, I guess nothing good came of our visit to the Masonic Hall today," Kurt responded. "I didn't like seeing Joice Heth being put on display. Seems to me that woman has earned a good long rest."

"So, you're not going to loan that Barnum guy any money?"

"No, I was never tempted. I don't think that man will ever make it by bamboozling people. Sooner or later, folks will catch on to him and run him out of town on a rail. Mark my words, he may make a name for himself for a while, but he has no chance of success in the long run."

Rian wasn't quite so sure. And Mr. Barnum had given her an idea about how to avoid being sent to Switzerland, at least for a little while.

Saturday, August 1

· RIAN ·

Two weeks had passed since the Joice Heth incident. Rian heard the tenor's lilting airs as she and her father rounded the corner onto George Street. The rich, melodious Irish brogue flowed from an open window of Seamus's apartment on the third floor of the dilapidated former mansion.

And all I've done for want of wit
To mem'ry now I can't recall
So, fill to me the parting glass
Good night and joy be with you all.

"Excited?" Otto asked her. "You've never attended a cèilidh before."

"I'd never heard of a cèilidh until Seamus invited us this morning. Sounds like a party to me."

"Oh, I think you'll find it a bit more than that. You can hear the music already. There will be storytelling, poetry, dancing. You'll meet a lot of your mother's family."

"Do you like them?"

"I liked all of them when your mother was alive. I'm not sure they liked me all that much."

"Why was that?"

"Oh, you know. I'm German; what they would call an ispini—a sausage. There's a lot of distrust between the two groups. They tolerated me because of your mother, but when she died, I think a lot of the goodwill died, too. I suspect your Aunt Lilly will tell some tales."

"Seamus's mom? How come?"

"She is a *shanachie*, a storyteller. Stories from old Ireland. It will be good for you to get to know her. She and your mother looked very much alike. Both raving beauties."

So many people attended Seamus's cèilidh that they spilled out onto the street. The apartments on the first floor, lit by candlelight, were crowded with people. It seemed like everyone—both men and women—had a glass in their hands. Rian looked behind her to her father, a silent query. *Where do we go?*

Otto pointed to the stairs. "Third floor."

People sat and stood, talked and drank, flirted and argued on the stairs. The tenor's song wafted down the stairs.

> *Oh, all the comrades e'er I had,*
> *They're sorry for my going away,*
> *And all the sweethearts e'er I had,*
> *They'd wish me one more day to stay,*

The apartments on the second floor were just as crowded with partiers as the rooms on the first floor. Many spoke Irish.

> *But since it falls unto my lot,*
> *That I should rise and you should not,*
> *I gently rise and softly call,*
> *That I should go and you should not,*

The closer they got to the third floor, the more Rian and Otto had to elbow and shoulder their way past people standing on the stairs. No one seemed to mind. Cousin Seamus stood at the top of the stairs, holding court with a half dozen young men his age. When he spotted Rian and Otto, he yelled, "Uncle Otto. Cousin Rian. You're just in time. Danny O'Rourke is singing."

> *Her rosy cheeks and ruby lips,*
> *I own she has my heart in thrall,*
> *Then fill to me the parting glass,*
> *Good night and joy be with you all.*

Seamus put his arm around the waist of a woman who clapped as the song ended and pulled her toward Rian and her father. She walked with a limp and looked like she was about sixty years old. "Rian, I want you to meet me mum, your Aunt Lilly. She is your ma's sister."

Otto and Lilly embraced. Rian was taken aback because her father had described this woman as a beauty who looked just like Rian's mother. Rian could tell right away that life had not been kind to her. Her face was lined, and her mostly gray hair descended to the middle of her back.

Lilly smiled warmly and wrapped Rian up in a hug. Then she held Rian by the shoulders so she could look at her. "My, you've grown like a nettle since I saw you last. I'd recognize you anyplace, though I don't see any of your ma in ye. Your Krieger blood obviously runs strong. Seamus tells me you're a scrapper, though, so I suspect Deirdre would take great pleasure in that."

"My mother was a fighter?"

Lilly nodded. "Aye, a fierce one, she was." Rian's aunt grabbed her by the hand. "Come, Darlin'. Seamus says me most important job this evening is to give you special attention." She pulled Rian into a less crowded room, guided her to two stools that sat under a broken window, and gestured for her to sit. She held both Rian's hands and looked her in the eye. "It's quieter here; a better place to talk. Ask me any questions you want."

Rian was a bit surprised by Lilly's attention and certainly had not planned to ask anyone questions. So as not to be rude, she said, "That song that the man was singing when we arrived. What was it about?"

Aunt Lilly smiled and squeezed Rian's hand lightly. "It's called *The Parting Glass*. It's about leaving. Leaving and probably never coming back. Did you know that when we left Ireland, our families held wakes for us?"

"Funerals?"

Lilly chuckled. "Not exactly. A funeral makes sure that you're properly sent off to heaven. A wake makes sure you're properly remembered by those left behind."

"So, there was a wake in your honor before you left?"

"Aye, and me husband, and your ma, and Seamus and his brothers and sisters who had been born. It was a joyous affair, but they celebrated our lives because they assumed they would never see us again. We were as good as dead, at least to them."

"Do you think you'll ever go back?"

"Doubt it. As hard as things are here, they're rougher in County Wicklow."

"*Vater* says you're a storyteller. What are your stories about?"

"Anything and everything. I can tell you stories about poor Irish girls who work in the textile mills that line the Schuylkill or your ancestors who fought battles three hundred years ago."

"I don't know anything about the Irish side of my family."

"Then it's a good thing you're here. You might be interested to know that your fifteen great-grandfather was Silken Thomas Fitzgerald, the Tenth Earl of

Kildare. Though he was a cousin of Henry VIII, Silken Thomas hated the English, for they had imprisoned his father in the Tower of London. He rebelled from his cousin's rule and holed up in an unconquerable fortress called Maynooth Castle. The evil Lord Deputy of Ireland, an Englishman named William Skeffington, promptly besieged the castle with his army. Silken Thomas made the mistake of entrusting the castle to his faithless foster brother Parris while he went out to recruit more men to his cause. Parris surrendered the castle to Skeffington for a hefty bribe. When the Lord Deputy's Englishmen took over the castle, they put Parris and the entire Garrison to death."

"What happened to Silken Thomas?"

"The snake Skeffington was an old man. He was replaced by the even more villainous Lord Grey, who dogged Silken Thomas until he had no choice but to surrender. The night before he gave himself up, Silken Thomas played his lute under a yew tree. I suspect he knew what was about to happen and grabbed a little bit of beauty for himself before the inevitable."

"Did the English kill him?"

"Aye. He was taken to the Tower of London, where his da had already died. He and five of his uncles were hanged and then beheaded. A sorry end to a great man."

"That's not a very happy ending."

"That's often what it means to be Irish, Darlin'. We have a weakness for lost causes, but we fight the good fight anyway. When it comes time for us to face our death, we do it with music in our hearts. Above all, we know that tales of our heroism, as desperate as it is, will be told for hundreds of years."

"Do you have other tales?"

"As many as you have ancestors. I'll be happy to tell them to you. I can stretch Silken Thomas' story out for an entire evening if you want."

"I want to hear more of everything." Then Rian went silent.

"What is it, Darlin'?"

"I just don't know if people will have anything to say about me in a hundred years."

"Oh, I don't think there's much doubt there. Seamus tells me you have a hero's heart."

"Seamus said that?"

"Aye. Your journey is just beginning, but your story will surely be told."

"Do you think so?"

"I know so."

Rian hugged her aunt.

Saturday, August 8

Inventions Change Philadelphia
Exclusive to the Philadelphia Independent
by Harold Foote

Philadelphia is changing before our eyes because visionary men are applying newly discovered scientific principles to everyday life.

Mr. Franklin's candlelit four-sided lanterns were marvels in their day but woefully inadequate for Philadelphia's streets in our modern era. Within months, our city will be much brighter at night, illuminated by lamps powered by coal gas piped under the streets from a central manufacturing site on the Schuylkill.

Such change is not new to the City of Brotherly Love, but it seems to be coming at a faster rate. Five years ago, there were no railroads and no Pennsylvania Canal. Now steam locomotives pulling as many as six cars leave Philadelphia's Broad Street Station multiple times each day to connect with the canal, 79 miles to the west. Travel time across Pennsylvania has been shortened from 14 days to 4.

And change will continue. Another railroad is being contemplated to the south, connecting Philadelphia to Baltimore and Washington and reducing travel time to our nation's capital from 4 days to 1. Steamships, which now ply our coastal waters and harbors by the hundreds, will become efficient enough to cross the Atlantic. Stone coal from the mines of Schuylkill County, which has been transported to Philadelphia on the Lehigh Canal for the past ten years, will soon outstrip wood as our city's primary source of heat. More powerful stationary steam engines, already prevalent in many factories around the city, will break factories free from their reliance on falling water for power. Steam-powered ice-breaking boats will turn the Delaware into a four-season port and break winter's grip on our city's commerce.

Applied Science—the application of scientific discoveries to everyday life—is changing Philadelphia and improving the lives of its citizens. One can only envision a time when Applied Science becomes a subject in the classrooms of our colleges and universities, and students are taught to use science to address practical problems in the fields of medicine, transportation, manufacturing, and agriculture.

· ·

· RIAN ·

A week after Rian attended the cèilidh, she was writing in her bedroom when Olivia Tucker and her cousin Trey knocked at the front door. Rian led them both back upstairs. Rian asked Olivia, "How are things with your father?"

"He didn't whip Topper, but he doesn't let him out of his sight much either. He's not very happy with me. The only reason I was allowed to leave the house was because Trey stopped by. But he didn't punish me for going to see Joice Heth, and I didn't tell Mama about him and that woman."

"Sounds like a standoff. Did you tell him you were coming here?"

"Are you kidding? No, he thinks we're walking over to the Fairmount Water Works."

Rian ushered her two friends into her bedroom. "Well, your father didn't tell my father about running into us either."

Olivia surveyed various newspapers and writing papers spread out on a small desk stationed at Rian's bedroom window. "It's a lot hotter up here than downstairs. What's so important that it needs to be done up here?"

"I don't want *Vater* to see it. I'm working on my plan. Making sure *Vater* doesn't send me to Switzerland."

"How are you going to do that?"

Rian showed Olivia and Trey a sheet of paper. "Here, read this."

The two read the short piece. "What are applied sciences?" asked Trey.

Rian handed a copy of the *Philadelphia Independent* to the two of them. "It's from an article by Harold Foote that was in yesterday's penny. I liked the sound of it."

"Do you think this is going to work?"

"I don't know. We'll find out if that man Barnum is right. If it appears in the papers enough times, Vater will assume it's true."

Olivia read Foote's article, then perused the rest of the page. "Hey, look at this. There's an article about Joice Heth here."

"I know. Read it. It's filled with lies."

Olivia scanned the article. "Trey, listen to this. 'Mr. P. T. Barnum, interviewed at the exhibition of Joice Heth in Hartford, Connecticut, has declared himself to be more than satisfied by the public's interest in the 161-year-old slave. Nursemaid to George Washington . . . Watched him take his first steps . . . Guarded him until she was sold down to Kentucky.' None of this is true."

"Including," added Rian, "that she's 161 years old, I bet. But read the last line. It seems like there's a lot of people who are willing to believe it."

"'Ten thousand people have seen Joice Heth since she started touring Connecticut. So many Hartfordians have flocked to see a woman born in 1674 that this exhibition has been held over for a second week.'"

"So, if it works for Mr. Barnum, why can't it work for me?"

"How are you going to pay for it?

"I've been on the payroll at Krieger Coach for a while, but now that I go in every day, I get paid on Friday, same as all the other workers. It's not like I have any expenses. I've got more than enough money right now."

Wednesday, August 19

Fire Companies Cause More Problems
Than they Solve
An Editorial by Harold Foote

Philadelphia's volunteer hose companies are little better than gangs of criminals who wear pretty uniforms on parade days. Originally established in colonial days to fight fires that often occur in our fair city, volunteer fire groups are now more apt to engage in arson, extortion, intimidation, and theft. On the surface, fire companies—with names like Moyamensing, Hibernians, Franklin, Lafayette, and Decatur—exist for the public good. They want you to believe that they are there to put out fires. Dig down a bit, and you find that they are social clubs formed around ethnic and religious lines. Protestant, Catholic, Irish, German, and native-born hose companies are numerous; just as common are hose companies that develop because of their antipathy to any aforementioned groups.

Then dig even further, and you find those hose companies are also intent on turning a profit, and therein lies the problem. Local insurance companies pay a bounty to the first fire company to set its hoses on a working fire. That system seems logical until you experience what has become too common in the City of Brotherly Love. Two days ago, the Moyamensing and Lafayette companies arrived simultaneously at the scene of a working fire on South Third Street. Rather than put out the fire, they engaged in a brawl to win the bounty. Members were so intent on declaring victory that the edifice burned to the ground. Undeterred, the brawlers continued the melee. No hose was ever put on the fire.

My research has revealed numerous heinous acts. Owners of burning homes were forced to pay extortion before hoses were engaged. Business owners are threatened with arson unless they pay up regularly. The very men charged with saving buildings instead ransack them of their valuables while they burn. Members of the Black community especially are targeted for random acts of violence.

The antipathy between hose companies has now descended to out-and-out maliciousness. Members of one hose company have deliberately set fires to lure competing hose companies into an ambush. The goal? Mete out black eyes. Bash their heads. Steal their pumps.

The larger goal? Controlling crime in the neighborhoods. Extortion. Breaking and entering. Petty theft. Looting of ships docked at the wharves.

Lost in all this mayhem are the citizens who merely want to feel safe in their homes and businesses. It is time for citizens to take a stand. These people are not heroes. They are common criminals.

· ·

· OTTO ·

Otto threw his hands aloft in a hallelujah gesture when Conor McGuire strutted into the Krieger Coach's office. "Why Conor, welcome home! How was your voyage?" He looked at the calendar. "My goodness, it has been eight weeks. We were getting a little worried."

"*Guten morgen.* It was an adventure. I loved Hamburg."

"So, I guess you learned some German along the way."

"*Nur ein bisschen* [Only a little]." Conor placed an envelope on Otto's desk. "Captain Ellison asked me to deliver this. I think it's important."

"Ah, yes, it is. Very important. It is confirmation that the carriages were delivered. Now we can receive the other half of the payment. Thank you. And thank you for making this trip for us. How did you make out with the carriages?"

"I put on three coats of varnish. The first on the first day just after we left Philadelphia. The second is on day six. I checked on day five, but it was still tacky. I think it takes a long time for varnish to dry in the hold of a ship. The last one I did on day eleven. It was good and dry when we arrived in Hamburg."

"How about the hardware?"

"The same."

"Wonderful. How was the rest of the trip?"

"I like Captain Ellsworth. He tried to teach me navigation, but I don't think that'll be me chosen profession. I also worked in the galley. I got to climb up the ratlines. I saw porpoises and whales. We were in Hamburg for five days and then sailed to Southampton before heading back to Philadelphia."

"So, do you want to become a sailor, or do we have a chance of keeping you on dry land?"

"No, sir. I think I'm a landlubber. We had a pretty big blow on the way home. It lasted for two days. I was puking. I thought I was going to die. Not sure I ever want to do that again. Where's Rian?"

"Rian is running an errand. I think Jules sent her out for something. Seems Trey Shippen was with her."

"Trey Shippen?"

"Yes, the two of them have been spending quite a bit of time lately. Trey's cousin, too. A little girl your age by the name of Olivia. Rian should be back soon."

Otto noted that Conor seemed a bit crestfallen at the news. "There is plenty of work if you would care to get back into it. And, of course, your room is waiting for you at our house."

"Thank you, sir. I'd best find at least one of me brothers first. Let 'em know I'm still alive. I'll probably be back later. And I'll probably be moving back in with you. Doubt me brothers'll have any room for me."

As Otto watched Conor depart, his thoughts returned briefly to Trey Shippen. *Oh, of course, you are rushing things. After all, they're only eleven years old. But Rian and the son of a bank president. Wouldn't that be a match.*

Seamus Gallagher entered the shop office. As Otto had stated during his interview with Seamus, Otto was serious about improving Seamus's reading, writing, and math. He had scheduled the first hour of each workday as a tutoring session with Aaron Bassinger. Otto smiled to himself with the thought that both his bookkeeper and Seamus had enthusiastically agreed to the sessions. "How did it go?"

"Most of it's coming back to me. Been a while since I had to use any of this. Was that Conor McGuire who just left?"

"Yes, he is quite filled with himself, as he has every right to be. I think he was more interested in seeing Rian than me, but that is no surprise. What did Aaron have you working on today?"

Seamus pulled this morning's *Philadelphia Independent* out of his rear pocket and placed it on Otto's shop desk. "Never found time to read the pennies before. Let's just say I'm expanding me horizons."

Otto noted that Seamus had folded the paper to the day's article about the hose companies. "What did you think about Mr. Foote's story about your friends?"

Seamus put his hands in his pockets and rocked back on his heels. "I've got two answers to that. He may have exaggerated a wee bit, but there's not much in there that's not true. However, when me friends at Moyamensing read it, they're gonna have some very strong objections. The darker aspects of the hose companies' business are best left in the shadows. If Mr. Foote continues to turn over rocks, he's likely to get some regrettable attention from me friends."

"Are you still intent on joining the Moyamensing Hose Company? I was hoping that we could change your career path with this job." Otto's smile implied that he was only half-serious, but he leaned across his shop desk, changing his tone. "Seamus, now that you've been here for a couple of months, I'm convinced that you do not share your friends' prejudices. You are capable of doing great things with us, but there is no room here for the hate that goes along with membership in your hose company."

"Well, I'm not in yet. They vote next week. But I hear what you're saying. I think I'll be able to keep me two worlds apart."

Seamus picked up his paper from the shop desk, used it to give Otto a wry salute, and left the office.

· · · · · · · · · · · · · · · · · · · ·

· OTTO ·

Three hours later, Otto sat at his usual table in the dining room of the United States Hotel when reporter Harold Foote approached the chair opposite him. Newspaper reporters were not exactly the cream of society, and Foote's worn, ill-repaired brown suit should have excluded him from admission to the dining room. Otto liked Foote and found he often provided useful information. Apparently, others felt the same way because James, the maître d', never prevented him from entering.

Today Foote was looking even shabbier than usual. He was also sporting a shiner that looked relatively new. He sat down with a grimace.

Otto half-rose to shake his friend's hand. "What happened to you?"

A small glimmer of Harold's usual jauntiness appeared. "Seems with one article I was able to do the impossible."

"Which was?"

"Unite all the hose companies in their hatred of the same thing."

"And that is?"

"Me."

"*Autsch* [Ouch]. Seamus Gallagher and I were just talking about that this morning. What happened?"

"I was attacked by three sons of Hibernia on my way home last night." He tenderly touched the shiner on his left eye. "That's how I got this. They really let me have it. Ruined my suit to boot. Then they told me to quit writing about Moyamensing. Didn't mention the other hose companies."

"How badly are you hurt?"

"This shiner's the worst of it. They didn't check in with their competitors because when I finally got home, the front windows of my house were all broken. One of the bricks had a note tied around it that threatened my life."

"What are you going to do?"

"I guess I overplayed my hand a bit. Philadelphia feels too hot for me right now. I think it's time I saw some other parts of the continent."

"Where are you going to go?"

"There's some interesting action in Mexico right now. Especially in Tejas. The area is huge. The Mexican government has offered a bounty to people who bring settlers into the area. Waves of Americans are moving in and bringing their slaves along with them even though slavery has been illegal in Mexico for six years. The settlers have more allegiance to the USA than to Mexico, and their numbers are growing. They're starting to flex their muscles."

"Harold, I am sorry to see you go. Will you be traveling as a reporter or as a private citizen?"

"I just got out of a meeting with my boss. He has agreed to give me a small stipend to send regular dispatches from my travels. I think it should be interesting. The slavery thing chafes the Mexican government."

"Sounds just as dangerous as what you would be leaving here. I have met a few slave owners, and they do not take well to criticism. Same as the hose companies."

Harold shrugged. "We'll see . . ."

"Krieger, hello." George Shippen towered over the two diners. "Enjoying your meal with the press, I see. I hope you've been paying attention to the value of the railroad stock you purchased in June. It's up fifteen percent in six weeks. Our construction is ahead of schedule. You should consider another purchase."

"Thank you, George. I think I have my hands full at the moment, but the offer is enticing."

Shippen turned his attention to Harold, oblivious to his bruises. "And you, Foote, you might consider writing an article about why investing in railroads is so important to Philadelphia. Important to all of America, really."

"Good idea, Mr. Shippen. I will consider it," responded Foote.

Shippen held out a penny paper to Otto. "I don't know if you have seen this. It seems Frau Gilbert has decided there are enough young women of a certain class in Philadelphia to advertise in Mr. Foote's Independent."

"I wrote her about Rian as you recommended. I have not heard back yet. May I see the ad?"

"I circled it for you. I am a little surprised because when Prudence was going there, I'm sure there were 11-year-olds." Shippen handed the paper to Otto.

Mrs. Gilbert's Finishing School for Young Women.
Ages 13 to 18. German, French, English. Latin.
Social graces. Discourse. Literature. Music. Art.
Applied Sciences. Staff management.
Contact Frau Gilbert. Lucerne, Switzerland

"Perhaps it is an error," Otto responded hopefully. "Such things happen all too often. You cannot really trust what you read in the pennies." He looked at his lunch companion. "Present company excepted, of course, Harold. However, I think the curriculum would be of interest to Rian. If the age is not an error, I suppose I will have to find another school. I am sure there are others."

"Not, however, with Frau Gilbert's reputation. Perhaps you should wait."

"Perhaps. Thank you for alerting me."

Harold Foote watched Shippen exit the dining room. "I have done some initial research into the *Philadelphia & Delaware County Rail-Road*. It is chronically undercapitalized. There are so many corporate layers that I cannot figure out who owns what or what owns what. I would think twice about further investment if I were you."

"Thank you for your advice, Harold, but as George implied, I have done very well so far."

· ·

Aaron looked up from his desk as Otto entered the office. "You've been gone a long time. Where have you been?"

"After lunch I walked up to the building lot."

"Any progress?"

"The brush is cleared. They are staking out the perimeter of the buildings now. I think we should all go up there tomorrow to make sure we are satisfied before they start on the foundations. I confess I would be sleeping a lot better if I had figured out what the interior layout of the new Krieger Coach was going to look like."

"What do you mean?"

"I think I am a pretty good designer of carriages—a good builder of carriages. I think I will be an equally good designer of railroad cars. But envisioning a space to build them efficiently, so far, that is a mystery to me."

"It will come to you in due time. Strickland is adamant about getting the buildings under roof before the snow flies. He says a factory is just a big box, anyway. We can decide how the box is to be broken up later."

"I believe Strickland. I just need to figure it out sooner or later, and I would rest easier if it were sooner."

"Hey, I was testing Rian about what she had read in the pennies this morning." Aaron held out the newspaper to Otto. "She showed me this ad in the *Das Philadelphische Patriot*."

Otto took the paper but didn't look at it. "Good, I'm glad she is reading the German pennies. That paper is a little strident, is it not?"

"It's no friend of the Negro. Or the Irish. I think she found it in the shop. One of the workers must have brought it in. Anyway, she pointed out this ad. It's for *Frau Gilberts Schule für Junge Frauen*. Isn't that the school you wrote to last month?"

"Yes, I have not heard back from Frau Gilbert yet. I just saw the English version of this same ad in the *Independent* when I was having lunch. Shippen showed it to me. What was Rian's reaction when she read it?"

"Oh, I think she was quite pleased. She assumes she won't be able to attend the school for another two years. What are you going to do now?"

"I do not know yet. Until this moment, I was hoping the age was an error." Otto looked at the German penny paper. "This ad also mentions *angewandte wissenschaften*. What do you think 'applied sciences' means?"

"I asked the same question myself. It sounds like manufacturing to me. Strange subject for a girls' school, but something Rian might be interested in."

"Did she comment about it?"

"No."

"Damn."

"Otto, you know my sentiment. I want her to continue to work with me here in the office."

"Yes, Aaron, that is no surprise."

· · · · · · · · · · · · · · · · · · ·

· SEAMUS ·

Seamus entered Clancy's Saloon and was pleased to see the owner start pouring a glass even before the door closed. He was surprised to see his friend Dylan already sitting at the bar. "No work today, Boyo?"

Dylan stared down into his whiskey glass. "Fooking foreman didn't pick me."

"Nothing else available?"

"Stopped by the hose company. Not enough ships in port to steal anything. Seamus, it's not nearly as much fun since you started working for the ispinis."

Dylan's comment put a smile on Seamus's face. "Have to admit I got lucky. It's a good job. I'm learning a lot. Might just be able to make something of meself."

Dylan looked down at his glass. He seemed to have something on his mind. "Hose company vote's coming up next week."

"You'll get in."

"Not so sure. I don't like to crack heads the way you do."

"I don't like to crack heads. I'm just willing to when the occasion calls."

"Well, you're good at it. I'm sure you'll get in."

Seamus confidently shrugged it off. "Hope so. Seems like the whole neighborhood belongs to the Moyamensing Hose Company. A touch ironic that acceptance is based more on our skills at breaking and entering and busting heads than putting out fires."

"I think I'm going to need some help to get in."

"What kind of help?"

"I need to distinguish meself. Get noticed . . . I've got an idea."

"Uh-oh. Clancy, I think we need another round here. Dylan's got an idea." Clancy refreshed their glasses and returned to the other end of the bar. Seamus took a sip. "Why do I think this idea includes me?"

"Seamus, you can read. I can't."

"So?"

Dylan conspiratorially leaned close to Seamus. "Did you hear about those abolitionist pamphlets that got burned up in South Carolina[14] last month?"

"Quite a ruckus, from what the penny papers said. Glad I wasn't the postmaster. Talk about being caught between a rock and a hard place. Duty said he had to deliver the mail, but he thought differently.

Dylan placed his glass down on the bar. "Well, the mob solved the problem. They broke into the post office, threw the pamphlets out into the street, and burned the whole lot of them."

Seamus pulled a penny paper out of his back pocket. "Says here that now Andy Jackson's involved. Told the US Mail not to send any more abo literature down South."

---

14. The American Anti-Slavery Society had printed a million copies of various anti-slavery tracts for distribution in the South via the US Mail. The literature prominently featured engravings of depredations inflicted on slaves by their masters. On July 29, 1835, an irate mob ransacked the Charleston, South Carolina post office, using sacks full of anti-slavery pamphlets to start a bonfire, which in turn set on fire an effigy of William Lloyd Garrison, among others.

"I wouldn't know about that. I just know we've got our own pamphlets."

Seamus looked up from the paper. "Whataya mean?"

"Here. In Philadelphia. You know Michael O'Shannessy?

Seamus nodded. "Sure."

"His sister's married to the postmaster on Chestnut Street."

"Didn't know. So?"

Dylan took another sip of his whiskey. "Postmaster told her, and she told O'Shannessy that there's tons of abo pamphlets been sent from New York for delivery here in Philadelphia. Just like Charleston."

"So, are you going to start a mob action and burn the pamphlets? Risky business assaulting government property."

"Nope. No mob necessary. I've got a better idea. I want to steal 'em."

Seamus finally connected the dots. "And, of course, you need me to help you because you can't read. But then what? Burn 'em?"

"No, it gets better. We take them to the Delaware and dump them in the water. Just like the Boston Tea Party. They'll love that at the hose company. That'll get me noticed."

"They won't love it if they don't see it. You'll need an audience watching you."

Dylan looked at Seamus and smiled. "So, we bring the pamphlets here first. A few hours after candlelight, there'll be a passel of our Moya boys here. Then we take 'em to the river. Then we have our Tea Party."

Seamus took a sip of his whiskey. "Your plan's only a little crazy. When do you intend for us to do it?"

"Us? Are you in?

Seamus nodded with bemusement. "We gotta do something to get you in. You're not a fighter. Present plan excepted, you're not a thinker. It's as good as anything I could have come up with."

"What are you doing tonight?"

"Reading mail, apparently."

• • • • • • • • • • • • • • • •

It was ten o'clock. Ten minutes ago, Seamus and Dylan had crowbarred into the post office on Chestnut Street. Seamus turned angrily to Dylan, who was creeping closely behind him in almost total darkness. "Jaysus, Dylan, will you hold the candle up so's I can see?"

Dylan stumbled over a partially filled mail sack but kept his footing. "I would if you'd move a little slower. I can barely see meself. This room's bigger than I thought."

Seamus turned and wrested the candle out of his hand. "Gimme that. Who the hell plans a two-man robbery with only one candle?"

Dylan straightened up in mock indignation. "Hey, I'm working on a limited budget here."

"Well, we need to make this quick. No sense getting pinched for raiding federal property." Seamus held the candle over a mail sack and read its tag. "I wish you'd learn to read so's I don't get included in your hair-brained schemes."

Dylan said nothing. He peered around helplessly at mail sacks as far as the candle threw light.

Seamus stooped over another mail sack. "What do these pamphlets look like anyway?"

"Dunno. Never seen any."

"How many of them are there?"

"Dunno. Thousands, I suspect. Postmaster said there were three mail sacks filled with 'em."

Seamus straightened up and held the candle to see Dylan's face. "Well, that might've been some valuable information that you could've told me at the start of this operation."

He then raised the candle high above his head and surveyed the mailroom. He spotted three bulging mail sacks sitting in a corner. "There we go."

He wended his way around islands of mail bags that littered the large room. The sacks that caught his attention were all by themselves. He read the tag on one. "This is promising. New York City."

Dylan peered over Seamus's shoulder. "Who are they to?"

"Lucretia Mott. 136 North Ninth Street. Is that it?"

"I dunno."

"That's up near where the Kriegers live."

"Your boss?"

"Yeah, I bet that's the Quaker woman who causes a ruckus every once in a while. Speaks about freeing the slaves."

Dylan started to untie the knot on one of the sacks. "Now we're getting somewhere. Do you think this is it?" He pulled out a printed pamphlet and handed it to Seamus.

Seamus and Dylan looked at the paper in the candlelight. There were two woodcut images on the front. One was a white man whipping a Black man tied to a post. The other portrayed a white man putting his hands on a Black woman. Seamus noted that the white man had a lascivious leer on his face. The Black woman looked afraid.

Seamus scanned the rest of the document. "American Anti-Slavery Society, New York City. Yup, this is it. Let's go."

Dylan lifted one of the sacks. "Jaysus, I didn't think they would be this heavy. How are we going to get 'em all the way down to Moyamensing?"

Seamus straightened up, held the candle aloft, and surveyed the building. "Well, fortunately, our friends in the US Mail Service have had to solve similar problems. There must be ten wheelbarrows in here."

"You're gonna steal a wheelbarrow?"

"Dylan, we're already breaking about fifteen laws here. Don't worry about a couple of fooking wheelbarrows."

• • • • • • • • • • • • • • • • • • •

Seamus and Dylan left the post office just after eleven o'clock. Those few people who were out expressed little interest in two workers pushing wheelbarrows of who-knows-what down the middle of the street. The boys took their time, acting like they were doing what they were supposed to be doing.

"Seamus." Dylan had the wheelbarrow with two sacks in it, so after a few blocks, he sounded like he was running out of breath.

"What?"

"Is that what they do? Whip their slaves?"

"Of course. What do you think?" Ironically, this was what Seamus had been thinking about as well.

"What about the other thing. With the girl slaves?"

"How am I supposed to know? Probably."

Dylan pondered this for a while. "That's not right."

"Of course, it's not right."

"Everybody says they're better off as slaves. They can't take care of themselves."

It was late. Seamus was losing patience with his friend. "Use your head. Does it make sense to you?"

"I don't know. Some of them, maybe."

"How would you like it?"

After a moment, Dylan said, "Well, me life ain't so hot. And I ain't no slave."

"Yeah, but you can wake up and walk out of this city anytime you want to. Or get drunk. Or learn to read. They can't do any of that."

"So, do you think the abos are right? That slavery should be ended?"

"Of course, I do."

"But what would it be like if all the darkies were free?"

Seamus didn't like the question because of his own mixed feelings. One of the first things the straw boss told his father when he got off the boat was that the Irish and the Africans were at war. Seamus's father passed that bit of lore down to him, and the lesson was reinforced the hard way when a bunch of Black kids beat the stuffing out of him. Seamus had since paid that one back many times. Until he started working for his Uncle Otto, he'd had to scrap for every job he could find. And there, right behind him, were the Africans, often willing to do the same job for less.

Yet, unlike many of his Hibernian brethren, he didn't hate Black people. He didn't generalize. He assumed that Negroes were just like the Irish or anyone else: there were good ones and some bad apples. They probably had hopes and fears, just like he and his family did.

The more Seamus worked with Jules, the more he respected the man. Jules was the best boss he had ever had. He didn't talk down to him. He had helped him learn a ton of things at work. Although Seamus had never spoken to him about this, because of the arrival of Cousin Elmo, he knew Jules and Maddie were sheltering runaway slaves, a hazardous undertaking. He had to respect them for that.

He finally gathered his thoughts. "If they freed the slaves, a lot of them would probably come up here. That'd be harder for us. It's hard enough for the Irish to find jobs as it is. Don't need more darkies competing."

"So, are you for abolition or against it?"

Seamus hesitated. "I don't think anyone should be a slave." As soon as he said those words, their implications became more apparent to him. "So, I guess what we're doing right now isn't such a good idea."

"Interesting time for you to find scruples."

"Hey, look. I'm here, ain't I? How many lads did you line up for the rest of this action?"

"Four or five. Hopefully, they'll be waiting for us at Clancy's."

· · · · · · · · · · · · · · · · · · · ·

There were so many patrons at Clancy's Saloon that they flowed out onto Plum Street. News of Dylan's plan had struck a responsive chord. The two were greeted with cheers and backslapping as they parked their wheelbarrows outside. The crowd parted so that Dylan and Seamus could make their way to the bar, and Clancy had their glasses waiting for them. "This one's on the house, lads. Haven't had a night like this since the strike ended."

Hugh Callaghan came up from behind and put his arms around their shoulders. "Simply inspiring, lads. Our very own Tea Party. This'll make a fine statement to the abolitionists and the darkies. When do we do the deed, Seamus?"

"Don't ask me. This is Dylan's operation. I just tagged along."

Callaghan shifted his attention to Dylan. "My my, Boyo, I may have underestimated ye. When are ye holding your Tea Party?"

Dylan drained the rest of his whiskey. "No time like the present. Let's march." He slammed the glass down on the bar and strode triumphantly out of the saloon; both fists raised high. Seamus reluctantly tagged along behind. Dylan grabbed his wheelbarrow and started down Plum Street toward the Delaware River. Seamus, feeling he had no choice, followed his lead.

Somehow, torches and shillelaghs appeared.[15] A crowd of fifty or so young Irish lads, fueled by drink and heartened by their numbers, set out noisily behind them. Someone started singing *The Rocky Road to Dublin*, and others joined in, heedless of the noise they were making in the otherwise quiet neighborhood. With one fighting song under their belts, they segued to *The Wearing of the Green*.

From his vantage point at the front of the crowd—which was just shy of becoming a mob—Seamus saw pedestrians turning down side streets to avoid the rowdy throng. "Dylan, you sure you know what you're doing?"

"Getting noticed. Just like we planned. It is a bit startling."

"Be careful. It's going to get out of hand."

"Who cares? This is me ticket into Moya. They gotta vote me in now."

Seamus didn't respond. As they passed other saloons, more lads joined the group.

At the end of Plum Street, they turned left on Second and then a quick right on Almond Street to continue toward the river. Two blocks later, they arrived at the wharf. Dylan dropped his wheelbarrow at the end of the dock. Seamus did the same. Dylan pulled out a knife and slit all three mailbags up their sides. Feeling the power of the crowd behind him, he dramatically picked up one of the pamphlets, balled it up, and tossed it into the river. "C'mon laddies! I need some help here! Let's start this Tea Party!" His face lit by torchlight, Dylan was feeding the mob, and they were feeding him. He was theirs now.

---

15. A shillelagh is a stout club with a knot at one end. Although it could be used as a walking stick, any Irishman who wielded the shillelagh was more than happy to knock an enemy over the head with it.

Greedy hands scooped up pamphlets and tossed them into the river. Some fed them to the torches first, then threw them, burning, into the river. When the crowd had thrown all the pamphlets, burning or not, into the river, Dylan pushed one of the wheelbarrows off the wharf, and it arced to the water. Someone else did the same with the second one to more cheers. Dylan grabbed a torch from one of his friends. "Thanks for attending me Tea Party, laddies! Let's go back to Clancy's!"

"No!" came a voice from the crowd. "Let's get some Africans!"

The crowd was now a mob, and Dylan was no longer in the lead. The rowdies left the wharf and noisily headed back toward Moyamensing. They sang more Irish fighting songs, only louder. Ash cans were upended. A white man and his prostitute were harassed but not seriously harmed. A wagon loaded with bricks was tipped over and set on fire.

Just inside Moyamensing, an unlucky Black man was beaten but escaped and ran away. Seamus followed the mob, aghast but not surprised. The mob stopped in front of two Black houses and started throwing bricks and stones through the windows.

Seamus found Dylan. "Boyo, you should try to stop this."

Dylan looked at him in consternation. "There's no stopping this. Nothing we can do about it."

Seamus thought about his next step only briefly. He knew this was going to be a life-changer. He wrested a torch from a man standing next to him and strode to the front of the crowd. "All of you, go home! We all should leave right now!"

The mob's blood was up. No one was deterred. A dozen bricks flew at him from different directions. He dodged valiantly, but one finally hit him in the head. Stunned, Seamus sat down hard. The crowd rushed past him. Someone picked up his fallen torch, stormed the house, and threw it through a window. Other torches followed.

Dylan bent over Seamus, who was trying to staunch the blood that was streaming from his forehead. "C'mon, Seamus. Nothing more you can do here."

"This isn't right, Dylan. These people didn't do anything to us."

"Of course, they didn't. But I guess that's just the way life is." Dylan helped his friend up. "Let's go. Our work is done here."

Seamus looked over his shoulder at the mob, now outlined by flames coming from both houses. "Was anyone in there?"

"I suspect they flew out the back. Here, lean on me 'til your feet start working right."

Wednesday, August 26

· JULES ·

Jules was a block away from Krieger Coach when he spotted Hans Schmidt leaning against a newly installed gas lamp post on the corner of Twelfth and Locust. He could have crossed the street to avoid trouble but sensed that Hans was waiting for him, and trouble would be hard to dodge.

He was right. As he approached the corner, Hans stepped into his path.

"Kind of early for you, isn't it, Hans? Man without a job and all? How long's it been? Two months since Otto fired you?"

"Otto didn't fire me; I quit. And I'm doing my job right now."

Jules shouldered his way past Hans. "Well, I'm not terribly interested, but if you're going to tell me about it, you'll have to walk with me because I've got to get to work."

"I'm not going to walk down the street with an African, so I'll tell you right now. I've teamed up with an old friend of yours."

"Who's that?"

"Austin T. Slatter. I'm in the slave-catching business now."

Jules stopped and turned. "I think that suits you, but why should that be of interest to me?"

"You know, there was always a rumor floating around the shop that you were just some fugitive slave Otto took pity on. That those papers you wave around are fake."

Jules froze. "That's an interesting rumor, Hans. Too bad for you it's not true."

"I think it is true, and I intend to prove it. Let me see your papers right now."

"It doesn't work that way, Hans. You know I have papers. What you need is to find the person I allegedly escaped from and get a warrant from him."

"Then I guess we'll just have to go by Austin's memory. Enjoy your days as a foreman at Krieger Coach. Pretty soon, you'll be back to being a slave again, or you'll be on the run."

WEDNESDAY, AUGUST 26 · 169

"And why are you warning me about this? That's not like you."

Hans smirked. "I just want to see you sweat."

"How am I doing? Do you see me sweating yet?"

Hans looked hard at Jules. "Nope, but I expect I'll see it soon enough."

"Not likely, Hans." Jules wheeled and walked away from his antagonist, his blood draining down to his shoes so fast that he saw stars. "Come see me when you figure out who I escaped from," he said over his shoulder. "That should take you forever because that person doesn't exist."

Jules listened for the rush of footsteps behind him, but they never came.

· ·

· RIAN ·

Olivia broke off from her family and a knot of well-wishers on the lower Gardiner Pier and walked over to Rian. "Thanks for coming to see me off."

"I see the *Carolina Princess* is back in service."

Olivia nodded. "New engine, new paint, new cabins. We'll be back in Charleston in four days. When will I ever see you again?"

Rian shrugged. "I still don't know if *Vater's* sending me to Switzerland. If he is, it will be years. If not, next summer, I hope."

"Well, my vote is for next summer."

"Mine, too. I hope your father doesn't punish Topper when you get home."

"Oh, my father will do what my father does. He says he's the king of his castle. I guess I'm lucky I got my way this time. Hopefully, by the time we return to Philadelphia next year, he will have forgotten about that day with Joice Heth, and you will be welcome in our house again."

"That would be nice."

Olivia hugged Rian and returned to her family.

· ·

· RIAN ·

Rian walked into the office. "Here's the morning mail, *Vater*." She put three letters on her father's desk. "It looks like they're all bills."

Her father looked up from his desk. "Rian, sit down. I would like to talk to you. I know you are aware that Frau Gilbert's School no longer accepts girls as young as you."

"Yes, I read the ad."

"I had hoped to hear directly from the school that perhaps they would make an exception. The curriculum looks like something you would enjoy and excel at."

Rian shrugged but felt her best tack was to remain silent.

"Anyway, I have heard nothing. Apparently, they are not interested in enrolling a child as young as you. Jules, Aaron, and Adrian have told me that you have become valuable to them this summer. Aaron says you are the best bookkeeping student he has ever had. Both Jules and Adrian like the work you are doing in the shops."

"Thank you, *Vater*." The compliments from Jules and Adrian were genuine. *I didn't ask them to tell Vater that.*

"So, I have come to a decision. I am not going to send you to Switzerland this fall. I would like you to work in the Krieger factories as you have done all summer long. Your studies will continue. We will be moving into the new factories in the spring, and Krieger Coach will start making railroad cars. It is an exciting time to be here. I am happy you will be here to witness it."

"Thank you, *Vater*. This makes me very happy." *But I don't want just to witness the move to the new factories. I want to be a part of it.*

"This issue is not over. You will still be going to Switzerland to attend Frau Gilbert's School, but not for two years. I trust you will use the time wisely."

"I will, *Vater*." Rian smiled to herself as she went to her table. Before she sat down, she took a letter out of her pocket and placed it in the table's shallow drawer. *I'll get to you later.* As she closed the drawer, she again glanced at the return address: *Lucerne, Schweiz* [Lucerne, Switzerland].

• •

· SEAMUS ·

Hugh Callaghan sat with Seamus at the bar at Clancy's Saloon. "There's no easy way to say this, Seamus."

"You've got to be kidding."

"No, no kidding. You didn't get in."

"Who blackballed me?"

"You know I can't tell ye that. But I can tell you this: there were two blackballs, and the rest were split down the middle. So you wouldn't have got in anyway."

"Was McLaughlin one of them? He hates me."

"You know what, Seamus? McLaughlin isn't your problem. You're your problem. The thing is, you don't stick with your own kind. The boys don't trust you. You're too busy looking out for the Africans and working for the ispinis."

"You mean I didn't get in because I didn't torch those houses last week?"

"I think that was a pretty good indication. You're either with us or you're against us. That night you weren't thinking about helping your mates. You tried to save the Africans. Never entered a house. Never took a swing at any of the darkies.

"What about Dylan?"

"Dylan's in. They loved that stunt he pulled last week."

Seamus slumped in his chair and looked vacantly at his whiskey glass. "All me friends are in Moya. Don't know what I'm gonna do now."

"Dunno, Kid. You're in a bit of a fix. I don't envy you."

1836

TUESDAY, MARCH 8

Americans Occupying San Antonio Mission
Massacred by Mexican Army
10 Pennsylvanians Amongst the Dead
Exclusive Dispatch to the Philadelphia Independent
by Harold Foote

American settlers in the Mexican territory known as Texas are in revolt against the Republic of Mexico. On March 1, 1836, 45 delegates representing 21 municipalities met in Washington-on-the Brazos and declared their independence. However, the nascent revolution was dealt a severe blow when the garrison of settlers occupying an outpost in San Antonio de Bexar was wiped out by General Antonio Lopez de Santa Anna, President of the Republic of Mexico. In the early days of the siege, Colonel William B. Travis, the Alamo's commanding officer, wrote the following letter to the world.

To the People of Texas & All Americans in the World:

Fellow citizens & compatriots—I am besieged, by a thousand or more of the Mexicans under Santa Anna—I have sustained a continual Bombardment & cannonade for 24 hours & have not lost a man. The enemy has demanded a surrender at discretion, otherwise, the garrison are to be put to the sword, if the fort is taken—I have answered the demand with a cannon shot, & our flag still waves proudly from the walls. I shall never surrender or retreat. Then, I call on you in the name of Liberty, of patriotism & everything dear to the American character, to come to our aid, with all dispatch—The enemy is receiving reinforcements daily & will no doubt increase to three or four thousand in four or five days. If this call is neglected, I am determined to sustain myself as long as possible & die like a soldier who never forgets what is due to his own honor & that of his country—Victory or Death.

William Barret Travis
Lt. Col. comdt

By March 6, after a thirteen-day siege, the entire garrison was wiped out. It is known that at least ten native Pennsylvanians were in the garrison of the massacred patriots. Events in the Republic of Mexico are still unfolding. Whether the settlers' revolution will succeed is in doubt.

Saturday, March 26

· OTTO ·

Seven months had passed since the mob threw the New York Abolitionist Society's pamphlets in the river and torched two Black houses in Moyamensing. Otto Krieger padded downstairs, still in his nightshirt, dreading the thought of going to work.

Rian sat at the kitchen table, dressed in her shop clothes and finishing up a breakfast of bacon and eggs. "Hello, *Vater*. You got in late last night. How was your trip?"

"Productive, thank you." *More productive than I have been at the shop for the past seven months.* "Both Baltimore and Washington are good markets for us. I signed contracts to build two new carriages. There is interest in railroad cars once we start building them."

"Why were you so late getting home?"

"Oh, I wanted to see the progress that George Shippen has been crowing about on the *Philadelphia, Wilmington, and Baltimore Railroad*. It was a mistake. Only a few sections are complete, and none of those are even being serviced by locomotives. The entire trip was horse-powered, sometimes on track, sometimes by stage. It was not an enjoyable experience. We missed several connections. The last six hours were by lantern light. Can you wait half an hour so we can walk to work together?"

"It's my birthday. Jules told me to take the day off and play with my friends. I've got one thing I need to do at work, and then I'm going to follow orders."

"Well, well, twelve years old. I'm surprised Jules let you out of the shop. He told me before I left that you are becoming quite valuable to him. He is a little jealous that you spend so much time at Krieger Forge. So which shop are you heading to, Coach or Forge?"

"Neither. I've got some bookkeeping to finish up for Aaron."

"Good news or bad news?"

"Excellent news, I think. I'm sure Aaron will have a report for you by the end of the morning."

Otto reached down and fished something out of the satchel sitting at the bottom of the stairs. "I may not see you at the shop. I have meetings scheduled all day. I bought this for you in Baltimore." He handed a clear glass bottle to Rian.

Rian took the bottle, which had a model of a sailing ship inside. The ship was much too large to fit through the neck of the bottle. "How did they get the ship in there?"

"I have no idea. This one was made in the Netherlands."

"My birthday is just getting started, and it's already one of the best birthdays ever." She hugged her father.

"Who are you going to spend the rest of your day with?"

"I talked Jules into letting Conor off too, so we're going to do something with Trey."

"Trey and Conor get along? Where is he, by the way?"

"I don't think they'll ever be best friends, but the three of us do okay. Conor moved back with his brothers. They found a new place, and it's got room for him."

Goodness, how long has he been with us? Seven months? "Well, I am happy for him, but if his circumstances change again, he is always welcome to stay with us."

"He knows that. He said to say thank you."

"Good. You should go now and get your task done. I will be there in an hour or so. I am sure there is a pile of work waiting for me since I have been gone for a week." *And I have got to face the music sooner or later.*

• •

· RIAN ·

Rian's nose had been buried in the company ledger for twenty minutes when Seamus strode into the office without knocking.

"Happy birthday, Rian. How's your day going so far?"

Rian looked up from her work and smiled. She was happy to see her cousin. "Not bad at all."

"Now you're sounding like a true Irishman. I think all the time we've been spending together is rubbing off on you."

"What do you mean?"

"You said, 'Not bad at all.' When an Irishman says that, it usually refers to something spectacular."

Rian put down her pencil and closed the ledger. "Let's just say my birthday started pretty spectacular. Vater gave me a ship in a bottle this morning. What if it hadn't been such a good day? What would I have said? You know, being an Irishman and all?"

"Why, you would have said, 'Not bad now.' Actually, it's more in the inflection thing." Seamus placed a light cylindrical object wrapped in an old copy of the *Philadelphia Independent* and tied with a piece of twine on her table. "Happy birthday."

Rian pulled on the bow and unwrapped the paper to find a copy of *The Dublin University Magazine*. She looked up at Seamus expectantly.

"I've started reading this meself lately. Graduated from the Philadelphia pennies. They send a few copies from Ireland over to the bookshop on Sansom Street every month, and now I buy them regular. I thought in your ongoing quest to explore what it means to be Irish, it would be helpful. There's a few poems in there by a man named James Clarence Mangan that I like."

"Seamus, this is very thoughtful of you. How are you doing?"

"Not bad now."

Seamus's response immediately caught Rian's attention. "What's wrong? Are you still staying away from Clancy's?"

"Aye. Not sure if they've exiled me or if it's me own doing. I just know there's not many kindred spirits there at the moment."

"Seamus, I think you did the right thing. The rowdies shouldn't have burned those houses. Have you found a saloon you like yet?"

"McSweeney's on Lombard Street serves whiskey that doesn't taste like swill. It's a little quieter than's to me liking. But no one from Moya goes there. I've made a couple of new friends. Rekindled relationships with some others."

"That sounds good. So, what's your problem."

"Well, I've got a bee in me bonnet. An idea I can't seem to get rid of."

"And what is that?"

"I'm thinking of starting me own hose company."

· ·

· LUCRETIA ·

Lucretia Mott was reading the *Philadelphia Independent*, which she had laid out on the butcher block table in the middle of the kitchen. She and James had followed through on their vows to cut ties with the slave economy, both in the South and the North. James no longer conducted business with cotton merchants in the South, and Lucretia had stopped purchasing goods produced by slave labor.

These decisions had disrupted domestic life considerably. James's importing firm, which had been quite lucrative, now barely showed a profit. Lucretia had resolutely tightened up spending but had found this incredibly challenging as "free produce"—any goods produced by non-slaves—was more expensive. It took significant efforts to find cotton, sugar, molasses, or rice untainted by the sin of slavery.

James descended noisily from the second floor, leaned over, and pecked his petite wife on the top of her head. "A little early for the pennies, isn't it, my dear?"

"I bought the paper when I was out buying butter for thy breakfast. Mr. Foote has written an article from Mexico."

James seemed more interested in starting his day with a good meal. "My goodness, it smells good in here. What has thee cooked up for me this morning?"

"A little surprise. I know how much thee misses thy sweets."

James sat down at the kitchen table, and Lucretia put the newspaper in front of him, folded to Harold Foote's article. She returned to the kitchen stove, the source of the wonderful smells.

James glanced at the article briefly. "This isn't good. Those frontiersmen tend to be a vindictive lot. Violence will only beget more violence."

"My heart breaks for those people, but I have larger worries than that."

"That they'll be crushed by Mexico?"

Lucretia flipped something in the cast iron fry pan, which sizzled and gave emphasis to her reply. "No, that the Texans will win and gain their independence."

"Thee doesn't support a man's right to self-determination?"

"Of course, I do. But I put a higher value on a man's right to be free. Slavery has been outlawed in Mexico for seven years. The Americans who are moving into that area are mostly slave owners. They are bringing those poor people with them and extending slavery to a much larger area. If that revolution is successful, then slavery wins as well."

"I didn't think about it that way. I'm sure thee is right."

"I'm sure I'll be even more unpopular in this city when I speak out against the revolution."

"Must thee do so?"

James didn't see her withering glance as she served him his breakfast.

"Ah, what is this, my dear?"

"It's called French toast. It's made with cinnamon. Slather some butter on it first. But the thing thee will most enjoy is this maple syrup. Pour it on over the toast, but don't use a lot of it because it is dearer than gold, and the children have not come down yet."

"Where did thee get this idea?"

"The ladies at PFASS[16] and I have been exchanging recipes. Alternatives to sugar and molasses, now that we are no longer buying them."

James took his first bite of the French toast and shut his eyes in delight. "Mmmm. My dear, this is wonderful. We should have this more often."

"Well, the first maple syrup of the season just arrived in town.[17] It's a springtime luxury."

James mopped up his last bite of French toast with the remaining drops of maple syrup. "What's the latest on the Free Produce movement? Any progress?"

"I'm afraid it has gained little support outside our little circle. Not even everyone from PFASS adheres to it. With summer around the corner, we will switch to linen, which is more expensive. And people are addicted to their sweets."

"Pity. A grand idea, but perhaps its time has not yet come."

"I remain resolute."

"That, my dear, is why I fell in love with thee."

· · · · · · · · · · · · · · · · · · · ·

· OTTO ·

Otto sat at his desk in the Krieger Coach's office, his face in his hands. Aaron leaned against his own desk, waiting for Otto to say something. Jules had joined them. The sense of gloom in the room was almost palpable.

Since their optimistic beginnings during the previous summer, the Krieger enterprises had stumbled badly. A monster November snowstorm had halted construction on the new factories. A harsh winter followed the early snow and kept the carpenters away until last week. Only one of the three buildings was yet under roof.

In their unrealistic plans of August, the factories would have been up and running by now.

---

16. The acronym for the Philadelphia Female Anti-Slavery Society, pronounced pea-fass.

17. European settlers first learned how to make maple syrup from the local Indian tribes. Sap from the ubiquitous maple trees was boiled down to make this sweet confection. As the sap ran only in the springtime, Americans could enjoy this luxury only when the weather turned warm during the day and fell below freezing at night.

Ironically, had the weather not been a factor, the project still would be far behind schedule, and the culprits were the two Krieger brothers. Both Otto and Adrian, brilliant at their respective crafts, were mystified by the tasks of growing their small shops into the modern factories of their dreams.

The three buildings were naught but huge rectangular shells. No interior walls had yet been put on paper, much less erected. Architect William Strickland had not yet designed the interiors of the Krieger Coach or Krieger Locomotive buildings because he was impatiently awaiting input from the Krieger brothers.

Aaron finally lost his patience and broke the lengthy silence. "Otto, this is a big day for us. Shippen has been demanding a progress report from us for weeks now, and we've been stalling him off. We're dead if he doesn't come through with a second loan. Then we meet Strickland at the job site. Today we fish or cut bait. You must either make these construction decisions or find the person who can."

Otto tossed his pencil onto his desk. "Aaron, I just do not have the time. My business trips have been important. I have to keep new orders coming in. The only way to do that is to meet with customers. In the little time I have leftover, I have been designing the new railroad coaches. It does not do Krieger Coach any good to have a factory if we do not have something to produce."

"Otto, I've seen your plans. You are a brilliant designer and a hell of a salesman. Between your long lunches at the United States Hotel and your trips away, you've launched us into the best year Krieger Coach has ever had. Our horse-drawn carriages are what's keeping us afloat. You don't have to be the one to make the decisions about the factory, but you must find the person who can."

"But how do you create a space for something that has never been done before? We are talking about building rolling stock on a scale with no precedent."

"I don't know how you do that. I'm busy making decisions for Krieger Rail. But at least my cousin has finished his design for the furnaces to make the rails. The artisans arrive next week to start building them. And that's even before the roof is completed, which is a huge risk."

"What about Adrian? He can make the decisions for both buildings."

"Adrian has his own problems. His guy has created a brilliant design for a locomotive, but the labor costs to build it will be huge. Unless he can figure out how to get his costs down, he will not sell a single locomotive."

Otto turned his attention to the third person in the room, who had been silent up to now. "What about you, Jules? You make Krieger Coach run like a clock."

Jules smiled. "Thanks for the compliment. I think I'm pretty good with the men on the floor. I can even anticipate the raw materials we'll need in enough time to keep things moving. I could probably do it, but I'd need a partner."

Aaron opened his arms wide, palms facing up. "And that, Otto, should be you or Adrian, but if you're not the guys to do it, you have to find the person who can be."

Otto put his face back in his hands. "*Scheisse* [Shit]! Okay, okay. I will figure this out. Is the meeting still on for Jules and me at the job site this morning?"

"As far as I know."

"If I do not go, I will find the person who can. Damn it. Do we have any good news?"

"Sure. A lot of it. You've been selling carriages at a record rate. So, if we hadn't decided to go into the railroad business, we'd be sitting pretty now."

"Glad to hear I am doing something right," Otto said, grateful for that bit of recognition.

Aaron ignored him. "As far as the railroad business goes, I've got letters of inquiry on my desk from outfits all over the country and even a few internationally. They're looking for engines, carriages, and track. And that's before we've done anything to get the word out. This is strictly by word of mouth. Railroads are starting up all over the world. Older railroads are extending their reach and building spurs. Many who have been in business for a while are adding a second track set. Mines are ditching their horses and converting to locomotives to do the work. It seems like the world is waiting for the three Krieger enterprises to start making something. All we need now are three fricking factories and products the railroads can afford."

Otto sat up a little straighter in his chair. "Anything else?"

"Did you hear about Heinrich's new engine?"

"The one that is going to drive the machinery in the factory? What about it?"

"He ran it for the first time on Thursday. Very successful. The thing's a monster. Of course, it isn't hooked up to anything yet, but it'll be able to drive every machine in Krieger Coach when it is. That is if someone ever figures out what the machines are supposed to be."

"That is wonderful. Anything else?"

"Well, yes, I guess if you count tragedy as good news."

"What do you mean?"

"Two boilers made by Olsen Locomotive exploded in the past few months. Killed a couple of civilians each. The accidents got a lot of press. The newspapers don't seem to mind so much when it's a railroad man who dies, but it's news when it's passengers. Olsen's stock is way down, and they may go out of business. If Krieger Locomotive were there to pick up the pieces, it would be a great way to start."

"Is that it?"

"No. There's more. There was another snakehead[18] accident last week. This one was more violent than usual. Took one man's head off. Never touched the guy sitting next to him. Injured a bunch of others."

"Why is that good news for us?"

"Krieger Rail is never going to make strap-iron rails. Ours will be shaped like an inverted T or perhaps an L. My cousin hopes to have his tests done in a couple of weeks, then he'll decide."

"Well, at least I am not the only one who has a few big decisions to make."

•   •   •   •   •   •   •   •   •   •   •   •   •   •   •   •   •

· SEAMUS ·

Seamus Gallagher leaned over a set of plans for a new landau but wasn't studying them. Instead, he was lost in thought.

Jules walked up to the desk. "Ernst said you were looking for me."

Seamus straightened, put his hands on his lower back, and arched. "Aye. Perfect timing. When I left ditch digging, I thought me days with a sore back were behind me. Leaning over these plans all day makes me ache in a whole new way."

Seamus was only complaining for effect. He had been a faithful employee at Krieger Coach for almost nine months and was grateful that Otto had taken a chance on him. The work was not as physically demanding as it was mentally, but Jules was an excellent—and patient—instructor. Jules had increased Seamus's responsibilities as his competence grew, and he had already received a pay raise.

The winter weather had been bitter, and he was grateful he was no longer freezing his ass off digging ditches. All winter long, he had been warmer during

---

18. The penny papers loved to report about snakeheads because they were so violent, and their destruction was so random. Most railroads in America ran on strap-iron track: flat strap-iron screwed to the side of thick boards. Over time, the heavy locomotives tended to weaken the seams between the wood and the strap-iron. If the worn rails weren't replaced, when a piece of strap-iron separated from the wood the weight of the engine bowed it upward like a spring. The loose end often penetrated the floor of the wooden carriages. It would flop around like a snake.

the workday than in his flat. Happily, even his home was warmer now that he could afford enough coal so his Mum could keep the stove running all day.

Seamus was benefitting from successes outside the shop as well. His talent for theft on the wharves was proving to be more and more lucrative. He was augmenting the steady income from Krieger Coach by "moonlighting" on the docks with his few remaining Irish friends. But not very many people knew about that.

"What's on your mind?" prompted Jules.

"I see three new carriages in the queue already this month. I can tell you right now we're gonna lose too much time because of the bottlenecks in your system."

Jules folded his arms. "What do you mean, bottlenecks?"

"Tasks that slow us down. Let's take the wheels, for example. We turn the wheel hubs on that lathe—the only one big enough to turn a hub, mind you—but make only four hubs at a time before we dismantle the lathe 'til the next order comes in. Maybe we do a fifth one just in case you're not happy with one of them. But taking down and setting up the lathe takes one of the boys half a day. That's a bottleneck. Instead, we should crank out a bunch of hubs, like sixty of them. They're the same size whether it's a cabriolet or a landau, front wheel or back. It makes no difference. The rate the orders are coming in, we'll go through them in a month."

Jules cracked the slightest of smiles. "What else?"

"We steam six or eight hoop sticks for the canopy of a landau, then bend them, then hang them over in a corner somewhere. Firing up the steam generator takes a lot of time, same as the lathe. If we've got it going, let's make a bunch of hoop sticks. Also, when it comes time to put a finish on them—after we've taken half an hour to find them—we have to choose a time when there's no activity going on in the shop that kicks up dust, which around here is never. That's a huge bottleneck."

"How would you solve that bottleneck?"

"I'd build two walls right over there in that corner. Build them tight so's no sawdust can get in. A double door so's you can wheel in an entire carriage. That would be a room used for nothing but varnishing so we could put a finish on anything, large or small, whilst the usual mayhem continues out here."

"Anything else?"

Seamus was just warming to his subject. "How much time do you have?"

"Wait right here." Jules disappeared into the office and was gone for a long while.

Careful there, Boyo. Bosses don't like to be told how to do their job better. Certain that he'd overstepped his place, he thought it possible the next person out of the office would be Uncle Otto to tell him things weren't working out, and he should collect his pay.

When Jules reappeared, he had a slight smile on his face. "Otto thought you might want to visit the new factories. Interested?"

Now, this is unexpected. Seamus knew the new factories, nine blocks to the north, were far from complete. Work had been halted for four months by the weather. With an early thaw and spring around the corner, carpenters had recently come back to work. Otto, Adrian, Aaron, or Jules made daily visits to the construction site.

Even though there was a ton of work to do in the shop, the idea of getting out on company time had appeal. *They haven't asked any of the other workers on the shop floor to go to the construction site.* "Sure. A walk would feel good for me back."

"No walking this time, I'm afraid. I've already hooked a team up to the cabriolet the crew just finished. I need to check it out before we deliver it tomorrow anyway."

Seamus froze. That cabriolet had one seat for two people. "That's okay; I need the exercise."

"I'm pressed for time. Plus, I want to talk to you along the way."

"What about me uncles?"

"Otto has a meeting with the banker first. He'll meet us there. Adrian says he's not leaving his office 'til he cracks some nut he's working on."

"I'd rather walk."

"What's the matter, Seamus? Afraid of sitting next to a Black man?"

It seemed like Jules could read his mind. *Why does it have to be the cabriolet?* If it had been a landau, Jules could have driven and Seamus could have ridden in the back. Half the coachmen in Philadelphia were Black, so no one would have given them a second look.

"Of course I'm not afraid, but Black folks sitting next to white folks—it just ain't done."

Jules seemed unperturbed. "It can be done because we're going to do it. You and me."

"But what'll people think?"

Jules seemed to be enjoying Seamus's discomfort. "Hopefully, they'll think we're heading off to inspect the new Krieger factories."

"Who drives?" *At least if I'm driving, it looks like I'm running the show.*

"Seamus, have you ever driven a team before?"

"No, but how hard can it be?"

"I'll tell you what: I'll drive up and teach you what you need to know. Then you can drive back."

With that, Seamus crossed an emotional and moral threshold. He had already been taking orders from this Black man for nine months. Jules had treated him fairly and with respect. He had recognized Seamus's increasing skills and rewarded him with more pay and responsibilities. "I hope Philadelphia's ready for this."

Jules abruptly turned and started walking toward the carriage. "I don't know about Philadelphia, but I think it's long overdue."

. . . .

With the slightest slap of the reins and a kissing sound, Jules encouraged the mare forward, and the cabriolet turned the corner onto Twelfth Street. "Pay attention, Seamus, because you're driving on the way back."

Seamus was more concerned about what people on the street would think about him sitting next to a Black man. However, he soon concluded that most people were too busy thinking about their own lives to pay attention to who was riding in a carriage. Sure, they got some stares, but most people didn't notice. "Why'd you invite me on this trip, Jules?"

"Isn't it obvious? Krieger Coach is about to move into a much larger shop. Although we're still going to make carriages, we hope that most of our business will be building railroad coaches within a year. We need to make them well, and we need to make them cheaper than anyone else."

"How are you going to do it?"

"Otto has a great eye for design. He's got a plan on the drawing board that will be a leap ahead of anything that you've ever ridden on."

"Well, that would be anything because I've never been on a train before."

Undistracted, Jules continued. "He's also got ideas for the next generation after that, once Krieger Locomotive invents more powerful steam engines that can pull heavier loads. Like the omnibuses you see on Walnut Street but built to ride on tracks."

"I still don't get why I'm going to visit the factories."

"Otto doesn't think much about production. That's always been my job. And I'm pretty good at keeping the workers moving, but today you demonstrated that you have a better feel for how production flows than I do. That's why you're coming with me today."

"What am I gonna do?"

"Seamus, wait 'til you see the shops. They're huge. But right now, they're just big empty shells with no thought about what goes where. What if we build that varnish room, so the rest of the shop doesn't have to shut down while we paint the coaches? What if we create a space for the lathe or the steam chamber to be set up permanently? What if the entire shop is configured so that all the work flows in an orderly fashion?"

"You're telling me that Uncle Otto hasn't already figured this stuff out?"

"I'm telling you that you have a better feel for how production flows than both Otto and me put together. We want your head in the planning process, starting right now. Think about where the goods will come in, what needs to happen to them next, and next, and next after that. And where the finished carriages—or the train coaches—get rolled out."

Seamus was incredulous. "You want me to help you design the inside of Krieger Coach?"

"Nope. Not help. I want us to work on it together. But you won't work for me anymore. As of today, and until all the production kinks are worked out, you're Krieger's production designer."

"I never heard of anyone being a production designer."

"That's because Otto and I just made it up. Today we'll introduce you to William Strickland, the architect who designed the buildings."

This news dumbfounded Seamus. "Wait'll I tell me mum. She's still amazed I'm not digging ditches."

After a lengthy silence, Seamus's curiosity got the better of him. "Jules, can I ask you a personal question?"

"You can ask. I might not answer."

"This Strickland fellow. The architect. How's he feel about meeting with a Black man?"

Jules didn't seem very perturbed by the question. "I guess you'd have to ask him. But what I think you're asking is 'How does a Black man get to meet with an important person like William Strickland?'"

"Aye. That's me question."

"I'm not sure. I think that's probably because your uncle knew he wasn't going to be able to answer Strickland's questions but hoped I might have some ideas. I started going up with Otto, Adrian, and Aaron to early meetings with Strickland. From the very beginning, the three of them asked me for my opinions. I guess Strickland took his cues from them."

"How did you do?"

"I guess well enough to get invited to the next meeting. To be honest, Strickland's pretty frustrated. He's been waiting for decisions from us for months. Right now, I think he'd be happy to work with someone from Mars if they could get this project moving. Last week was my first meeting with him without one of the others. I think it went pretty well. Truth be told, I think I'm better in the shop than at this job. I'm happy you're going along with me."

Seamus let this information sink in. Jules's candor was unexpected. His willingness to give Seamus a shot at this job was very flattering. Surprisingly, Seamus wasn't very intimidated by the task. "Me. Seamus Gallagher. In a business meeting. Who woulda thunk it?"

By this time, Jules had steered the mare onto James Street, and the new factories' tall outlines loomed a block ahead. The carpenters had rigged up a scaffold and winch to hoist up a massive truss that spanned from wall to wall. An army of carpenters started trueing it up and securing it to the walls as it settled into place.

Seamus was just starting to marvel at it all when he noticed a crew of ditch diggers working on a gas line trench that led to the new shops. His old friend Dylan worked at the front of the line with a pick. Seamus hadn't had much to do with him since being rejected by the Moyamensing Hose Company.

The crew, including Dylan, stopped work to watch the carriage approach, with Seamus and Jules sitting next to one another. Jules noticed the noticers. "Want to take the reins, Seamus?"

Seamus thought about it for only a second. "No. I'm good. But thanks, Jules."

· · · · · · · · · · · · · · · · · · · ·

· ADRIAN ·

Adrian Krieger was in a quandary, almost to the point of panic. For the past twenty minutes, he had stared at the object sitting next to his desk.

Four months ago, Heinrich Aldrich, the machinist whom he had hired away from Baldwin Locomotive, had unveiled the steam engine that was going to drive the first generation of Krieger locomotives. The engine was a thing of beauty. This one-quarter-sized prototype did everything Heinrich had said it would and was more powerful than Heinrich had predicted.

After Heinrich proved this petite, working steam engine was viable, Adrian had it placed next to his desk for inspiration. Instead, it frustrated him daily.

Nine months ago, he had rashly predicted that Krieger Forge would become Krieger Locomotive and manufacture more innovative and less expensive engines than anything produced in the world. Surprisingly, innovation had come readily. Heinrich's machine was a leap ahead of any steam engine ever created. However, it was going to cost a bundle to build. Try as he might, Adrian could not get the cost of the engine down to a reasonable price. Krieger Locomotive was going to fail before it even opened its doors.

There were two problems, as Adrian saw it. First, a steam engine was a complex machine with hundreds of parts. Each part had to be milled by hand and custom fit to the component next to it. This was a laborious process that took the time and patience of skilled craftsmen. The second problem was the scarcity of the craftsmen that Krieger Locomotive would need. Philadelphia had become a manufacturing town, and skilled workers were in high demand. Training fifteen or twenty workers to build a steam engine would take years.

In the months that the prototype had been sitting next to his desk, Adrian had made no progress on either problem. He was about to call a meeting with his brother and Aaron Bassinger and admit defeat.

His niece Rian entered his office with her friends Conor McGuire and Trey Shippen. The three of them had been thick as peas in a pod since Conor returned from his voyage to Hamburg last year. Adrian looked up from his desk and noticed that Trey held something behind him. "Happy birthday, Rian. How old are you today, anyway?" Rian didn't seem to be her usual smiley self, but Adrian ignored it.

"Twelve. Uncle Adrian, we need your help."

"I'm a little busy right now, Rian. How about asking Jules?"

"I tried. He and Seamus just left for a meeting at the new shops."

With a sigh, Adrian put down his pencil. "I've got five minutes. What's going on?"

Rian looked distressed. "We did something we weren't supposed to do, and now we can't put it back together, and Trey's father is going to kill us."

Despite her youth, Adrian had always found Rian to be a very cogent child. The random way she blurted out this information got Adrian's attention more than the "going to kill us" part. "Hopefully, it's not going to go that far. What's the problem?"

Trey held out a polished walnut box about twenty inches long and twelve inches wide. He put the box on Adrian's desk. "It's my father's dueling pistols."

Adrian carefully opened the lid to the box to find a jumble of parts in disarray. "What happened here?"

"It was a surprise for Rian's birthday. I wanted to do something special. I borrowed my father's pistols so we could have a duel."

"Borrowed?" interjected Adrian.

"Well, Father doesn't know I borrowed them. We were going to have a duel—you know, a pretend duel. But if you're going to have a duel, you need to have seconds, and Thomas Mott wouldn't have anything to do with guns, even though we were just playing."

"I would say your Quaker friend made a good decision."

"So, without a second, we couldn't have a duel. Instead, we decided to take the pistols apart. When my father shows the pistols to his friends, he always tells them that the parts are interchangeable. Well, I guess they are, but now we can't figure out how to get them back together again. Can you help us out?"

Adrian didn't own a pistol, and he certainly had never taken one apart. But with his machinist's eye, he could tell an object of quality when he saw it. He picked up two oily pieces of steel that appeared to be part of a trigger mechanism and put them next to each other. They were exactly the same.

"Idiot!" Adrian yelled as he jumped up from his desk. "Idiot! Interchangeable parts! Interchangeable parts! Heinrich! Heinrich!"

The three children had taken a step back, probably fearing this lunatic. Adrian calmed down only slightly. "Trey, your father's not going to kill you. I'll put the pistols back together, but I want to look at them for a bit first. Can I have them for a few hours?"

The kids readily agreed and scooted out of the madman's office. Adrian shut the lid of the box and scooped it up.

Heinrich Aldrich warily entered Adrian's office.

"Heinrich, all this time, I've been assuming that one or two craftsmen would build an entire steam engine. That was all wrong. What if we set up workstations? What if we have to teach each man how to do only one task but do that task precisely and quickly? Grab your coat. We're heading to the new shops."

. . . .

· SEAMUS ·

Seamus sat at the bar in McSweeney's Saloon, the only patron of the establishment. For the past half hour, he had been telling McSweeney about his new responsibilities at Krieger Coach. Then his friend Dylan sauntered in. Seamus immediately cut off his conversation and buried his nose in the *Philadelphia*

Independent. Just great. I go a month without seeing him, and now it's twice in one day.

Seamus signaled to McSweeney to set the newcomer up with a drink. Dylan slid onto the stool next to him, but Seamus didn't look up from his penny paper. "Lombard Street's a bit out of your territory, ain't it? What're you doing here, Boyo?"

"Looking for you. You don't come around Clancy's anymore."

Seamus kept his eyes on his paper. "Clancy's might as well be the Moya office." Seamus now viewed Moya as a fork in the road that he never got to take. "I didn't feel very welcome after I got shut out."

Dylan lived with the silence for a bit. "What're you reading?"

"Remember Harold Foote? That reporter some of your boys roughed up last year? He's down in Mexico writing about a little dustup that happened last week."

"I heard about that. Turns out Hugh Callaghan's cousin was there. He got killed."

"Tell Hugh I'm sorry for his loss."

"Yeah, about that . . . A few of the boys and me, we're on Hugh's shyte list."

Seamus still kept his nose in the paper. "Hmm."

More silence.

"Seamus, people are talking about you."

"I hope it's all nice things."

"I guess it's mixed. It depends on who's doing the talking. We saw you hanging with the African today, acting all buddy-buddy."

"Fook you, Dylan," Seamus said without much emphasis, making it clear he didn't want to hear more of that kind of talk. "Jules is a good boss. He treats me well. He deserves the same."

Dylan got the message. "Word around Moya is you're forming a new fire company."

'What's it to you?"

"We heard you've recruited a couple of the other boys who didn't get into Moya. Who weren't so keen on beating on the Africans."

"That might be part of it. Mainly, I think the neighborhood needs another hose company, that's all."

"Yeah, okay. That and swiping cargo off the Walnut Street Pier."

Seamus was only mildly surprised that word of the group's latest caper had already gotten back to Moya. "Not me fault the pier is poorly tended at night. I just use the opportunities the good Lord makes available, that's all."

"We also heard you're looking for a pump."

"Wouldn't be much of a hose company without a pump, now would we."

"I might have a lead for you."

Seamus's eyes left the paper for the first time, and he turned toward his friend. "Keep talking."

"Me cousin was visiting from New York last week. He was telling stories. He belongs to a fire company there. They get involved with the same shenanigans that we do—fighting the other hose companies. Muscling into each other's territory. Occasionally putting out an actual fire."

Seamus tossed the paper on the bar. "So what?"

"Well, they also steal each other's pumps. They're doing quite well in that regard. They've got four pumps sitting in a warehouse that they've usurped from the competition."

"That doesn't do me any good. I can't afford to buy a pump."

"Listen to me. That's me point. You can get one of them for free. They're certain the machines are gonna get stolen back sooner or later—right out of their warehouse. They don't want to burn them. They've got too much respect for the machinery for that. They're selling three of them. Well, they're ransoming one of them back to the company they wrestled it from. But the last one is a wee bit beat up. They're looking to give it away, but they want it out of town. All you've got to do is go and get it. I've already broached the subject with me cousin. He said he'd talk to his president."

"So, all I gotta do is get it here? That's still gonna cost me a pretty penny. Where am I gonna get that kind of money?"

"You're a bright guy, Seamus. You'll figure something out. You always do."

"Why're you telling me all this, Boyo? How's this help Moya?"

"Well, that's Part 2 of what I'm getting at. Me and a couple of the boys aren't thrilled with the way things is going right now. Truth be told, Callaghan ain't very high on us, neither. Kind of ironic since we scrambled so hard to get in."

Seamus ignored the thought that Dylan understood the concept of irony. "So?"

"Callaghan gets a special joy out of tormenting the Africans. More than some of us is comfortable with. We're looking to get out."

Seamus smiled. "You never liked busting heads anyway. Your pals the same way?"

"Naw, some of them are happy to scrap it up a bit. They don't especially mind going after Africans if there's a reason. But they don't like beating up the innocents."

"How many?"

"Me and three others. Collins and the two Fitzpatrick brothers."

"Kind of young, aren't they?"

Dylan shrugged. "They're seventeen and eighteen. Just a couple of years younger than us. Another year or so, we'll probably get Angus."

"Ain't this a wonderment. And I've got five counting me. That would mean nine. I think that's enough to declare ourselves an actual organization. Hugh Callaghan ain't gonna like it; you boys deserting Moya like this."

"Well, not so much as you might think. Last week he gave the four of us an ultimatum: start busting African heads or get out."

"Hmm, that one's gonna blow up in his face."

"Moya'll survive. There're plenty of lads looking to get in."

"Still, seems you should tell him you're getting out before you tell him you're going with me."

"Aye. That part's gonna be a bit ugly. I think Callaghan's already got you in his sights. He wasn't pleased when some of the boys came back empty-handed from the Walnut Street Pier the other night. He doesn't like it when folks muscle in on Moya territory."

Seamus broke the hint of a smile. "We expect he'll try to put us in our place soon enough. We'll be waiting for him."

"You got a name yet?"

"For my group? Yeah, I guess I do. How's the No Name Fire Brigade sound?"

· · · · · · · · · · · · · · · · · · · ·

· RIAN ·

Conor stopped walking when he and Rian arrived at the Assembly Building. A broadside tacked to the display board in front said:

One night only
The magic and wonder of
World Famous
Signor Antonio Blitz

50¢

"Happy birthday," said Conor.

"I thought my birthday present was a duel."

"Well, that was mostly Trey's present. I want us to see this guy. My brother Mikey saw him the other night, and he said he was amazing."

"Do you have a buck to get us in?"

"Uh-uh, but Mikey told me how we can sneak in."

Conor led Rian around the corner of the building into an alley, where someone had propped a door ajar. "Even on a cool night like this, all the bodies in the hall can make it pretty hot in there. They leave this door open for ventilation."

Conor led Rian through the door. Before they had a moment to get oriented, a male voice to their right called out, "Hey, you two, turn right around and go out the way you came in. Pay admission just like everyone else."

"Run!" whispered Conor.

Without thinking further, Rian ran away from the voice toward the stage.

"Hey, stop those two!"

Rian dodged around people looking for their seats and a woman selling popped corn out of a picnic basket. No one tried to stop her. When she reached the stage, she looked fleetingly behind her. Conor beamed back at her, his face a mixture of excitement and glee.

"Other side," he said.

Walking as if they both belonged in the theatre, Rian and Conor crossed the hall in front of the stage, skirted around a three-man band, and slid into the two right-hand-most front row seats. Rian eyed the rich purple stage curtain. She could tell that their line of sight would be terrible when it was raised. *Nuts. No wonder nobody was sitting here. We won't be able to see a thing.*

Conor craned his neck to the rear of the auditorium. "Do you see the guy who was after us?"

Rian looked to the left, along the front of the stage. A burly man in vest and cravat but no jacket dodged around people and headed purposefully toward them. "Yeah, and he's coming our way. We've got to go." Rian waited until another popped corn vendor momentarily obscured the man's view, then shot out of her seat and ran into a hallway that flanked the stage.

"Rian, what are you doing?" Conor whispered as he ran after her. "That's the wrong way."

Rian leaped a set of six steps two at a time. "Making it up as I go along," she said as she found herself in the stage's wing. She eyed a scaffold that overlooked the performance area, the purple curtain now between them and the audience. "Come on," she said as she started climbing.

"Rian, we're going to get caught. We'll be trapped."

"It's dark up here. No one will ever see us."

Rian and Conor climbed the scaffold until they were engulfed in shadows at the top, about fifteen feet above the stage. They dangled their feet over the edge, confident that no one below could see them in the darkness.

Conor elbowed Rian and pointed down. The man in the vest was standing at the base of the scaffold. Conor put his finger to his lips in a *shhh* gesture, but Rian could also make out a big grin. "Best birthday present ever," she whispered in his ear. She again peered down at the man from the darkness. She could see him but knew he couldn't see her.

A stagehand started lighting candles on a candelabra lowered by rope and pulley next to the curtain. Rian counted sixty candles. The more candles he lit, the more light found its way to the top of the scaffold. Conor again nudged Rian and changed his position to sit cross-legged so that his legs no longer dangled over the edge. Rian did the same, except that the scaffold moved ever so slightly when she shifted her weight.

The man in the vest detected the motion and looked up. It was still dark enough that Rian assumed the man couldn't see them, but she suspected that soon she would not be able to look down at him with impunity.

The stagehand finished lighting the candles and walked to the other side of the stage. He and another man hoisted the candelabra, so it lit up the stage but, to Rian's horror, also threw light on Rian and Conor.

The stagehand crossed to their side of the stage. With an exaggerated count of 1-2-3, both men pulled on ropes. The curtain parted. The band started playing. From the opposite side of the stage, Signor Antonio Blitz, a man heralded as the finest magician in the country, walked out to loud applause. He was carrying a stack of white china plates.

Without saying a word, he placed the plates on a table in the middle of the stage. He picked up one plate with both hands, tossed it—spinning—six feet in the air, and caught it on the tip of his finger. The tempo of the music sped up. Blitz transferred the spinning plate from the tip of his finger to the end of a bamboo pole. He tossed the plate aloft and caught it on the pole again. The audience applauded. He tossed it and caught it on another pole. The audience oohed and clapped. Blitz stuck the pole in a hole in the table. The plate continued to spin. He positioned another pole in the stand next to the first one and started a second plate spinning. Then a third, and a fourth. The first plate started wobbling to the point that it was moments away from falling off the pole and breaking. The audience became agitated and started calling his attention to the plate. Blitz feigned obliviousness, took out his pocket watch, and checked the time, never looking at the plate. At the last second, he turned, grabbed the middle of the pole, gave it a few quick circular motions, and started the plate spinning merrily again. The audience loved it. They clapped and they whooped.

Rian and Conor were entranced by the act but couldn't clap and whoop for fear of discovery. Rian peered over the edge to check on the man in the vest. He was still there.

In just a few minutes, Blitz had nine plates spinning steadily. He extended his arms wide, and the band punctuated the gesture with a thunderous TA-DA. Blitz rescued the spinning plates by popping them off the poles, catching them, and stacking them onto the table. He bowed. The audience screamed their approval.

"Good evening, ladies and gentlemen. My name is Signor Antonio Blitz. I have been performing on both sides of the Atlantic Ocean since I was thirteen years old. I have learned a lot from men much more adept than I. Magic is a craft, just like cutting a priceless diamond. And just as a fine diamond reflects light to give the illusion of fire, so do I."

Blitz extended his right arm, and suddenly a sparkly diamond about the size of an orange appeared in his hand. The audience oohed. "But I will let you in on a little secret. Fundamental to the craft of magic is misdirection. A good magician will attract your attention to his right—" Blitz twitched his right hand to make the diamond disappear, and again to make it reappear "—to distract you from what is really going on to his left." He pulled his left hand from behind his back and displayed a bouquet of flowers. The audience applauded. "So, my friends, I warn you, when you think I'm trying to distract you—" He held the bouquet aloft "—check out what my other hand is doing. You might learn something about the craft of magic." Rian was still looking at the bouquet when the audience applauded again. In Blitz's right hand, where moments before he had held a diamond, now there was a lit candle.

Rian concluded that she and Conor had the best seats in the house. Although she didn't know how Blitz did the trick with the diamond, bouquet, and candle, she occasionally could see behind his back, and she was confident she would learn how he pulled off his tricks.

Then the scaffold shook. Rian looked down. The man with the vest was climbing toward them.

Rian and Conor both stood up. The scaffold shook even more as the man got closer. They scrambled to the other side of the scaffold and half climbed, half slid down the side. They reached the stage before the man could reverse direction, only to find that another man blocked their escape route to the stairs.

"C'mon. This way," said Rian. She ran across the lit stage, behind Signor Antonio Blitz, and to the opposite wing, Conor following right behind her. And behind Conor ran the man in the vest and his confederate.

The audience erupted with glee and consternation. Blitz, the consummate professional, didn't miss a beat. "And while you were being distracted by my two young friends, you allowed me to do this." The audience clapped and stomped their joyous approval.

Rian never learned what "this" was, but clearly, Blitz altered his act just enough to make it seem like the interlopers were merely one more misdirection ploy.

Rian and Conor flew out the stage door, ran back up the alley, careened onto the street, and ran another block before they assured themselves their pursuers had given up the chase.

"Happy birthday again," said Conor, as he held out Blitz's bouquet.

Monday, March 28

· SEAMUS ·

Two days later, Seamus entered the Krieger shops with a plan. He wasn't sure whether it was brilliant or his stupidest idea ever. Carrying out his plan would mean turning his back on many of his own kind and making an alliance that he had never heard of anyone doing before. Just the thought of going through with it put him on the verge of throwing up.

As he was walking through the shop, he saw three workers on a task, but in his haste to talk with Jules, he didn't stop to investigate.

As usual, Jules was standing at his shop desk when Seamus approached him. "What're those three ispinis doing?"

"Building your new desk. I figured if you're going to take your new job seriously, you'll need a proper desk. It'll be a standing desk, like this one. No more complaining about your back. We can move it over to the new shop as soon as it's under roof."

Jules's gesture threw Seamus off guard. The meeting with William Strickland and Jules had gone extremely well. With Seamus's fresh energy and insight, the trio had broken the three-month logjam of decisions. They had developed a shared vision for how the Krieger Coach factory would become a modern manufacturing facility. Then Uncle Otto arrived with the news that the Bank of Industry had okayed an additional loan.

Right after that, Adrian and Heinrich Aldrich unexpectedly showed up, and the group did a walk-through of the future Krieger Locomotive building. Seamus's ideas about permanent workstations fit neatly with Adrian's new ideas about interchangeable parts. Seamus was surprised at how often the five others asked for his opinion. Before they left, the group had decided that Heinrich would design and install two more stationary steam engines, so there would be one in each of the three buildings.

However, after Saturday night's conversation with Dylan at McSweeney's, Seamus had barely thought about his promotion or the many tasks ahead of him at the Krieger enterprises. Instead, he had been distracted by the problem of transporting the fire pump from New York City to Philadelphia for the No Name Fire Brigade. Seamus felt as though his head was about to explode. Two worlds were calling him. During the day, he was going to solve problems for the Kriegers. During the evenings, he was consorting with his kind and solving problems of a different sort.

Seamus yanked himself back to the present. "Thank you, Jules. I've never had me own desk. That's very kind of you. It was a good meeting, wasn't it? Jules, I've got a question for you. What do folks in your neighborhood do when a house catches fire?"

Jules looked Seamus right in the eye, clearly mystified by the change of topics. "Not much we can do. The Moyamensing Hose Company would never help us out. Hell, they're probably the ones who started the fire. So, people just form a bucket brigade. There are buckets hanging at the front door of almost every house just for that purpose. Young or old. Man or woman. Doesn't matter. We run to a well down the street. Do the best we can. Why?"

"What if I start a new fire company. One that will help to put out your fires."

Jules tossed his pencil onto his standing desk. "With all that we've got going on here, you want to start a fire company? And why're you interested in putting out Black folks' fires?"

"We wouldn't be there just to put out Black folks' fires. It would be anyone in the area. I think Moya needs some competition."

Jules hesitated for a bit. "I heard you got shut out of Moya."

"I did because of that ruckus in your neighborhood last August. I was stupid enough to try to stop it. The boys at Moya didn't like that. So, I didn't get in."

"So, this is payback?"

"In a manner of speaking. I've got some other irons in the fire as well."

Jules folded his arms in front of him. "So, where are you going with this?"

"There's a pump in New York City. I can get the pump, but I need to bring it here. Most likely on the *Camden & Amboy*."

"You want the Black community to front you the money to get this pump here?"

Seamus swallowed hard. "No, not front. Give."

Jules rubbed his forehead, clearly thinking. "Seamus, nothing like this has ever been done before. We're better off keeping to ourselves. We've been burned too many times."

"Jules, just yesterday, you told me something could be done because we were going to do it. Whatsamatter? Afraid to trust a Hibernian?"

Jules was quiet for a few long moments. "I might have some ideas. Let me get back to you. Meanwhile, do you want this desk or not?"

• •

· JULES ·

At home that evening, Jules explained Seamus's proposal to Maddie. She was much more enthusiastic about it than he was. "Jules, this is an opportunity. How many times have the Irish reached out to the Black community?"

"None that I know of. But this isn't 'The Irish.' This is an Irish kid with a couple of friends who want to start a fire company."

"You said yourself that he's a capable young man."

"Very capable. Surprisingly so. But he's only twenty. He lacks focus. The Kriegers are giving him a ton of responsibilities at work. He could really make something of himself. But here he is, choosing instead to get involved in things that have a pretty unsavory reputation."

"He went out on a limb for us before when he brought Rufus home."

"Actually, I learned today that he also went against his kind last summer when that Irish mob burned the two houses down the street."

"What more do you need to know? His heart is in the right place. Let's help him."

"We don't have that kind of money. I was thinking about asking Robert Purvis."

"I think that's a perfect idea. But don't ask Robert for his money. Ask him for his advice. The money will follow."

• •

Harriet Forte Purvis escorted Jules into Robert's study. "Well, I'll leave you two men to your important discussions. Jules, it's good to see you after such a long time. Please give my best to Maddie."

"Oh, I will. She enjoys working with you and Mrs. Mott at PFASS."

Harriet sighed. "Our progress at the Anti-Slavery Society is incremental. But it is a worthy pursuit. I am undeterred by occasional setbacks."

"As is Maddie. Thank you for all your work on our behalf."

Robert Purvis unfolded his lanky frame from his overstuffed chair and rose to shake Jules's hand. "Jules, it's been far too long."

"I haven't seen you since you returned from England, Robert. How did your trip go?"

"Mixed, to be honest. I got a great reception from the abolitionist societies when I spoke about our efforts here. They are very supportive. A bit skeptical about how our wives have become involved. I think they're somewhat stuffy in that regard. Also, while I was there, I was approached by a delegation advocating Irish independence from England. The Brits continue to abuse those people terribly. Many parallels between our people and the Irish. My reception at the abolitionist meetings wasn't quite as warm when I pointed that out to them."

Jules immediately saw his opening. "Do you think there's hope for us and the Irish? Here in Philadelphia?"

"You know me, Jules. I'm always the optimist. Is this what's on your mind? The Irish?"

"Well, actually, it is. I need your advice. A young man has approached me—an Irishman who has been working with me at Krieger Coach for the past nine months. A good lad, as they would say. He wants to start another hose company in Moyamensing. It would give the boys at Moya a bit of competition. He wonders if we'd be interested in having his outfit protect the Black community."

"What'd you tell him?"

"I stalled. I'm honestly ambivalent. We're doing pretty well on our own right now. It seems like when we get too far ahead of ourselves, somebody makes a point of knocking us down." Jules gestured to the expanse of Robert's parlor. "Such a project is just the sort of thing that will call attention to all this."

Purvis hesitated a bit. "Jules, did you know that Philadelphia is the home to the largest population of free Blacks in the country?"

"I had no idea."

"Odd, isn't it. Philadelphia might as well be a southern city. We're butted right up next to Delaware and Maryland, two slave states. There are hundreds of Southerners who come here every summer to get away from the heat of South Carolina and Georgia. We're also the home to thousands of recent Irish immigrants. Blacks and Irish are clinging tight to the bottom rung of the economic ladder, trying to loosen each other's grip. Philadelphia is a powder keg, just waiting to explode."

Jules waited patiently for Robert to continue. Even though Robert was more than ten years younger than Jules, Jules paid deference to his host's wealth.

"We need to form alliances. To reduce the number of sparks in our little powder keg. Do you trust this man? He's only a couple of years younger than I am."

"I think so. It's not him I'm worried about. It's the forces that will be marshaled against all of us when word of such an alliance gets out."

"It sounds like a great idea to me. Why is he interested in helping us? Surely his motives weren't purely for the good of the Black community. What's in it for him?"

"He needs a pump to fight the fires. He's found one in New York City, but he can't afford to get it here."

"That shouldn't cost even a hundred dollars. I can give that to you right now if that'll make it happen."

"I'm sure he would appreciate that immensely. Thank you." Jules got up to leave.

Pervis put his hand up, signaling to Jules that he still wanted to talk. "One more thing before you go. What was your last name before you changed it to Freeman?"

"Taney. I came to Philadelphia still calling myself by my first enslaver's surname. But I changed it soon after I met Maddie." Jules suspected what Purvis was fishing for, "Why?"

"Did you read in the pennies that the Senate has finally confirmed the successor to John Marshall as Chief Justice of the Supreme Court?"

Jules nodded. "Roger B. Taney."

"I note he's originally from Calvert County, Maryland. Same as where you hailed from before you self-emancipated."

Jules shifted uncomfortably. "Roger Taney is my former enslaver's son. He went off to college before I was born."

"Did you ever meet him?"

"I was in his presence a few times. He and his wife lived in Baltimore, so they occasionally visited Taney Place."

"What can you tell me about him?"

"He was always kind to me. I was sold away from the plantation when I was twelve, so I saw him only once after that. I've been watching his career since Andy Jackson appointed him Attorney General in '31. He had a short stint as Secretary of the Treasury. He's no admirer of the National Bank."

"When was the last time you saw him?"

"A few months before I self-emancipated, so 1819. I was in a general store in Adelina. That's the nearest town to Taney Place. I was twenty or so. Roger was buying some supplies. I assume he had come to town to settle up some legal matters. His daddy had killed a man in a knife fight and run away to Virginia to escape prosecution. It was all people were talking about—even the slaves—all over Calvert County. I recognized him, and he recognized me. He asked me how I was doing. That was about the only time anyone from the Taney family ever asked me that question."

"I see he freed his own slaves."

"Yeah, I read that, too."

"Jules, I'm just trying to read the tea leaves here. He was kind to you when you were little. He asked you how you were doing when you saw him in the store. He freed his slaves. Perhaps someday that will work in favor of the Black man if a slave case ever gets to the Supreme Court."

"I doubt it."

"Why do you say that?"

"He never put up a fuss when I was sold. I probably wasn't even twelve years old."

"Why would he care about a slave kid on a plantation that he hadn't lived at for the past fifteen years?"

"Why? Because he's my father."

. . . .

On his way home, Jules shoved aside the unpleasant memories of his child-hood. Instead, he chose to marvel at his wife's words of wisdom. *Want a person's money? Ask for his advice.*

Monday, July 11

· Jules ·

More than three months after his meeting with Robert Purvis, Jules looked around the shop somewhat wistfully. It was uncharacteristically quiet for the tail end of a workday. Some of the workers had already moved up to the new factories and were installing the workstations he and Seamus had designed. Jules knew all too well that his work-life was about to change. Here in the old shop, he was looking at the past. With few exceptions, this shop looked the way a shop would have looked a hundred years ago. All the tools in the old factory were powered by hand or foot.

Part of him looked forward to moving to the new, modern Krieger Coach. And part of him knew he would be giving up some things he cherished.

He walked by Rian as she sharpened a chisel and poked her in the back. "C'mon, I need your help."

Rian dropped what she was doing and followed Jules like a puppy. "What're we doing?"

"I've sent too many people up to help Seamus install machinery. I need to finish a wheel to stay on schedule. Besides, this may be the last time we do this together. It'll be done differently in the new factory."

Jules and Rian had probably made fifty wheels together. More often than not, it became a chance for them to chat.

They walked to a wooden wheel hub sitting on a workbench. One of the workers had previously rimmed the hub in steel on both edges and had bored out the mortises for the spokes. The next task was to fit twelve spokes into the mortises.

"Great," said Rian, as she looked over the job. "This is my favorite part."

Jules was no longer surprised at how competent this wild young pre-woman was. "I'll chisel the tenons, and you hammer them into place." Jules knew from experience that if they'd traded tasks, she still would have done a good job. It would have just taken longer.

They set about their respective tasks. Jules had made so many spokes in his life that he could now chisel a tenon to the right size just by eye. He rarely used a ruler or calipers for anything anymore, although he would have chastised a worker for doing so. "I'm going to miss this, Rian."

"Won't we still be able to do it at the new factory?"

"You might, but my job's going to be different. I'm afraid I'll spend more time in the office than actually doing jobs like this."

"How's Cousin Elmo?"

The abrupt change of topic took him aback. "Who?"

"Your cousin. He was at your house last year when Billy Schiffler hit Rufus with a rock."

Jules worked on his spoke for a few seconds, collecting his thoughts. "I don't know. I haven't heard from him lately."

"He's not really your cousin, is he? He was an escaped slave who you were hiding."

Jules hesitated. *How much about the adult world do I want to expose to this twelve-year-old?* Perhaps he sensed that he was at the end of an era. He would never do this job—one that he could almost do with his eyes closed—quite the same ever again. Or perhaps he and Rian might never again share such a task. "Yes, he was an escaped slave."

"Where is he now?"

"Not sure. Probably Canada."

"Have you helped other escaped slaves?"

I should have known. She's tenacious. "Yes."

"Why do you keep it a secret?"

"Why? Because it's illegal."

"How illegal? Like spitting on the street illegal? Or killing someone illegal?"

Despite the seriousness of the subject, Jules chuckled to himself. "More toward killing someone illegal. It's part of the US Constitution."

"Honest?"

"Honest. Article 4, Section 2, Clause 3. Look it up next time you're at the library. Then in 1793, Congress passed another law that tightened up penalties for people who helped fugitive slaves. I could get thrown in jail for doing it."

Rian concentrated on whacking a spoke into place with a mallet for a minute. She applied stout, precise strokes, wielding the mallet with a surprising amount of strength.

"How did Cousin Elmo find your house? How did he know you are a good guy? That you wouldn't turn him in?"

"There are two men who bring escapees to us. Actually, I don't like the word escapee. I prefer to say they have self-emancipated."

"Freed themselves. I get it. Is that a real term?"

"We use it in our house."

"Who are the guys? The ones who bring them in?"

"Rian, I would love to tell you. But the less you know, the better it is for everyone. That way, if you ever get found out, you can't tell because you don't know. Your father doesn't even know about our activities."

Rian paused for a few moments. Jules suspected she was making sense of knowing a secret that her father didn't know.

"Then where do they go?"

"To the next station."

"What station is that?"

"It's just an expression. Lately, people have been calling what we do the Underground Railroad. Because if we do it right, it's like a self-emancipator gets to Philadelphia and then disappears like they just got on a train and vanished."

"So, you and Maddie operate a station?"

"Mmm-hmm. And the people who bring the self-emancipators to us are conductors."

"When I get older, can I help you out?"

"You are helping me out."

"No, not this. Can I help you get escaped slaves to Canada?"

Jules shook his head in amazement. "Nothing would give me greater pleasure. But it isn't a game. You can end up in jail doing this. You might have to drop what you're doing instantly when a fugitive comes knocking at your door. And when your first plan doesn't work out, you have to make up a new one right on the spot."

"I can do those things."

"Let's wait a few years, though. To make sure you still feel the same way."

Rian set her mallet down on the workbench. "I'll never change my mind about this, Jules."

· ·

Two hours later, Jules and Rian walked north on Broad Street toward the new Krieger shops.

Rian reached over and put her hand in his. The gesture wasn't unusual, but Jules suspected this was another part of their lives that wouldn't last much longer. Sooner or later, this tomboy was going to grow up. She wouldn't want to hold hands with him, and others would think it unseemly.

Jules squeezed Rian's hand gently. "Last year, the day John Marshall died, remember we talked about our heroes?"

"Sure. You said two of your heroes were Maddie's grandfathers."

Of course, she remembered. She never forgets a thing. "Well, now I want to tell you about some of my other heroes."

"How come now?"

"Because of what we were talking about before. About Maddie and me being stationmasters."

"Good. Who are your other heroes?"

"Every enslaved person who has ever resisted their enslavers."

"Why?"

"Think about it. The consequences of resisting are so significant. Say 'no,' and you might get beaten. Try to escape, and it could be worse."

"So, you've met a lot of heroes. Every person who got as far as your house."

"Yup. Every one of them is a hero. Everyone who tried to escape and didn't make it is a hero. Everyone who had too many family members to think about escaping but resisted in other ways. They're heroes."

"I bet that's a lot of people."

"I know it's a lot of people."

"Do you think they will ever make it into the history books? As heroes? Like George Washington?"

Jules smiled. "Someday, maybe. Yeah, someday. Rian, thank you for listening to me ramble on."

"It's not rambling. It's important. Thank you for trusting me about this. Everyone should have heroes."

The two walked in silence for two blocks. Then Rian said, "So a hero is someone who risks a lot to do what they think is right."

Jules thought for a moment. "Yes, I think that's a good definition."

"And what you are doing is illegal. You could get thrown in jail for it."

"Yes, that is true."

"Jules, you're *my* hero."

Jules smiled. They didn't say a word to one another for the rest of their walk to the new factory.

· · · · · · · · · · · · · · · · · · · ·

· RIAN ·

Twenty minutes later, Rian and Jules arrived at the new Krieger Coach factory. An unroofed shell only four months ago, the massive building was now filled with rows of beefy but untested machinery and slated to start production in one week.

It was just after 6:00 in the evening. Exhausted but upbeat workers had left the factory after their ten-hour day. A beehive of activity fifteen minutes ago, the building was now blessedly quiet except for the hiss of steam coming from the regulator valve of Heinrich Aldrich's massive steam engine.

A group of men had gathered to admire the factory's new power plant and witness the first-ever startup of all the tools of Krieger Coach.

Rian's father smoked his pipe and joked with William Strickland, the architect. Uncle Adrian had walked over from the under-construction locomotive factory. Seamus Gallagher chatted with Aaron Bassinger, whom Rian knew was still getting used to his dual role as the bookkeeper for all three Krieger companies and president of Krieger Rail.

Rian had recently worked with Heinrich Aldrich's crew as they built this steam engine. The machine was a beast. Its firebox and boiler together were the size of an omnibus. Aldrich had started a fire in the firebox a few hours ago, which added to the heat of this July evening.

Directed by Aldrich, Rian started monkeying around the metal scaffolding that surrounded the machine. With a bucket of tallow lard in one hand and a slather stick in the other, she smeared lard onto any piece of steel that would soon be moving against another piece of steel. She lost her cap, and her light brown hair cascaded down to the middle of her back. Tallow lard streaked her blouse, pants, and cheeks.

Rian jumped from one ladder to another while still holding the bucket in the crook of her arm. Seamus yelled, "Jaysus, Rian. Be careful!" but she rewarded him only with an over-the-shoulder smile.

High above the shop floor, Rian looked down to see that Aldrich had turned to address the group. She noticed that Aldrich had borrowed her father's lumber rule to use as a pointer. "Gentlemen, we approach the moment of truth," he announced, his English thick with the accent of his native Westphalia. "As soon as Rian finishes her acrobatics, I will pull this lever, which will engage the clutch that begins to drive the piston. This pair of flywheels will keep the machine's momentum at an even rate. They are approximately five feet in diameter, and each weighs almost four hundred pounds." Aldrich used the lumber rule to point to a twenty-foot loop of leather that ran from the steam engine to a shaft overhead. "Power from the engine's pulley will be transmitted to that overhead shaft by this continuous belt."

Rian marveled that so much had been accomplished in such a relatively short time. Just last week, workers had installed the overhead shaft, which ran from above the steam engine to the other end of the building. More continuous belts descended from the shaft back down to individual machines, the workstations that Seamus and Jules had designed.

Rian finished the slathering, climbed down from the machine, gathered up her cap, and took her place between her father and Jules. She wiped tallow from her hands with a rag.

Aldrich gestured grandly to his left as if there were trumpeters assembled for this august occasion. "Fanfare, please!" he announced with a smile, and everyone laughed nervously.

Aldrich pulled the clutch, a lever almost as tall as he was. The steam engine started its deafening *choosh . . . choosh . . . choosh*. The machine strained. The flywheels ever-so-slowly started rotating, then rotating faster, then faster yet. When the *chooshes* became regular, Aldrich pulled a second clutch that shifted the drive belt from its idler pully to engage with a pulley affixed to the overhead shaft. The shaft started rotating. The giant steam engine barely noticed the new load.

"Seamus, if you will . . . ," yelled Aldrich above the din. He used Otto's lumber stick to point to a wood lathe.

Cousin Seamus walked to a wood lathe and pulled a lever, which shifted a stout continuous belt from its idler pulley onto a drive pulley. The belt started rotating, supplying power from the overhead shaft to the machine. The lathe started humming.

Aldrich pointed to the next machine in line. "Start another one, Seamus!"

Seamus put a second lathe in motion. And then a third and a fourth. Then a shaper. And another. Then a drill press. And another. The steam engine *chooshed* away happily. The machines whirred. The din was deafening, but everyone was smiling.

Aldrich nodded to Seamus and, with a flourish, swept the lumber stick along the second row of machines, all powered by the same overhead shaft. Seamus walked down the row, pulling levers as he went. Circular saws. Planing machines. Metal lathes. The steam engine chugged. The overhead shaft whirred. Twenty machines hummed.

Everyone smiled.

Then suddenly, a clatter chat-chat-chatted from up above. Rian looked up to see a section of the shaft had separated from its mate. Still powered by the steam engine, it kept rotating. Loud reports occurred every time the shaft hit the ceiling. Bang! Bang! Bang! Bang! With every rotation, the shaft bent more and struck the ceiling harder.

Aldrich sprinted for the steam engine and shoved hard on the lever to disengage the clutch to the shaft and then the other to the steam engine.

Rian's father yelled, "Everybody back!" and the group stepped away from the racket.

The tortured metal of the shaft finally failed, broke completely from its bearings, and flew across the room, landing with a clang thirty feet away.

The flywheels and machines began to wind down ever so slowly. "Anybody hurt?" yelled Jules.

A quick assessment indicated that everyone was okay.

Rian was crestfallen. She looked around and was surprised to see smiles coming from the adults.

Jules was the first to speak. "Okay, folks. Let's clean up the little that we can. The rest of this mess'll have to wait until morning. It's been a long day. Time to go home."

Within a short time, the group had done what cleanup they could, turned out the gas lanterns, locked the doors, and started their respective walks south. It was already dark, but Rian could see faint cones of light from the new gaslights for a few blocks on Broad Street. Then another one flickered, and Rian could make out the silhouette of a lamplighter working his way south.

Otto, Jules, and Adrian were involved in a conversation that Rian didn't understand; she fell back to walk with Seamus.

Despite the setback, Seamus seemed unperturbed. "Thanks for your help today, Girl. That jump from one ladder to another with a bucket of lard was pretty impressive. But you scare me a bit."

"Seamus, I don't get it. Why is everyone so smiley? The shaft broke."

"Aye, it did, in spectacular fashion. But nobody got hurt. That's the important part. Everything else can be fixed. None of us really thought it would work on the first try. In truth, it worked much better than we feared. Adrian's crew'll have a new shaft and better connectors ready for us to install tomorrow. Remember, Darlin'; no one's ever done half this stuff before. We're inventing the future here. Bound to have a setback or two along the way."

"You knew it was going to fail?"

"We had a lot of bets going. I won a nickel from Jules. He didn't think the belts would work from the shaft to the tools. I had confidence in me system. Made a bet with him."

"So, now what?"

Seamus used the light of a streetlamp to check his pocket watch. "So . . . now I go on to me other job."

"The hose company? How's it going?"

"Going great. But I'm tired. Not getting much sleep. We've been first on the scene at three fires in two weeks. Two of them were the homes of Black folks."

"I don't get it. How do you get paid for putting out fires?"

"It's the insurance companies. They'd rather pay us ten dollars to put out the fire than pay their clients a few hundred dollars for a burned-out house."

Rian slowed down to let a horse and buggy pass as they crossed Sassafras Street. "Black people can get insurance?"

"Sure, same as whites. The insurance folks're happy to take their money. But they'd prefer never to pay out for anybody's fire."

"How do they decide who gets paid if there are two fire companies that show up?"

"It's easy. The first one that trains their hoses on the fire gets the reward. You can see how there might be a bit of competition to get there first. Sometimes it gets a little dirty."

"How come the Moya folks don't do it? Race to the fire to beat you to get to the fires of the Black houses?"

Following the group ahead, Seamus turned left onto Cherry Street. "I guess you'd have to say their dislike for Black folks outweighs their love of the money. Sometimes they even race to the scene and then figure out it's a bunch of Black folks. Then they just stand there. They've never been interested in helping out the Black community all that much."

"How's the pump doing?"

"Aah, the pump. Well, that's a story all its own. I guess you heard that Jules's friend, Mr. Purvis, came through with enough money for me to hop the train to New York City. First time I've ever been on a train, mind you. An experience all its own. Me heart sank when I saw our little pump. It was a sad little specimen. I knew right away that it would need a lot of fixing before it could generate even a meager stream at a fire."

"Yeah, I saw it. Remember? I helped pull on the bar when you tried to pump the pump. It was a lot of work."

"Well, Darlin', I dare say it's harder when you don't yet weigh a hundred pounds. Me boys quickly got the hang of it. Two on a side going up and down in coordination, and we get a pretty nice stream. Dylan even painted *No Name Fire Brigade* on its side. I think that was one of the proudest moments of me life. We'd brought that little pump back to life. Made it useful again. Two months earlier, it was headed for the ash pile."

By this time, Rian and Seamus were approaching the Krieger home. There seemed to be some activity next door, and Rian's father, Uncle Adrian, and Jules had stopped to chat with some people who were taking advantage of the blessed coolness of the evening and the light of the gaslit street. "Seems like your neighbors is having a party, Rian," said Seamus.

When Rian and Seamus arrived, the knot of partiers opened up to accept them as well. Rian recognized Mrs. Mott but no one else. Her father, Adrian, and Jules were paying the most attention to a short, bald man with bushy side-whiskers.

Her father put his arm around her. "Mr. President, this is my daughter, Rian. Please excuse her appearance. She has been working on a steam engine this evening and smells of tallow lard. And this is my nephew, Seamus Gallagher. Rian, Seamus, this is President John Quincy Adams."

"Ex-president," Mr. Adams corrected. "I'd prefer not to take the blame for any of the current mess in Washington."

Mr. Adams extended his hand to both Rian and Seamus. He grasped Seamus's hand warmly. "So, you're the young Irishman everyone is talking about."

"Excuse me, sir?" said Seamus.

"Why this is the story of the hour inside." He gestured with a jerk of his head that he meant the Mott household, where another dozen or so people, most in Quaker garb, were chatting. "An Irish hose company that's putting out fires in Black neighborhoods. It gives me hope for the future of our country."

"Thank you, Mr. President," Seamus stammered.

Adams continued. "Seems I'm putting many faces to the names I have heard this evening." He turned to Jules. "Mr. Freeman, I assume you are the man Mr. Purvis has been talking about. The bridge between him and Mr. Gallagher here."

"I believe I am, sir."

Jules also had nothing further to say. Rian filled the void. "What brings you to Philadelphia, Mr. Adams?" Her father squeezed her into his side as if to tell her that a child should not get involved in adults' conversations.

Mr. Adams seemed not to mind in the least. "Well, my dear, I came to Philadelphia to celebrate the beginning of my seventieth year. Mr. Lundy here," Adams hooked his thumb toward a tall man in Quaker garb who smiled and nodded his head slightly, "stopped by and escorted me here to his friends, the Motts. We've been having a marvelous time, and I'm pleased to hear about your family's endeavors." He returned his attention to Seamus. "'The No Name Fire Brigade.' An interesting title, sir."

"Aye. Afraid so. Moyamensing Hose Company was already taken."

Adams chuckled at Seamus's quip. "How many men do you have in the No Name Fire Brigade, Mr. Gallagher?"

"We're up to twelve now, sir."

Adams seemed a little surprised. "Is that a lot or a little?

"Moya has over one hundred, sir. We are small but mighty."

"Well, bully for you, Mr. Gallagher. I'm proud of you."

"President Adams, Mr. Lundy," interjected Rian's father. "It was very nice to meet you both. It is late, and my daughter needs to rest up. We have a long day ahead of us again tomorrow. Good evening to you as well, Lucretia."

Adams was clearly having a good time and not interested in letting the new arrivals go right away. "Ah, at the new shops. I understand the Krieger family will dominate the railroad world in a few years."

"It seems that word of our endeavors is starting to spread, sir." Her father paused for dramatic effect, "At least as far as our next-door neighbors. Perhaps the next time you come to Philadelphia, you will arrive on a Krieger coach."

"Or be pulled by a Krieger locomotive," chimed in Uncle Adrian.

With that, the knot of partiers broke up. Rian hugged Seamus and Jules and Adrian good-night, and she and her father walked next door to their home.

"Well, *Liebling*," her father said as they walked up the steps to their house. "It is not every day that we meet a US president."

"*Vater*, how did Mr. Adams know so much about us?"

"Philadelphia's a small town. We're trying to change things—a good many things. Quakers like the Motts want us to succeed. I am pleased but not all that surprised they were talking about us next door. Now, up to bed. Beforehand, though, wash off whatever tallow you could not wipe off at the shop. We are up early again tomorrow."

· · · · · · · · · · · · · · · · · · · ·

· SEAMUS ·

Seamus left the Mott's front yard in a mammoth quandary. Admittedly, he respected Jules, and he liked Jules' wife Maddie, though he had met her only when he had carried the injured Rufus back to their home. *How did you get yourself here, Bucko?*

He made the proposal to Jules because he needed money, not because he wanted to be all buddy-buddy with Black people. Truth be told, he didn't really know any other Black people, and his offer to put out fires in Black neighborhoods was strictly a business deal. *Gotta admit, though, when we put out those folks' fires, they were pretty grateful, just like a white person.*

And now, here he was, receiving accolades from the President of the United States. Like he was some hero or something. *Well, I'm no hero.* In fact, his intention for the rest of the evening was to find out what ships had come in today and see what he could shake loose on the docks. *That's not hero stuff.*

He headed to McSweeney's, the unofficial headquarters for the No Name Fire Brigade. Five of his mates were already there, seated around a table.

Dylan was the first to speak. "Kind of late, aren't you, Boyo? We figured you weren't gonna show tonight."

"Big day at work. Then I had a meeting with President John Quincy Adams."

That declaration got a collective whoop of derision from the other No Names, all of whom knew of Seamus's fondness for exaggeration.

Dylan couldn't resist the easy target. "I'm sure he wanted some advice on what to do about the Republic of Texas." Another whoop of joy came up from the group.

"No, I'm serious. I met him on me walk home. He knows the neighbors of the Kriegers. They told him about us. Us meaning No Name. He said he was proud of us."

That quieted the boys down a bit.

Jimmy Collins ran in the door, all out of breath. "Fire bell's ringing.[19] Time to make some more money."

Those with a glass in front of them downed its contents, and they were off. As they exited McSweeney's, Seamus counted rings coming from the State House. *Two plus four. That's southwest.* "That's our territory, lads. Let's get a move on."

---

19. When it wasn't tolling to mark important occasions, the State House bell also acted as the fire bell, using the following code: 1=north, 2=south, 3=east, 4=west. 1+3 = northeast, and so on.

They grabbed the pump, stashed under lock and key in a warehouse a block away, and dashed toward the fire. Seamus was happy that the pump was relatively small because hauling it by hand took two men. Running hard, as one would do when racing to put out a fire, was so exhausting that pairs of men rotated between the traces every few blocks. Three more No Names caught up, and a few blocks later, they could hear the commotion and smell smoke, seemingly just around the corner.

They took the turn at full speed and came to an abrupt halt. There, in the middle of the street, was Hugh Callaghan holding a shillelagh. Arrayed behind Hugh were thirty or so members of the Moyamensing Hose Company.

"Evening, Seamus. Fancy meeting you here on this beautiful, warm summer night."

"Get out of our way, Hugh. We're putting out a fire."

"Don't think so. We started that fire at one of your African friends. Thought you and your boys might show up."

With that, thirty or so other Moya boys came up from behind them, blocking any chance of a retreat. Seamus's heart sank. They had fallen for a very old trick. "Real brave, Hugh. Looks like about sixty to eight of us."

"'The supreme art of war is to subdue the enemy without fighting.' Did you ever hear that one, Seamus? We don't want to beat you up, Seamus. We'll just settle for your pump."

Seamus defiantly put his hands on his hips. "We're not giving up our pump. We'd rather die fighting you."

"You sure, Seamus? Look around. Don't think your boys are keen on getting a thumping tonight."

Seamus didn't have to look around. He knew the score. He turned to Dylan and Jimmy Collins, who were between the traces. "Give 'em the pump, Dylan."

As soon as Dylan and Jimmy handed over the pump, men with sledgehammers started smashing it to bits.

"No!" yelled Seamus.

"What'd you think, you little shit? That we'd store it someplace so's you could steal it back?"

The Moya boys descended on Seamus, Dylan, and Jimmy and started pummeling them to the ground. Another group blocked the rest of the No Names but didn't beat them.

Hugh Callaghan sauntered up to Seamus, who was curled into a protective ball, and kicked him hard in the head. "I always liked you, Seamus. But even as a kid, you were too big for your britches. A piece of advice: You're down now. Stay down. C'mon, boys."

Callaghan stepped over the prone body of Dylan as he left. "Not crazy about traitors, neither. Fook you, Dylan. You shoulda stuck with your own kind."

The Moya boys withdrew with a shout and the beginnings of an Irish fighting song.

Seamus got back up to his hands and knees and then stumbled to his feet. "Any broken bones?"

Other No Names helped Dylan and Jimmy up. They shook their heads but otherwise didn't respond.

"Let's go then. We've got a fire to put out."

Dylan was barely able to stand. "You serious, Boyo?"

Seamus winced in pain. "That fire was started because of us. The least we can do is help them put it out."

To Seamus's gratification, all seven joined the bucket brigade to help put out the fire.

Wednesday, July 13

· SEAMUS ·

Two days after the disastrous altercation with Hugh Callaghan and the Moya boys, Seamus sat at the bar by himself, his glass all the way empty. Mc-Sweeney uncorked a bottle and poured him three fingers. "C'mon, Boyo, you gonna sulk the rest of your life?"

Seamus winced as he reached for the glass, his ribs still tender from the thrashing he had received.

"Don't know what I'm gonna do, Braden. I got no boys. I got no pump. Can't even pilfer anything at the piers cuz I don't have a lookout. Good thing I got a day job."

"Why aren't you there right now?"

"They kicked me out early. I couldn't even lift me arm to point. I've taken the omnibus the past two days. Not used to riding like the impatient class."

"Dylan was in here last night. He hasn't deserted you. Says none of the rest have either. They're just awaiting orders."

Seamus swirled his finger around the rim of his glass. "That's a miracle in itself. But what's the sense of resurrecting a hose company of twelve guys? We're just gonna get creamed again the next time."

"Why do you have to get back into the firefighting business? Just work the docks."

"Ah, that's just for pin money. The real action's in fighting fires. It ain't just the insurance companies. Folks was offering me money for protection. Offering. I didn't even have to shake 'em down. They came to me."

"Then just stick to your day job. Why even bother with the extracurricular stuff?"

"Dunno, Braden. Dunno. I guess I always thought I would belong to a fire company. I'm having a hard time putting it down."

Then a beautiful young woman walked out of the kitchen, tying an apron around her thin waist. She had the blackest hair that Seamus had ever seen, and it flowed down to the middle of her back. Seamus perked up just a bit.

"Who's the bird?"

"Siobhan Callaghan. Hugh's daughter."

"What's she doing here? She should be working at Clancy's."

"Hugh's got four daughters older than her, all unmarried, all on Clancy's payroll. Clancy finally put his foot down, so Hugh asked me a favor."

"Why'd you say yes? You've never needed a girl before."

"Look at her. She could be the worst kitchen wench in Moya, and the customers would come in just to gaze at her. Just like yer doing now."

"How old is she?"

"Seventeen."

"Maybe I should say hello."

"Watch it. She's scrappy."

"Then this is a good time to meet her." Seamus got up from the bar stool with a wince. "Right now, I'm pretty harmless."

Seamus tried to disguise his limp as he ambled over to the other end of the bar, where Siobhan was polishing glasses. "Good afternoon. Thought I should introduce meself. Me name's Seamus Gallagher."

Siobhan held a glass up to the fading sunlight streaming in the window to check for spots. "I know who you are. I haven't seen you at mass recently."

"Haven't been recently. Maybe I'll get back in the habit."

"It'll probably do you good. How come you're gimpy?"

Seamus didn't feel like revealing to Siobhan that her father had kicked the shit out of him two nights ago. "I fell off a wagon."

"That's not what me da says. He says his boys kicked the shit out of you and your boys the other night."

"If you knew how I got hurt, why'd you ask?"

Siobhan leaned over the bar and made eye contact for the first time. "Wanted to see what you'd say."

Seamus thought that he could stare into her beautiful black eyes forever. "What answer were you hoping for?"

"There's no good answer. The truth doesn't put me da in a particularly fine light. A lie's a lie. Now I know which one comes to you most easily."

"No credit for not exposing your da?"

"I know me da's an arsehole."

Seamus looked down at his drink. "You got that right."

"But he's a good judge of character. And he told me when I left the house this morning that you hang out here and to give you a wide berth. So, this is me, giving you a wide berth." Siobhan picked up her tray of glasses and headed back into the kitchen.

Seamus sauntered back to McSweeney's end of the bar, no longer trying to hide his limp. "I think she likes me."

McSweeney snorted and draped a bar towel over his left shoulder. "You'll have better luck at the piers than you do with her. And if she does take a fancy to ya, which is highly unlikely, that thumping you got from Hugh the other night will feel like a kiss on the cheek."

· ·

· RIAN ·

"I've got to talk to you, but you can't tell Trey." Olivia Tucker spoke to Rian in a conspiratorial whisper as they walked a few yards ahead of her cousin Trey Shippen and Conor McGuire.

After work, Rian and Conor had met Olivia and Trey for a walk to look at the newly opened Philadelphia Gas Works. This walk was the first time Rian had seen Olivia since last summer when Rian still feared her father would send her to Switzerland. Conor seemed more interested in playing gotcha-last with Trey.

As they strolled west on High Street, Rian and Olivia had paired up. Olivia had grown an inch since last summer. She wore a yellow, purple, and red plaid sundress that ran well below her knees. Her brown hair fell in curls to her shoulders. Rian, of course, was dressed in her shop clothes.

"What's it about?" asked Rian.

"I can't tell you. Can we meet someplace later?" Rian had forgotten how Olivia's syrupy South Carolina accent mesmerized her.

"Can you give me a hint?"

"No, it's too important."

Trey and Conor caught up with the girls. "What are you two whispering about?" asked Trey.

"We sailed directly from Charleston," Olivia stated loud enough for the boys to hear as if she were merely carrying on a previous conversation. "It took less than four days. A new record for the Tucker family."

Rian played along with the ruse. "How was your ship?"

"Fine. The *Carolina Princess*. It was just mother and me. We had our own stateroom. The steam engine kept me awake a bit."

"Where's your father?"

"He had to stay behind for business. My father always has business to attend to."

"How long are you up for?"

"Only about four weeks this year. I'm still not old enough to go to the balls, but Mother says we'll miss the last week of the social season. We sail back in the middle of August."

Rian didn't care about balls.

The foursome arrived at the Gas Works on the east bank of the Schuylkill River. Barges of coal lined up end-to-end along docks next to the plant. It was almost six o'clock in the evening, and workers still shoveled coal into wheelbarrows that another set of workers hauled up wooden ramps to the plant. A steam whistle sounded, and all the workers stopped what they were doing and started putting away their tools.

The Irish dominated the coal docks of the Schuylkill. Rian scanned the workers to see if she could spot any of her Irish cousins. Her mother had had nine brothers and sisters, and each of them had a lot of kids. The only one of her cousins that she knew well was Seamus. "Conor, are any of your brothers down there?"

"Redmond might be."

Rian knew Conor was proud that he was already better educated and more gainfully employed than his three older brothers, even though he was only twelve.

With no activity to entertain them, the foursome moved on to the Fairmount Waterworks. The waterworks, a marvel of modern engineering, supplied water to the entire city of Philadelphia. The youngsters joined a sedate stream of strollers attracted to the beauty of the reservoir and the classical structures that hid the industrial nature of the facility.

Especially during the cool evenings of summer, a pathway surrounding the reservoir attracted strollers. The foursome stopped at a bridge that crossed an aqueduct to watch three waterwheels lift water from the Schuylkill into the vast reservoir.

Speaking just loudly enough to hear one another above the sound of the cascading water, Rian and Olivia made their plan to meet after Rian finished work the next day.

•   •   •   •   •   •   •   •   •   •   •   •   •   •   •   •   •   •   •   •

· JULES ·

Jules swallowed his last bite of berries at the dinner table. The children had rollicked out of the house, leaving him and Maddie alone for the first time that evening. "I had an interesting conversation with Rian Krieger the other day."

"Our favorite ragamuffin? What did you talk about?"

"Oh, it was wide-ranging. Honestly, that young woman amazes me sometimes. She knows we harbor self-emancipators, by the way."

"Because of the day Rufus got hit by a rock?"

Jules nodded.

"I guess I'm not surprised. She's a sharp cookie."

"Well, she was sharp enough to keep it under her hat. That eventually led us to the topic of heroes. Since slaveholders are automatically excluded from my list of potential heroes, she asked me who my heroes are. After a bit, I said that any enslaved person who ever resisted their enslavers."

"That makes you a hero."

"That made me a hero fifteen years ago. I don't feel very heroic right now."

"My goodness, Husband, what has gotten into you? You are a wonderful provider. You come home every night without stopping at a grog shop. You help self-emancipators find freedom. You are a hero to our children. What more do you need to do?"

"I don't know. I just feel it's not enough. You are more of a hero than I am."

"How do you figure that?"

"Your work with PFASS. You have taken a public stand. You open yourself to all the hatefulness in the world, yet you remain resolute."

"Jules, where is this coming from? You and I have had this discussion a hundred times. You have always maintained that every time our people get a little ahead of themselves, someone smacks us down. Do you think differently now?"

"No, I still believe that hateful people will try to smash us. But our cause needs heroes. Our children need heroes who look like them, not some white man who enslaved people because of the color of their skin."

"Jules Freeman, our children idolize you."

"I want to be worthy. I believe I should be doing more."

"Patience, Husband. The way will make itself known to you when it is time. But please know, you are a heroic man to your children and me. I wish that were enough."

Thursday, July 14

· SEAMUS ·

Still in pain from the thrashing three days ago, Seamus had again ridden a sequence of omnibuses to work. At this moment, he stood with his hands in his pockets, watching two Germans connect one section of the overhead shaft to another.

Jules joined him and assumed a similar pose. "How are they doing?"

"Aw, Jules, I expected something was gonna break the first time. I was disappointed by the second break. I bet this third time'll be a charm."

"We're running out of time. We're supposed to be up and running on Monday."

"We will, even if I have to work on Sunday."

"You better hope not. You're in no shape to climb these scaffolds. Let's just hope everything goes perfectly today. Remember, once we get this one up and running, we do the same thing across the alley."

"We've learned a few lessons on this one. Hopefully, the next one will go faster."

"Robert Purvis said he wants to talk to you."

"What's he want to talk to me about?"

"Don't know for sure, but I can guess. He asked me to come, too."

"Well, there's a bit of a conundrum. I can't walk two miles, and Negroes aren't welcome on the omnibus."

Jules smiled ruefully. "I'll make the walk and meet you there. I don't know, Seamus. I think you like riding the omnibus. You becoming a member of the impatient class?"

"Not likely. I figure today's me last day, 'though the ladies is fun to look at."

•　•　•　•　•　•　•　•　•　•　•　•　•　•　•　•　•

· SEAMUS ·

Seamus was greeted at the door of Robert Purvis's house by a maid. As they wended their way to the back of the house, Seamus marveled at the opulence. Wallpaper with deep rich colors. Portraits and engravings on the walls. A bust of someone on a pedestal. He passed a large room dominated by a pianoforte.

As he entered the study, the maid announced, "Mr. Gallagher is here to see you, Sir." Despite walking rather than riding, Jules had beat him there. He held a coffee cup and saucer and perused Purvis's library, which covered an entire wall of the room.

Purvis rose to greet Seamus and extended his hand. "Thank you for coming, Mr. Gallagher."

Seamus shook Purvis's hand and noted a firm, comfortable grip. "No one calls me that, Sir. Just Seamus is fine." Seamus was a bit surprised at two things: Purvis appeared to be only a few years older than him, and his skin was so light that he could easily pass as a white man.

"Then please call me Robert. Seamus, pour yourself a cup of coffee and sit."

Seamus followed orders but sat rigidly in his chair, unsure of how he was supposed to act in such rich surroundings.

Purvis continued. "It's good to finally meet you. I understand we almost met at the Motts' party the other night."

"Never thought I'd meet a president. Lots of ups and downs that day."

"I wish we'd had a chance to chat. I was disturbed to hear of the events that occurred later that evening."

"Yes, Sir, er, Robert. Bad business. We got nicked up pretty bad. They made a point of destroying the pump. I'm sorry we didn't do a very good job protecting it. Afraid that wasn't a good investment for you."

"I didn't think I was investing in the pump, Seamus. I was investing in you. I am most interested in fostering cooperative arrangements between the Black community and the Irish."

"Afraid I don't speak for all the Irish, Robert. Matter of fact, not many. 'Though me boys seem to be sticking with me."

"Are you looking for another engine?"

"I'm still heartsick about the one we lost. Also, we're only twelve. Even if we did find another pump, how would the next time end up any different?"

Purvis leaned forward in his chair. "I have a thought. What if I recruited some men from the Black community to join you?"

Seamus crossed his arms and leaned back a bit. "That's a tough one, Robert. A hose company is as much a social club as it is a firefighting organization. Afraid me boys'd balk at socializing with a bunch of Negroes, no offense. Not sure that would go over very well with the general public, either. You might get some resistance on that."

Purvis looked at Jules, whose shrug seemed to confirm an earlier conversation.

"A pity," said Purvis.

Seamus reached for his coffee. "Why don't you just organize your own hose company?"

"My father-in-law tried to organize a Negro fire company fifteen years ago. It barely got off the ground. Not because of us, but there was too much resistance from whites—even in the press. There was sporadic violence. It collapsed after a short run. Last night, he told me that nothing has changed in our City of Brotherly Love. What if a bunch of men just showed up at a fire to help out? They wouldn't officially be members of the No Name Fire Brigade."

"How many are we talking about? I'd still have to protect me pump. If we had one, that is."

"There are 15,000 free Blacks in Philadelphia. Many of them in Moyamensing. I bet we could recruit twenty-five. Maybe fifty."

"That's still light. Robert, I'll be honest with you. I took a real thumping the other night. I should just drop this and pay attention to me day job." He nodded toward Jules. "Which is going quite nicely, by the way. But I haven't been able to put this thing down. Let me ponder this a bit. Give me a week or two."

"That's all I ask."

"Robert, I've got a question for you." Seamus gestured toward the wall of books. "You seem to be a pretty educated man."

Purvis waved his hand dismissively, as if owning a lot of books didn't make an education.

"Before he gave me the thrashing, Hugh Callaghan said something about the art of war and beating the enemy without fighting. Does that ring a bell?"

Purvis shifted in surprise. "Your Mr. Callaghan may be a more formidable opponent than we thought. I believe you are referring to Sun Tzu, a Chinese military strategist who died 2,500 years ago. Sun Tzu wrote a brilliant treatise called *The Art of War*. I've never seen a copy in English. There's a version in French somewhere over in that bookcase. I could loan it to you if you're interested."

"It wouldn't do me much good. I'm just now mastering English. But thank you. I guess I've got another question for you."

"Of course."

"I hope you don't take offense at this. You think of yourself as a Black man. But I'm looking at a white guy. A rich white guy. You can do anything you want to. Ride the omnibus. Attend other rich people's parties. Travel the world. Why do you do what you're trying to do now?"

Purvis sat back in his chair and looked momentarily at the ceiling. "I've been asked this question many times, so no offense taken. Here's the best I can come up with. My mother's mother was born in Morocco, in northern Africa. When she was twelve, she was kidnapped and thrown onto a slave ship.

The next time she saw the light of day was when she was sold at an auction in Charleston. She was a slave for over a decade. Fortunately for her, she was freed when her owner died."

"Tough story," said Seamus.

Purvis nodded. "I don't even think Grandma Dido was Black, although she was much darker than Jules. She claimed to be a full-blooded Moor, but she certainly looked Black, which is all that matters in the South. Although being a free colored person in South Carolina in the 1770s was no picnic, she did okay. She fell in love with my grandfather, who was the son of a wealthy Jewish merchant."

"So, your black-skinned grandmother, an ex-slave, married a wealthy white man. This is storybook stuff."

That elicited a smile from Purvis. "So my mother was half Moor and half Jewish. In South Carolina, that still means you're colored. As you can imagine, she and my father, who was white, could never marry. Grandma Dido lived with us until she died, just before we moved to Philadelphia. She raised me as much as my mother did. Because of her, I have an appreciation for the plight of all oppressed people, not just Blacks. She was proud of her Moorish blood, and so am I. I don't believe anyone, regardless of skin color, should feel inferior to another. I have great sympathy at how your brethren are suffering in Ireland."

Seamus was silent for a bit. "Thank you. That helps me understand this a lot." With that, he and Jules rose to leave. They exited onto the street; both lost in their own thoughts.

They walked slowly south together on Ninth Street until it was time to go their separate ways.

Jules broke the silence. "You going to be able to make it home?"

"Oh, sure. I'll stop off at McSweeney's for a bit of a rest. What do you think of Robert's scheme?"

"What do I think? I think you're both crazy."

With that, the two smiled at one another and parted.

• • • • • • • • • • • • • • • • • •

· RIAN ·

"What's he doing here?" Olivia asked in an accusatory voice. She was staring at Conor.

At work that day, Rian could not keep Olivia's secret from her best friend. She told Conor about her impending meeting with Olivia. Always happy to be part of a conspiracy, Conor had insisted on coming along. As planned, they found Olivia sitting on a bench in Washington Square near a small pond covered with lily pads.

Rian joined Olivia on the bench. "You only said I couldn't tell Trey."

Conor remained standing, waiting for Olivia's judgment: stay or go.

"This is really important. My father will kill me if he finds out."

Conor took her response to mean "stay," and sat down on the bench and crossed himself. "I swear to God I'll never talk."

"What's going on?" added Rian.

Olivia sighed and hesitated for many long seconds. "My Mammy. She wants to be free."

With no idea what Olivia was talking about, Rian stared blankly back at Olivia.

Having crossed her Rubicon, Olivia became more forthcoming. "Ever since I was a baby, it's really my Mammy who's taken care of me. Not my mother."

For Conor's benefit, Rian asked the obvious question: "Mammy's a slave?".

Olivia nodded. "We call her Mammy, but her real name is Rose. She raised my mother. Now she's raising me. Last year, when we went back to South Carolina, I told Mammy about Cousin Elmo at your friend Jules's house.

"Why did you do that? You said you were going to keep it a secret."

"I said I wasn't going to tell my father. You told Conor about it. He wasn't there."

Rian looked down sheepishly.

"I didn't think telling a secret down in Charleston would do any harm. Mammy knows all my secrets. Anyway, she wasn't supposed to make this trip to Philadelphia. She'd come with us a couple of times when I was little, but not recently. Mother's favorite is Mathilde now. She wanted to bring her."

"She brought Mathilde last year."

Olivia nodded. "Then Mathilde got sick. Mother said our trip had been delayed long enough, so she told Mammy to pack up and come with us. It was all real sudden. But when we were on the Carolina Princess, we had a lot of free time to talk. Mammy asked me if I would help her escape."

"You mean she'd planned to escape after she heard about Cousin Elmo and Jules and Maddie?

Olivia shook her head. "I think she's stewed about it forever, but it was just a dream until we were on the steamship."

"Jaysus," said Conor.

"I told Mammy I would help her. But there's a problem. Her grandson Topper—remember him from last summer? My half-brother? She doesn't want to escape without him."

Conor leaned in and whispered, even though no one was near them. "How can she do that if Topper's down on your farm?"

"That's just it. Topper's still my father's groom. Father will bring him north with the horses on the Carolina Princess in a couple of weeks. When Topper comes north, Mammy wants me to help them escape."

· ·

· SEAMUS ·

When Seamus entered McSweeney's, he spotted Siobhan pouring a drink for William Fitzpatrick.

Seamus ordered by pointing to William's drink and giving Siobhan a nod. "Where's Braden?"

Siobhan poured him a generous three fingers. "Attending some political meeting. I think he's rooting for Mr. Harrison."

With the presidential election coming up in a couple of months, both political parties were ratcheting up their campaigns. The Democrats had nominated Martin Van Buren of New York to succeed Andrew Jackson. The Whigs, barely a national party, had nominated three different candidates in three regions of the United States. Whigs convening in Harrisburg, Pennsylvania chose William Henry Harrison of Indiana on a platform of internal improvements and support for the Second National Bank.

With other things on his mind, Seamus didn't want to get drawn into a political discussion. "It's only your third day of work. You know what you're doing back there?"

"Not flirting with you, that's for sure." She turned on her heel and walked into the kitchen, leaving Seamus alone with William.

William stared at the open kitchen door. "McSweeney told me you were sweet on that one."

"McSweeney talks too much."

"How's it going so far?"

"She loves me. She just doesn't know it yet."

SATURDAY, JULY 16

· RIAN ·

Rian felt bad that she couldn't tell Trey about Olivia's secret, but she and Conor agreed they shouldn't test his loyalty to his family. Trey's mother and Olivia's mother were sisters. If anyone in the Shippen family found out, it would surely get back to the Tuckers. Then Rose and Topper would never become free.

The pair sat on the conspiracy for two days before talking to Jules. Neither had yet been able to get to him. With final tests of the Krieger Coach production line in full swing, things were hectic all day long. Their responsibilities at the factory kept getting in the way. In Rian's case, her most important job was assisting Seamus or Jules as they plowed through an ever-churning list of tasks. Today was her Seamus day.

Even so, Rian lost track of Seamus for an hour or so. When she finally found her cousin, he was standing at the opposite end of the Krieger Coach factory from the steam engine. All the machines in the building were humming, some with workers in attendance, some just running. Seamus had his hands in his pockets and his eyes shut.

"What are you doing?" Rian yelled.

Seamus didn't bother to open his eyes. "Listening. Trying to hear anything that ain't right."

"Whataya think?"

"For the first time, I'm pretty sure we're going to start on time next week," he yelled over the din. "One down, two to go!"

"Who are all the new guys?" asked Rian.

"Some Irish, some Germans. They officially start on Monday. I've had 'em testing out individual machines all afternoon. The older guys are training them on their own specialized tasks. We should be ready to go the day after tomorrow. If nothing else breaks, tomorrow will be a day of rest for all of us."

Rian was impatient. "Come on; it's time to go."

"Go where?"

"To the locomotive factory. It's three o'clock. You've got a meeting. Uncle Adrian just got back from his trip to Mauch Chunk.[20] He wants an update."

Rian walked behind her cousin but pushed him in the back to hurry him along a little. He tended to get distracted, so it became her mission to keep him on schedule. They walked across the alley to Krieger Locomotive. Compared to the coach factory, the locomotive factory was relatively quiet. They entered Adrian's office to find him seated at his desk. Jules was already there, reading a set of shop plans. The one-quarter-sized steam engine prototype had been moved to the new factory and placed right next to his desk, even though Adrian no longer needed it for inspiration.

"Sorry we're late," Seamus said as he pulled up a chair. "I think things across the alley are finally in good shape. For now, anyway."

"Good to hear," said Adrian. "Jules tells me we're on schedule to open the locomotive factory in two weeks."

Seamus looked over Jules's shoulder to see if anyone had changed the shop drawings. "Hope so. We learned a lot of lessons across the alley. We may be up and running before that. No promises, of course. How was your trip to the mines of Mauch Chunk?"

"You folks should go some time. Even traveling there is a story—canal most of the way. Then railway; horse-drawn, of course. I got a tour of the anthracite mine. It's fascinating, but if you think we work hard, those Irish have it ten times worse. Barely see the light of day. Tons of things to worry about—cave-ins, gases that can kill you, flooded shafts. They were using a steam engine to pump out the water. If things don't go well here, we can always go into the mine pump business."

Rian hoped he was joking, but she wasn't sure.

Seamus settled into a chair with a muted grunt. "Did you make a sale?"

In response, Adrian produced a bottle of champagne that had been chilling on ice behind his desk. "I did. My first sale. A locomotive for hauling their cars from the mine to the canal." Adrian pushed on the cork until it popped and flew toward the office door. Jules and Adrian cheered.

Adrian poured champagne into four coffee cups, then distributed them to everyone. "It wasn't hard to convince them that the future's in steam. Horses are on their way out. They'll probably need some track as well. How're you feeling, by the way, Seamus? You don't look quite as gimpy."

"I walked to work today. That's a good sign. Me ribs are still a mite touchy."

---

20. Mauch Chunk, a mining town in eastern Pennsylvania, was renamed Jim Thorpe in 1954.

"So, I guess you're out of the fire-fighting business for a while."

Seamus gave Jules a sidelong glance. "I'm on the fence about that. Me boys are still with me, but I could use some more hands. And of course, we don't have a pump."

Rian took a sip of her champagne and decided she didn't like it. When she heard the word pump a second time, she looked at the shiny, one-quarter-sized steam engine sitting next to Adrian's desk. "Does it have to be a hand pump, like your old engine?"

"Of course," responded Seamus curtly. "What other kind of pump is there?"

In response, Rian pointed to the prototype. "That kind."

Seamus barely looked. "That's not a pump. That's a toy."

Adrian stiffened a bit. "It's not a toy at all. It wouldn't take much to modify it so it could pump water. Now that I think about it, I imagine it could generate quite a stream."

Seamus got up and walked over to the steam engine, touching it reverently. "Do you mean this specimen or something like this?"

"I mean this one. It's just sitting here. It's too small to pull a railway car, but it would be perfect as a pump to fight fires. Has anyone ever done that?"

"Not that I've heard. Not in the whole world," whispered Seamus, still running his hands over the metal. "Course, we would need a carriage to transport it."

Jules looked up from his plans for the first time. "Hell, we've got a carriage's worth of spare parts down at the old shop. I'm sure we could cobble something together for you."

Seamus straightened and looked at Jules. "You told me yesterday I was crazy. Which side are you on?"

Jules smiled. "Can't see a good engine just sitting here like an oversized Christmas ornament. It'd be good to put it to work."

Adrian placed his coffee cup on his desk. "My locomotive guys are pushing hard to get us going in two weeks. You can't steal their time for any of your harebrained schemes."

"But if I can get them to work on this after hours, you're okay to let the engine go?"

Adrian ran his hand through his hair. "I should talk to Aldrich first, just out of courtesy. After all, he built it. But I imagine he'll be pleased. But otherwise, sure."

Since it was her original suggestion, Rian's imagination was already running a mile a minute. "The firemen's parade is coming up in two weeks. Could we have it ready by then?"

Seamus protectively put both his hands on the machine. "Whoa, girl. I'm not sure this is even a good idea yet."

Rian was undeterred. "We could make a banner."

Adrian suddenly grasped what Rian was thinking. He spread his arms out wide to indicate the expanse of a banner. "'This Pump Built By Krieger Locomotive.' Overnight the whole town would know we're open for business."

Seamus started to chuckle. "I think I better go talk to me boys." He raised his coffee cup in salute and drained it of its champagne.

· ·

· JULES ·

Jules was often the last to leave the factory, long after the other workers had left, but this Saturday was different. Now that the machinery at Krieger Coach seemed to be ready to go, tomorrow would be a day of rest. He was happy to be locking up the shop promptly at 6:05.

Rian and Conor were waiting for him outside. The two matched his pace as he walked south on Broad Street. Jules knew something was up but had no guess what the twelve-year-olds were plotting. "I know you two aren't here because you love my company."

"We need your help," said Rian.

"Somehow, I'm not surprised."

"No, this is serious."

"How serious?"

"Cousin Elmo serious."

Jules stopped walking. Broad Street was relatively deserted, typical for a Saturday evening. He could see one man on horseback two blocks south. A pair of oxen pulled a wagon far to the north. Folks would soon be coming out for after-dinner strolls. *I was looking forward to an evening with Maddie and the kids, but now, I think that's about to change.* "How much does Conor know about my business?"

"Conor's my best friend," was Rian's only explanation.

"I thought I told you we could talk about this in a few years, not a few days."

"We didn't know it was going to come up. Do you remember Olivia Tucker?"

"Olivia. Of course. She's Randolph Tucker's daughter. She was at our house the day Rufus got hit by a rock."

Rian nodded. "She just came back up North from Charleston."

"You haven't told her about my private life, have you?"

Rian shook her head. "Didn't need to. She figured it out on her own."

"Jesus Lord. You're saying the daughter of a slave owner knows I shelter fugitive slaves?"

"Yes, and that's why we need your help."

· · · · · · · · · · · · · · · · · ·

· SEAMUS ·

That evening Seamus sat with Dylan, Jimmy Collins, and the Fitzpatrick brothers at McSweeney's, telling them about the quarter-sized steam engine at Krieger Locomotive. "And the kicker is there's nothing like it in Philadelphia. Maybe even all of America. In two weeks, everyone'll be talking about the No Name Fire Brigade."

The table reacted with muted *hear hears* and lifted glasses. But Seamus interrupted his story to watch Siobhan Callaghan delivering meals to a noisy table nearby. "Who's the gump sitting with the Murphys?"

Dylan put down his drink. "The arsehole feeling your girlfriend's ass right now? He's their uncle from Baltimore. He's been acting like he owns the place ever since he walked in the door."

Seamus got up from the table, wincing a bit from the pain in his ribs. "Think I'll go have a talk with him."

Dylan shook his head. "Oh boy, here we go. Careful, Seamus. You're not exactly at fighting strength."

In reply, Seamus picked up his drink and winked. "Just a talk."

Two seconds later, Siobhan dumped an entire bowl of beef stew onto the lap of the Murphys' uncle. He sprang up from his chair and pulled back his fist to strike the young woman. Seamus grabbed his fist from behind with his left hand just as Siobhan kneed him in the groin. The uncle doubled over, and Siobhan broke the bowl over his head. He crumpled.

None of the Murphys moved. Seamus set his drink down on their table, leaned over with a wince, and pulled the uncle back up by his collar. "You might wanna take your uncle home, boys. I think he's had a mite too much to drink."

Seamus turned to Siobhan. "You okay?"

"I didn't need your help."

"I think you're right."

"Look at me dress. I got beef stew all over it when I kneed that arsehole."

Seamus flashed her a wolfish grin. "I could wipe it off for you."

"Fook you, Seamus. I gotta clean this mess up. And Braden's gonna charge me for the meal. And the bowl. Go back to your stupid friends."

. . . .

Seamus was sitting at the bar two hours later, the last patron in the saloon. Siobhan finished sweeping and leaned the broom next to the door to the kitchen. She poured Seamus another three fingers. "Last one. I'm tired, and I want to go home. I've gotta get up early tomorrow to go to mass."

"Was it worth it?"

"Was what worth it?"

"Kneeing that gump in the nuts. Was it worth the cost of the meal? And the bowl? And the mess?"

"Suppose I wasn't thinking about it at the time. I just knew I didn't want him feeling me ass anymore. I'd already told 'em twice."

"Seems that shoulda been enough."

"I think me da would approve. Word'll spread. It'll keep the handsy customers off me for a bit."

Seamus lifted his drink in salute.

Siobhan hesitated, then met his eyes. "Thanks for your help."

"It was my privilege. But you didn't need it." He got up from the barstool with a wince.

"You're still hurting."

"Aye. I was getting better. Pulling on that arsehole's fist strained me ribs a bit."

Siobhan hesitated. "You've got another couple of sips in that glass. Give me five minutes. I'll walk with you for a bit. Suspect your route goes right by me house."

. . . .

As they exited from the saloon, Seamus noted ruefully that the gas line crews hadn't yet worked their way this far south. The street was much darker here than in the northern part of the city. *The impatient class gets all the improvements before we do.* "Do you walk home alone every night?"

"Mostly. You worried about me?"

"Given what I saw tonight? Not much."

"Most everyone in the neighborhood knows me da. Doubt they'd be foolish enough to mess with me. . . . Why'd you do it?"

"Do what?"

"Throw in with the darkies? You're turning your back on your own kind."

"Not doing that at all. I just don't think it's fair to make meself better off by making someone else worse off."

"But the darkies are takin' jobs away from us. It's a war."

"Number one: most of those darkies have been here longer than we have. Number two: now you sound like your da. Does he read French?"

"Why do you ask that question?"

As they walked into the faint cone of light cast by one of Franklin's old street lanterns, Seamus noticed that she was looking up at him. "The night he kicked the shit out of me, he quoted something from Sun Tzu. The Art of War. I don't believe that's been translated into English yet."

Siobhan stopped in her tracks. "You know that book? Me da quotes Sun Tzu all the time. He thinks the Irish are at war with just about everybody."

"How'd your da learn French?"

"He grew up in France. Me grandfather hated the English. He hated that they've had their boot on our neck for two hundred years. The United Irishmen organized to resist the English. They sent me grandfather to France. Me gram and da went with him. The French were at war with the English anyway. Me grampa spent fifteen years trying to convince them to support Irish independence. Finally gave up after Napoleon got beat the second time. Things were too hot back in Ireland, so the whole family sailed here in 1818."

"Now ain't that a wonderment," Seamus said with only a touch of sarcasm.

"Me da doesn't let people know much about his education. He doesn't talk like he just got off the boat at home. Speaks the king's English. But out on the streets, he talks like you and me. He'd prefer that folks underestimate his intelligence."

"Hugh, you sly old fox. What about you? Do you speak the king's English?"

"I can when the situation calls for it. So, you dodged me question. Why'd you do it? Throw in with the darkies."

"It's complicated. I work with a Black man, Jules Freeman. I think I know him pretty well. He's no different than you or me. Works hard. Loves his family."

"Yeah, but now you're going out of your way to help a lot of 'em. Not just one guy."

"I have to admit, in the beginning, with this fire brigade thing, I was helping the coloreds out because they helped me pay for the pump—the one your da's boys busted up. It was a business deal. But that same night, just before I got beat up, I met John Quincy Adams."

"The President?"

Yes, the very same. This is no lie. He'd heard about me. He knew about the No Name Fire Brigade. He said he was proud of me. That I was trying to make the world a better place."

"No lie?"

"No lie. I think that changed me. Siobhan, I'm not interested in turning me back on me own kind. I just don't want us to better ourselves by crawling over the backs of others. It seems like there should be a better way."

By this time, they had arrived at the Callaghan house. Siobhan turned to him. "You're a strange one, Seamus Gallagher. Don't know if I should shoot ya or kiss ya."

"I'd prefer to be kissed."

"That's not gonna happen."

Sunday, July 17

· SEAMUS ·

The next morning, Seamus sat in a pew at the Church of St. Philip de Neri with his mother and three sisters. He hadn't attended mass for months, but the family always occupied the same pew. Five minutes later, Hugh Callaghan, the rooster with his hen and five chicks, led his family down the aisle and into their usual pew five rows in front. Seamus attempted to give the procession little notice but failed. He had eyes only for Siobhan. Before he sat down, Callaghan turned and surveyed the congregation. He spotted Seamus and nodded. If anyone had seen the momentary interaction, they never would have guessed that Hugh had kicked Seamus in the head less than a week ago.

The priest and altar boys, two of whom were Seamus's little brothers, began the service by entering the church in silence. That's when Siobhan looked back at Seamus. His heart skipped a beat. Five seconds later, Hugh Callaghan looked back as well. This time, his look was not nearly as friendly.

Shit. How the hell does he know by just one look?

• •

· JULES ·

Maddie often knew Jules was in a mood before he did. Usually, she let him stew until he was ready to talk. This time she seemed to know things were different. She broke the silence. "Jules, you've been quiet all morning. Is everything okay at work?"

"Rian Krieger and her friend Conor corralled me yesterday." With that, Jules launched into his story. That Olivia Tucker, the daughter of a slave owner, knew they were stationmasters on the Underground Railroad. That a slave woman who wasn't supposed to come north was spending the next four weeks just ten blocks away. That the woman was hoping Jules and Maddie would help her escape to freedom. That nothing could happen until her grandson arrived with Olivia's father.

Maddie listened to him without interrupting. When he had finished, she said, "And of course, you told them you would help this woman." It was a statement, not a question.

"No, I told them I would talk to you first. This little girl is twelve years old. What if she changes her mind? Or panics?"

"She's the one who was here last year after Rufus got hit with the rock?"

Jules nodded.

"And Rian vouches for her?"

"Another twelve-year-old," Jules responded, verbalizing how tenuous he thought their situation was. "This isn't like us putting up some raggedy-assed yokel from the Tidewater who's passing through. We'd be swiping this woman from right under their noses. The Tuckers'll turn Moyamensing upside down looking for her. It's going to stir up a hornet's nest."

"That just means we'll have to plan a bit differently. Get her out of town right away. You've got to admit, the stars aligned to make this possible."

Jules nodded. It was unheard of for slave owners to bring two slave family members North together. By dividing slave families—keeping loved ones in the South—owners tied their slaves with an emotional leash that almost guaranteed the slaves wouldn't bolt for freedom.

A knock on the door interrupted their conversation. Jules was only slightly surprised to see Rian Krieger, Conor McGuire, and Olivia Tucker on his doorstep. "You three are pretty far from home. Come in."

Jules escorted the youngsters into the kitchen. He settled them at the kitchen table and introduced his wife to Conor. "I assume this isn't a social call."

Rian acted as spokesperson for the group. "We were wondering if you had reached a decision yet. Will you help Olivia's Mammy?"

Jules remained standing and folded his arms. "I guess we need some answers from Miss Tucker first."

Olivia nodded and met Jules's gaze directly.

"Child, this is very serious stuff. Why do you want to get mixed up in adult business?"

"Because of your Cousin Elmo. Last year. I knew he was an escaped slave right away and that you were helping him out. I knew it was a secret I couldn't tell my family because you would get in trouble. But I didn't think you were doing anything wrong. When we went back to South Carolina, I told my Mammy because she would know what to do. Mammy said I should keep it under my hat. But then I guess she kept thinking about it. I don't think Mammy ever thought she'd be free until she heard that she and Topper were going to be in

Philadelphia at the same time. I know I'm going to miss her, but I think it's what should happen."

Maddie leaned across the table and took Olivia's hand. "How old are you, Child?"

"I'll be thirteen next month."

Jules made eye contact with his wife. *Thirteen. We're putting our lives in the hands of a thirteen-year-old.*

Maddie gave her silent assent. "Okay, Miss Thirteen-year-old, we're going to help you out."

"Mammy wants to meet you."

"When?"

"Mother sends her to High Street on Mondays to buy vegetables. That's tomorrow. She wants to know if she can meet you then."

"When does she do the shopping?"

"She can go anytime. The markets close at 5:00."

Jules shook his head. "Tomorrow's a big day at the new carriage factory. We're starting production tomorrow. I can't get out then."

"I can make it," Maddie said. "But High Street is a pretty public place. Free Blacks in Moya generally don't shop that far north. I'm not sure it's very wise for me to just strike up a conversation with a slave. It would be noticed."

Olivia was undeterred. "What if I were with Mammy and you were with Rian? And we just bump into one another?"

"You mean we pretend that I'm Rian's slave?" Maddie smiled and shook her head. "I suppose I can dress down for the occasion. I just hope my Momma doesn't see me. Think you can act like you own a slave, Rian?"

"I can't; I've got French lessons with Professor LaForce."

Jules chuckled. "Welcome to the Underground Railroad. I guess you better get your lies lined up."

Monday, July 18

· SEAMUS ·

The next day, Seamus and Rian stood at the end of the new Krieger Coach building, watching and listening. The first day of production had gone well. Jules had run the men while Seamus paid most attention to the machinery. Rian had divided her time between them, a self-appointed assistant who took on any job asked of her, no matter how trivial. When not on assignment, Rian kept them both on task.

Mercifully, there had been no breakdowns. Rian helped Heinrich Aldrich install a whistle on the steam engine that signaled break time. With the lunch whistle, machinery started to wind down, and Seamus could speak without yelling. "Some of the guys have said they'd stay after a bit to work on the fire pump. You staying too?"

Rian's shoulders sagged a bit. "I can't. I've got to go to my French lesson."

"French lesson. Since when have you been taking French lessons?"

"Since I was eight. After my mother died, Vater thought it would be good for me. It's really French, Latin, and Greek. I go see a professor down at the University on Ninth Street."

"How good are you at it?"

"*Le Francais? Un peu.* Not as good as my German. Better than the Latin and the Greek."

"Good enough to translate a book for me?"

"Maybe. I'd probably need some help."

"Robert Purvis has a book that I'd like to read. He said it's not very long."
"When?"
"Dunno. I'll have to ask when we can stop by."

· · · · · · · · · · · · · · · · · · ·

· RIAN ·

Welcome to the Underground Railroad.

The lies had already started to pile up. Yesterday afternoon Rian left her meeting at the Freemans and walked directly to Professor LaForce's home near the University of Pennsylvania. She told him that she couldn't take his lesson because she had to work late. When she and her father walked to work this morning, he asked her about her French lessons, and she let him assume she was going to her Monday lesson as usual. Then today, she told Seamus that she couldn't help him out with the fire pump because she had to see Professor LaForce.

As expected, High Street was bustling at four o'clock in the afternoon. Vendors had long ago built semi-permanent structures between the eastbound and westbound portions of High Street. Of course, there were all sorts of foods; it looked like lettuce, radishes, squash, peas, and beans were in season—also cured hams, chickens both live and plucked, and meat cakes. But lots of other things: peacock feathers, puppy dogs, newspapers, ice, bolts of cloth, pottery, glassware, even wallpaper.

Rian rendezvoused with Maddie Freeman on the corner of High and Third. She was unsure how a twelve-year-old should interact with a woman who was supposed to be her slave. For lack of any definitive social rule, they walked side by side to Fifth Street, where most of the vegetable stands were.

"There they are," said Rian with a sigh of relief. Olivia and a Black woman who appeared to be in her fifties were looking at vegetables at a stand but getting little attention from the vendor. Rian noted that the two were chatting easily with one another, much as she and Maddie had been doing.

Rian approached Olivia from behind. "Hi, Olivia. What are you doing here?" She winced inwardly because her tone sounded so contrived.

Olivia played her part. "I'm just helping my Mammy buy some vegetables."

And thus, the subterfuge continued. Rian and Olivia stood back while Maddie and Mammy/Rose talked as they fingered the vegetables. After what seemed an eternity, the two women paid for some vegetables and placed them in their baskets, which they handed to the girls. They moved to the next stand. Rian and Olivia followed at a distance.

"What do you think they're talking about?" Rian asked Olivia impatiently.

"I don't know. I hope Mammy will tell me when we walk back to our house."

The two women bought more vegetables and passed them back to the girls. From Rian's vantage point, no casual observer would think they were doing anything but talking about produce. Maddie and Rose worked their way down to two more stands. The girls held the baskets and chatted about nothing consequential.

"Rian. Hello. It's been so long."

The unexpected voice jolted Rian. She turned to see Eilish Cavanaugh smiling at her. Eilish was one of Rian's many cousins from her mother's side. She was only a few years older than Rian, but they hadn't spent much time with one another in years. *Yeah, since Mother died.*

Rian composed herself. "Eilish, what are you doing here?"

"Oh, Cook sent me over for some vegetables. Just a quick trip, but good to get out of the house."

"Where are you working these days?"

"At Shippen House," she said with what seemed to be a touch of pride. "Been there for over a year." Eilish looked at Olivia as if waiting for an introduction.

Rian felt as if she had no choice. "This is my friend Olivia Tucker."

"Oh, I've seen you before, Miss Tucker," Eilish said, even though she addressed a twelve-year-old. "You're the Missus's niece. I've seen you at Shippen House many times. Surprised you're over here."

Olivia seemed as panicked as Rian felt. "Oh, I'm just keeping my Mammy company while she buys some food for dinner. We bumped into Rian."

Eilish nodded in the direction of Maddie Freeman. "And who are you with?"

"Oh, that's just a friend." Rian inwardly winced because her response sounded so false to her. She added, "Who I bumped into," which didn't sound true either.

With that awkward response, Eilish seemed to get the hint. "Well, I'd best be doing me job. Don't want to piss Cook off. Nice to finally meet you, Miss Tucker." She turned and danced away.

Rian watched Eilish bounce down High Street. "Do you think she knew anything?"

"I don't know. If she does figure anything out, I hope she keeps her mouth shut."

Twenty minutes later, Maddie and Rose parted with polite nods and headed for home. Rian caught up with Maddie. She noticed that Olivia and her Mammy were walking on the other side of the street.

Rian's curiosity was killing her. "What did you two decide?"

"I've got some sewing to do. New outfits for both Rose and her grandson. I've got sizes for both."

"Do you know how you're going to help them escape?"

"We've got some ideas. Nothing is going to happen until Topper gets here. That's at least a couple of weeks. The key will be getting her out of Philadelphia as soon as they bolt. No hiding them here in town because all hell will break loose."

"How are they going to get out of town?"

"Don't know yet. Could be on a steamer that's headed to New York. Maybe even the train now that they've got cars for colored folks. Maybe the back of a farmer's wagon. We'll figure it out."

"What if they get stopped?"

"We have a friend who has an embosser. A stamp. It's a fake, but it looks official."

"Who is your friend?"

"Rule Number 1 in this business is that if you don't need to know something, you don't get told, and you don't need to know that. We write up some fake manumission papers and stamp them. They'll have physical descriptions of Topper and Rose, but with different names. That'll get them past any nosy slave catchers, and hopefully, the two of them will be ahead of the wanted posters."

"Do you know what their new names are going to be?"

Maddie smiled as she walked. "Rule Number 1."

• •

· SEAMUS ·

After work, Seamus dropped off a note at the Purvis residence and then walked to the Church of St. Philip de Neri. He was pleased that he could walk almost entirely without pain.

Thankfully, there was no line at the confessional. He entered the compartment. "Forgive me, Father, for I have sinned. It has been six weeks since me last confession. I accuse meself of the following sins. I'm afraid I haven't attended church much recently."

"I've noticed. That saddens me," said the priest from behind the wooden lattice.

"I have had impure thoughts."

"How many times, my son?"

"More than I can count, Father."

"Anything else, my son?"

"I stole, father. Goods from the piers."

"How many times?"

"Just once."

"Anything else, my son?"

"I took the Lord's name in vain."

"How many times?"

"I don't know. Maybe twenty."

"The impure thoughts are new. Is there a girl?"

"Yes, Father."

"It isn't Siobhan Callaghan, is it?"

"Yes, Father."

"Be careful, my son."

"I know, Father."

"You've already crossed the line by deserting your own kind and consorting with the coloreds, Seamus. You're traveling down the wrong road."

"Father, could you please let me know me penance and give me absolution? I don't know anything about the wrong road."

"Watch yourself, Seamus. You're getting too big for your britches."

"I've heard that before, Father."

· · · · · · · · · · · · · · · · · · · ·

Seamus's next stop was McSweeney's. He was disappointed that Siobhan wasn't behind the bar to greet him as he walked in. He ducked into the kitchen—no Siobhan.

Just then, McSweeney walked up the stairs from the basement carrying a crate of whiskey bottles.

"Braden, where's Siobhan?"

McSweeney walked past him to the bar. "She quit."

Seamus felt like the breath had been kicked out of him. He had to lean against the door. "Quit? When?"

McSweeney started unloading bottles from the crate. "She stopped in at lunch. Left me high and dry. Too bad. I was getting used to her." He shook his head ruefully. "Business has gotten better too. No surprise. I think you overplayed your hand, Seamus."

"Why? Why'd she quit?"

"Officially? One of her sisters is in a family way and quit her job at Clancy's. Opened up a space for her. Unofficially, her daddy didn't like you mooning over her at church yesterday. I think Sunday dinner at the Callaghans got a little heated."

"Whataya mean?"

"Whataya think I mean? Your little girlfriend didn't want to quit. I think she likes you, Boyo. What are you gonna do now?"

Seamus was both devastated and elated by the news. "Dunno. Things just got a little complicated."

Wednesday, July 20

· OTTO ·

Two days later, Otto Krieger dined with Nicholas Biddle, former president of the Second Bank of the United States. In April, the Second Bank's charter had run out, and it had been reorganized as the Bank of the United States of Pennsylvania. Even though Biddle's status was dramatically reduced, Otto loyally supported his friend. They had just ordered the turtle soup and settled into their luncheon conversation.

"Thanks for making the trek down here, Otto. I know it's not as convenient as it used to be."

"I must admit that when we decided to move the factories nine blocks north, I was not thinking about my daily lunches here. However, the walk does me good."

"Have you started production yet?"

"Yes. On Monday. I can already see the first passenger coach shaping up. It is going to be a beauty. I think the efficiencies that arise from our modern production methods will serve us well."

"How about the locomotive and rail shops? When will they open?"

"Krieger Locomotive in about two weeks. Krieger Rail in a month, plus or minus."

"How are orders?"

"About what you would expect. We already had a good reputation for building horse-drawn carriages, so the railroads have readily ordered our railway cars right off the drawing board—more freight cars than passenger cars, which has been a bit of a surprise. Most have taken a wait-and-see for Krieger Locomotive, although Adrian sold one engine to a mining operation in Mach Chunk. There is a demand for our engines. We just have to prove that the locomotives can do what we have predicted. The success of the rails will go hand-in-hand with the engines. Heavier engines will demand heavier rails."

"I must say, Otto. I think you are running a grand experiment. I approve of your industrial innovations. I think they are going to dominate the industry. I have to admit I'm skeptical about your hiring practices. First, a Black man. Now I hear you're hiring the Irish."

Otto stuffed down an impulse to verbally lash out. He was used to this from most people in town but hoped for better from Biddle. "It all seems to be working out fine. Jules Freeman has been essential in this transition. He is working closely with Seamus Gallagher, my late wife's nephew. The two of them together are industrial production geniuses. They have the coach factory up and running. Now they are pushing hard to open Krieger Locomotive."

"How's your cash flow?"

"We are feeling a little pinched right now. Frankly, even though I intend to eventually move out of the horse-drawn carriage part of the business, that has kept us afloat during this transition. Why do you ask?"

"I'm worried. Have you read about the Specie Circular?"

Otto shook his head and was distracted briefly as the turtle soup arrived.

"A couple of days ago, Andy Jackson issued an executive order called the Specie Circular. In a few months, all western lands will have to be paid for by paper money backed by gold or silver."

Otto took a sip of his soup and added a little sherry while he pondered this. "You are talking about land in states like Indiana and Mississippi. They are a long way from here. Why should that worry us?"

"Remember when Jackson withdrew all the federal funds from the Second Bank and placed them in his pet banks around the country?"

"Of course. He was trying to kill your bank."

"Well, he was only partially successful. But those banks—banks like your friend Shippen's Bank of Industry—haven't adhered to a conservative monetary policy as we did. They've just printed money without attempting to tie the amount of paper to the amount of gold they had sitting in their vaults. People, especially speculators, are paying for land out West with paper money that isn't backed by gold."

Otto took a sip of his soup and tried to absorb the implications. "So?"

"So, all of a sudden, all that paper money issued by the banks won't be able to buy a single acre of land. It will be worthless. Overnight, there will be a lot less sound money in the system. The money that is backed by gold is going to be sucked to the West. There won't be enough for internal improvements like railroads, bridges, and canals in the East. That is going to directly affect your business."

"When do you think this is all going to take effect?"

"I've been working on that question. Best guess? One year. Maybe less."

"What do you suggest I do?"

"Don't get too overextended. Build a cash reserve. Vote for Harrison."

"I have paid little attention to the election. Why Harrison?"

"The Whigs have stated clearly that they are in favor of federal financing of internal improvements. The opposite of Jackson, and we assume his heir apparent, Mr. Van Buren."

"Any chance Mr. Harrison will recharter the Second Bank of the United States and pull federal money back from Jackson's pet banks?"

"That is my hope. Our economy is unruly. It needs some degree of discipline. The pet banks are printing money without regard to the long-term consequences. Only a national bank has the clout to impose appropriate regulations. Since Jackson withdrew the funds from my bank, the country has enjoyed quite a party. I'm afraid we'll soon suffer from an even bigger hangover."

"What happens to you if Van Buren wins?"

"My bank will remain what it has been since its charter ran out in April: just a regular bank, same as Shippen's bank. Watch out for him, by the way. He's flying high right now, but I predict he will crash hard along with many, many others."

"Thanks for the advice. I will keep it in mind."

. . . .

· JULES ·

After work, Jules found Maddie in the kitchen sorting through remnants of cloth. He guessed she was already starting to create outfits for Rose and Topper. "Well, who are they going to be?"

"This is the most fun part of our job, making up new identities for our fugitives until they can get to Canada. Neither Rose nor Topper can read or write. Rose felt comfortable posing as a domestic traveling to Albany to work for a lobbyist. I don't think she understood what a lobbyist is, but she was okay with it."

"Do we know the names of any lobbyists in Albany?"

"Nope. I'll just make one up." Forged documents weren't part of the standard service the stationmasters provided to the escapees who passed through. If possible, they gave them a safe place to rest up for a day or so, clean clothing, and a guide to the next stationmaster. Only on two previous occasions had Maddie written out official-looking documents in her precise penmanship. She had completed the forgery with an even more official-looking stamp.

"Where's the embosser?" asked Jules.

"Not sure. I imagine Robert Purvis has it."

· ·

· SEAMUS ·

The Purvis's maid escorted Seamus and Rian to his study. As Purvis wasn't present, they spent the time perusing his library. He had a vast array of books in French and English. They couldn't find *The Art of War* and eventually sat, each with a book they had pulled from the shelves.

Purvis arrived ten minutes later, and the two rose from their chairs as Purvis introduced himself to Rian. Seamus was impressed that Purvis was gracious to his twelve-year-old visitor, treating Rian as an honored guest.

"I'm so sorry I'm late," Purvis said. "I had an unexpected meeting that couldn't be delayed." He gestured for both of them to re-seat themselves.

Seamus sat back down, only slightly more comfortable in the opulent surroundings. "Everything okay?"

"Oh yes, in the grand scheme of things. Before my father died, he invested heavily in Philadelphia real estate. My mother hung on to most of them and bought some others. When I reached adulthood, her choices still proved to be quite sound, so I kept most of the properties that she purchased. However, two in particular are on the verge of collapsing. I had to meet with a man who can tear them down for me."

"Is he going to do it?"

"I don't think he wants the job. He gave me such a high price; if I say yes, it will put a smile on his face."

"Well, thank you for meeting us so soon, Robert. It looks like your days are very busy."

"I was pleased to receive your note, Seamus. When we parted last week, I wasn't sure what you would decide."

"Me boys and me are back in. But I've got some major problems to solve."

"Do you have a lead on a new pump?"

"We're building one this time. At Krieger Locomotive. And it's gonna be a doozy. It'll still have a hand pump, but we'll use that only until we get a chamber of water boiling. Then, we'll have a pump that's powered by steam. Should be more powerful than what we can generate by hand."

Purvis slapped his knee and laughed a hearty laugh. "A steam-powered fire pump! Only in America. Has anyone ever done this before?"

Seamus shook his head and smiled. "Not that we've ever heard of."

"Are you sure it will work?"

"Heinrich Aldrich, the guy who designed the steam engines at the factories—he built a smaller model of the real thing to make sure he got all the parts right—he says this model will work like a charm. I'm taking his word for it. Jules is running a crew of volunteers as we speak, making a new carriage out of spare parts from the old coach factory."

"This is brilliant. A major problem solved. What else?"

"I've got some recruits for the hose company. Some of the workers at the factories. Word spread around the shops that we're building a steam-powered fire pump. Men just came up and volunteered. Said they wanted to be a part of it. Most of them live here in Moya. They know we're gonna be helping out your people."

"Wonderful. How many?"

"About a dozen. Mostly ispinis."

"Germans. Do you think that's going to be enough?"

"No, Robert. Nowhere near enough. I'd like to make use of some men from your community."

"Whoa. A change of heart?"

"No, sir. But the seeds of an idea. Me problem is that as soon as the first Black man strikes an Irishman, we've got a race riot on our hands."

"How are you going to avoid a fight? Callaghan has already knocked you down once. He's going to show no mercy the next time."

"That's why Rian and I are here. We'd like to read *The Art of War*."

"You think you can find the answer to this problem in a book that's 2,500 years old?"

"Callaghan reads it. Worst case is I learn a little bit about how he thinks."

Purvis rose from his desk. "We can start right away if you would like." He walked to one of his bookcases and, after only a few seconds, pulled out a slim volume and handed it to Seamus.

The cover of the book said *L'Art de la Guerre, Textes Originaux de Sun Wu, Jean Joseph Marie Amiot*. Seamus reverently opened the book and noted its year of publication: 1772. "I wonder if George Washington read this."

"There's no record of that. But Napoleon certainly did."

Sitting next to Seamus, Rian spotted an American eagle embossed over the signature William Purvis on the first page. "What's this?"

"I inherited at least half these books, that one included, when my father died. He frequently loaned his books to friends, but when he did, he would emboss the first page to make sure the books found their way back to him."

Rian ran her finger over the circle of stars that surrounded the eagle. "How did he make it?"

Purvis opened his desk drawer and pulled out a cast-iron gadget with two handles. "With this. It's called an embosser. I found it in this desk when my father died. Here, let me show you."

Purvis handed the embosser and a sheet of paper to Rian. "Put the paper between these two plates." The plates were little metal circles about two inches in diameter. "Now squeeze," Purvis said. "Harder. Harder. Just a few more seconds."

When Rian removed the paper from the embosser, there it was: an American eagle surrounded by a circle of stars. She handed the paper to Seamus. He had never seen such a thing, nor could he imagine being so rich that he could own so many books that he would just freely loan them out. He ran his finger over the raised bumps of the eagle and the circle of stars. *Maybe someday I'll have an embosser.*

• • • • • • • • • • • • • • • • • • • •

That evening and the next, Seamus, Rian, and Robert sat in his study. Rian did her best to translate the French. More often, just to move things along a little faster, Robert translated fluently on the fly. Occasionally Seamus took notes.

"Appear weak when you are strong, and strong when you are weak."

"The supreme art of war is to subdue the enemy without fighting."

"Pretend to be weak, that he may grow arrogant. If he is taking his ease, give him no rest. If his forces are united, separate them. If sovereign and subject are in accord, put division between them."

"All warfare is based on deception. Hence, when we are able to attack, we must seem unable; when using our forces, we must appear inactive; when we are near, we must make the enemy believe we are far away; when far away, we must make him believe we are near."

As Rian or Robert read, Seamus marveled at the sophistication of this man who lived before the time of Christ. Only occasionally did his mind wander.

He smiled to himself as they plowed through the treatise. They made an odd trio: The wealthy 26-year-old Black man who could pass as a white; the on-the-make Irishmen six years his junior; and the half-German half-Irish half-wild pre-woman. Seamus was impressed that his twelve-year-old cousin stuck with the reading the entire time and showed no sign of roochiness. And her curiosity seemed to be boundless.

Rather than stretch her legs during a break, Rian continued to leaf through the book.

They got back to their reading.

"The greatest victory is that which requires no battle."

"Let your plans be dark and impenetrable as night, and when you move, fall like a thunderbolt."

"Attack where your enemies are not prepared; go to where they do not expect."

"When the enemy sees an advantage but does not advance to seize it, he is fatigued."

"If your enemy is quick tempered, you can make a fool of him."

"One who knows how to unite upper and lower ranks in purpose will be victorious."

When Robert read the last passage and closed the book, he looked expectantly at Seamus. "Well, what do you think?"

"Only seen a couple of Chinese before. Over on the wharves. Don't think I'll ever look at them the same again. That Sun Tzu was one smart cookie. Don't understand how come they're letting the English kick the shit out of 'em so bad right now."

Purvis shrugged. "Did the book help?"

"I think it did. It seems I've got to learn a lot more about Callaghan before I make me move."

"Did you know Callaghan is one of the largest landowners in Philadelphia? We often find ourselves competing for the same buildings."

This was new information to Seamus. "What does he do with them?"

"Rents them. Same as me. They're mostly apartments."

"Only to Irish?"

"Heavens, no. Callaghan rents to anyone who will pay. And he threatens anyone who falls behind on their rent. It doesn't matter the color of their skin."

"Now that's an interesting piece of information. I'll need some more help from you."

"What do you have in mind?"

"I need some uniforms for me boys. The flashier, the better. About fifteen of them. I need them by August 6."

"That's a tall order, but it can probably be done. There are many seamstresses in Moya. Your men will have to come by for measurements. Anything else?"

"Yes, I'd like to talk to you about those properties you're going to tear down."

FRIDAY, JULY 22

· RIAN ·

As was often the case since the move to the new factory, Rian and her father walked home together. A light rain had started during the walk, so the two were happy to get to the house. Rian always enjoyed this time with her father, and as usual, they were planning to practice their violins together.

When Rian mounted the porch steps, she saw Olivia sitting on a chair near the front door. Something was wrong. Olivia had been crying.

Otto walked up the brick walk two steps behind Rian. "*Wer ist das* [What is this]? Why, Rian, it is Olivia Tucker. You have grown so much since last summer. What is the problem, Child?"

"I need to talk to Rian."

"Please come inside. It is drier there."

"I'm fine, sir. Thank you."

Otto smiled and opened the front door. "Then do not let me get in the way of your important business. Rian, Alice should have dinner on the table in ten minutes. Please do not be late."

Rian waited until Otto closed the door. "Did Rose tell Topper about the plan?"

"Topper didn't come. My father lost him in a card game last week. Topper. My brother. My father didn't even bother to tell Mammy or me. Didn't think it was important enough. Mammy heard about it from the boy Father brought as his groom instead. She's crushed. I hate him."

"What is Mammy going to do?"

"I don't know. She wouldn't talk to me."

· ·

· SEAMUS ·

It was two o'clock in the morning. Seamus had been standing in the rain for so long that he was shivering, even though the day's heat had barely broken.

Someone extinguished the last candle in Clancy's Saloon, and he watched Siobhan and Clancy exit the building. Siobhan raised an umbrella and held it over Clancy as he locked the door. Clancy said something to Siobhan that Seamus couldn't hear, and the two parted. As Siobhan crossed the street, Seamus stepped out of the shadows.

Siobhan saw him, quickened her pace toward him, and extended her umbrella to cover him as well. It wasn't big enough to do its job. "What are you doing here, Seamus? Jaysus, you're soaking wet. How long have you been out here?"

"Dunno. Couple of hours. I've got to talk to you."

"Me father's gonna tan your hide, Seamus. He doesn't want us to see each other."

"Yeah. I know. But what do you want?"

Siobhan hesitated. With the umbrella half sheltering her and half sheltering Seamus, she was getting soaked too. "I think you're trouble."

"No more trouble than any of the other Irish lads around here."

"Yeah, but some of them me da actually likes."

"Like who?"

Siobhan's black eyes sparkled. "I don't know. Mikey McGuire's pretty nice looking."

Seamus snorted. "Mikey? He's going no place. You'd be better off waiting for his little brother Conor."

"Whataya want, Seamus?"

"I need to talk to you."

"You blew that in church. Me da caught what was going on right away."

"You're the one who looked back at me."

"You're the one who showed up at mass after not coming for months."

"How was I supposed to know your da had eyes in the back of his head?"

"I've got four older sisters. He's had plenty of practice. You said you gotta talk to me. So, talk."

"I can't see you for a while."

Siobhan looked up at him with incredulity. "You're a fooking idiot, Seamus. You waited in the rain for two fooking hours to tell me you can't fooking see me?"

Seamus let the ridiculousness of his statement sink in. "All right, that didn't come out so good. I meant I want to see you, but I can't. For a while."

"How long's a while?"

"Dunno. Couple of weeks."

"What makes you think I'm interested?"

A wolfish grin crept onto Seamus's face. "Not sure. Maybe you like trouble."

"Trouble's okay when it's worth it. I'm not sure you're worth it."

"Look, I've got some problems to solve. I can't do that and see you too. I can't tell you why I can't see you until I've solved the problems. After that, you'll either know I'm worth the trouble or know I'm not."

Siobhan looked Seamus hard in the eye. "You hurt me da, and I'll kill you."

"Your da's a problem, but he's not me only problem. Will you just wait for a couple of weeks?"

Siobhan cracked a smile for the first time. "You think I'm standing out here getting soaked with you for nothing? Yeah, I'll wait."

Seamus matched her warm smile. "That's good. That's real good."

"Go home. If any of me da's boys see us, there'll be hell to pay."

WEDNESDAY, JULY 27

· OLIVIA ·

"I just decided I don't want them to hurt me anymore."

It had been six days since Randolph Tucker had arrived in Philadelphia without Topper. Olivia had approached Rose numerous times, but she always shut her out. Today, though, Olivia found her alone in the kitchen and ready to talk. "Mammy, Topper's your grandson, but he's my half-brother. I love him too."

Rose sat at the kitchen table, oblivious to the flour she was smearing onto her face as she wiped her tears. "Lady's daddy sold off Ben and then Abraham."

Rose had raised Olivia's mother, just like she had raised Olivia. When Olivia's mother was an infant, Rose had started calling her *Lady* and never stopped. *Ben? Abraham?* Olivia was embarrassed at how little she knew about her Mammy. She didn't know how old she was. She didn't know who Ben and Abraham were. She didn't know if one was her husband and the other was a child. She just didn't know.

"Lady put up such a fuss when she married Mister Tucker that Mister Hayne, your grandfather, just sent me over to Long Pond. Lady didn't want to be without me, but she didn't ever think that I left three children back at Bobbit Hall."

Bobbit Hall was six hours from Long Pond. There were more slaves there than at her home. Olivia and her mother visited her grandparents perhaps once a year. To the best of her knowledge, they had never bothered to bring Mammy back to her old plantation. As far as she knew, Olivia had never run into any of Mammy's relatives at Bobbit Hall. But she had never asked.

"Then Mister Tucker sold Rebecca. Then Palidore. Then Jenny. The only blood I've got left is Topper. And now he gone lost him in a fucking card game. I don't care what happens to me no more. I'm going to get out of here and walk to Canada."

"Mammy, I think we can get you to Canada."

"Don't know. Your daddy hasn't let me out of the house since he got here. That man's got eyes in the back of his head. He just sniffs, and he knows what the slaves is thinking."

"We've got a couple of weeks yet. Let me talk to my friends."

. . . .

· JULES ·

Jules leaned forward and handed Seamus a nickel. "Best bet I ever lost."

They sat facing one another on the bench seats of the first railroad car built in the new Krieger Coach factory. Each of its three passenger compartments, accessed by a side door, could seat six people.

The car was parked in the finish room, isolated from the dust and mayhem of the production floor. Tomorrow, workers would roll it back onto the factory floor to install the last of the hardware. In the afternoon, with the assistance of horses, the beefiest men in the factory would hoist it atop a wagon built for one purpose: transporting railroad cars to the sidings and wharves of Philadelphia. In this case, the first delivery would be to the *Camden & Amboy* across the river.

Seamus accepted the nickel and smirked. "You keep losing bets like this, and you're gonna make me a rich man."

"I never imagined we could build an entire coach in ten days. I figured twelve at the fastest. How did you know?"

"Oh, I stacked the deck a bit. When me boys were practicing on their new machines, I had them working on the benches. Had Conor varnishing them in this room a week ago. Same with some of the trim before it was installed. I was working pretty closely with Adrian's crew to make sure they delivered the hardware in time. Question is, can we keep it up?"

Jules ran a practiced eye over the craftsmanship. Although he saw flaws, he was generally pleased with the finished product. "It helps my planning to have sales so strong. I'm ordering materials now that we won't get to for another three months. Unless you keep speeding things up, that is."

Seamus shrugged as if he might still have some tricks up his sleeve. He produced a sheet of paper from his breast pocket that Jules recognized as the factory's work schedule for the next three weeks. "While we're here, we might take advantage of the quiet. Care to talk about what's coming up? I've got some questions."

Jules nodded and moved over to Seamus's bench to look at the paper together. "Whataya got?"

Seamus pointed to the top item on the list. "What the hell is this?"

"That's your Uncle Otto wheeling and dealing. *Camden & Amboy* has a coal tender that somebody else built. Not us. Well, it's already falling apart. The wheel assemblies are fine, but the body's all but shot." Jules pointed to the following five cars listed on the work schedule. "To sweeten the deal for these five passenger cars, Otto said we would pick up that old tender in Camden, bring it here, build a new body, and deliver it back as soon as we could. I guess they liked the idea because they paid cash money upfront for everything."

"Jaysus, Otto."

"Can't complain too much. He's designing great cars. And he's a great salesman, despite his thick accent. He would still be the best craftsman on the floor if he did any of that anymore."

"And when were you going to tell me about this little coal tender thing? Do we even have a design for it?"

"Otto's working on that today. The plans will be ready by the time the wreck gets here."

"Jules, I'm already pushing the boys pretty hard. I'll probably have to hire some of me Irish lads to go pick that wreck up."

"That one I've already figured out. When we deliver this car tomorrow, we just leave the wagon by the railroad siding. We'll walk the horses back but not the wagon. I told the *Camden & Amboy* folks that when the tender arrives in Camden, if they hoist it aboard the wagon and tie it down, we'll take it from there. With all the heavy lifting done, we'll just send Rian and Conor over to pick it up and bring it back."

"Nice plan, Jules. When do we send the kids?

"We figure two weeks. Anything else you need to know?"

Seamus folded the work schedule and placed it in his shirt pocket. "Nope, the rest is straightforward. The shop's working just like we planned. The workers are settling in. We've got enough materials to build at least half this list. I'm good." Then Seamus shifted to the bench seat opposite Jules. "While we're by ourselves, I've got some information that might be of interest."

Jules took his appraising eye off the woodwork and focused on Seamus. "What's up?"

"Hans Schmidt."

"The guy Otto fired last year? He's in the slave-catching business now. What about him?"

"He was at a meeting at George Shippen's house a couple of days ago."

"You consorting with the impatient class these days, Seamus?"

"Nope. Me cousin Eilish is a maid in the Shippens' house. Rian's late mum Deirdre, my mum, and Eilish's mum are sisters. Eilish knows I've taken a recent interest in the welfare of your people. Not sure she approves, but I guess family loyalty wins out over prejudice. At least in this instance."

Jules knew that sometimes he just had to allow Seamus to prattle on before getting to his point.

"Eilish was serving lunch to Shippen and his brother-in-law Randolph Tucker—that's Olivia's father—and a couple of others. I don't think they were interested in breaking bread with the likes of Hans, so they discussed business over lunch before he arrived."

"Eilish eavesdropped on their meeting?"

"Not really. More like these gentlemen just talked as if the help wasn't in the room. The staff might as well be wallpaper. The men weren't very . . . what's the word?"

"Discreet?"

"Yup. Discreet. Even when they disparage the Irish, they just speak as if there's no Hibernians there to overhear it."

Jules smiled ruefully. "I'm familiar."

"Well, anyway, this group of men is concerned about the growing number of Negroes in Philadelphia."

"How concerned?"

"Concerned enough to hire Hans Schmidt to figure out who is helping escaped slaves settle in Philadelphia."

Jules sat back and crossed his arms. "Why should that worry me?"

"Because of Cousin Elmo, for one."

Jules knew there was no sense pretending that he wasn't a stationmaster. He decided to take the new reality with grace. "We never talked about that day at my house. So, you knew Cousin Elmo was an escaped slave?"

"Right away. And I assume you and Maddie have been harboring fugitives for a while."

Jules nodded. *Damnit. Maddie and I have been so careful for so many years. That one day changed a whole lot—Rian, then Olivia, then Conor, now Seamus.*

"These gentlemen are intent on putting an end to it, Jules."

"Not many fugitives remain in Philadelphia. Most self-emancipators just keep on heading north."

"They're concerned about both—free Blacks and the runaways passing through. The group wants to stop the network of folks helping out the runaways. I think that's why Mr. Tucker was invited. Shippen had a name for it."

"The Underground Railroad?"

"Yes, that's it. And I have more piece of info."

"Shoot."

"The Tuckers have a maid named Rose."

Jules stiffened but didn't say anything.

"She's planning to bolt. One of the other slaves ratted her out. They're going to use her for bait. They've hired Schmidt and Austin Slatter to follow her."

"Why are you telling me this?"

"Just putting two and two together. I guess I have another bit of information. Eilish said she bumped into Rian the other day on High Street. Rian was with Olivia Tucker."

"That's not unusual these days."

"Yeah, but it was last Monday afternoon, the first day we worked on the new fire pump. Rian told me that she couldn't help because she had to go to her French lesson."

Jules grew more uncomfortable. "Keep talking."

"So, Olivia was with a Black woman who I'm betting was Rose."

"And . . ."

"And Rian was also with a Black woman. I'll bet you this nickel that it was Maddie."

Jules shook his head. "City's a bit smaller than we figured."

"Watch yourself, Jules. I don't think these folks are going to play nice."

 •   •   •   •   •   •   •   •   •   •   •   •   •   •   •   •   •   •   •

· SEAMUS ·

At the end of their workday, Seamus and Dylan walked to the old Krieger Coach shop to admire the just completed steam-powered fire engine. Seamus couldn't help but notice how dim the old place was, compared to Krieger's new gaslit shops.

Even so, the beauty of the new engine bounced out at him. The cherry red paint looked almost liquid in the candlelight. The steam engine, polished to bright silver, glistened. The traces were just big enough for three men to haul the engine to wherever it needed to go. He reached out to stroke their graceful lines.

"Watch it, Seamus. Is the varnish even dry?"

"Dry as can be. It's perfect."

"Lookee here." Dylan pointed to an oval-shaped brass medallion that stated Krieger Locomotive, Philadelphia U.S.A.

"Jules brought that down the other day. He says it will be the best advertising Krieger Locomotive can get."

"There's no other writing on this beautiful little machine. How come they didn't write No Name Fire Brigade on it?"

"I told 'em not to. I've got plans."

"Whataya gonna call it? You gotta name it. How about Lilly, after yer ma?"

"Nope. I'm saving that for the next one."

"Yer already planning the next one? What? You afraid Callaghan's gonna swipe this one too?"

"Callaghan won't have the chance to swipe this one. I can guarantee that."

"How?"

"Sorry, Dylan. Let your plans be dark and impenetrable as night."

"What the fook's that supposed to mean?"

Seamus smiled to himself. "Don't worry about it. Just stick with me, okay? I think I know what I'm doing."

· ·

· RIAN ·

Olivia's mother kept a watchful eye on the girls as she pruned roses a mere twenty feet away.

Rian gave Olivia a gentle push on a swing that hung from the limb of a majestic chestnut tree in the Tuckers' backyard. "How's Rose doing?"

Olivia didn't respond until she had arced back to Rian. "She'd leave tomorrow if the plan were in place. Now she's just angry."

Rian gave Olivia another push. "I've got a message from Jules. Somebody ratted her out." She had to wait until Olivia swung back to her. "Your father knows she's planning to bolt." Another pause. "He wants to catch the conductors and stationmasters on the Underground Railroad." And another. "So, he's having Mammy followed whenever she leaves the house."

"Who's going to follow her?"

"A guy by the name of Hans Schmidt. He's a partner with Austin Slatter." Olivia arced back again. "He's the man with the manacles who wanted to get into the fight with my family the day we met."

"I remember him. He's big."

"Yes, he is. And mean, too."

Monday, August 1

· SEAMUS ·

Seamus was dog-tired. Work and fire brigade business demanded so much of his time that he was getting by on three hours of sleep a night. Social time at Mc-Sweeney's and extracurricular activity on the wharves were just a fond memory.

Just as he finished his first lap around the production floor of Krieger Coach, someone poked him from behind. He turned to find Rian. Even yelling was useless with the steam engine and every machine at full clatter. Rian merely pointed to a figure two hundred feet away, walking toward them.

Seamus's heart leaped. *Siobhan.* He signaled her to follow him out the door to the alley. Rian floated away, on to her next mission, whatever that was.

Seamus tried to suppress a wide grin as he held the alley door for Siobhan. "I thought we weren't supposed to see each other for a few weeks."

"I just came here to tell you you're an idiot."

Seamus was dumbstruck. "What are you talking about?"

"I had to talk me da out of kicking the shit out of you again."

"But I haven't done anything yet." Seamus could still feel the pain of Hugh Callaghan's wrath and certainly didn't make light of it.

"Swiping stuff right in our own backyard ain't the way to keep out of me da's way."

Siobhan must have read the blank expression on his face. "The Pine Street Pier? Two nights ago? Two wagon loads of Ferris china?"

Seamus spread his arms in sincere innocence. "That wasn't me, Siobhan. Not me, not me boys. But tell your da I'll find out who it was."

"I'm not sure he's gonna believe you."

"Tell your da I'm too busy getting ready for the parade to be lifting stuff off the wharves."

"He told me you reserved a spot. Must say, you've got him wondering where you've found a new fire pump. None of your boys is talking."

"That's good. I want it to be a surprise."

• •

· RIAN ·

Rian was out of breath when Rufus ushered her into the Freemans' kitchen. She found Maddie seated at the kitchen table that seemed to be where the Freemans conducted all their business. Maddie put down a quill pen and greeted Rian warmly. "Good lord, Child. Did you run the whole way down here?"

Rian nodded. "You told me to bring you the biggest parasol I could find. How is this one?" Rian didn't know the Freemans' entire plan for abetting Mammy's escape, but she knew the umbrella was a piece of the puzzle. *"People get used to seeing an umbrella in a crowd, but they forget to look at who's holding it,"* Maddie said.

Maddie grasped the umbrella and opened it, eyeing its expanse. "It's not as big as I was hoping for, but its red color works to our advantage. I think it will do. Where did you find it?"

"Mrs. Mott loaned it to me. She was very proud that the fabric is made of slave-free cotton."

Maddie smiled. "Good for her. Does she suspect anything?"

"Hard to say. Maybe. It's not something I would use, but I didn't tell her what I wanted it for. I figured Rule #1."

That made Maddie smile. "Hey, your timing is perfect. I could use your help. I'm about to make a document look very official. Here, read this." She handed Rian a sheet of paper filled with words written with quill and ink.

Certificate of Manumission
March 1, 1830
To Whom it may concern,

> This document certifies that the bearer hereof, the negro woman known as Mazie, has purchased her freedom from the widow Meredith Barry for the price of $550. She is 50 years old, 5'6" tall, of dark complexion, and of strong constitution. She has a prominent scar on her upper right arm.
> It is mandated by law that Mazie leave Prince William County and the Commonwealth of Virginia within two weeks of this date. She may take any worldly possessions belonging to her or granted to her by Widow Barry. Mazie shall hereafter be considered and treated as a free woman and shall move at will in areas outside the Commonwealth of Virginia.
> Percival H. Warren
> County Clerk
> Prince William County
> Commonwealth of Virginia

"Who is Mazie?"

"That's going to be Rose's new name."

Holy mackerel, thought Rian. *She trusts me enough to violate Rule #1.* "Did you just write this?"

Maddie smiled. "Mmm-hmm. What do you think?"

"I don't know. The words sound official. Who's Percival H. Warren?"

"Nobody. I just made him up."

"But what if they check? And there's no Percival Warren?"

"Well, that's just it. Chances are no one's going to ever check. The important thing is that it looks genuine. And that's where this comes in." She held up a heavy cast iron gadget.

"What's that?" said Rian, although she knew exactly what it was.

"This, Child, is an embosser." Maddie placed the embosser over the fake signature of Percival H. Warren and clamped it down. "Help me squeeze." Rian grasped the long handle of the embosser. "Squeeze harder," Maddie said. "Harder. Harder." When Maddie released the paper, there it was: the image of an American eagle clearly defined by a series of bumps surrounded by a circle of raised stars.

Rian ran her finger over the bumps. "This is the same embosser you used when you made Jules's fake papers."

Maddie looked at Rian with surprise. "You've seen my husband's papers?"

"Yes, a year ago. He said you made them. I love the embosser. It makes the paper look official."

"I wish my husband would tell me who knows what around here." She rolled an ink blotter over the page. "Yup. It almost doesn't matter what I write in this document. The people most likely to be reading this are train conductors or ticket takers on a boat. But even if a bounty hunter reads it, he'll see the eagle and assume that this document is genuine. As long as the description on the paper matches Rose, they're going to let her pass."

"Does Rose have a scar like that? On her upper arm?"

"Yes, she does. When she and I were at the market, that's one of the things I asked her for."

"Where'd you get this stamper?"

"It's called an embosser. A friend loaned it to us. He found it when he went through his father's library after he died. He's loaned it to us a couple of times for situations like this."

Rian chose not to reveal that she knew the friend was Robert Purvis. *It's kind of fun to apply Rule #1,* she thought.

Saturday, August 6

· RIAN ·

For ten years, the city's hose companies had held a firemen's parade on the first Saturday in August. Even the bitterest of rivals declared a day of truce and instead competed in other ways. The parades became more of a spectacle each year, with fancy uniforms, bands, floats, and fire equipment on display. In 1835, the parade had attracted ten thousand spectators along its route. Following the parade, hose companies held contests: the longest flow of water, the hose carry, axemanship, ladder climb, and a battle royale. Expectations were that this day would be the most memorable ever.

Rian had recruited Conor McGuire and Trey Shippen to walk with her and carry a banner she and Jules had created the night before by painting an old bedsheet. The staging area for the parade was Washington Square. With a 10:00 start time, hose companies began arriving around 9:00 to find their assigned places in line.

The three friends stood on Walnut Street opposite the Square's entrance. Firemen were striding into the square in all sorts of regalia—some brigades dressed as medieval courtiers, others as Indians, others as pioneers with axes. Band members in plumed helmets practiced their instruments. Men hauled in brightly polished fire equipment. A white stallion pranced by, towing what appeared to be a brand-new piece of equipment that said Moyamensing Hose Company on its side. Right behind it, three other men hauled the old Moya pump, which now looked shabby by comparison.

"Holy mackerel," muttered Rian when she eyed the new engine. "That's a six-man pump."

Conor stuck his chin forward, ever so slightly, as if to point across the street. "You see that guy over there? The big one standing next to the entrance? That's Hugh Callaghan. He's the one who organizes this thing every year."

Rian was impressed by the size of the man. He was a giant. "That's Hugh Callaghan? How do you know?"

"Me two older brothers just joined Moya. They introduced me to him the other day."

"Holy smokes. Does that mean you're gonna join up when you're old enough?"

"Dunno. Maybe. Come on. Let's find out where we're supposed to go."

The trio dodged around another fire pump, escorted by firemen dressed as Revolutionary War soldiers, and entered the Square.

With Conor leading the way, they walked up to Hugh Callaghan, who stood next to a stake that said Moyamensing. There were easily eighty Moya men already there, chatting idly. "Hello, Mr. Callaghan. Where's the No Name Fire Brigade supposed to start?"

Callaghan looked down at the trio as if they were mosquitoes he might swat. "You're Conor, right? The McGuires' little brother?"

"Yes, sir."

"Whaterya doing hanging out with No Name for? You'll be with us in a couple of years."

"Probably, sir. I'm just helping with a banner today."

Callaghan's eyes surveyed the arriving paraders as he gestured behind him with his thumb. "Follow the path to the back, next to a pond. That's where Seamus Gallagher asked to be put. The least I could do since we'll shortly own whatever new pump he manages to get his hands on." Callaghan chuckled, clearly amused by his own joke.

Just then, the rhythmic sound of massed drums echoed down Walnut Street from the west.

"What the hell is that?" Callaghan mumbled to himself.

Rian smiled because she knew what it was: the Third Company of Washington Guards, the premier Black marching band in Philadelphia. Composed originally of veterans of the War of 1812, their leader, Francis "Frank" Johnson, had continually recruited and taught young Black men to play the drums, bugles, and lately, trumpets. Rian had been at the Purvis residence when Purvis had recommended his friend Frank Johnson to Seamus. She was amazed that Seamus had readily agreed.

Moments later, the drummers arrived at Washington Square, decked out in purple uniforms and hats with long peacock plumes sticking out. Now spare and rhythmic, the drumbeat defined a rapid pace that propelled the band members forward, drummers first, then brass, which was still silent. Behind them marched Seamus, Dylan, and thirteen other members of the United No Name Fire Brigade, all dressed as Turks in wide, flowing pantaloons. Three Turks hauled the shiny, cherry red steam-powered fire pump. The pump's boiler already had a good head of steam. Cinders flew out of its short smokestack. Two other firemen carried furled fire hoses draped over their shoulders.

Callaghan stood there, mouth agape.

Rian signaled her two friends to unfurl the banner, which proclaimed "The World's First Steam Powered Fire Pump, Built by Krieger Locomotive."

Trey read the banner. "Is that true?"

Rian thought of the lesson she learned from Phineas T. Barnum. "I don't know. It might be. But starting today, a lot of people are going to believe it is." She waved to the drum major to follow the banner, and without breaking stride, the band members narrowed their ranks to march toward their designated place in line. Rian passed stakes denoting the staging area for each hose company: *Moyamensing . . . Hibernia . . . Lafayette . . . Franklin . . . Decatur . . . Quaker City.* Each group stepped back only slightly to make way, first for the noisy drum onslaught, then in awe of the first steam-powered fire pump they had ever conceived of or seen.

Rian and her friends arrived at the stake marked *United No Name.* They dropped the banner and signaled with wild, jumping gestures that the band and fire brigade had arrived at their spot.

Seamus and his crew smartly wheeled the pump around. One hose carrier dumped his burden into the pond and waded in to fill it with water. Leaving one end of the hose in the pond, he hooked the other end to the pump. The second hose carrier hooked his hose to the pump's discharge valve. Without hesitation, he aimed the hose so a stream of water arced over a nearby grove of trees. Almost immediately, angry cries sprung up from the other side, where other fire companies were getting doused with water.

Hugh Callaghan stormed down the path. "Knock it off, Seamus."

Seamus smiled at Callaghan and waved back to the men at the pump. The stream of water immediately trickled to a halt. "Whatsamatter, Hugh? Jealous?"

"Save it for this afternoon. Meanwhile, behave yourself. Or I'll just take your new toy right now rather than at the next fire."

Seamus's fists were resting on his hips. "We'll see about that."

Hugh smirked. "I see you added *United* to your name. What? Ya think you add a couple of ispinis to your ranks, and you've got something special?" He disdainfully surveyed the No Names. "I still only count fifteen. That's not gonna cut it, Seamus."

"See you this afternoon, Hugh. Better field your best hose team."

· ·

The parade traveled north on Seventh Street from Washington Square to Franklin Square, turned left on Sassafras, marched half a dozen blocks to Broad, then turned south to get back to Walnut. When they passed the old Krieger shops on the corner at Twelfth Street, they found that all the employees of the three factories had been given a break in the middle of the day to leave work and watch the parade. The Krieger workers enthusiastically applauded the United No Name Fire Brigade and the Third Company of Washington Guards. Rian waved to her father, Jules, Aaron, and Uncle Adrian. Seamus rang the pump's bell in appreciation of the turnout.

Back at Washington Square, the hose companies shed their colorful costumes and re-outfitted for the real business of the day: the competitions.

Rian, Conor, and Trey were watching the hose teams compete in the distance contest when someone tapped her on the shoulder. She turned and was delighted to see Olivia. They hadn't seen each other much since the evening she pushed Olivia on the swing, when she told Olivia that someone would tail Mammy whenever she left the house. "How did you get let out of the house? I thought your mother had you on a tight leash."

"I'm with Mammy. Mama sent us to High Street for vegetables, but I saw you in the parade. I talked Mammy into coming here instead. It wasn't hard. She wanted to see No Name compete. She knows it's about the only fire company in the city that puts out fires in Black people's houses."

"She does? How's she know that?"

"Every Black person in the city knows that. Look around."

Rian assessed the crowd for the first time, which looked to be about ten-percent Black by her reckoning.

"They're all here to see the No Name Fire Brigade beat Moyamensing," Olivia explained.

Rian's danger sense kicked in. "This is bad."

"Why?"

"The Battle Royale always gets people's blood up. Fights can break out in the crowd after the contest, especially if they think someone cheated. You know who they'll take it out on if things go wrong."

"Every Black person in the crowd. The only thing the English and the Irish agree on. We were followed here, by the way."

"Who's following you?"

"Austin Slatter." Olivia subtly hooked her thumb over her shoulder. "He's been behind us since we left the house. I think that's another reason why Mammy was happy to change plans. She just doesn't care what my father thinks anymore. And if she makes the slave catchers work hard for nothing, then she's happy to do it."

Rian did her best to scan the crowd without making it look like she was looking for anyone in particular. She didn't see Slatter, but she did spy Hans Schmidt. "Does your mother know what Rose is planning?"

"I'm not sure. I don't think Papa's told her."

Trey turned his attention to the two girls. "Hi, Olivia. What are you two talking about?"

"So," said Rian, as if she were carrying on a previous conversation. "The No Name's steam pump has been a real hit. Our stream is by far the longest. Even Moya's six-man pumper couldn't touch it."

"Have any other competitions taken place?"

"The hose carry. Moya won that. Decatur took the ladder climb. Axemanship went to Quaker City, so it's tied 1 to 1 to 1 to 1. If any of those four take the hose war, they get the trophy. Otherwise, it'll be a five-way tie, and no one gets it."

"Do you think No Name will win?"

Rian shrugged. "A couple of Germans from the factories just joined No Name. They're big and beefy. I think we're going to make a good fight of it."

"How's the hose war work?"

"It's the grand finale, a battle royale. All seven fire brigades gather around the fountain in the center of the square. Everyone has their hose dipped in the fountain, each connected to their pump. Then out the other side of the pump comes another hose with the guy at the end holding the nozzle." Rian pointed to a pebble walkway about thirty feet away that circled the fountain. "Anyone who gets forced out beyond that walkway is out of the competition. The last team with a man in the circle wins."

"Sounds like fun."

"Wait 'til you see. There are only three other rules. Each team gets only ten men, no weapons allowed, and you can't hurt the pumps."

. . . .

· SEAMUS ·

Seamus set down the nozzle of No Name's fire hose and walked around the fountain to Hugh Callaghan, who was at the nozzle of the Moya hose. "Little old for this, aren't you, Hugh? You should let the younger lads take that job."

"Not a chance, Seamus. I want to have a front-row seat when we wipe that smile off your face."

"You'll have a seat all right because you'll be sitting on your ass when the stream from my hose knocks you off your feet."

"Care to place a bet, Kid?"

"What have you got in mind?"

"A hundred dollars to whichever of us gets knocked out of the ring last."

A hundred dollars was far more than Seamus had been able to save since he had started his job with Krieger Coach. *About ninety bucks more.* "I'll take that bet. I already know how we're going to beat you."

"Care to tell me?"

"Sure. You've got that shiny new six-man pump. I know it generates a hefty stream. Not as much as our little steam pump, but hefty. Trouble is, it takes six men to get it up. You're number seven. You need at least two men to help you haul a fully charged hose around. That leaves only one of your lads to guard your hose and pump. Good luck with that."

Hugh contemplated Seamus's strategizing for a few moments. "Tell you what, Kid. How about a side deal? Moya and No Name lay off each other until all the others are out. Then we'll see how well your strategy works."

"I think that's a fine plan. Make sure you hold your boys to it."

"By the way, did you take a look at the crowd?"

Seamus surveyed the gathering, which was mostly male, most of whom he assumed were members of one fire brigade or another. "Yeah, so?"

"So, there's a lot more Africans here than usual. I think they're here to see you beat the tar out of us."

"Wouldn't that be nice."

"No, that would be regrettable. If you win, me boys—and a few others, I suspect—will happily take it out on your African friends."

"And what if we lose?"

"Then I just made a real enjoyable hundred bucks."

A wave of applause swelled from the crowd as Mayor Swift stepped to the fountain and turned to address the crowd. Seamus took the opportunity to walk back around the fountain and talk to his boys. Dylan, Jimmy Collins, the two Fitzpatrick brothers, Silken McDonald, and four of the beefiest Germans from the factory looked like a pretty solid team to him. The steam pump idled merrily, sounding a modest *choosh . . . choosh . . . choosh* that was easy to talk over.

Seamus reeled from this new fix. *Whaterya going to do now, Boyo? Win, and we've got a race riot on our hands. Lose, and I owe Hugh a hundred bucks that I don't have.* He shoved his dilemma out of his mind and faced his boys. "Okay, here's how I look at it. Our disadvantage is that the other teams know we've got the best pump in the competition, so they'll come after us early, probably all together. I just scared the pants off Hugh, so he'll lay off us until it's just us two teams standing, assuming we last that long. Our advantage is that we don't need anyone pumping the pump, so the seven guys who aren't hauling the hose around are free to attack or defend. That puts us in the catbird seat."

The mayor concluded his remarks and yielded the scene to the competitors. The hose companies wheeled their pumps next to the fountain; Moyamensing, then Hibernia, Lafayette, Franklin, No Name, Decatur, and Quaker City, which put them next to Moya. Each team placed a hose in the fountain and signaled to the mayor that they were ready.

The mayor waved a yellow flag, signaling to the companies that it was time to start pumping.

Dylan pushed the clutch on the steam pumper. The machine strained, then the chooshing got louder and more rapid. Six other teams started pulling up and down on their side handrails, desperately trying to be the first to get a stream going. Moya's larger, more powerful engine took six guys; everyone else took four. The crowd roared.

No Name's pump was the first to generate a stream. Seamus trained it on the men hauling up and down at the Franklin pump next to him. That slowed them down momentarily, but seconds later, Seamus was knocked off his feet by two streams, one from Decatur and one from Lafayette.

The fall caused Seamus to drop his nozzle, which waggled harmlessly on the ground until he regained control over it. Meanwhile, the Fitzpatrick brothers waded into the fountain and pulled out the Decatur hose, ending their ability to generate a stream. With the Decatur boys defenseless, Seamus started pushing the men one-by-one outside the circle with a concentrated stream of water. Yells coming from behind him pulled his attention back to his troops. Two Germans and Dylan were shoved to the edge of the circle by the streams of a coalition of three teams that had ganged up on them. Seamus trained his stream on the attackers, but he was too late. Just like that, No Name was down to seven guys.

The three teams turned their firepower on Seamus and drove him toward the circle's edge. The Fitzpatrick brothers pulled another hose out of the fountain, thus killing one of the three streams that nearly knocked Seamus out of the ring. The remaining two Germans, who were supposed to be Seamus's backup by hauling the hose around behind him, left their posts and attacked two men pumping one of the other pumps. They physically dragged the men to the circle's edge and threw them out. Streams of water immediately hit the Germans and forced them out of the circle. No Name was down to five.

Seamus assessed the playing field. Franklin was done. Moya had wiped out Hibernia. Decatur and Quaker City appeared to be at half strength. Moyamensing had lost a couple of guys but was going at Lafayette. Seamus called to the Fitzpatricks. "Move into the backup positions!"

He went after the Decatur guys with a stream, shoving two of them out, leaving the nozzleman with no backup and only two men to pull up and down on a four-man pump. He turned his attention to Quaker City. Moya went after Lafayette with such ferocity that they said uncle and voluntarily walked out of the circle. Hugh nodded to Seamus, and they ganged up on the remaining Quaker City boys who couldn't withstand the combined hose power of Moya and No Name.

"Just as we suspected," Hugh yelled over the din and the cheering, "it's down to you and us. At least we know it's going to be an Irish outfit that'll take the trophy. Get ready, Kid. Here we come."

Seamus had little time to assess. No Name had five men standing: himself, the two Fitzpatrick brothers, Silken McDonald, and Jimmy Collins. Moya had seven men left, all big beefy Irish.

Without hesitation, four Moya boys started running through the fountain directly toward No Name's hose. The four No Name boys charged at the Moyas and met them in the fountain. Hugh trained his diminished stream on Seamus. One of the Moyas broke free from the melee and waded laboriously toward the No Name engine.

Seamus wasn't particularly concerned about him because even though the Battle Royale often got pretty rough, Moya would automatically be disqualified if they harmed another team's pump. The Moya guy reached the No Name pump and opened the door to the pump's firebox. Hugh switched his stream from Seamus to the firebox, effectively dousing the fire in a heartbeat. Seamus briefly hung his head because Hugh had outsmarted him. He knew he probably had two minutes before his pump died altogether.

He trained his stream on the guy who opened the firebox door and shoved him out of the ring. Silken McDonald held his man underwater so long that he held up his hand in a sign of surrender. That left two Moya guys and four No Names in the fountain.

"It's four against two, lads!" Seamus yelled. "Throw 'em out of the ring."

With the crowd yelling, the four No Names hauled the Moyas toward the circle's edge.

The No Name pump started to lose power. With only two men to heave on his six-man pump, Hugh didn't have much of a stream either. The No Names were on the verge of tossing two Moyas out when the remaining two Moya men left their pump and, with a mighty heave, pushed at the knot of combatants, and all eight of them fell out of the circle.

Hugh had no one to pump his pump. Seamus had no fire in his firebox.

Seamus dropped his nozzle. "Well, Old Man, this is a bit poetic. You want to get drowned in the fountain or tossed outside the circle?"

Hugh started walking around the fountain. "Let's try dry land, Kid."

The fight wasn't much of a contest. Even though Hugh was twenty-five years older than Seamus, he outweighed him by forty pounds, and he was all muscle. Seamus put up a worthy fight, but Hugh dragged and punched him toward the circle's edge.

The two adversaries were inches away from the edge when two other men tackled them, and all four collapsed outside the circle. Seamus looked up from the pile to see the nozzleman from Decatur dancing around in victory.

Hugh sat up next to Seamus. "I thought you finished them off."

"I thought you did," said Seamus, suppressing the slightest of smiles.

Monday, August 8

· OTTO ·

It was two days after the Firemen's Parade. Otto sat at his usual table in the United States Hotel. His dining companion this day was newspaperman Harold Foote. "Good to have you back, Harold. I assume things have died down with the hose companies?"

"Yes, we've reached a bit of a truce. I don't write about them, and they'll leave me alone. I met with Hugh Callaghan yesterday to make sure I wasn't stepping back into a hornet's nest. It turns out he was more concerned with an outfit named the United No Name Fire Brigade. I guess there's some connection between it and the Krieger factories. What's the story there?"

"That is my nephew Seamus Gallagher and a few of his friends. He has launched a new hose company to compete with Moyamensing. Krieger Locomotive made their pump, apparently the first steam-powered fire pump in America. Maybe the world. Rian and her friends marched in the parade two days ago. She came home from the Firemen's Day all filled with herself. And we got a lot of free publicity."

"Hugh didn't sound very pleased with the outcome of the games."

"Oh, as Seamus Gallagher would say, he was a mite upset. Seamus baited him all afternoon long. I do not know what that young man has up his sleeve, but he certainly wants to piss Hugh off. I hope the results are not the same as the last time."

"The last time?"

"While you were in Mexico, Hugh's men suckered No Name into a trap. They busted up their first pump and thrashed Seamus pretty badly. He could barely walk. Anyway, Seamus says Hugh expected Moya's big new pump to be the talk of the town in the saloons that evening. Instead, all anyone wanted to talk about was No Name's new engine. If I were not so busy expanding my coach business into railroad cars, I might consider going into that business as well."

"It was that big a hit?"

"No doubt about it. By the end of the day, every hose company approached my brother Adrian about buying a steam engine to pump water. Adrian just smiled and said he was too busy building locomotives."

"He turned down all that business?

"Yes. To all of them. Except one."

"Who was that?"

"I think I should keep that information to myself for the moment. How was your time in Mexico? It seems like you were gone a long time."

"Almost a year. Mexico was fascinating. Though where I was isn't Mexico anymore. It's the Republic of Texas now. It was a pretty ugly little war. Given what I've been through there, I don't think the hose companies will ever intimidate me quite in the same way again."

"What do you think of the new republic?"

"I don't think this fight has been over independence. It's all about slavery. Slavery has been outlawed in Mexico since 1827. The Mexicans were happy to have the Americans come in, but not their slaves. The Americans revolted because they knew their slaves would be legal in an independent Texas."

"Interesting point of view."

"Texans are different from you and me. They're frontiersmen. Self-reliant. Headstrong. Defiant. They've successfully fought off the Mexicans, although animosities still run deep. There are Mexican landowners who used to rule the roost who are now considered second-class citizens. Of course, the Mexican government doesn't recognize Texas's independence. But I'm sure that's a lost cause."

"I am surprised Mexico allowed so many Americans to settle in the area."

"They didn't just allow it. They encouraged it, hoping to get more taxes. The federal government granted huge tracts of land to *empresarios*—promoters—but to get the grant, the empresario had to bring in a minimum of two-hundred families to settle on the land. Well, they got their taxpayers, mostly Americans with a distrust and dislike of authority."

"How about Indians?"

"Lots of them. Wichita, Apache, Comanche. Other sub-tribes. They don't care who it is, Mexican or Anglo; they hate us because we're invading their homeland. Mostly they're fighting the whites tooth and nail. Sometimes they form alliances with the whites, but they don't last long. The Americans are just flooding into the area. It's a tidal wave of humanity. There'll be no denying their numbers. And, of course, they're bringing their slaves."

Otto winced at the thought. "Sad. Lucretia has been trying to call attention to this for years. Do you think they will join the union?"

"Many of them are already pushing for that. You'll notice that President Jackson has been mum on the subject. Texas would undoubtedly be admitted as a slave state, which would upset the balance of power in the Senate. Arkansas got admitted this year, so there's already one more slave state than free, but the balance will return next year when Michigan joins."

Foote took a while to cut his steak, then returned to his narrative. "I don't think Jackson wants Texas to become an election issue. He wants to make sure Mr. Van Buren gets elected, and Texas would surely divide northern and southern Democrats."

"So, you think Mr. Van Buren is pro-slavery?"

"I certainly do. But then again, I think Mr. Harrison is, too. If you are anti-slavery, I don't think you have a good choice."

"What a pity."

Harold nodded. "And whoever wins will certainly have to deal with the issue of expansion of slavery. If we ever annex Texas, it will mean war with Mexico. Mexico can live with Texas as an independent republic, but having the United States knocking on their door would be unacceptable."

"So now that you are back, what will you do?

"I'm back at the *Independent*. There's a lot going on in Philadelphia that interests me. Same with Harrisburg. I'm sorry to say that many of our state representatives are selling their votes to the highest bidder. There's a lot to write about. But I'll also travel to Washington to keep my eye on national politics."

"Sounds exciting."

"I'm looking forward to it. Travel is so much easier than it used to be. I can be in Harrisburg in ten hours. Washington in less than a day: steamship to Baltimore via the canal, railroad to DC. Once Shippen's railroad is finished, that will probably put the canal out of business, at least as far as passenger service is concerned. No matter what, the stagecoach days will soon be over, at least here in the East. Too slow. Too expensive. Too hard on the passengers."

"Did you travel through Washington on your way back from Texas?"

"No. Stage from Austin to Galveston. That was by far the hardest part of the trip—steamship from Galveston to New Orleans, steamboats up the Mississippi to Cairo, Illinois. Steamboat up the Ohio River to Pittsburgh. Then canal packet to Columbia and train here."

"How long did it take to get home?"

"From New Orleans, exactly two weeks. And what about you, Otto. How are you and Rian doing?"

"Rian has settled down. She likes working in the Krieger shops. Has not been involved in a fistfight for a year. I think for the first time in a long while, I am not worried about her impulsively doing something dangerous."

· · · · · · · · · · · · · · · · · · · ·

· RIAN ·

Rian found Seamus at the other end of the Krieger Carriage Shop from the steam engine. Seamus had his eyes closed and his hands in his pockets. He was listening to the machinery. She gave Seamus a nudge. He opened his eyes, and she yelled, "Dylan said you wanted to talk to me."

Seamus indicated with his thumb to follow him outside.

Rian already had a suspicion that big things were about to happen. Seamus took his time. He made a production of tapping his pipe on the brick wall to empty some spent tobacco. "I could use you and a friend tonight."

"Is tonight the night?"

"The night for what?"

"The night for us to do to Moya what they did to us. Steal one of their pumps."

Seamus looked surprised. He tamped some new tobacco into his pipe. "What makes you think I'm planning that?"

"I paid attention when we were reading *The Art of War*. 'Make your enemy think you are weak when you are strong.' Remember? Mr. Callaghan saw only fifteen No Names, and I know a lot more have joined since you built the steam pump. If you count Robert's friends, we've got a lot more than Mr. Callaghan thinks. I think you made such a big splash on parade day to piss him off. To make him reckless, just like Sun Tzu said."

"You haven't told anyone about this, have you?"

"Uh-uh. Your plans are as dark and impenetrable as the night."

"That's good." Seamus took a metal tin from his pocket, pulled a small stick out of the tin, and scraped it on a piece of sandpaper. A ball of fire appeared at the end of the stick as sparks flew off. Seamus casually lit his pipe.

Rian had never seen this before. "What's that? What did you just do?"

Seamus took a drag on his pipe. "This? This is called a loco-foco. Saw the first one meself at McSweeney's last week. Some factory in Massachusetts is making them. You can pretty much light a fire anyplace now. It's gonna change the world. Flint and steel will soon be a thing of the past. So, can you get Trey to help us with a little reconnaissance tonight?"

"Sure. I can get Conor, too."

"No. Conor can't do this."

"Why not? He's trickier than Trey by a long shot."

"Think about it. Then tell me why this can't be."

Rian hesitated for a long while. She put her head down. "Conor's brothers have joined Moya. You're afraid he'll tell them something's up." She looked up at Seamus. "He would never do that."

"Honestly, I'm not a bit afraid that Conor would tell his brothers. But this way, he'll be able to look them right in the eye and tell them he didn't know anything. I don't want Conor to have to choose between you and his brothers."

"This is gonna kill him."

"It'll kill him worse if he knows and has to choose. Don't let him know anything's going to happen tonight."

· ·

· JULES ·

Rian found Jules at his standing desk. "Jules, there's two guys outside who want to talk to you, but I don't think you want to talk to them."

"Who are the guys?"

"One's Hans Schmidt."

Despite the heat of the day, Jules felt a cold chill run down the back of his spine. "Let me guess. The other one is Austin T. Slatter."

"Yeah, the slave catcher."

"Do me a favor, will you? Rian, you go to the office. Tell your father we have visitors, and I would like him to watch my back. Then get those two gumps and invite them in. Actually, that sounds too polite. Tell them I'm busy, but I can spare two minutes. And take your time." That made Rian smile as she sauntered toward the office.

Five minutes later, Otto, Adrian, Seamus, and Aaron flanked Jules when Rian ushered in Schmidt and Slatter. She noticed Otto held his lumber rule with the heavy end resting on his shoulder.

Slatter strutted in with the obvious intention of intimidating Jules but then eyed his allies. Massively outnumbered, his demeanor changed, but not much. "I've been looking forward to this day for over a year," said Slatter with no pretense of warmth. "I recently delivered a runaway to Albemarle County, Virginia. One of your brethren who had been on the loose for three years, but I tracked him down and returned him to his rightful owner."

"So, what does that have to do with me?"

"Next county north of Albemarle is Greene. I stopped at the courthouse to check on the papers you showed me last year. Turns out they have no record of a Jules Howland ever buying his freedom. I believe that's what the name said on your paper. And by the way, there's never been a prothonotary in Greene County by the name of Cyrus R. Talbot. They don't have anyone on their tax records by the name of Marion Pruett. I did get the names right, didn't I, Mr. Putting-On-Airs?"

Jules's shoulders slumped. "Yes, you got the names right."

"So, I guess you'll be coming with us."

Rather than acquiesce, Jules straightened. "I don't think so. You got all the names right, but you were in the wrong county."

"What do you mean?"

"I'm not from Greene County. I'm from Greensville County. That's south of Richmond on the North Carolina border. You missed the right courthouse by, oh, probably 200 miles or so."

Slatter was unconvinced. "Let me see your papers again."

"I let you see my papers once when you were fishing for any Black man who might be a runaway. Come back and see me when you find the person I allegedly ran away from. Good luck on that because it won't happen."

Otto stepped forward, his lumber rule at the ready. "Okay, Hans, you and your friend have had your fun. I told you never to come back. Consider yourself lucky that I have not beat the shit out of you a second time."

Otto and Seamus escorted the two intruders out of the shop while Jules retreated to the safety of the office with Adrian, Aaron, and Rian.

"Quick thinking," said Adrian.

"Not that quick. I've had that ploy in my hip pocket since Hans told me they intended to check on my papers. I'm afraid Slatter's dander is up now. It won't be another year before he contacts the Greensville County courthouse."

"What are you going to do?"

"Beats me. I'm really dug in here. I sure don't want to run again after all this time. Why did this have to happen now, with everything else that's going on?"

Adrian sat on Otto's desk. "What do you mean? What else have you got going on?

Jules looked at Rian, then shook his head. "Oh, you know, just the usual production worries."

· ·

· RIAN ·

Rian and Trey hid in an alley off Plum Street where they could keep an eye on both Clancy's Saloon and the warehouse where the Moyamensing Hose Company stored their pumps under lock and key.

Rian had told so many lies that she feared she would no longer keep them straight. She had lied many times to her father to cover her tracks in the conspiracy to free Rose. She lied to Seamus about going to her French lesson. She couldn't tell Conor about the caper with No Name because of his brothers. She couldn't tell Trey about the Rose/Mammy conspiracy because of his family. She didn't tell Maddie that she knew who loaned her the embosser because of Rule #1. *I think my head is going to explode.*

At 10:30, right on schedule, the bell at the Statehouse started to ring, alarming all of Philadelphia that there was a fire. Moments later, calls of 'Fire! Fire! Fire!' came from two different directions. Hugh Callaghan and a score of men streamed out of Clancy's and walked briskly toward the warehouse, counting the dongs—which ever since the day Rian cracked the bell sounded to her more like a clong—emanating from the statehouse bell tower as they strode ahead.

Callaghan was in the lead when his group passed their hiding place. "Looks like we're going to make some serious money tonight, boys. Didn't even have to set the fires. I'll take half the men and the old pump to the one to the west. Davey, you take the others and the new pump to the south."

More men streamed toward the warehouse from all different directions. About fifty Moya men had arrived within minutes and were preparing to haul the pumps and hoses to the two fires.

Rian and Trey casually left their hiding place and walked away from the warehouse. As soon as they were out of sight of the Moya men, they started running as fast as they could. They found Seamus right where he said he would be, at the corner of Fitzwater and Fifth Streets.

Rian's heart was pounding, a mixture of excitement and exertion. "They're going after both fires. Hugh's heading to the one on Catherine Street!"

Seamus pulled his derby down snugly on his head. "Perfect. Trey, that means you're telling the folks to the south that it's time to skedaddle. Rian, you find the boys with the pump and tell them to come to Catherine Street right away. Okay, start running, lads."

In the excitement, Rian only vaguely noticed that Seamus had called her a lad, but kind of liked it.

She ran half a block to the alley where Dylan and the two Fitzpatrick brothers hid with the steam-powered pump. Dylan had just thrown a few lumps of coal in the fire chamber. The water was already boiling.

"Hugh's heading to Catherine Street with half the Moya men. Seamus wants us to get there as soon as we can."

Dylan shut and latched the door to the fire chamber. "I don't get it. If we're gonna put out the fire with the pump, how come we're not there already, putting out the fooking fire?"

· ·

· SEAMUS ·

It took just a few minutes for Seamus to run to the scene of the fire on Catherine Street. The flames had climbed to the second story of an old house, but Seamus gave the conflagration passing notice. Fifteen members of the No Name Fire Brigade were standing in the middle of the street. They made no effort to attack the flames. Instead, they greeted Seamus enthusiastically with raised shillelaghs, hammers, and pitchforks as he jogged the last fifty feet to join his troops. Seamus noticed a few pistols.

Like the fire to the south, No Name men had set the fire on Catherine Street in one of Robert Purvis's abandoned buildings. *If this evening goes right, we'll even save Robert a little money.*

"Gentlemen, thank you all for your support tonight. Callaghan and half his men should be here in just a few minutes. It is very important that you not attack the Moya men until I give the order. But if that happens, feel free to attack with enthusiasm."

All eyes shifted toward the sound of approaching steel-rimmed wheels clattering on cobblestones. Seamus turned in time to see Rian Krieger round the corner at a dead run, followed by Dylan and the Fitzpatrick brothers hauling the steam pump as fast as they could.

Rian ran directly to Seamus. She was so out of breath that she could barely put words together. "They're coming. They saw us. I bet thirty seconds."

Seamus pointed to the side of the street away from the burning building. "Go stand over there, Rian. Whatever happens, don't get involved. Just watch. I don't want to get through this only to have your da kill me for getting you roughed up." Then Seamus straightened and faced his troops. "Make room for the pump, gentlemen. And get ready."

The phalanx parted, and the three No Name men hauled the steam pump through the gap. They wheeled the machine around and set down the traces. Dylan elbowed his way to the front of the group. "I sure don't want to miss this."

For the second time in less than a minute, the sound of steel rims on cobblestones echoed down Catherine Street. This time it was accompanied by the sound of scores of leather boots, yells of encouragement, and an Irish fighting song.

Hugh Callaghan trotted around the corner, followed by twenty-five or so members of the Moyamensing Hose Company and their old fire pump. Hugh got halfway down the block before he sensed something was amiss. He put up his hand to halt his men.

"Evening, Seamus. Surprised your pump beat us here. I see we've got you outnumbered again, even with half me guys. Now you're gonna lose your fancy new pump and the bounty for getting to the fire first. Makes me almost feel sorry for you."

Seamus stood his ground. "Not going to happen, Hugh."

Hugh eyed the group of men arrayed behind Seamus. "Big words. Looks like you've got fifteen guys this time. I've got at least twenty-five. See you brought a couple of pistols. That ought to make things a little interesting."

"We don't want to fight you, Hugh. But we're ready for you." Seamus raised his hand, and thirty men, mostly Black, walked up behind the No Name phalanx.

Hugh struck a defiant pose. "You think a couple of Africans is gonna be a problem for us?"

"More than a couple, Hugh." Seamus raised his hand a second time, and another thirty men rounded the corner onto Catherine Street and formed behind the Moya men. Seamus smiled just a bit more when he saw Jules Freeman and Robert Purvis in front of the group. Hugh and his men were trapped.

Seamus assumed a more relaxed stance than he felt. "Appear weak when you are strong, and strong when you are weak. You aren't the only one who's read *The Art of War*, Hugh."

Callaghan looked behind him and saw the second group of men. "Whataya want, Kid? Our pump? A race war? You wanna kick me in the head? What?"

So far, everything had gone according to Seamus's plan, but the next few minutes would determine whether he got out of his dilemma or started a race war, the effects of which would last for years. "Sorry to see you brought your old pump, Hugh. I was kind of looking forward to getting my hands on the new one. But for now, let's just talk. Tell your boys to relax a bit. Nobody's gonna do anything until I give them the word."

The two adversaries walked toward one another until they were almost eyeball to eyeball. Hugh put his hands on his hips. "Whataya want, Seamus?"

"We want to be left alone."

Hugh smiled a bit. "You're a fooking idiot, Seamus. You go to all this trouble just to tell me you want to be left alone?"

Seamus smiled since he had heard something like this from Hugh's daughter not long ago. "Yup. I guess I wanted to get your attention."

"You talking about leaving your No Name boys alone?" Then a sneer crept over his face. "Or your African friends here?"

"Both."

"You might even beat us here tonight, but you'll start a race war that will end with every Black house in Moyamensing getting burned out."

"Really, Hugh? Everyone?" Seamus handed a paper to Hugh. "Including the properties you own?"

"What's this? It's just a bunch of numbers."

"Not just numbers, Hugh. House numbers. Of every house you own in Moyamensing, I figure half of them are currently occupied by Black families."

"Them? I'll just throw those folks out. It's called eviction."

"That's a lot of rent to lose out on, Hugh. There's not enough Irish families to take their places. At least that can pay the rent. Might wanna rethink that idea. I've got another proposal."

"So, make it."

"A truce. We all walk away from here, and no one gets hurt. We don't even take your pump. You promise to quit beating the coloreds. You promise that when we're racing to a fire, if you beat us, you beat us fair and square. The first outfit to a fire wins. No traps like we've now sprung on each other."

"You're kidding."

"Nope, fair and square competition between hose companies with no tricks. No beating up Black folks for the fun of it. That's the deal. Take it or leave it."

"What about the docks?"

"No Name gets Walnut Street to High Street. You don't get up that far north very often anyway. Your turf is farther south."

Seamus watched Callaghan as he turned to look at his boys behind him. He knew that Hugh was doing his numbers again.

Hugh sullenly shoved his hands into his pockets. "Okay, but it ain't no open-ended truce. Six months, then it's off."

"Twelve months. Then we talk again to see how we're doing." Seamus stuck out his hand.

"Okay. Twelve months." Callaghan reluctantly took Seamus's hand.

"Oh, Hugh, one more thing."

"No. We shook. No more of your crap."

"Just listen a minute." Seamus turned to face his men. "Dylan, bring up the steam pump!"

A wave of consternation rippled through his group. Dylan and the Fitzpatrick brothers reluctantly picked up the traces for the pump and walked it to Seamus and Hugh.

Seamus put his hand protectively on the steam engine. "Take it."

"What?!"

"Take it—a little icing on the cake. We mean business. We don't want to be constantly looking over our shoulders. If this seals the deal, it's worth it."

Hugh just stood there, obviously dumbfounded. "You're serious?"

"Couldn't be more serious. Look. Our name's not even on it yet."

"How long have you been planning this?"

"A while. Had to read *The Art of War* first."

Hugh cracked the smallest of smiles. "Didn't read it very well. Sun Tzu would have killed me while he had the chance."

"Sun Tzu didn't care about starting a race war. Also, he didn't want to start seeing your daughter."

Hugh stopped smiling. "You're pushing your luck, Seamus."

"Just putting you on notice. Chances are she's too much of a woman for me anyway, but I'd like to give it a try."

"I already know she's too much of a woman for you. But I'll tell you this: you hurt her, and this whole deal is off. You'll be sorry you were ever born."

Seamus smiled and looked Hugh right in the eye. "Deal. . . . Now you want to try out your new pump? It's fired up and ready to go. Don't worry so much about the fire; just dowse the houses on either side real good. Purvis said he would feel real bad if the fires spread to the neighbors."

· ·

Both hose companies had remained on Catherine Street until the fire had burned itself out. Then the Moyamensing boys turned both pumps on the embers to finish the job.

Seamus and Callaghan had stood together, watching the men do their work. Callaghan kicked at a charred board that had tumbled to the middle of the street. "I assume Purvis knows the insurance folks ain't gonna pay for this."

"Yeah, he knows."

"Suppose you're gonna need a pump 'til your new one's finished."

"What makes you think we're building another one?"

"You've been ahead of me all night. Offering up your steam pump was a stroke of genius. Now, not only did you beat me, but I'm beholden to you. But, given that you've plotted this caper out so well, I think you wouldn't have done it unless you had a new pump in the queue."

"You're catching up, Hugh. Aye, I've got one in the queue. It's still on the drawing board, but Krieger Locomotive should have it done in a month or so. Robert Purvis is paying for it."

"Purvis . . . has he been in this from the beginning?"

"Pretty much. I read *The Art of War* at his house."

"Gotta hand it to ya, Seamus. You handled yourself well. Now I'm kind of sorry you didn't get into Moya."

"Ah, that wouldn'ta worked out so good. You and me woulda got on each other's nerves soon enough. This is better."

Callaghan watched as his men started packing up their hoses. "Take our pump for the month."

"What for?"

"To use, you idiot. How'm I gonna beat you fair and square if you don't have a pump?"

"For a month?"

"Just until you get your pump finished. Then bring it back."

Seamus looked up at Callaghan and held out his hand. "Deal."

• • • • • • • • • • • • • • • • • • •

The United No Name Fire Brigade hauled Moyamensing's old fire pump to the warehouse, locked it up, and retired to McSweeney's to recount the evening.

It was 1:00 am. Seamus sat at a table with seven other No Name Fire Brigade members. The mood was mixed.

Dylan stared down into his glass. "It's still a hard one to swallow, Boyo. We won the night, yet Moya walked away with that beautiful pump."

Seamus smiled. "Dylan, we won the battle, and we won the war. I loved that pump as much as you did. But the pump is not important. Besides, we'll have a better one in less than a month."

"If you say so."

Kevin Fitzpatrick lightened the mood when he walked into the saloon with his arms around Rian and Trey. "Hey, lads, look who I found outside."

A collective cheer went up from the table.

Seamus stood up and walked toward the youngsters. "Me scouts! Me scouts! Rian! Trey! We couldn't have done it without ye!" Then Seamus noticed that they weren't smiling. "Kind of late for ye to be out, ain't it?"

Rian looked up at him with a forlorn expression. "Why'd you do it, Seamus?"

"What, the pump?"

"Yeah. The pump. You had your enemy destroyed. He was beaten. You didn't have to give him anything."

"You're right, but all the time you and I were reading Sun Tzu, I felt that he didn't totally apply to our situation. I didn't want to start a war we couldn't finish. I didn't want us Irish to be fighting amongst ourselves. I didn't want to drag the coloreds into this because a lot of innocent folks would have gotten hurt. For all of that, I gave up our lovely little steam-powered fire pump."

"I loved that pump."

"So did I, Rian. So did I. It's time for you two to be getting home. If you get caught, just tell your folks you were with me. I'll take the heat."

Seamus walked the two youngsters out the door, just in time to encounter Robert Purvis and Jules.

"Good evening, Seamus. We're here to thank you." Robert extended his hand.

Seamus grabbed Robert's hand enthusiastically. "Longest day of me life. I'm glad we've got some breathing room."

"Do you think the truce will last?"

"It'll last as long as it lasts. But tonight, we made the world a better place, at least for a while."

"We won't push things to ask to come in."

"If it was up to me, I'd invite you in for a drink. Imagine McSweeney would even make an exception tonight. But that would be an example of winning the battle and losing the war. Word'd travel back to Hugh soon enough, and he'd get all bothered that the two races are fraternizing."

Purvis smiled. "We were thinking the same thing. A pity. Would you care to come to my house for a drink?"

The gesture genuinely touched Seamus. "That is very kind and more than I deserve, Robert. But I think I'll stay with me boys tonight. Some other time, I hope."

Seamus shook hands with the two men and was about to return to his friends when he noticed Siobhan walking toward him through the light of the nearest streetlamp. He leaned against the wall and pulled his pipe out of his pocket.

"See you're still hanging with the coloreds."

Seamus didn't rise to the bait. "It was a good night. They just stopped by to say thanks. How are things at Clancy's?"

"Quiet. Me da's holding the troops in line. Some of them wanted to start burning stuff up."

"He's doing okay?"

"For now. You played this beautifully, Seamus. I want to thank you for stalling off wherever you and I are heading for these past few weeks. First thing he asked me when he walked into Clancy's was if I knew anything about your shenanigans this evening."

"So, where *are* you and me heading?"

"Beats me. But I don't want to shoot you anymore."

"And the alternative to that is . . . ?"

"This." With that, Siobhan stood up on her tiptoes and kissed him lightly on the lips. "Now go back to your boys, Seamus." With that, Siobhan turned and started walking back down the street.

Seamus realized he had never lit his pipe. He called after her, "I'm sure you can have your old job back. Braden hasn't hired anyone yet."

Siobhan didn't break her stride, nor did she turn around. "Don't press your luck, Seamus."

Tuesday, August 9

· Rian ·

The next morning the shop was abuzz with stories about the confrontation between the Moyamensing Hose Company and the United No Name Fire Brigade. The last evening's events became more dramatic and perilous after each rendition. Conor listened to the stories, first with incredulity, then with ire.

He was so frosty toward Rian that she was apprehensive when Jules told them to rent two horses, take the ferry to New Jersey, and pick up a broken-down coal tender at the Camden train station.

Conor walked beside Rian as they led the animals south on Broad Street. "You should have told me about Seamus's plan."

"What would you have done if you had known?"

"I would have helped."

"What would your brothers have done if they'd seen you with us?"

"They would have cuffed me around a bit. Kicked me out."

"So, I saved you a licking. You're still living with them."

Conor shouldered playfully into Rian. "They cuffed me around anyway because they didn't believe me. They just didn't kick me out."

Rian smiled. "So, are you still mad at me?"

Conor never answered her question. "Hey, is that Olivia?"

Rian looked ahead and spotted Olivia three blocks away. Olivia ran a bit, slowed to a walk to wipe her eyes, then started running again. She was still crying when she reached them.

Rian hung on to her horse's reins. "Olivia, what's wrong?"

Olivia wiped her eyes with the back of her hand. "Mother is leaving for home with Mammy tomorrow. Papa told her that Mammy wanted to run away. She flew into a hissy. She's already booked us on the *Carolina Princess*."

"Us? You have to go, too?"

Olivia nodded through her tears. "Tomorrow."

Sensing that Olivia's agitation would upset the mare, Rian stroked her muzzle. "But Jules and Maddie's plan is to get her out next week. They've got everything lined up for then."

"Mammy is crying. I don't know what to do."

"We can do something," said Conor. "I've got an idea. We're going to New Jersey to pick up an old coal tender. It will be the perfect hiding place to get Mammy out of the neighborhood. Olivia, go back to your house. Get Mammy ready to run." Conor issued a piercing whistle through his teeth that startled his horse. "When you hear me whistle like that, send her out the back door and tell her to jump into the wagon. It'll take us at least a couple of hours to get back here."

· · · · · · · · · · · · · · · · · · · ·

Preoccupied, Rian barely noticed Philadelphia's receding wharves on the ferry.

Conor shifted his weight from one leg to the other, then back again, a sure sign he was nervous. "What are Jules and Maddie going to say?"

"I already know because he warned me. 'Welcome to the Underground Railroad. When your first plan doesn't work out, you have to make up a new one right on the spot.' Well, that's what we did. Well, actually, you did. I'm really happy we don't have any secrets between us anymore."

"You mean you don't have any secrets. I never had them."

· · · · · · · · · · · · · · · · · · · ·

At the railroad siding in Camden, Rian and Conor found the transport wagon with the coal tender already loaded and lashed down.

"Jaysus," said Conor as he looked at the decrepit railroad car. "They better have tied that car down to the wagon real good because it's likely to fall apart before we get it back to the factory."

They hitched the horses to the transport wagon and drove it down the steep hill, with Rian pushing hard on the brake the entire way. The coal tender creaked and swayed just inches behind them. *If this car breaks free on the hill, we'll be squashed like bugs,* Rian thought.

They passed the schnitzel man and arrived back at the ferry landing just as the Falcon returned to New Jersey.

The ropes held.

They caught the *Falcon* back to the Walnut Street dock just as Jules had instructed them. But then, they deviated from orders. They were supposed to bring the coal tender back to Krieger Coach by the shortest route—west on Walnut to Broad; north on Broad to the shop.

Instead, they headed south one block to Spruce Street, then west toward Ninth. As they approached Carolina Row, Rian's danger-sense kicked in. She directed the horses to the side of the street, reined them to a halt, and secured the brake.

"Why are you stopping?" asked Conor. "We're already running late."

"You see that guy on the street corner?"

"Yeah, who is he?"

"His name's Austin T. Slatter. He's a slave catcher."

"The one who Hans Schmidt has teamed up with? What's he doing down here?"

"I don't know, but I don't like it. How about if you take a walk down Spruce Street. Don't get noticed. My guess is you'll spot Hans someplace."

Fifteen minutes later, Conor ran up to the transport wagon from behind and climbed back onto the driver's seat. "I had to run around two blocks. You were right. Hans is farther down the street. What are we going to do?"

"If your enemy is quick-tempered, you can make a fool of him."

"What's that supposed to mean?"

Rian hopped down to the street. "You know what your brothers did to you last night?"

"Yeah, they cuffed me good."

"Well, that's what I'm going to let Slatter do to me."

Conor looked down at Rian. "That's a bad idea."

"Do you have a better one?"

"No. So what am I supposed to do?"

"You're going to pick up Rose. When you make the turn onto Ninth Street, whistle your whistle. She comes running. You slow down just long enough for her to hop on."

"Rian, that's a terrible plan."

"That's the only plan I can come up with."

"No, you don't get it. I don't know how to drive a team of horses."

Rian took off her jacket and hat, allowing her long hair to cascade down her back. She handed them up to Conor. "Don't lose these. You've been with me often enough when I've driven a team of horses. It's easy. You only have to make one turn, and it's a right. First, make sure you let the brake off. Slap the reins and give the horses a little kissing sound when you want the horses to start. Gently pull both reins when you want them to slow down. Pull on the right rein to make your turn. Pull harder when you want them to stop. These horses will know what to do."

"What are you going to do?"

Rian bent down behind the horses and picked up two freshly dropped horse turds. "When you hear the ruckus, you'll know it's time to start. Don't forget to whistle when you get close to Olivia's house." She turned and started walking toward Austin T. Slatter.

. . . .

Rian sauntered toward Slatter. He was leaning against one of the city's new gas streetlamps, keeping half an eye on the Tucker residence across the street while smoking a cigarette. She directed her attention toward an omnibus, pulled briskly by two gray horses and heading south on Ninth. It was an elaborate coach, like the ones she was familiar with on High Street. Its driver sat high in front. A conductor stood on a stoop in the back. The only entrance was a rear door. A narrow staircase curved steeply from the rear stoop to a second, open-air level. Slatter momentarily looked at Rian, didn't recognize her, followed her gaze to the omnibus, saw nothing of interest, and returned his attention to his cigarette.

As Rian walked to Slatter's rear, she threw her first horse turd as hard as she could at the back of his head. It found its mark and disintegrated with a satisfying *thunk*. "If you ever come to my father's shop again, you're going to be sorry!" she yelled at the top of her lungs.

Stunned, not realizing what had hit him, Slatter turned, only to get the second horse turd in the face.

"Fook you! I hope that shit went in your mouth!" yelled Rian.

Slatter took a moment to wipe his eyes and realize what he had been hit with, which gave Rian a solid head start as she ran south on Ninth. In half a block, she caught up to the omnibus and leaped aboard the rear platform. "How much?" she asked the conductor as she looked back to see Slatter thirty feet back and gaining on them. He was puffing hard.

"Whatsamatter, Arsehole? Out of breath already? You only ran half a block! I hope you die!" she yelled.

"Five cents," said the conductor.

Rian heard Conor's piercing whistle from Spruce Street, now a few hundred yards away.

"Hey, grab that kid!" yelled Slatter.

Rian handed the conductor a nickel. "Mister, that man's going to whale the tar out of me."

"I imagine he is. What'd you do to him?"

She started climbing the steps to the second level. "I told him his breath stunk."

"There's no way off the upper deck but this staircase," the conductor called after her. "He's got you trapped. You're going to catch it."

Rian didn't answer. She walked to the front of the upper deck, turned, and waited for Slatter. Two blocks to the north, she saw Conor turn the transport wagon onto Ninth Street. Rose walked briskly from the house to the wagon. Conor gave her a hand up, and, using his bench as a step, she rolled herself over the side of the coal tender.

Slatter appeared at the top of the stairs. Knowing that he had her trapped, he stopped to catch his breath. "You little shit, I'm going to whip you 'til you're dead." He reached to his waist, unbuckled his belt, and pulled it out of the pant loops.

Rian was resigned to taking a licking from Slatter. No matter how much he hurt her, she had already beat him because Rose was free. "Come and get me, shit for breath." Hopefully, he would never know it was she who engineered the escape. *The longer you beat me, the farther away Rose will be when you realize she slipped out of the house.*

The omnibus started to slow down. "Lombard Street!" yelled the conductor from the platform.

Another omnibus—a double-decker, just like this one—had drawn to a halt while heading in the opposite direction on Ninth Street to take on a passenger. Only four feet separated the two vehicles. Rian decided there was no reason to take a licking if she didn't have to. She stepped up on a bench, then the deck railing, and poised to leap to the other omnibus. Slatter charged and swung his belt at her. His buckle dug deep into her back.

The northbound bus moved forward. Rian leaped, but the blow of the belt buckle took all the energy out of her leap. Her jump was woefully short, but she was able to grab the rail of the northbound bus for just a moment before she fell to the street. She picked herself up and looked at the southbound omnibus, which continued on its route. Slatter watched her from the upper deck. He bent over, breathing hard, with his hands on his knees.

When the enemy sees an advantage but does not advance to seize it, he is fatigued, she thought. The distance between the omnibus and Rian grew.

· ·

· CONOR ·

Conor was driving the transport wagon at a sedate pace when Rian crossed the street in front of him and flagged him down. He directed the horses across High Street and then to a halt at the side of the street. Rian stumbled toward the wagon. She was obviously hurt.

Conor put on the brake and jumped down from the wagon. "Jaysus, Rian, what did he do to you?"

"One shot with his belt. That's all he got, but Jaysus, it hurts."

Conor noted a rip in Rian's shirt, surrounded by a fresh bloodstain. "Can you make it up onto the wagon?"

"I think I'll need your help."

"Is he still looking for you?"

"I don't think so, but I should put my jacket and hat back on. Are you still okay to drive?"

"Sure, it's only two more blocks. Let me help you up."

. . . .

· LUCRETIA ·

Lucretia opened the front door and was surprised to see Conor McGuire nervously shifting his weight from one foot to the other and back. "Why Conor, dear, is thee all right?"

"I'm fine, Mrs. Mott. But Rian and I need your help. Can you come next door, please?"

As Lucretia walked across the front lawn, she noticed a team of horses tethered in front of the Kriegers' house. They were hitched to a beefy wagon, and atop the wagon was a rather decrepit-looking railroad car. *What have these children gotten themselves into?*

Conor ushered Lucretia into the Krieger's house and down the hallway to the kitchen. Rian rose from a chair and greeted her.

"Rian, Conor says thee needs my help."

"Yes, we do."

Rian directed Lucretia's attention to a Black woman standing near a window. Coal dust covered her hands and dress. "This is Rose. She is running away, and she needs a place to stay for a few days. We couldn't take her to Moyamensing because they'll soon be looking for her. The plan was to get her out of town next week, so we need a place for her to stay until then. We were wondering if she could stay at your place."

Lucretia looked at Rose. Without hesitation, she walked over and shook her hand. "My name is Lucretia. Let's get thee over to my house, and we will figure out how we shall get thee to safety."

"Uh, Lucretia," said Conor, "Could you take a look at Rian, too. She took a pretty good shot from the slave catcher."

· ·

· SEAMUS ·

Seamus followed Dylan into the alley between Krieger Coach and Krieger Locomotive, away from the din in the factory. Dylan started tamping some tobacco into his pipe. "Little shy on sleep, Boyo?"

"I've been shy on sleep for months. It was a good night, though. What's up?"

"That china you were looking for, that Hugh thinks you stole off the docks. I think I might have something for you. Me sister Glennis cooks for some richies out on Eighth Street. Turns out the missus just bought a new set of china for the household. Ferris China."

Seamus lit his friend's pipe before he lit his own. "Do you know where she bought it?"

Dylan nodded. "From a stall on High Street. Toward the east end, the dodgy end, where the merchants are a little less reputable."

"I should be able to find it."

"What are you going to do?"

"Guess I'll lean on the vendor a bit. Find out where he got it."

"Good luck with that. Doubt he's in the habit of ratting out his suppliers."

"I can be very persuasive, Dylan."

· ·

· JULES ·

Not all the Germans at Krieger Coach approved of the No Name Fire Brigade's activities the night before. After lunch, a fight broke out between three Germans and three members of No Name; surprisingly, two Germans and an Irishman.

Jules waded into the melee, almost got pulled into it himself, then wasted half an hour—three man-hours, he groused to himself—settling things back down again. He stood at his shop desk, machinating about how he would get production back on schedule, when Rian and Conor returned with the coal tender.

"It took you long enough. Any problems?"

"No, not with the tender," responded Rian. "Jules, Conor and I need to talk to you."

Jules noticed that Rian held her back awkwardly but didn't think any more about it. "Not now, Rian."

WEDNESDAY, AUGUST 10

· RIAN ·

It was late morning the next day before Rian could finally corner Jules at Krieger Coach. "Jules, I need to talk to you."

"Yeah, I remember. Sorry about yesterday. I had a lot on my plate. You never told me why it took you so long to pick up the coal tender."

"That's what I want to talk to you about. It's got to be in private."

Jules looked at her quizzically, then turned on his heel. "I know just the place."

He led Rian to the varnish room, where the workers had hauled the next passenger car in the queue. "The guys aren't going to get to this car until after lunch to make sure all the dust has settled. So, talk to me. How come you were so late yesterday?"

"Conor and I. And Olivia. We kind of stole Mammy."

· · · · · · · · · · · · · · · · · · · ·

· JULES ·

Jules flew out of the shop and ran down Broad Street toward Moyamensing. Blocks before he arrived at his house, he knew that people were looking for Mammy, and they weren't being gentle about it. Some of his neighbors swept up debris from the front of their houses. He saw broken windows. A man consoled a woman who was in tears.

He arrived at his home to find his front door bashed in. He stormed in to find tipped-over furniture and some broken pottery. Maddie walked toward him, holding a kitchen knife. She wiped tears from her eyes and calmly put the knife down.

Jules ran to Maddie and embraced her. "Did they hurt you?"

"No. They never touched me."

"The children?"

"They're all okay. Scared but okay. I sent them upstairs."

"Did they find anything?"

"No. They were looking for Rose. I think they just enjoyed breaking things."

"Did you know any of them? Were they Irish?"

"No. Not Irish. One was a German. He said to tell you he'd be back. He said his name was Hans. The other had a Southern accent. Sounded like Virginia."

Jules nodded. "Hans Schmidt and Austin T. Slatter. Otto fired Schmidt last year. I was glad to see him go. Slatter's a slave catcher."

"Well, he certainly isn't afraid of getting caught. He knows there's nothing a Black family can do about this."

"They paid me a visit at the shop yesterday."

"What about?"

"Slatter checked up on my papers in Virginia. I threw him off the scent for a bit, and now he's distracted by Rose's escape, but soon enough, he's going to be on my tail again. He's like a bloodhound."

"Do you know where Rose is?"

Jules nodded. "I just found out an hour ago. Lucretia is hiding her until we can figure out how to get her out of town."

"Dear Lucretia. That may be a bit more than she bargained for. How did Rose get there?"

"Our favorite ragamuffin made up her own plan on the spur of the moment. The Tuckers were going to take Rose back to South Carolina today. I can't believe all the destruction this has brought on."

"Jules, we knew this would happen when we helped Rose escape. We've never helped an enslaved person flee from someone in Philadelphia before."

"I know. I just thought we'd be better prepared for it."

Rap rap rap. A knock at the front door. Maddie reflexively grabbed for her kitchen knife.

"Put the knife down," Jules said. "The people we're worried about don't knock."

Jules opened the door to find Rian Krieger. He pulled her into the house a little more roughly than he meant to. She winced. "Moya isn't a very safe place at the moment, Rian."

"I know. I saw some bully boys a couple of blocks from here, but I skirted around them."

"What are you doing here?" Jules looked at Rian a little more closely this time. "Are you hurt?"

"Yeah, a little bit. Slatter caught me with his belt buckle before I jumped off the omnibus. It still hurts quite a bit."

"Let me see it, Child," said Maddie.

Rian pulled up her shirt in the back, revealing a deep gash about two inches long.

"Has anyone treated this?"

"Lucretia washed it yesterday. She wrapped a bandage around me, but it came off while I was sleeping last night."

"Come with me. Something we have a lot of in this house is fresh bandages."

Rian dutifully followed Maddie, then stopped and turned to Jules. "I've got an idea about how to get Mammy out of Philadelphia. Do you still have the embosser?"

. . . .

Jules and Rian walked to Robert Purvis's house, lost in their thoughts. Every Black household they passed seemed to have some sort of destruction, although Jules had seen worse.

The timing of Mammy's disappearance was regrettable. Men from the Moyamensing Hose Company were still smarting from the confrontation on Catherine Street. Although Seamus had engineered the evening perfectly, the Irish were not pleased to have been bested with the assistance of a phalanx of Black men. The hunt for Rose was their opportunity to even the score a bit.

Jules wondered about the morality of abetting one person's freedom, only to bring such mayhem down upon his friends and neighbors. *What is good luck for one man is bad luck for another,* he thought to himself, quoting one of his mother's Ashanti proverbs.

He knew the Irish and people like the Shippens and Tuckers hate each other but give them a chance to rain down punishment on the Black community, and they somehow found a common cause. Almost every Black household suffered destroyed furniture and broken windows. But no one had been killed, and no houses burned. He fumed but, at the same time, felt guilty for his role in the destruction. He and Rian occasionally stopped to check in with friends and assist with the damage. The bully boys had roughed up some folks. Two Black women had been accused of being Mammy and hauled to the Tuckers' home, only to be tossed into the street when Randolph Tucker declared them not to be "his African."

Jules hoped the situation was blowing over but suspected that knots of hotheads would patrol Moyamensing until Rose was found or judged to have escaped from Philadelphia.

When the two arrived at Robert Purvis's house, the first thing Jules noticed was the shattered front door. He knocked, and a subdued Robert holding a pistol greeted them. "Come in. Quickly. Have they been to your house yet?"

"An hour ago. Everyone's okay. They just broke things. What about here?"

"The same. Don't know if we'd been better prepared—put up more resistance—perhaps it would have been worse. I'm just thankful no one was hurt."

"Robert, I'm sorry to barge in on you like this. Rian came to our house looking for the embosser. When Maddie told her we'd returned it, she already knew it was yours. She claims to have an idea to get Rose out of town but says I wouldn't understand."

Purvis looked down at Rian. "You know where Rose is?"

"Yes. I helped her escape yesterday. I had to. They were going to ship her back home today."

Purvis took a few moments to right an upended chair. He turned and faced Rian. "Well, now that you've taken the lead on this venture, I guess we'd better hear what you have in mind."

"If your enemy's forces are united, separate them. If sovereign and subject are in accord, put division between them."

· ·

Jules had to admit the twelve-year-old had the beginnings of a pretty good escape plan. But, by the time the three conspirators finished, he had injected his own twist. He read the carefully crafted letter one last time as it lay on the library table in Purvis's office.

August 10, 1836

Dear Mr. Tucker,

Today I came into possession of a slave woman who answers to the name Rose. She was arrested this afternoon here in Harrisburg, Pennsylvania, without papers of manumission or any other identifying paperwork. Upon interrogation, said woman admitted that she ran away from your residence yesterday and made her way to Harrisburg, traveling by both railroad and canal boat with the assistance of a man named Hans.

As this woman was delivered to me and captured through no effort on my part, you can reclaim your property by coming to Harrisburg, presenting yourself to this address with proper identification, and reimbursing the City of Harrisburg for the cost of her meals starting with dinner on this date.

As Negroes are not typically found on either canal boats or railroads, it strikes me that this woman was particularly motivated to escape enslavement. I recommend that you come with irons to prevent her from escaping again.

Your humble servant,

Ezekiel H. Cornfelder

Constable

112 Front Street

Harrisburg, Pennsylvania

Rian was looking over Jules's shoulder. "Ezekiel Cornfelder. Where did that name come from?"

"He was a blacksmith in the town near where I grew up. I didn't like him very much."

"And the address, 112 Front Street. Is that a real place?"

Purvis opened and closed drawers at his desk, looking for the embosser. "Front Street is. I have no idea what house or business is at 112. Rian, when did you say that newspaperman is leaving for Harrisburg?"

"Mr. Foote? He said he was going to catch the one o'clock."

Purvis found the embosser and brought it to the library table. "And he'll take the letter to Harrisburg and drop it at the post office?"

"Yes, he said he would do that as soon as he got to Harrisburg. I think he knows something's going on."

Purvis handed the embosser to Rian. She was about to clamp it over the signature of Ezekiel Cornfelder when Jules put his hand on hers and said, "No, don't do it."

"Why not? This is what's going to make this so convincing."

"When Tucker figures out this letter's a fake, it's not a stretch to see him showing it to Slatter."

Rian hit her forehead lightly with her fist. "And Slatter has already seen the stamp on your manumission paper."

"This letter is going to do the job without the stamp, at least long enough for us to get Rose out of town." He folded the letter, sealed it with wax, and addressed it to Mr. Randolph Tucker, Spruce and Ninth Streets, Philadelphia. "This has taken a lot longer than we anticipated. You don't have much time to get it to Mr. Foote. And congratulations, by the way."

"For what?"

"Think about it. Yesterday you escorted a slave to freedom. That makes you a conductor on the Underground Railroad. Not bad for a twelve-year-old."

· ·

Rian found Harold Foote already aboard the one o'clock train at the *Philadelphia & Columbia* train station at Broad and Vine.

Foote descended from the coach. "Rian, I figured you had changed your mind."

"No, it just took longer than we thought."

"We?"

"I can't tell you who else."

"You led me to believe I am now part of a conspiracy to assist a fugitive slave gain freedom. Is this true?"

"Yes."

"Does it have anything to do with the woman who fled from the Tucker residence on Tuesday?"

"I can't say, sir."

"Can't or won't?"

"Won't."

"Okay, the train is about to leave. I will deliver this letter to the post office before I check in to my hotel. Whatever it is, I hope it helps."

Thursday, August 11

· RIAN ·

The next day, Rian's Uncle Kurt had sailed into Philadelphia and walked uptown to get a tour of the new factories. With Otto and Adrian both out of the office on business, he fell asleep with his feet propped up on Otto's desk. Rian and Jules whispered in the corner, partly not to disturb Kurt, partly to talk privately about their conspiracy.

Yesterday, Jules didn't return to work. He spent the rest of the day cleaning up the damage to his home and trying to settle his family back down to some semblance of normal.

Rian had never divulged to her father that she had anything to do with Rose's disappearance, even though it was all anyone talked about in Philadelphia. *More lies.*

"How's your back?" asked Jules.

"It still hurts. Jules, Slatter only hit me once, and the pain was awful. I've been thinking. What if he had hit me ten times or a hundred?"

"I suspect it would have crippled you for weeks. Maybe forever."

"But that's what happens to lots of slaves."

"Sadly, yes."

"Jules, no one should be allowed to hit someone else like Slatter hit me. I said a while ago that I wanted to help you. You said that you would be happy if that happened someday. I don't want to wait. I want to start now."

Jules nodded. "I believe you already have, Rian, and I am honored to have you by my side."

Rian straightened in her chair. "Now, what are you going to do about Austin T. Slatter?"

"I think I've done all I can do. I've packed a bag so that I can light out of town at a moment's notice if I get wind that he's going to come after me. I've signed over ownership of the house to Maddie, so all the legalities are taken care of."

"You'd just leave her and the kids? Just like that?"

"If I had to. It beats walking to Calvert County in chains."

"If Rufus is the son of an escaped slave, does that mean he's a slave?"

Jules shook his head. "Slave status passes through the mother. Maddie's family has been free for three generations. Maddie and the kids are safe."

"How long do you think you'll have to keep your bag packed?"

"As long as Slatter's in town, I guess. Hans, too, unless we can throw them off the scent."

"I've got an idea. Do you know where Slatter lives? Where does he spend his time when he isn't tracking down slaves?"

"I know a couple of years ago he used to stay at a rooming house on Locust Street. That's about all I can think of."

"Think he still stays there?"

"I don't know. Why?"

Before Rian could answer, Seamus entered the office and shut the door. "Good, I need to talk to both of you. Jules, I heard there was some trouble in your neighborhood yesterday. How'd you make out?"

"A lot of Black households got hit. The bully boys and Irish. Slatter and Schmidt visited my house in person, just to let me know they still have me in their sights."

"Did they find the woman?"

"Nope."

"Did you have anything to do with it?"

Jules looked briefly at Rian. "Nope."

Seamus followed Jules's eyes. "Jaysus, Rian. Did you swipe her?"

Rian could not make eye contact with her cousin. "No."

"You wouldn't be lying to your Cousin Seamus, would you?"

Rian looked at Jules, who shrugged. "Maybe."

"Where is she?

"At Mrs. Mott's"

Seamus cracked a smile. "Brilliant, they're looking in the wrong part of town."

Jules got up from his desk. "Yeah, but that presents us with a bit of a problem. Our original plan is in shambles. Once we sprung her, we intended to spirit her out of town right away before they could upend Moya. Rian and Conor grabbed her early because Tucker was going to send her home."

"And now you don't have a way to get her out of the city."

"Exactly. And I've got Slatter breathing down my neck."

Seamus started pacing around the office. "Now this is getting a wee bit interesting. And I've got me own problems to solve. I need a little bit of reconnaissance, and I was wondering if I could pry Rian out of the office to help."

Rian fished into her table drawer, pulled out a cylinder about eight inches long, and placed it in her left hand. "Last year, Conor took me to see Signor Blitz, the magician." *You don't need to know that we snuck in and got chased out of the theatre.* "He said that one of the secrets to magic is misdirection, making the audience watch the left hand—" She pushed a button on the cylinder, and a bouquet of artificial flowers popped out "—while the important stuff is happening with the right."

At that moment, the forgotten Kurt Krieger stirred. "I'll be in town for at least two days. Any way I can help?"

. . . .

· RIAN ·

"Come on, Uncle Kurt. You were supposed to be here half an hour ago."

Rian sat on a bench near the corner of High and Front Streets, which at least was busy enough to be interesting, but when she sat still, the wound on her back began to throb again.

From the Delaware to Eighth Street, High Street was a wide, double-laned boulevard with a grassy strip down the middle. One hundred and fifty years ago, William Penn's surveyors designed the center strip to accommodate farm stands on market days. But these days, vendors had built semi-permanent stalls that were open six days a week. Rian doubted Penn envisioned that the stalls nearest the river would become less reputable, selling used, broken, and stolen goods.

Finally, Uncle Kurt, dressed in a frock coat, showed up at a stall that sold used housewares. Rian sauntered across the street to be close enough to hear the conversation.

Kurt addressed the vendor. "I'm hoping you can help me out. I'm looking for some china."

The vendor, a lean man with a pinched face, looked at him with suspicion. "Sorry, Mister. I sold all I had a few days ago."

"Oh, drat. See, I'm in a bit of a fix. Our clumsy maid just destroyed our current set. Broke everything to smithereens. My wife is preparing for a dinner party on Friday. I need a full set of twelve. Dinner plates, salad plates, dessert plates, cups, saucers. Anything else in the same pattern. I won't haggle about the price."

The vendor hesitated. "I might be able to help you out. Come back this time tomorrow."

Uncle Kurt thanked the man and left. Rian noted that the pinch-faced man asked the vendor next door to watch his stall. She followed him east on Walnut, then south on Seventh, until he turned right on Sansom. Two buildings down, he entered the Sansom Street Brauhaus. Rian paced up and down the block for fifteen minutes until the vendor exited the tavern with—Rian reflexively ducked behind a delivery wagon—*that's Hans Schmidt.*

Pinch-face headed back north. Rian followed Hans. He walked south to a warehouse at Pine Street. He unlocked a door big enough to swallow a wagon but slid it open just enough to slip inside. Half an hour later, he emerged with a wheelbarrow that held a large wooden crate.

Bingo, said Rian to herself. She wasn't surprised when Hans delivered the crate to the vendor.

• •

· AUSTIN T. SLATTER ·

Austin T. Slatter sat down in the rocking chair on the porch of Mrs. Barner's rooming house. Usually, he would have smoked his after-dinner cigar with the other men at the table. Tonight, however, a new boarder, a businessman, had kept up an irritating chatter the entire meal. Rather than cause a ruckus, Slatter escaped to the porch, only to realize that he had neglected to light his cigar from a candle before he left.

The salesman appeared on the porch. Now that the man was standing, Slatter noted that the stranger was quite a bit bigger than he was. He was tanned and muscular but walked with a limp so bad that he had to support himself with a cane. The man allowed the screen door to bang, lit his own cigar with a loco-foco, and offered to light Slatter's cigar.

"Thanks," said Slatter, grateful not to leave his rocker but irritated that the man had followed him out of the house.

"Have you seen these loco-focos before?" asked the businessman. "They're quite a marvel. I just saw my first one a few weeks ago. Now everyone uses them. They seem to be taking the country by storm. I didn't catch your name at dinner."

"Austin T. Slatter," he said, giving the man no encouragement to continue.

The stranger handed Slatter a business card. "Glad to make your acquaintance, Mr. Slatter. My name is Marion Pruett."

Slatter read the card twice.

Marion Pruett

Import/Export

Hicksford, Virginia

Slatter's desire to avoid the man evaporated. "I pride myself on deciphering accents, Mr. Pruett. You don't sound like you are a native of Virginia."

"Yes, I've heard that before. I was born and raised right on the North Carolina border, so there may be more than a touch of the Old North State in me, but I also spent four years attending the College of New Jersey. My classmates did their best to beat my accent out of me, but I persevered."

"I have seen your name before. You were cited on a manumission paper that I read well over a year ago. You're from Greene County."

"Close. Greensville County," Pruett corrected. "I haven't sold a slave in quite a few years, but there are any number of slaves from years ago who you could have bumped into."

"This one's name was Jules Howland. He calls himself Jules Freeman."

Pruett's demeanor changed from convivial to serious. "Jules Howland? I've been looking for Jules Howland for fifteen years. Do you know where he is? I would like to speak with him."

"I believe I could locate him for you. For a fee, that is."

"What is your profession, Mr. Slatter?"

"I help people recover lost or stolen property."

"Reading between those lines, I assume you are a slave catcher."

"That is exactly what I am."

"In that case, I would like to engage your services. In former days, I would just confront Jules Howland myself if you told me where I could find him, but with this gimpy leg and all, he would just run away. I need a professional and a more private setting to talk to him."

"I'm sure I can arrange that."

"Can you think of a private place for us to talk?"

"Kent's Livery. It's a stable on the corner of Broad and James Streets, catty-corner from the Krieger Coach factory. We will be there with Jules before 6:30 tomorrow evening."

Pruett nodded. "I am not familiar with it, but I'm sure I can find it. I will talk with the owner and make sure we are not disturbed."

306 · ROGER A. SMITH

Slatter put up his hand. "We should discuss my commission. I charge twenty percent of the value of all property returned."

"That seems a bit exorbitant to me. It's not like you have to escort him back to Hicksford. Five percent would seem more appropriate."

"Ten percent, and it's a deal."

"Then we will meet again after six tomorrow evening. It will be good to see Jules again. I have been looking forward to this for fifteen years."

· · · · · · · · · · · · · · · · · · · ·

· SEAMUS ·

That night, Hugh Callaghan stood in the middle of the street, directing his firemen as they worked to put out a house fire on Christian Street between Seventh and Eighth. The blaze silhouetted him as Seamus sauntered up behind and waited until the time was right. "Good evening, Hugh. No rest for the wicked, I see."

Callahan turned. "Too late, Kid. We've been here for fifteen minutes."

"Ah, no worries. Me boys had a busy afternoon. I told them to take the evening off. Let you guys have this one."

"The way I look at it, your crowd didn't do anything today. They should have been out banging heads, looking for the escaped slave woman."

"Afraid me boys' sensibilities don't run in that direction."

"So, what are you doing here?"

"That load of Ferris china that got swiped from under your nose last week. I think I might be able to help you out. Did you have a buyer in mind?"

Hugh looked hard at Seamus, then returned his attention to his men. "Had a great plan. Couple of retail establishments in New York City were all lined up and ready to buy. I was going to take them up there meself in the wagons they were packed in. Spend the night with me brother. Then sell the wagons and take the *John Bull* back here."

Seamus shook his head. "This is like a gift from God."

"Talk to me, Seamus."

"How about if I get you the china and the person responsible for swiping it?"

"There's got to be an *and* in here someplace. What do you want me to do?"

"You don't need to know that yet."

FRIDAY, AUGUST 12

· AUSTIN T. SLATTER ·

Austin T. Slatter and Hans Schmidt half walked, half dragged a bloodied Jules Freeman into the stable. Pruett was already there, sitting in a chair that looked like it belonged in a kitchen, not a stable.

"Very good, Mr. Slatter. Right on time." He pointed to a second chair that was facing him. "Please set Mr. Howland down there."

They roughly forced Jules into the chair.

"It's Mr. Freeman now," said Jules. "I don't go by my slave name anymore."

Pruett held out three pieces of rope. "Mr. Slatter, please tie Mr. Howland to the chair so we can have a chat. His legs to the legs of the chair. His hands behind his back. That way, I won't waste any more of your time."

Slatter accepted the pieces of rope and handed them to Schmidt, who knelt to tie Jules' legs.

Pruett stared at Hans's face. "Mr. Slatter, it appears that Mr. Howland put up a fight. Are those new wounds to your associate's face?"

Hans stood up and wiped some blood from his upper lip. "Nothing I can't handle."

Slatter wasn't much interested in banter. "Time to pay me, Pruett. I figure a runaway buck like this one is worth about $1200. That means you owe me $120 cash on the barrelhead."

Pruett's visage darkened. "Apparently, there has been a misunderstanding. Mr. Howland isn't a runaway. He bought his freedom from me fifteen years ago."

Slatter's ire, never far below the surface, kicked in. "If he's not a runaway, what are we doing here?"

"We are here because when he bought his freedom, he left Greensville County, taking his little sister along with him. He never bought her freedom." Pruett turned his attention to Jules. "I figure Cassie was worth about $800 at the time, Jules. It's taken me fifteen years to track you down, but I still want my stolen property back. Where is Cassie?"

"I don't know. Canada someplace."

"As I feared. Then you have a choice. Pay me $800, or I will happily pay Mr. Slatter 20% of the value of your sister to take you back to Greensville County. You will find there is a warrant out for your arrest for theft."

Slatter interrupted. "I wouldn't trust this African one bit. His sister's probably still here, just like him."

Jules ignored Slatter. "I don't have that kind of money."

"But I suspect you can get your hands on it," Pruett countered.

"You wouldn't consider a payment plan, would you?"

"You always did have a sense of humor, Jules."

"No. Look, I'm dug in here. I've got a good job. I own my own house. I'm not going to run away to avoid paying you a lousy $800. I could get back to even with you in a couple of years."

Pruett seemed to consider the proposition. "What do you think, Mr. Slatter?"

"What do I think?" Slatter struck a downward blow at Jules's cheek with his fist. "I think this has been an enjoyable afternoon for me. That last little tap is a message for your little friend. She better hope I never catch her alone again. Pruett, do whatever you want. Pay me my commission, and Hans and I will get out of your hair."

Pruett handed Slatter a wad of bills. "I thank you both for your time."

"Come on, Hans. Our job is done here." *The easiest $80 I've ever made*, Slatter chuckled to himself as he strode out of the stable.

· ·

· RIAN ·

Rian's Uncle Kurt walked into the dining room of the Krieger household. "Where's Otto?"

Rian set two plates of beef stew on the table. "*Vater* has a meeting. Alice made dinner and went home. It's just you and me for dinner tonight. We'll have to do cleanup."

Kurt opened the silver chest on the sideboard and pulled out two spoons. "Well, that allows us to catch up without working your father into a lather. How's your back?"

"It still hurts. I hope I never get whipped again. Not ever. Did you give Slatter the business card? The one that said *Marion Pruett*?"

"I did. I was afraid the ink would smear; it was so fresh. So, it seems like Robert Purvis knows every tradesman in Philadelphia who leans toward abolition."

"I watched the printer make up the cards. He set the type while I was right there. I ran them right to you."

"You're learning some rather unsavory skills for a twelve-year-old. Forgery, surveillance, lying."

Rian smiled. "I don't like the lying part. It hurts my head because I've got to keep all my lies straight. How did things go in the stable?"

"I think Jules and I were both convincing. Sadly, Slatter and Schmidt took the opportunity to rough Jules up more than a bit. He struggled mightily when they snatched him. He gave Schmidt a fat lip."

"Is he okay?"

Kurt took his first taste of the stew and reached for the salt. "Banged up a bit. More angry that we had to cough up $80 to sell the charade."

"Do you think they swallowed it?"

"Hook, line, and sinker."

Rian got up, walked to the kitchen, and returned with a glass of cold milk. "I just hope Mr. Foote did his job and put the letter to Olivia's father into the mail in Harrisburg."

"I bet it will work. Tucker should get the letter with a Harrisburg postmark tomorrow. Hopefully, that will help to calm things down in Moyamensing. What about the china?"

"Seamus told Hugh Callaghan about Hans. I think Hugh's going to talk to him."

"Hmm, I suspect they'll do a bit more than chat." Kurt wiped his mouth with his napkin. "So, my work is done here, as Austin Slatter would say. Tomorrow I return to the *Vestal*, and we sail on the evening tide. I'll probably be back in a couple of weeks. I'm sure all these shenanigans will have played out by the time I return.

SATURDAY, AUGUST 13

· OTTO ·

Otto was writing a letter at his desk when Jules entered the Krieger Coach office. "Boss, you got a minute?"

Otto put his quill down, looked at Jules, and rose from his desk. "What happened to you?

Jules touched a bruise on his cheek. "I had a little altercation with Schmidt and Slatter. I think my problems are behind me for the moment."

"I am happy to hear you say that. Tell me what is on your mind."

Jules handed Otto an envelope. "Adrian got this in this morning's mail. It's another request for Krieger Locomotive to build a fire pump."

Otto scanned the letter and tossed it to the side of his desk. "Adrian turned down half a dozen requests on Saturday. This one does not seem to be any different."

"Well, except this one is in writing. Your brother asked me to bring it to you to make sure you aren't interested either."

Otto shook his head and picked up his quill to get back to his letter.

But Jules wasn't finished. "It just seems a pity to be turning away business."

"Jules, we are too busy. We have not even ironed out all the kinks in this factory. We have to open the two others in the next few weeks."

"That's what Adrian said you would say. So, I've got a proposal."

"And that is?"

"Let me take the requests for fire pumps. I can build them separate from the Krieger companies."

Otto shook his head. "No, that is out of the question. I just said we do not have time to build the coaches—and I am talking about horse-drawn carriages and railroad cars—that we already have orders for. I need you on the shop floor, undistracted by another new business. And with the 10-hour day that we agreed to last year, we do not have the workers."

Jules persisted. "Have you rented out your old Krieger factory buildings yet?"

"We have had some nibbles, but no. They are too antiquated."

"What if I rent them and build fire pumps down there?"

"Jules, that would be ridiculous. You would be taking a step backward. You would need a modern facility to make fire pumps of the quality that has attracted all the attention. Those buildings would need a steam engine to drive the machinery."

"This would be a much smaller operation than what we're running here. I could install a smaller steam engine to drive one or two of everything: lathes, drill presses, saws, shapers."

Otto sensed that Jules had done more than a casual amount of thinking about this. "Are you talking about owning a business? Of this magnitude?"

Jules nodded.

"That would be unprecedented. No Black man in Philadelphia, in America even, owns an operation of that size."

"Well, that's not really true. James Forten, Robert Purvis's father-in-law, owns one of America's largest sail-making businesses. On the Delaware, right here in Philadelphia. There are others."

Otto shook his head. "It would take significant capital investment. No bank will lend that kind of money to a Black man."

"I may not need a bank. Purvis and Forten are willing to back me."

"When did they tell you this?"

"Yesterday. Maddie and I visited both of them after my little meeting with Slatter and Schmidt."

"Maddie?"

"My wife would be involved too. She would keep the books."

"Where will you find the workers? Good workers are scarce these days. And if you could find the workers, who would run them?"

"There are plenty of workers out there who I could train."

"Seamus already has his fingers out in the Irish community. He is hand-picking lads who he feels will fit. They are few and far between."

"I'm not talking about Irish."

"Then who?"

"Negroes."

"Jules, no. Blacks in skilled positions. Your wife running the office. A Black man owning a business of that size. This is too much. It is out of the question."

"Please, just sleep on it." Jules placed a shiny golden object on Otto's desk, turned, and exited the office. Otto sighed and picked up the heavy brass oval. It said

Freeman Hydraulics
Philadelphia U. S. A.

· ·

· RIAN ·

The search for Rose evaporated almost overnight. Randolph Tucker left the city on the *Philadelphia & Columbia* the day after receiving the letter from the fake Constable Cornfelder. Rian heard from three different people that the escaped slave woman had been captured in Harrisburg. With no prospects for a reward, the nativists and Irish broke off their tacit alliance and retired to their own neighborhoods.

When Randolph Tucker returned empty-handed from Harrisburg, no one bothered to renew the search for Rose. Olivia reported that her father knew someone had duped him but had no idea who. The Tuckers had to wait another week for the *Carolina Princess* to return to Philadelphia before sailing to Charleston.

Knowing that Olivia would shortly be returning to South Carolina, Rian, Conor, Trey, and Olivia spent as much time with each other as they could. Rian had developed a genuine affection for Olivia and would be sad when she returned to Charleston. It also saddened her that she still had a secret to keep. Trey knew nothing about the conspiracy to free Rose.

Rian and Olivia walked a few paces behind Conor and Trey on the pathway around Fairmount Water Works. "What are you going to do when I leave?" Olivia asked Rian. "It won't be nearly as much fun without me."

"I think I've got to make a decision."

"Whether to continue working with Jules and Maddie on the Underground Railroad?"

"Nope. I'm doing that for sure."

"What then?"

"I've got to choose. Which factory do I want to run when I grow up? Krieger Coach or Krieger Locomotive?"

"I like that," said Olivia.

"Like what?"

"That even though you are only twelve years old, and you are a girl, you are already certain you will run a factory."

Olivia's statement of confidence felt good to Rian but prompted her to make another confession. "That is unless Vater sends me to Switzerland next year."

Sunday, August 14

· SEAMUS ·

Seamus left morning mass directly but waited for Hugh when he exited the Church of St. Philip de Neri with his family. With a slight gesture, he indicated he wanted to talk to Hugh, not Siobhan. Hugh smiled. Siobhan humphed and flounced away with her mother and sisters.

"Good to see you've become a regular at church these days, Seamus. What do you want?"

"I understand you got your china back."

"Only one wagon. Mr. Schmidt took some persuading, but he came around. Where's the other wagon?"

"Oh, I've got it. I'll be happy to deliver it to you. But I want to cash in the favor."

"I've got to do you a favor to get me own china back? I don't think so."

Seamus put his hands into his pockets and rocked back on his heels. "Well, technically, it was never your china. Hans stole it before you could steal it."

"Yeah, but he stole it from my territory."

"And then you falsely accused me of stealing it."

"Yet here you are, in possession of the china you didn't steal, asking me for a favor."

"Let's call it a finder's fee."

"Enough banter, Seamus. What do you want?"

"I think you want to take that trip to New York to see your brother tomorrow. First ferry leaves Chestnut Street at sunrise. I suggest you be there with the wagon. The other wagon might just appear."

"So, what's this favor I'm doing for you?"

"I'll tell you tomorrow. You're not going to like it, so I don't want to give you time to back out."

Hugh shook his head. "It's a good thing you amuse me, Seamus. I think my life might be a lot easier if I just squashed you like a bug."

"What'd be the fun in that? And Hugh, you want to come alone. See you tomorrow. Don't be late."

· ·

· JULES ·

The Freeman family had finished Sunday dinner, and Maddie had shooed five of the children from the house. Jules and Rufus were replacing the front door that had been badly abused by the rowdies five days ago.

"Ahem. Good afternoon, Jules. Good afternoon, Rufus."

Jules turned to see Otto Krieger standing in the street in front of his house. "Hi, Boss. What brings you to this part of town?"

"I would like to talk if you have a little time. I suppose with you and Maddie both."

Jules dismissed Rufus. He picked a shard of the old, shattered door off the porch and invited Otto into his home. He called to Maddie, who greeted Otto warmly. The three seated themselves in the parlor, with Maddie and Jules sitting next to one another on a settee. Jules absentmindedly laid the shard on the table beside him.

Otto looked around the room with a craftsman's eye. "It looks like you have repaired whatever damage was done."

"It was mostly furniture. A fairly easy fix. And the door, of course."

"Then I should get down to business. Maddie, I assume Jules told you about his proposal to make steam engines to put out fires."

Maddie nodded. "Yes, we have put a lot of thought into it. I'm in favor of it."

"As Jules requested, I slept on it. I talked to my brother. We would like to explore the idea of renting our old shops to Freeman Hydraulics."

Jules looked at Maddie. They made eye contact, both nodding. *Here we go.*

"But I have questions," Otto continued. "Why do you want to do this?"

Jules straightened. "The brass plate didn't answer that question? I want to have my name on something as fine as the carriages that we are producing at Krieger Coach."

"Oh, I understand that. The brass plate was a brilliant touch. That is what convinced me to have this discussion. Let me rephrase my question. You and Maddie are becoming a force in Philadelphia's Black community. You own this house. You have six beautiful children. Jules, your job at Krieger Coach pays better than almost any other Blacks in this city. From what Lucretia tells me,

Maddie is helping to drive PFASS forward. What motivates you to risk all that to have your name on a plaque?"

Jules leaned forward, putting his elbows on his knees. He looked Otto right in the eye. "Because of Rian."

"My daughter? I do not understand."

"She has blossomed in the factories. She has become so capable at so many things. I look into the future, and I see nothing but opportunities for her. She is going to light the world on fire."

"But that is not what I want for my daughter. Her role will be to become a good helpmate to a fine husband."

Jules shook his head. "Otto, you may have plans for her, but your daughter is a force of nature." *Do you even suspect that your 12-year-old daughter has already helped an enslaved woman find her way to freedom? That she is a conductor on the Underground Railroad?* "When the time comes, my friend, she will make those sorts of decisions for herself."

"And how does my daughter inspire you to make the leap to Freeman Hydraulics?"

"Because I want my own children to have the same opportunities. I am not naive enough to think it would work out by bringing them to the Krieger factories. We are already stretching things to mix the Irish and the Germans. But if this were a Black enterprise, owned by Black people, employing mostly Black people, my children might have a chance to flourish. Just the same way Rian is flourishing."

"But this is such a departure. You have always told me you did not want to stick out. You said that as soon as a Black person gets a little ahead, someone makes a point of smacking him down. What has changed?"

"What happened?" Jules reached for the piece of the shattered door that he had rested on the nearby table. "This happened. For years since I first arrived in Philadelphia, I have believed that the best thing for us Negroes was to keep our heads down and not attract too much attention. Even Maddie's work with PFASS made me nervous. I was afraid that sooner or later, we would get swatted like some irritating fly."

"It seems that almost happened five days ago."

"It did happen. It also happened to many of our neighbors, rich, like Robert Pervis, and much poorer than we are. It didn't matter which. The bully boys took it out on all of us. But it convinced me that until the Black man in America approaches some semblance of equality, there will be dark forces that always want to smack us down. I learned the other day that the only way through this is to go forward. If that means that I occasionally get smacked, so be it. But my goal is to change things so that my children do not have to live in fear of a shattered front door."

Jules realized his words came out with more vehemence and conviction than intended.

Maddie put her hand into his. "This is the man I married. His words frighten me, but I have never been prouder of my husband than I am right now."

Otto stared at Jules for many seconds. Then he stood and offered his hand to Jules. "And I am proud to call you my friend. Let us go forward, then, and figure out how we will make the world a better place for all our children."

"Whatever they choose for themselves?"

Otto laughed. "I am not on board with all your foolishness about my daughter's future. Her time in the factory is coming to a close. This time next year, she will be on a boat to Europe to attend finishing school. But I like what you are saying about a better life for the next generation. Let us go on from there."

MONDAY, AUGUST 15

· SEAMUS ·

Seamus was nervous. This one last thing had to fall into place.

Ten minutes ago, he had parked the wagon on Water Street, just around the corner from the Chestnut Ferry Dock. He sat on the wagon seat, gripping the stem of his unlit pipe between his teeth. Reflecting his own mood, the horses stirred uneasily. There was only occasional rustling underneath the tarpaulin behind him.

The plan would be a step closer to success if the girls came back with word that Hugh had come alone.

As if on cue, Olivia and Rian rounded the corner and waved him on. He released the brake and gave the reins a slight slap. *My, how things change. A little over a year ago, I didn't even know how to drive a team of horses.* The horses seemed grateful to be finally moving forward. When he turned onto Chestnut Street, he could see Hugh already in line to board the first ferry of the day.

Seamus felt no need to hurry. The horses plodded, then halted of their own accord. Seamus set the brake. "Good morning, Hugh. Ready to head to New York?"

Hugh stood with arms crossed. "Not so fast. I know there's a condition attached to this. What do I have to do for your—I guess we could call it—largess?"

Seamus hopped down from the wagon. He walked to the rear of the wagon and pulled back the tarp. Rose sat up and climbed out of the wagon.

The enormity of the favor dawned on Hugh. "No, I'm not doing it."

"That's the deal, Hugh. Take it or leave it. You get the wagons. You get the china on the wagons. We paid $50 for the horses. If you sell them for more than that in New York, you can keep the profit. All you have to do is deliver Rose to New York City."

"There is no way I'm going to do that."

"How about if I sweeten the pot a little bit?"

Seamus pulled up the other side of the tarp, and Siobhan sat up. She climbed out of the wagon and walked over to her father. "Come on, Da. This isn't that big a deal. She's leaving Philadelphia, for fook sake. What do you care? She'll be in Canada by the end of the week."

"I assume this is the African woman we've been turning Moya upside down looking for the past few days."

"Not as far as you're concerned. She's carrying manumission papers. It's all proper."

"Have you been in this from the beginning?"

"Did I help her escape? No, that wasn't me. Let's just say I'm re-paying me own debts here. But I guess I'm happy to do it."

"I'm not sure you know what you're getting yourself into, Seamus. The folks who are looking for her, they're determined to put an end to the runaways. And they are very powerful."

"Can't see that you have an incentive to rat me out. They're not crazy about the Irish either."

Hugh shrugged. "Naw, I won't rat you out. But how do you know I won't just turn this woman into some constable once we get to New Jersey? The reward is pretty hefty."

"Because you're going to have company," Seamus said. "Siobhan's going with you."

Hugh's shoulders sagged. "Siobhan doesn't know how to drive a team of horses. Seamus, you told me I wouldn't need any of my boys. There's two wagons here. Who's the other driver?"

"Rose. She has driven teams since she was a kid. You get her to New York. You sell the wagons. You sell the horses. You and Siobhan spend the night with your brother. You come home on the train. Just like you planned, except you get some time with your daughter."

Hugh turned to his daughter. "Aren't you working at Clancy's the next two nights?"

"Jenna's filling in for me."

Hugh still wasn't mollified. "Every captain on the Delaware is on the lookout for this African woman and two wagons filled with china. You aren't setting me up, are you, Seamus?"

"It would be fun to watch you try to squirm your way out of a fix like that, but no. Siobhan's presence should assure you of that. Anyway, Captain Ames is properly bribed. No extra charge for that, by the way."

The Falcon's whistle gave one long and one short blast. "Fish or cut bait, Hugh."

Hugh shook his head at his predicament. "Now I've got a condition for you."

"And what's that?"

"None of my boys ever find out about this."

"Deal."

With the deal sealed, Hugh climbed aboard the wagon. He held a hand out and helped his daughter into the seat. He slapped his reins, and his horses obediently climbed the planks onto the ferry. Rose walked to the horses hitched to the second wagon and grabbed one by the halter. "C'mon, we're going to have a long day," she said to the horses. With a kissing sound, she led them up the planks to the ferry's deck.

· · · · · · · · · · · · · · · · · · · ·

· RIAN ·

Rian watched as Rose's team followed Hugh onto the ferry. She turned to her cousin. "Seamus, Olivia and I want to cross the river with them."

"That's another hour of work you're going to miss."

"Jules said he'd cover for me."

"See you at the shop. Don't dawdle. We need you."

Rian and Olivia were the last two to board the Falcon before the crew winched the planks up and loosed the lines. Olivia walked forward to find Rose, now known as Mazie, and climbed aboard her wagon. She sat down on the driver's seat and snuggled next to her. Mazie put her arm around Olivia and pulled her close. Rian figured it was better to let them have their last minutes together by themselves.

The Falcon left the wharf and churned across the Delaware. Rian turned away from the headwind and watched the outline of Philadelphia diminish. She eyed the docks, busy with longshoremen unloading cargo from ships with furled sails. She watched a crane haul a large crate aboard a ship headed for some exotic destination. She felt the ferry bob slightly as it crossed the wake of a steamboat chugging down the Delaware. Then she shut her eyes and listened, identifying sounds she loved. The call of seagulls. The faint cries of workers. The *choosh! . . . choosh! . . . choosh*! of the steam engine.

Choose! . . . choose! . . . the steam engine seemed to urge her. *Which one are you going to choose, Rian? Run Krieger Coach or Krieger Locomotive?*

She arched her back to test the week-old gash from Slatter's belt buckle. *Not bad, not bad at all,* she said to herself, using a phrase she knew would please her Irish cousin.

Slatter, I beat you, and you didn't even know there was a contest. You were up against Rian Krieger, a Warrior by name and a warrior by nature. I am a follower of Sun Tzu, the greatest general who ever lived. I am twelve years old, and I'm a conductor on the Underground Railroad. And one day, I will run one of the finest factories in America.

Rian pulled herself out of her reverie and chided herself *unless Vater sends me to that ridiculous finishing school in Switzerland.*

Author's Notes

When I taught high school American History, I often struggled to incorporate groups ignored in the history books into my curriculum. As a reader of historical novels, I am frequently disappointed by two things. That characters were not impacted by more significant events—economic change, intellectual movements, and especially technological innovations—taking place in their world. And that the characters often displayed anachronistic sensibilities that were a reflection of our own time rather than the era the novel was set in. When I started writing Rian Krieger's Journey, I hoped to address these issues.

I take special pleasure in weaving real historical characters and venues into my stories. I want these figures to espouse opinions they held at a time and place where they were. I want the venues—some of which still exist, some that have long ago disappeared—to come alive to the reader.

- I have tried to describe Philadelphia in the antebellum period as accurately as possible. I leaned heavily on an 1830 map entitled *Plan of the City of Philadelphia and Adjoining Districts* by William Allen. Today's Market Street was originally known as High Street, but even in the 1830s was occasionally referred to by its modern name. Bainbridge Street used to be Shippen Street, South Street used to be Cedar Street, and Race Street used to be Sassafras Street.

- Although my library is now filled with many books relevant to this era, I was fortunate that very early in this journey, I discovered the book *Philadelphia, A 300-Year History*, written by Russell F. Weigley, et al.

- The John Bull locomotive served the *Camden & Amboy Railroad* for many years. It is currently on display at the Smithsonian National Museum of American History.

- Windmill Island lay between Philadelphia and Camden. In 1838, a channel was dug through Windmill Island so that steam ferries had a more direct route between the two cities. The northern island created by the division was named Smith. Both islands were later dredged to oblivion to allow more straightforward navigation in the Delaware.

- The General Strike of 1835 took place as described.

- Lucretia Mott is the only one of my <u>major</u> characters who was a real person. She lived at 136 North Ninth St. in Philadelphia, next door to the fictional Otto and Rian Krieger. Through Lucretia, I have the opportunity to introduce a score of other famous people with whom she interacted in real life. In this book, we met William Lloyd Garrison, Benjamin Lundy, and John Quincy Adams. More will follow in future books.

- The population in Philadelphia shifted during this period. Wealthy families left their sumptuous homes near the Delaware River and moved west of Seventh Street. Their former homes were divided into apartments and rented to whomever.

- The Flying Horse riots occurred as described.

- It was undoubtedly unwise for Maddie and Jules to keep a journal of the fugitive slaves they had sheltered. Such evidence could incriminate them in significant crimes if it were ever found. But some stationmasters believed that the records would become important for historical purposes. Most notable among them was William Still of Philadelphia, who documented the stories of 800 fugitives whom he had sheltered.

- The cholera epidemic that took Rian's mother and Conor's parents raged through Philadelphia in 1832. The massacre of Irish workers at Duffy's Cut most likely did occur as Seamus described during his meeting with Otto at Clancy's Saloon.

- The United States Hotel existed on Chestnut Street directly across from the Second Bank of the United States Building from 1826 to 1856.

- William Strickland was an architectural and engineering renaissance man. He designed the Second Bank of the United States and the Merchants Exchange, which still stand in downtown Philadelphia. As described in the book, he was sent to England to study canals and returned instead as a proponent of railroads.

- Slave owners during this era were allowed to bring their slaves into Pennsylvania. Any slave who remained in Pennsylvania for six months was legally free. When Philadelphia was the capital of the United States and George Washington was president, he circumvented this rule by swapping his slaves out before they reached their sixth month of Pennsylvania residence.

- Above all, I love finding those moments in history that are the unknowns, the grey areas that I can slip my characters and storyline through. Historians have speculated for years about how and when the Liberty Bell was cracked. Perhaps it was in 1824, when the Marquis de Lafayette made a triumphant return to America. Or 1832, on the hundredth anniversary of George Washington's birth. And, of course, 1835, during the funeral procession of John Marshall. I decided to borrow from the latter two theories. Memories of Emmanuel J. Rausch, as recounted by his widow, appeared in newspapers in 1915:

> "My mother had sent me to the shop that morning," Rauch said, "and I heard 'Major Jack'—that's what we boys called Jack Downing, the keeper of the steeple, who was quite a character in Philadelphia—calling me. He corralled a lot of youngsters beside me and then asked us, 'Say, boys, do you want to ring the Liberty Bell today, in honor of Washington's birthday?' Did we want to! 'Major Jack' climbed up into the steeple and tied a rope around the clapper. When he came down, we took the other end, as he told us to, began pulling with all our might. And to make a long story short, the boys pulled with such might that the old bell cracked under the strain! We never said a word about our exploit. It seemed one of those things that 10-year-old boys who aren't looking for trouble had best keep silent about. And I guess 'Major Jack' wasn't inclined to talk about it, either."

The most glaring inaccuracy in Rauch's recollection is that the State House Bell wasn't called the Liberty Bell until 1839, when William Lloyd Garrison reprinted an article in his newspaper, *The Liberator*.

- I'm not sure the interrelationship between stouter rails, more powerful locomotives, and heavier rolling stock was an identified phenomenon in the 1830s. However, it seems quite evident when viewed from the era of personal computers. During the early days of the desktop computer, consumers were made dizzy by more powerful computers that appeared regularly, only to see them filled almost to capacity with new, more voluminous software. I believe there is a direct analogy between the two eras.

- Omnibus drivers were wildcats. The omnibuses were a new phenomenon in Philadelphia in this era.

- Joice Heth was a formerly enslaved person exhibited as the reputed 161-year-old nursemaid to George Washington. P. T. Barnum purchased her contract in 1835 after he traveled to Philadelphia to see her in person. She was his first entry into showcasing oddities and fantastical, often fake, products of nature. The article about Joice in the *Pennsylvania Inquirer* is quoted verbatim from Barnum's autobiography, *Struggles and Triumphs, or Forty Years' Recollections of P. T. Barnum*. When Heth died in 1836, an autopsy estimated she was more likely in her 80s, which would mean that she could not have been George Washington's nursemaid. Barnum even made money off her death, charging 50 cents to witness the autopsy.

- William Lloyd Garrison frequently visited Lucretia Mott in her home when he came to Philadelphia. After a disastrous speech, early in their friendship, Lucretia and James Mott encouraged Garrison to speak from the heart rather than from notes. Garrison did have a $5000 price on his head, courtesy of the Georgia state legislature.

- In July 1835, the American Abolitionist Society in New York City flooded Charleston, SC, with anti-slavery literature. The postmaster, citing the literature as inflammatory, sorted this mail out before it was delivered. A mob stole the mail sacks and burned the literature in a public demonstration. In August 1835, a Philadelphia mob inspired by the Charleston action ransacked a post office, tore stolen abolitionist literature into bits, and dumped it into the Delaware River. That action led to further violence in Moyamensing. I chose to place Seamus and Dylan in the center of this action.

- Mailing massive amounts of printed literature was only possible because of innovations in the printing industry. Higher quality and consistency in paper in the 1830s made faster presses practical for the first time. More rapid presses were only possible with the advent of steam power.

- In December 1835, President Andrew Jackson recommended that Congress pass federal legislation that prohibited sending incendiary publications (that was the era's code for anti-slavery literature) through the mail.

- Lest you think that Seamus Gallagher and Hugh Callaghan's story arcs are a bit fantastical, read *Philadelphia Politics from the Bottom Up, the*

Life of Irishman William McMullen by Harry C. Silcox. McMullen, who will appear in future books, became the president of the *Moyamensing Hose Company*.

- Fire brigades in this era were a combination of social clubs, gangs, and extortionists. The rivalries among fire companies in Philadelphia were well documented. Stealing one another's pumps was common. The histories I have read provide no record of white fire brigades created to serve the Black community, but records exist of a sizable number of Irish who did not turn their backs on their Black neighbors.

- Robert Purvis lived in Philadelphia as described. His mixed-race ancestry was a source of pride to him. His marriage to Harriet Forten, the daughter of a prosperous Black sailmaker, put the couple at the peak of Philadelphia's Black community. Robert's trip to England—the positive reception from the abolition societies and the adverse reaction when he tried to establish a parallel between the English treatment of the Irish and the American treatment of enslaved people—is well documented.

- Purvis' father-in-law, the sailmaker James Forten, was likely the wealthiest Black man in America. He attempted to create a Black fire brigade in the early 1820s. His efforts were vilified in the Philadelphia press, which generated anti-Black turmoil, and the brigade was soon disbanded.

- Signor Antonio Blitz, who maintained a home in Philadelphia, was the premier magician in America during this era. Born in England, he started his career as a magician at age 13 in Hamburg and emigrated to the United States in 1834. He wrote an autobiography, *50 Years in the Magic Circle*. Blitz died in 1877 in Philadelphia.

- John Quincy Adams was escorted to Lucretia Mott's house by Benjamin Lundy on July 11, 1836. Defeated by Andrew Jackson in his bid for a second term as President of the United States, Adams served in the House of Representatives from 1831 to his death in 1848. He became a tireless advocate of abolition, to the point that the House instituted a gag rule, automatically tabling hundreds of anti-slavery petitions, most of them presented by Adams.

- Benjamin Lundy, a Quaker, devoted his life to the anti-slavery movement. In 1827, he was severely beaten by a slave trader in Baltimore who objected to a series of articles Lundy had written about him. The slave trader was fined one dollar for his assault, the judge stating that Lundy had brought the assault on himself by criticizing the slave trader's lawful occupation.

- *The Art of War* was translated into French in the second half of the 1700s. No English translation existed until the early 1900s.

- The first steam fire pumper was built in England in 1829. They did not become practical until the 1840s.

- The Black marching band known as the Third Company of Washington Guards, which led the fictional *No Name Fire Brigade* into Washington Square before the firemen's parade, was real, as was Frank Johnson.

- The *Philadelphia & Columbia Railway* functioned as described.

- I am sure that this book includes numerous historical inaccuracies. I apologize in advance and would appreciate hearing others' feedback on this. Feel free to contact me by visiting my website: rogerasmith.com. The only errors that I have purposely included are that

  ○ I know that William Lloyd Garrison traveled to Philadelphia in March of 1835. I have no evidence that he was there again in June. By 1835, travel between Boston and Philadelphia had shortened to a two-day affair, and I felt that having Garrison meet with Lucretia on the opening date of the book was a minor transgression.

  ○ The church St. Philip de Neri was built in 1840, so Seamus could not have attended mass there in 1835.

On a personal note, my maternal grandmother's maiden name was Warrior. She was feisty and opinionated. Numerous times I heard her declare, "I'm a Warrior by name and a warrior by nature." It seemed only fitting that I weave this little bit of family lore into Rian Krieger's family history.

While writing this book, one of my many joys has been "going down the rabbit hole." That is what happens when I want to get a fact right, buy a book or go online, keep following reference after reference, and then realize that three hours have gone by, I haven't written a word, but I know a lot more about stuff than I used to. If any of the historical figures or events in this book intrigue you, I encourage you to go down the rabbit hole yourself. I hope you will find it as rewarding as I have.

ACKNOWLEDGMENTS

I want to thank the many people and organizations who have supported me during this journey.

- The Writers Group of New Cumberland, especially Don Helin, for launching me and giving me confidence.

- The Brewster Writers Group, for sandwiching criticism between praise and helping me tinker, improve, and appreciate nuance.

- The Cape Cod Writers Conference and (Boston's) Muse and the Marketplace, for educating me in the art and the business of novel writing.

- Piper, Tempest, and Nisi, whose course Writing the Other gives me ongoing inspiration and has cautioned me to approach my subjects with respect and humility.

- My readers/critiquers—Linda Bailey-Davies, Brooke Carroll, Jeff Drake, Becky Fischer, Don Helin, Maggie Mallan, Clyde McGeary, Elenita Muniz, Maureen Osborne, Alex Smith, Matt Smith, Susan Smith, Ted Spevak, Leslie Morgan Steiner, Steve Szaraz, Joan Talmadge, Rob Teplitz, and Sally Wyner—for their time, perspective, insight, praise, and criticism.

- Jeff Talmadge and Jake and Louise Warner, for their constant encouragement from the moment I started writing my first pages.

- Magician John Westford allowed me to peek behind the curtain just enough to ground the scene with Signor Antonio Blitz in a magical reality.

- Maureen Murphy, who gave me insights into confession.

- Sid and Margaret of Two Step Approach, editors who made the macro comments I needed to hear.

- Brooke Carroll, for her help with Quaker speech.

- Katherine Talmadge Sallé, copy editor extraordinaire, who was the last person to polish The Conductor before I sent it off to the publisher.

- John Kilbride, retired passenger railroader and Camden & Amboy historian, for leading me to historical references that enriched my descriptions of the railroad, its equipment, and depots.

- Cathy Jordan, for giving generous encouragement, offering a timely critique of important passages, and opening doors.

- The staff at Sunbury Press, who believed in me and the importance of Rian Krieger's Journey. Editor Abigail Hensen for her insightful comments and suggestions. Ashley Walkowiak for her engaging cover design. Taylor Berger-Knorr for her counsel and perspective. And Lawrence Knorr for writing the words that every aspiring author dreams of reading: "We are very pleased to inform you our editors wish to move forward with the publication of your manuscript."

- My family—Susan, Matt, Alecia, Alex, and Courtney—for their constant support and encouragement.

Rian Krieger's journey is far from over.

In Book 2, *The Blackmailer*, we will spend more time with Rian, her friends, and her enemies. Rian stabs a mugger, runs away to tsarist Russia, and finds herself in the center of events with historic implications.

If you want to read a transcript of an interview in which 91-year-old Rian reminisces about the events portrayed in *The Conductor*, contact me at rogerasmith.com and ask for **Book 1 Bonus Materials**. I will send you a PDF of Rian's first words recorded on Thomas Edison's new office dictating machine. I promise no spoilers (but I might tease you a bit).

If you are a member of a book club, I have created a set of questions to facilitate discussion. Contact me at rogerasmith.com and ask for **Book 1 Discussion Questions.**

About the Author

ROGER A. SMITH started his professional career as a high school history teacher. After ten years of inspiring young people, he yielded to passions for which he had no formal training: co-owning a summer camp, farming, founding a participatory science museum, co-owning a wilderness expedition program for teenagers, teaching entrepreneurship at the college level, woodworking, and leading a rural arts organization. Now an author, he draws lore and wisdom from those professions and joy from the thought that he is once again making history come alive to his constituents.

Mr. Smith and his wife lived and worked on a farm in Central Pennsylvania for 41 years. They currently reside in Massachusetts with their Great Dane and two cats. They have three adult children and two grandchildren.

Made in United States
North Haven, CT
15 November 2022

26685141R00200